The
HOUSE
of the
SEVEN
HEAVENS

& Other Stories

MARK MORGANSTERN

Once again to Susan, who made it all possible, even if she disagrees. If my book were a song to her, I'd have called it: *I Would've Had Nothin' Without You*. And to my beautiful children, Luke, Lily, and Harry, who've filled my cup over so many times I've had to buy more cups. You all surrounded me with love, even at times when I might not have deserved it. And to Arnold, our rescue canine, who sits by my desk and looks at me quizzically, as if to say, *And what exactly is it that you're doing in here?*

CONTENTS

THE HOUSE OF THE SEVEN HEAVENS

I t was once an imposing three-story home in a neighborhood that had long since seen its luster dimmed in the decades following the Second World War. The white paint had peeled from the pine siding to reveal the dried wood underneath, which resulted in the house appearing to be of no discernible color. A steep, spiral staircase led up to the solid oak door. Below the first floor, off to the side, was a basement entrance, where once a thriving business operated, Rudy Stine's Swap Shop and Refurbished Appliances. A few of the adjoining rooms in the cellar had been previously used for kosher butchering, or for storing Goodyear Tires and cases of Quaker State motor oil. The house, long ago deserted, sat there waiting for the next phase of urban renewal off the I-890 corridor. It looked dismayed with its cracked windows, faded curtains signaling in the breeze, and asphalt shingles having succumbed to the years of harsh northeast winters.

Behind the house, in the distance, is an imposing thirty-six-foot wide rooftop emblem with ten-foot tall letters spelling out *GE* in script. The monogram contains 1,399 twenty-five watt light bulbs. It's mounted on top of Building 37 on the General Electric campus and is visible up to one mile away. It can be seen day and night, a glowing sphere that has summoned vehicles and pedestrians down Erie Boulevard since 1934. The emblem, which fades in and out, was visible from the back of the house and between the cross streets on Broadway, including Edison Avenue, and from the upper neighborhoods, an intrusive orb that branded the sky and transfixed all those who lived beneath its menacing corporate glow.

The house belonged to Sarah and Ivan Rosensweig, who, with their seven children, had survived to inhabit those rooms in the new world. The family had emigrated from Szemud, Poland, just before the murderous late nineteen-thirties. Ivan, a tailor by trade, an astute man, took a hard look at what was festering in Germany, and in his own country. One night, as the children slept, he told Sarah, "The Germans will come. They will murder us. And our neighbors will help them." The next day he sold the family heirlooms, the furniture, a 14k gold menorah, all of Sarah's jewelry except her wedding ring, and a grandfather clock of fine German craftsmanship, the irony of which was not lost on him. Sarah cried and begged Ivan to let them stay. It was the only home she'd ever known. Her parents were buried in the Jewish cemetery. "If we stay," he told her, "our home will be a pile of ashes—ours and the children's."

Soon after, the family left Szemud and traveled to the seaport town of Gdyniac where they departed for America. After clearing Ellis Island, where the anti-Semitism was at least slightly hidden beneath the smiles of the condescending officials, the family stayed with Ivan's distant relative just off Canal Street. Ivan's second cousin, Noam Coblentz, the patriarch of his family, after arriving from Poland prior to the Rosensweigs, had managed to get himself set up in Tammany Hall as a precinct leader, once the Jews started to take it over. Between his powerful position and his dry goods business he'd done well for his family. A gaunt, humorless, austere man, who shunned his wife's "peasant banquets"—strawberry blintzes with pints of sour cream—he adored his daughters and denied them nothing. He wanted for them to have everything besides the right to their lives, which they would have forfeited in Poland. Shana and Rima took music lessons from musicians from the philharmonic, dance and theater lessons from the finest troupes and acting companies in the city. And both attended the High School of Music and Art. Shana excelled at singing and was considered to have an operatic vocal quality. In the short time the Rosensweigs stayed on Canal Street, Shana and Davora, the youngest daughter of Ivan and Sarah, became close friends. Shana would say, 'you are my sister.' Sometimes she would call her Sophie. On the morning they left to move upstate to Schenectady, Shana pressed a piece of paper into Davora's hand. "Here's our address and phone number. You'll come back," she cried and kissed her. "You will find me again." Davora wouldn't find out until much later that there had been a third Coblentz sister, Sophie, who had contracted diphtheria on the ship and had died on the way to the new world. It devastated the two remaining sisters, Shana in particular, that Sophie never saw the Statue of Liberty, that she never achieved the security they had. It had caused irreversible emotional damage to Shana.

Despite the generosity Noam rained on his daughters, it wasn't extended to Ivan and his family for long. He gave them one week to get their bearings and then they would be back out on the street. As usual Ivan had done his homework. He'd studied the trade journals and read about scientific innovations taking place in companies like General Electric. He determined that there would be more opportunity upstate than on the Lower East Side, where thousands of new arrivals were vying to carve out an existence. His plan was that he and the two older boys, now in their teens, would get jobs at the General Electric plant. Ivan intuited that the future was going to be about incandescent light bulbs, electric fans, heating and cooking devices, and turbines. They would need skilled workers, and his sons were skilled. When they got upstate, he tried to rent out a small store front with bedrooms in the back, but could only secure a one-bedroom, which they shared for almost a year. There was a kitchen that consisted of a sink, a hot plate, and some mildewed cabinets. The bathroom was a regrettable stall plumbed into the back porch, making for brisk visits in the winter.

Ivan converted the storefront into a tailor's shop. The girls, since they were young, had been well-trained to sew clothes and fabrics, make alterations, and hem and mend all types of garments. They were competent and worked quickly. Ivan was highly skilled and could make suits, coats, and fancy dresses. In Szemud he was often called upon to make suits for the local rabbis and rabbinical students. He called the new shop Fine Alterations and Tailoring, foregoing their surname that might put some patrons off. There were certain folks who were reluctant to trade with Jews. When he wasn't working the assembly line at the plant he was in the shop. Word about the quality of their work got around and they attracted customers from the more affluent Union Street neighborhood, and folks from the working class neighborhoods who constantly needed denim jeans and jackets patched, and zippers replaced. The family focused on nothing but work, making the long, arduous climb upward.

Within a year they'd earned enough money, along with the residual cash Ivan had socked away from selling the family's belongings in Poland, to purchase the new house at 580 Broadway, a more desirable location than the one-bedroom storefront on Kaiser Avenue. Broadway was a wide, historic thoroughfare with a mix of cultures, many shops and bars, and a premier movie theater / playhouse. Their new home bordered the GE turbine plant campus, behind which the Mohawk River wound moodily south as if disgruntled about having to combine with the greater Hudson River, known as the Rhine of America—another German allusion

Ivan didn't embrace. It was an immense relief to the family after a year in a one-bedroom storefront with a freezing bathroom, to inhabit a grand home in a fine neighborhood.

The house was situated diagonally across the street from a curious structure, a bit of an architectural monstrosity. It was called the Klondike Ramp, circa 1905, a spiral ramp supported on concrete piers. It stood sixty-four feet in height. Each level provided seven feet of clearance. The concrete walkway was pitched at a grade of almost eight percent to accommodate foot traffic, bicycles, and kids racing wagons. There were seven complete turns in the structure, which connected the 11th Ward neighborhoods high above to Broadway below. Observing it for the first time, a visitor might describe it as a huge, inverted flour sifter without a hand crank.

The alternative to accessing those neighborhoods above was a notoriously steep hill, known for multiple accidents and injuries, especially in the winter. The 11th Ward included Strong and Summit Streets along with Hamilton Hill, once famous for its speakeasies and tenor sax men like Lester Young and Coleman Hawkins when they were passing through town. Unfortunately, the ramp was constructed next to an unstable clay hill prone to landslides, and littered with trash deposited from the back porches of homes on Strong and Summit Streets. Heavy rainfall over the years saturated the soil, eventually causing a landslide that demolished a gas station at the bottom of the hill. But at the time, the ramp served an almost singular purpose. It provided a useful covered passage for the workers to travel to and from the GE Plant below. Each day a steady stream of employees would descend the ramp, lunch pails in hand. At the bottom of the incline was a viaduct that deposited them out onto Broadway—a short walk to their jobs. After their shifts ended, the workers would ascend the ramp to get home. They would pass the Rosensweig house everyday, streams of them, in various conditions of well-being and mood, endlessly making their way to and from the GE facility.

Some of the workers who traversed the Klondike ramp referred to it as the Seven Heavens because of the seven levels of ramps. There was a strong Catholic presence in the town that held to beliefs they'd been raised by, the Jewish and Christian cosmologies, the concept of the Seven Heavens, and the Pauline Arts, though they might not have recognized or understood those terms. Stories circulated that a few of the folks who regularly made their way through the ramps experienced indescribable feelings, strange passions, or had sightings of a sort they could hardly explain or describe. But given the day to day hardships, the necessity of making a living, the drudgery and repetitive work at the plant, little thought was given to it. It was passed off as fatigue or just anomalies. Some of it was attributed to frequent stops on the way home at The Sanctuary, a dive bar convenient to the ramp's entrance, which featured a shot and beer for seventy-five cents.

Ivan remained focused on his long-term plan, which was also to set up his three sons in their own businesses. He bought a vacant gas station a few doors down from the Klondike Ramp and set Ben up in it because Ben was good at mechanical tasks; he could fix almost anything. Ben took to it quickly; he was clever at negotiating oil and gas purchases and soon established his own automotive repair and heating oil delivery business, Electric City Oil & Gas. Josh, the quiet one, who was always hiding behind the Daily Gazette, was, Ivan determined, going to own a printing shop. Ivan found a location, bought the printing presses and typesetting pieces, and installed Josh there. What Josh wanted was to be a reporter and work for a newspaper. Ivan was intent that he should make a living first. So Josh cranked out stationery, business cards, pads, signs, and promotional materials for the local businesses. Soon he was able to buy his own home and move out of the house on Broadway. But he married a woman, Mimi, from the reformed temple, instead of someone from the orthodox community. Ivan disapproved of the marriage and threatened to withhold support money until the business took off. But Josh possessed good social skills and did well right away. He also made it a point to support community organizations and charities, which made him well-thought-of.

Jake was another story. He was the least capable of the three brothers, or so it seemed. He didn't make it past the fifth grade, after which he was enrolled in a vocational school to learn tool and die making, but he couldn't adequately read the complicated manuals or master the metric system. He had not been able to learn Hebrew sufficiently, and memorize his Haftarah. He had to listen to the rabbi recite it for him at his bar mitzvah. Unfortunately for Jake, it was a time when learning disabilities weren't recognized or respected. A young man was either thought to be smart or dumb. Jake's talents lay hidden. He probably would have made a great athlete with his physical strength and agility. He always beat his brothers at wrestling or impromptu races. But nothing added up for him. Ivan assigned Jake to make the deliveries for Ben's heating oil business. Jake spent his days driving around the company truck listening to the Yankees and Dodgers games on the radio. After he moved out, Ivan and Sarah learned that he was living with a shiksa, a non-Jewish woman, who, it was rumored, would berate him and call him a 'dirty Jew.' Ivan was enraged and said to Sarah, "I saved him for this?" Sarah said nothing. But when she made brisket or stuffed cabbage she'd tell Ben to tell Jake that she'd leave some on the back porch for him. Ivan wouldn't allow him in the house anymore.

The career choices for the four sisters were not as well thought out as they'd been for the brothers. They could continue working as seamstresses, or they could get married, which Ivan preferred, so they'd be provided for. Galena, the oldest sister, married a butcher, a harsh man, who thought himself devout and righteous before God. But he belittled her constantly, and struck her on occasion. She became a virtual kitchen slave striving to keep everything glatt kosher. Hannah married a fabric salesman who wanted nothing to do with the family and relocated her and himself to Pennsylvania immediately after the wedding. Rose, the next to the youngest sister, did somewhat better. She married an accountant who cared for her and provided a more genteel lifestyle than Galena enjoyed. Her boys were the first in the family to graduate from college. Rose and her husband vacationed at the Catskills resorts, a luxury none of the other siblings enjoyed.

The youngest sister, Davora, wanted since childhood to become a nurse or perhaps a teacher, or, if it were possible, a world traveler. She wanted something beyond what destiny seemed to have planned for her. She was the adventurous one, the curious one, and the secret rebel. She kept a private journal and wrote copious entries whenever she was alone, recording her thoughts, the events of the day, and the family's dynamics, which ranged from even-tempered to volatile. She liked to slip out on warm evenings to explore the neighborhood. She was fascinated by the people they shared the place with but never got to interact with. Ivan forbade the kids to talk to folks who lived nearby. The fear and suspicion he experienced in Poland, and their escape, stayed with him. He'd adopted a severe countenance, ever alert to danger, and always questioning the motives of strangers. He stood erect and watchful in his black suits and ties, with his quick birdlike movements, his snappy pace, and his sharp facial features.

Davora was particularly attracted to The Three Aces, a social club and music room frequented by the Black community. She didn't dare enter it as she thought her presence might seem inappropriate, or worse, disrespectful, but the music enthralled her. She'd listen to the jazz in the alleyway by the side of the building, tapping out the rhythm with her fingers. She had a thought, but had no one to share it with except her journal: jazz music and klezmer had much in common. Both were lively and made up on the spot—she didn't know the term "improvise." Once or twice a large man named Big Daddy Flanagan, the house pianist, would notice her listening, intent on the music. He'd always smile and say, "What you perched out here for, little chickie? You like what you hear?" She was embarrassed at first, almost frightened, and then she understood—his acknowledgement, his kindness. He didn't see her as some skinny white girl eavesdropping. Her people struggled to show warmth or encouragement. It was all just work and obedience. Hadn't these people also suffered oppression and hatred for who they were, like her people had, though without the systematic extermination? She liked hearing the spirited laugher coming from inside the club as much as the music itself. The music spoke to her. It said: *this is life.*

In twelfth grade, just before graduation from the Edison High School, Davora was accepted to the nursing program at St. Clair's Hospital, with a partial scholarship, and was excited to train to be a registered nurse. But Ivan decided that she would work at Ben's gas station doing the books and pumping gas. The business was doing well and Ben needed help. And he didn't want her walking home from the hospital at night anyway. Disobedience was not an option at the time. The patriarch ruled the household here, just as he had in Eastern Europe. Davora complied as she made alternative plans. She would not live her life this way. They were, after all, living in the 'land of the free,' and that is what she wanted most, *freedom.*

Reluctantly, and somewhat angered, she went to work for Ben but was surprised to find some liberation in that. She didn't just pump gas and clean windows. That was too boring. Before long she'd become proficient at oil changes and replacing struts and spark plugs. She could even patch or install new radiators. She became the most competent mechanic in the garage, even surpassing Ben. He took advantage of that and assigned her much of the specialty work. The men who brought their vehicles to the garage got a kick out of watching a competent young lady repair their cars. Especially a pert little thing in mechanics coveralls, an Electric City Oil service cap, cocked smartly to one side of her head, and work boots. Some of the men with underworld connections would ask her out. But she always came up with a reply that outfoxed them: "I can't, my boyfriend's boxing tonight at the Casino. He's a heavyweight, you know."

The Klondike Ramp, aka the Seven Heavens, also had a reputation for trouble. It could be dangerous. Groups of teenagers sometimes harassed and robbed unsuspecting travelers. Homeless men would urinate in the ramps. Occasionally, perverts were hauled out by the police for soliciting sex. It was not a good place to be after dark. Ivan had decreed from the time they moved into the neighborhood that the children would stay out of the place. It was not a playground, though some of the local kids, unsupervised by their full-time working parents, would race their bikes down the ramp, often with disastrous consequences like broken legs and cracked skulls. Ivan's rule was enough to tempt Davora to explore the peculiar structure and its various levels. She was drawn to it. The stories she'd heard intrigued her. It became a challenge to foray into the ramp and return home without Ivan discovering her disobedience. She'd visited multiple times before she began to realize that the place was somehow *affecting* her. She would experience things there that would open her up, change her in ways she would not have expected, though she might never fully comprehend what they meant. She sensed that it was much more than just a passageway for laborers to tread. It was a gateway to other worlds.

*

The boys prospered in their businesses. On Sundays the family, except for Jake, would gather at the house for Sarah's offerings: gefilte fish with fresh ground horseradish, chicken soup with matzo balls, kugel, kasha varnishkes, and delicious rugelach. After dinner the family would sit uncomfortably on the flower-patterned sofa and chairs in the living room and listen to the Philco standing radio, a rounded brown coffin with knobs. First it was the Klezmer

Hour followed by the news delivered in Yiddish. The news was grim. As Ivan had predicted, the Jews, not just in Szemud, but all over Europe, were hunted down in their homes, in the beautiful hills and pastures Sarah had roamed as a child, in the barns and forests where they hid; hunted and killed, or turned over to the Nazis for "prizes," most often the clothing or jewelry from the people they murdered. Their synagogue was torched—the torah and prayer books burned with it. The cemetery where Sarah's parents were buried was desecrated. There was something in the Polish zeitgeist that instantaneously ignited their taste for blood and blind obedience to their German bosses. After the broadcast Ivan would retreat to his bedroom. One time Davora pressed her ear to the door and could hear him sobbing as he recited the Kaddish.

Davora felt sorry for her father. She understood the struggle and sacrifice he'd gone through to save his family from certain death. She forgave him his authoritarian nature, but yearned for her freedom. She struggled herself to understand how the Nazis' who had families of their own, wives and children whom they certainly must love, could visit such murderous acts on the Jews. How could their own countrymen have turned on them like that? There was no answer, but she intuited that there was something about the Seven Heavens that could explain such things. Something was awakening in her; she was frightened, but drawn to whatever there was about the Seven Heavens. Why did she feel so different when she was in there? Was there something she was supposed to learn in that place? It might have to do with the freedom she craved so much. One time Galena came to her crying over her terrible choice in marriage. Davora comforted her and encouraged her to divorce the butcher, something almost unheard of in their tradition. "You don't need him," she told her sister. "You could have a different life. You could be free."

Galena became angry. "Free? I don't know what you're talking about."

Beyond the horror playing out in Europe and her growing interest in the Seven Heavens for what she described in her journals as "my education," an event took place in the winter of 1940 that further impacted Davora's life. There was a tremendous blizzard in mid February that all but shut down the city. The *GE* emblem was literally blotted out for thirty-six hours. And, Rudy Stine arrived from Florida. By the time he reached the train station, the storm was so intense he had to sleep on top of his suitcases. The next morning, after the plows had made the streets passable, he made his way to his aunt's house on Stanley Street. He'd left Florida, and his absentee parents, to seek his fortune up north. Rudy's Aunt Anna, his dad's sister, was married to Sol, a short, sturdy, Russian immigrant, a hardcore business man who owned a secondhand shop. Rudy was offered a position as a salesman, but what he really did was bid on and buy used furniture, metal, tools, and jewelry. He'd return with it in Sol's Mercury Station Wagon, then he'd clean and polish it up, and create an eye-catching display. Sol paid Rudy half of minimum wage, fifteen cents per hour, barely enough to buy cigarettes. But he had free room and board. The cigarettes, unfiltered Camels, that he started smoking at age fourteen, would catch up with him three decades later. He'd switched to Carlton filtered by then, but it was too late.

Rudy had big plans. He wanted to make something of himself. What he wanted most was to be an educated gentleman, a deep thinker, which was a tough call with only a sixth-grade education, growing up knocking about St. Petersburg, doing odd jobs and following his father around, a salesman of sorts and sometimes a featherweight boxer if the money was right. His mother was mainly interested in shuffleboard matches and cocktails, usually Rum Runners and Daiquiris, there being an abundance of fresh fruit year round. When he wasn't planning his career, Rudy practiced vocabulary words, the bigger the better. Words like sycophant, untenable, paradox, malaise—but he'd misuse and confuse them in sentences like, "The box of old tools was untenable, so I didn't buy them," or, "I skipped over the used snow tires because they had a malaise about them."

The first time Davora met Rudy she thought he was a performer of some kind. He pulled up to the house in a maroon La Salle Series 50 Coupe, which he referred to as "a sweet boat." He'd put down twenty dollars at the dealership and convinced the manager he'd be making way more than the monthly payments he'd agreed to, which he did not at first. Like his dad, he knew how to sell used furniture, junk iron, appliances, and himself. He hopped out of the car and approached the house. Davora was sitting on the stoop thinking about the first level of the seven heavens, where supposedly the Garden of Eden was located. She wondered if Adam and Eve had experienced a romantic union or was it just carnal. She imagined what their attraction to each other might have been like. Maybe it was just a thought a young, inexperienced girl might have. It was not until later that she would actually see... *something*.

Rudy strutted up to Davora and said, "Are you the girl in the jitterbug dress?" Then he laughed. She felt her cheeks redden. "You live here? I'm answering the ad in the paper. I'm Rudy Stine and I'd like to rent a storefront in the basement of your house." Davora looked him over. He was wearing a poorly tailored double-breasted suit which she could have fixed in her sleep. He sported a hand-painted silk tie featuring a peacock, and two-tone, wing-tip, lace-up Oxford dress shoes. He had reddish hair combed neatly back over his head and a thin moustache carefully trimmed. It occurred to Davora that he was a bit of a peacock himself, this Rudy Stine, suddenly presenting himself before her, all new and strange. She'd never met anyone like him before. He liked to describe his style and manner as being "snazzy."

"You have to ask my father."

"What's your name?"

She hesitated, "Davora."

"I'll bet that means pretty in Spanish."

"No, it means bee, like a bug. And it's Hebrew, not Spanish."

Rudy smiled; he knew exactly where that name came from. He rested one foot on the stoop and leaned forward on his knee. "Oh, and a pretty little bee if you ask me."

She blushed, "I'll get my father."

Soon after, Rudy Stine's Swap Shop and Refurbished Appliances opened up in the basement of the house. Rudy then began a prolonged and strenuous courtship of Davora, who wanted nothing to do with him. Ivan was not that impressed with the flashy young man either, but he'd rented the space to him because it brought in additional income. Davora felt that Rudy just seemed too silly for her. The man, she thought, doesn't have a serious bone in his body. She avoided him and continued to explore the Seven Heavens.

*

It was the last week of February, a bitterly cold, overcast day with another storm threatening the town. Davora had wandered up to the third level ramp and was looking out at the Mohawk River, which was churning in anticipation of the front moving in. She felt drawn back down to the second level where she experienced something that affected her deeply. She didn't know how to describe it. Was it something she saw in her mind's eye or was it a waking dream? Or something completely *other*? And it wasn't necessarily within the second ramp, but more just outside in the darkness as if she were viewing a diorama or a drive-in movie. She saw what she thought to be an angel floating in the midst of a hailstorm. She'd been working her way through the catalogue of books on religion at the library. She made the connection instantaneously. The name simply was there as if she were reading it off of a page: Nuriel. Nuriel was the Fire of the Lord and responsible for hailstorms.

And, according to the text she'd read and scribbled notes about in her journal, Moses encountered Nuriel in the second heaven. The idea of coming across Moses made her shiver. She stared at the specter of Nuriel for some moments until the flames were extinguished by the hailstorm. Then he was gone, but the hail remained, hard nuggets pelting the exterior of the entire structure, like a giant resonating snare drum. She realized that in fact it was a hailstorm, immediately followed by a snowstorm that dropped like an impenetrable, suffocating curtain. She ran down the ramp and crossed the street to the house. She lay on her bed recording the event in her journal, trying to make sense of what she'd just seen, what she thought she'd seen. She was frightened but knew she would not be able to resist going back in. Just not for a few days.

Davora's return to the Seven Heavens was delayed by Josh's murder. He was working late one night printing posters for the local Mardi Gras parade on March 5. A young man knocked on the shop door. Josh recognized him from the neighborhood. He had given him money a few times for food. The kid displayed a gun and told Josh to open the cash register. There was only two dollars and ninety-seven cents in it. Josh put it on the counter and offered to take him to a restaurant around the corner and buy him dinner. The young man shook terribly and Josh realized his mistake. Drug dealers had started moving into the neighborhood and some of the young men, unemployed, over-policed, and subject to ethnic bias, had become addicted. Most likely the trigger was pulled because the kid started to shake violently. Mimi, Josh's wife, called to see why he was still at the shop. When he didn't answer she went there and found the door open, and Josh on the floor bleeding out. The money was still on the counter.

The next shock came when the family found out that Josh's wife, Mimi, would not be honoring the tradition of sitting Shiva for seven days, nor had she covered the mirrors in their house. She'd had

Josh's body taken to a non-denominational funeral home and embalmed. She'd also allowed for viewing hours, a brazen departure from Jewish orthodoxy. For some reason she avoided the Jewish cemetery and had him buried in a non-denominational cemetery. Josh had been a well-liked member of the business community and the chamber of commerce wanted to honor him posthumously with a Community Service Improvement Award for his donations and volunteerism to the Boys and Girls Clubs. The local American Legion Band played at his funeral. Ivan was enraged and forbade any of the girls, including Sarah, to attend Josh's funeral. This precipitated a rare confrontation, something unheard of in the family structure. Sarah and Davora told Ivan they were going to the funeral home to see Josh before his interment. "You will not leave this house," he ordered them.

Sarah spoke quietly, but firmly, "He's my son. I will see him."

Ivan shook with rage. "That is not our son in a gentile funeral home. You will not go to him."

For the first time in her life Davora spoke up to her father, her voice trembling. "Papa, we will never have Josh again. You must let us see him."

Ivan swung his arm back, his hand flat, about to strike Davora across the face. "No," Sarah stepped in front of her, "don't touch her."

Slowly, he lowered his arm. He seemed to shrink into his body. "I have no children," he said bitterly.

"You had seven children," she said. "Now one is gone." Ivan turned away and went to the living room. They heard the radio crackling and the news was on, urgent and horrific.

On the way to the funeral home Davora told her mother that it was her intention, if it were possible, to take over Josh's printing business. She had saved up money from what Ben paid her, plus tips she'd earned from customers who were impressed with her service. She hoped that Mimi would like the idea of keeping the business in the family. Beyond that, it would be her path to independence. She could rent an apartment near the business and establish herself, a woman who didn't need a man to provide for her. She was determined; she would not allow herself to be dominated. In the back of her mind was the idea that when she learned what was actually happening in the Seven Heavens she would write about it, but in a more formal manner than her journal. A printing press could be useful. Two days after Josh's funeral she learned that Mimi had put the business on the market with a broker who'd sold it immediately for a large sum of money.

Davora was not familiar with the darkness of depression until it suddenly dropped upon her, a dark, ominous weight. Losing Josh, and what she thought might have been her only chance to obtain her freedom, brought her low. Even as a young girl in her village in Poland she'd been resilient, brushing off the occasional anti-Semitic remarks from fellow students and even some of her teachers. She believed in the basic goodness of people, and that she would somehow grow up to realize her dreams. She wanted to believe that someday there would be no persecution of innocent people. But that was not the case. She'd stopped listening to the radio broadcasts about Europe. People were full of hate and she lived in a joyless family where all that mattered was work, the synagogue, and obedience to the patriarch. Jake, whom she loved dearly, had been banished by Ivan. After what the family had been through, how could he turn his back on any of his children?

The only thing in her life that was different, that promised something unusual, an escape from drudgery, was the *exploration*. Her spirits were lifted by the return of spring. The winter, a particularly bitter one, had finally died off. Late one afternoon she found herself back on the third level. She was in an unusual mood, somewhat buoyant because of the weather. And also because she'd just finished replacing a push-button starter on a Ford and completely serviced a Buick Century, including shocks and struts. The owner of the vehicle offered to let Davora take a *spin* in it. It had a hundred and sixty-five horsepower, eight-cylinder engine that could reach a speed of ninety-five miles per hour. She got into the driver's seat tentatively and started it up. It purred like a kitten, to everyone's satisfaction. She drove around the property a few times, hopped out of the car and tossed the keys to the owner and skipped off. After that Ben made her chief mechanic of the garage and gave her a raise. Suddenly she was making more money than most women and some men at that time—even Rudy, who was doing better himself. She wasn't going to tolerate a man paying her way. All this accounted for her upbeat mood that day as she wandered through the third level.

She was reflecting on that positive thought when she saw a tree, or rather thought she did. Again, she couldn't differentiate between what was actually before her eyes and what she was seeing in her mind. It was a beautiful tree, lush with green shimmering leaves that were illuminated by an ethereal light. She noticed a group of figures surrounding the tree and one particular individual who was unusually tall. His arm was extended up into the branches of the tree. She moved closer, or rather the scene became more vivid to her sight. The tall figure had withdrawn his arm from the upper branches and held something in his hand. A shock wave went through her as she remembered what she'd read in Genesis 2:3. The Tree of Life aka The Tree of Souls, located in the Garden of Eden. It was said to blossom and produce new souls which would fall into the Guf. The angel Gabriel would reach in and take hold of the first soul he touched.

Suddenly anxious, she resisted an impulse to flee. Something held her there. One of the forms standing before the tree turned around and moved, or rather floated toward her, which increased her anxiety. She felt as if she were being engulfed in a warm mist. The form came closer and seemed to reach out to her though it didn't have arms. But there was a countenance, a face; it was Josh, his face pulsing as if it were composed of energy, thousands of atoms swirling in and out as though it was taking on form, but undeniably his face. His lips were moving. She heard words but couldn't decipher them, and she felt a calmness overtake her being. She could only describe it as *peace*, peacefulness like she'd never known before. "All right. It's all right," is what she thought she heard. Then something grabbed her arm tightly. She screamed. It was a police officer. "Miss, are you all right? You shouldn't be in here alone. It's not safe."

"No, no, I'm all right. Thank you."

"I'll walk you down."

"No, I'm sure I'm fine." The officer followed her down the ramp anyway. She looked back. Everything she'd just seen was gone—vanished. Obviously it looked normal to the police officer.

When they got to the bottom of the ramp, the officer said: "Aren't you the Rosensweig girl? Your father made a suit for my boy for his confirmation. It was just perfect. Tell him I said thanks, Officer Jansinski." She crossed Broadway in a trance-like state and sat on the porch stairs attempting to parse out what she'd just witnessed. On one hand it was completely frightening, but also, shouldn't she take solace that Josh was there, wherever that was, and he seemed to be OK with his situation? She went into the house and wandered into the kitchen to see if there was any milk in the ice box. Sarah was seated at the table before a bowl of potato peels. She rocked back and forth sobbing, her tears falling into the bowl. "My boy, my boy," she murmured. Davora wrapped her arms around her shoulders and cried into her mother's hair, "Oh, mama, mama." They both wept.

Sarah sat the bowl down and held Davora's hands. "My Josh, my Jake, gone."

"No, mama, we still have Jake."

"He won't let him come into the house...his own son."

"I'll talk to him. I'll make him see." After the fact, Davora thought maybe it would better to write her father a letter to avoid another confrontation. Since the previous argument about going to see Josh at the funeral home, she'd noticed a change in him; he seemed like a different man. He'd never been talkative, but now he was almost taciturn and more distant. He'd begun taking long walks. He'd leave the house in the morning after he'd had his tea, without announcing his departure. He'd follow Broadway to Albany Avenue, and then take the steep hill up to Central Park where he'd sit for hours watching the fountain in the middle of the small lake. It was quiet in the daytime as school was in session, just the sound of splashing water and the occasional honking of snow geese and chattering of squirrels. Sometimes he'd bring a sandwich or an apple; otherwise he'd eat nothing. as the vendor only sold hotdogs, potato chips, and soda. He'd arrive home late in the afternoon and sit in the living room until dinner. He'd doze or stare out at the traffic. Usually, by that time of day, a steady stream of people would be entering the ramp to return home to the upper neighborhoods unless they stopped off at The Sanctuary for a shot and a beer to mitigate some of the drudgery of factory work.

On a morning at the beginning of April, Ivan arrived at the park and noticed a man sitting on a bench nearby. The man had two shopping bags from which he fed the pigeons and squirrels peanuts and the snow geese with wads of white bread. As Ivan observed him he realized he'd seen the man many times before, always feeding the wildlife. But he thought nothing of it. This time it was different; the man waved and smiled and shrugged his shoulders as if to convey, 'what else would I be doing?' Ivan avoided the man's gestures and preferred to be left alone. He got up and walked around the path and took a seat on the other side near the rose garden. The man walked counterclockwise around the path and sat down on the same bench and continued to throw treats out to the squirrels and geese that had followed him. Ivan diverted his eyes and watched a woman push a baby carriage along the perimeter of the park. He remembered that he'd always carried his children in his arms. They'd never had a carriage.

"I am," the man announced, as if addressing an audience, "Oliver Kent Crosswright."

Ivan observed the disheveled man in his stained trench coat, his decidedly pockmarked Sephardic face and carved nose. "The hell you are."

The man chuckled. "Of course I'm not. I adopted the name when I got here, very Christian. "They don't like us much better here than they did over there."

"And where is there?" Ivan asked, coldly.

"Kielno. Ever hear of it?"

Ivan gasped. "Who the hell are you?"

"Shmuel Krakoff, at your service." He extended his hand to Ivan who refused it. "And you, sir, did you take on a Christian name, or did they bastardize it at Ellis Island? Schwartz they turn into Smith, hah! The goyim, they think they're the cat's meow."

Ivan snapped, "I don't need you at my service. What do you want from me?"

Shmuel turned his head sideways as if he was trying to think of what he wanted. A squirrel jumped on his shoe and scurried back quickly. Shmuel chuckled, "They get impatient. Here..." He threw more nuts and the animals devoured them. The snow geese honked for more wads of bread. "What do I want? What I always want, to connect to another Landsman. I want," he said, in a whisper, "to feel that there's something left to live for...if you follow me."

Ivan left Shmuel on the bench to connect to the squirrels and walked home in a strange mood. *Kielno,* how in all the places in the world could he be from Kielno? Out of his habit for self-protection, never revealing anything about himself because of the inherent danger, he didn't tell Shmuel that their towns were just a few kilometers apart. And who was this man anyway who accosted him, disturbed his meditation at the fountain? If Ivan wanted anything, it was to be left alone. The world, or rather the behavior of some of those in it, the war against his people, had cost him too much. The one source of peace for him was that he'd saved his family. But who were they to him now, turning against traditions, against their... God, the God which Ivan, when he admitted it, believed in less and less?

The next time he visited the park it was a bright, warm morning. Shmuel was already there with his bags of nuts and white bread feeding his animal friends. Ivan took a bench halfway around the lake away from Shmuel, who waved cordially at him. Ivan ruminated, 'What business do I have with this man anyway?' Shmuel finished his feeding and made his way around the path toward Ivan. He crumpled his bags up and dropped them in a trash can. Shmuel stopped at the concession wagon and made a purchase. He approached Ivan conspiratorially, smiling, a man who, in his vagrancy, seemed to be in comfortable possession of himself. He sat down. "I got us a snack." He handed Ivan a hotdog wrapped in tissue. Ivan stared at it then pushed it away.

"Traif? I don't eat traif."

"It's got everything on it, mustard, pickles, kraut."

The word *kraut* made him cringe. "How could you eat that?"

"It tastes good, a reasonably priced meal for a man on a limited budget. Here, have a soda pop, orange."

Ivan stood up. "Who the hell are you?"

Shmuel had taken a large bite of his hot dog and mumbled something. Ivan stood over him, determined. "What are you saying?"

Shmuel swallowed his mouthful and took a sip of soda. "Szemud, I finally remembered."

Ivan shuddered, a disabling wave of fear rising from his stomach. "How can you know Szemud?"

"You, Mr. Rosensweig, made a suit for my little brother...for his bar mitzvah."

Ivan sat down slowly, a memory starting to pour in. It came to him. "Your father, Mortachai, he was..."

"The rabbi of our town. My mother had the bakery, and my brother and sister..."

Ivan waited; the memory that had come to him had turned dark and forbidding. "What happened?"

Shmuel stared into the fountain where the sunlight caught thousands of dazzling drops raining down onto the surface with a pleasing sound. "What happened? What happened to them all, my father and mother, my sister, and my brother...his bar mitzvah was consecrated at Belzec. He and the others were gassed there. He probably wore the suit you made for him."

Ivan gasped; he felt something unknown to him, a strange feeling behind his eyes. He had never cried before. He thought of himself as someone who just didn't cry or didn't know how to cry. But tears fell from his eyes. He cried, not just for Shmuel's family, but for Josh gone now forever, and Jake, whom he'd banished from their home. And for Sarah, whom he owed more than just a roof over her head. She was, he understood, the heart of the family. He was the pragmatist, the lawgiver, and did it all matter? For what? "And you?" he asked, Shmuel. "What happened?"

Shmuel wiped his mouth with his sleeve. "I wasn't there when they came for them. I was in a barn with a girl I was seeing. We would meet there to... we had to hide. She wasn't Jewish." His hands started shaking. "I was having pleasure as my family was..."

"How did you get away?"

Shmuel took a long drink of soda and tossed the can into the trash next to the bench. "I didn't get away. None of us did. You didn't; we're walking dead, dragging more corpses behind us. The question is how did I get out? I couldn't go home, they'd be waiting. I never saw them again... my family. I knew a man in Gdyniac, a longshoreman. He managed to get me on a ship. I pretended I was on the crew. I didn't even know where I was going. I wound up in England of all places. Eventually made it to the States. "I..." he hesitated. "I should not be alive. I wouldn't be if I had the courage... if I could bring myself to..." Slowly he lowered his face into the palms of his hands. Involuntarily, Ivan slid over to him and put his arm around the man's quaking shoulders.

"Don't talk like that. You must live on for them if nothing else."

*

It took most of the spring, but Rudy finally persuaded Davora to take a spin in his La Salle Series 50 Coupe, his 'sweet boat,' as he put it. Davora considered the offer from several angles. Rudy seemed somehow less offensive than when he'd first appeared after a record-breaking snowstorm. He was slightly more serious, probably as a result of working sixty hours a week in his shop, just to pay off his fancy car. He was doing good business by then. Though it still irritated her when he said things like, "I'd swim to Panama for you." But she decided to trade in her garage mechanic's coveralls and work boots for her favorite flower-patterned dress, with buttons rising from the waist to a bow tied in the middle, her beaded necklace, Mary Jane shoes, and her wide-brimmed sun hat. Ivan, who was the treasurer for their synagogue, was at a meeting, so she didn't have to ask for permission to go. There was also an idea she was just starting to consider, but was far from articulating it, especially to Rudy. "Hold on to your hat," Rudy blurted as they sped away from the curb. The warm spring air caressed her body and it felt good. The further they traveled north on Route 9 the lighter she felt. With the windows open, the fresh green fields and budding trees added to her exhilaration. *This makes me happy,* she thought. Their destination, Rudy announced, was the beautiful and historic Ballston Lake.

Rudy's plan was to drive Davora around the lake as he delivered a tutorial he'd worked on for the better part of a week. An erudite presentation that he hoped would impress her. He'd finally gotten it through his head that she was a serious girl and thought about things. Therefore, she might appreciate a knowledgeable talk on the biology of the lake. Ballston Lake, he'd read off a brochure he'd picked up at the Saratoga Race Course, was meromictic, meaning that the layers of water didn't intermix—as opposed to a lake that was holomictic, where the levels of water did intermix. Rudy had practiced the terms studiously, but wound up pronouncing them like *mirrormiktic* and *halomiktic*. He'd given up on the fact that Ingo Findenegg, the Austrian scientist, had coined the term meromictic in 1935. It was just too much to remember. He'd also decided to leave out the part about Big Tim, a monster fish who allegedly lived in the caves at the bottom of the lake. It might scare her, though it was nothing compared to what she'd already seen and would see in the Seven Heavens. The rest of Rudy's plan was to take Davora to Villago's Restaurant for what he hoped would be the first of many romantic lunches and dinners.

Davora stared at him astonished as he recited the hydrology facts of the lake and mispronounced the terms that he used to describe them. His bumbling and inadequacy touched her in a way that surprised her. "You don't have to do that for me," she said kindly. Rudy blushed, "I was just trying to... say, are you hungry?" Normally, she would have said no, but she felt bad for him, felt perhaps something for him for the first time. He was trying so hard. They got a table outside at Villago's, overlooking the lake. Rudy ordered a bottle of Chianti. He didn't attempt pronouncing it; he just pointed at it on the wine list. The only alcohol Davora had ever tasted was at her bat mitzvah, sweet concord Mogen David, the taste of which sickened her immediately. Rudy assured her that this wine was nothing like that. It was from Tuscany, which he thought was located near Albuquerque, New Mexico. The waiter brought it out and stood next to the table until Rudy asked him what he wanted. "The wine is to your satisfaction, sir?" he said. He'd poured a small amount into Rudy's wine glass.

Davora nudged him. "He wants you to taste it." Rudy did and nodded. The waiter poured out the glasses. He held up his glass to her: "To the prettiest little bee I've ever met." She clicked his glass suspiciously and sipped the wine. It was not sugary, but full-bodied, dry, and smelled wonderful. It reminded her of the green fields they'd passed on the way up Route 9. Rudy insisted on ordering for both of them, but she refused, reluctant to give up her autonomy. He ordered the chicken parmesan. Davora got a salad and angel hair pasta with marinara sauce. She'd never heard of angel hair, but liked the way it sounded. At least, she thought, it was sort of kosher, which of course brought up Ivan's stern countenance to her mind. Just the fact that she was far from home, drinking wine with a man Ivan didn't approve of, was enough. But she was enjoying herself. It was as if a knot had unraveled in her stomach. The wine warmed her chest and produced a sudden voracious appetite. A basket of warm bread came first and she dove in. The crust was crispy and delicious. She swabbed slices of it through the olive oil with drops of balsamic dressing and devoured them. "I love this bread." She also loved her mother's challah bread, braided and still warm from the oven. She loved dipping it in chicken soup. But this bread with the crispy crust was something else.

"It's Italian," Rudy announced triumphantly.

Davora reached for the bottle. "I'll have more of that."

Rudy laughed, "Take it easy, little bee. I can't bring you home all buzzed up."

She took another sip. "To the heavens," she toasted.

He gave her an uncertain glance. "If you say so, to the heavens."

The next morning Davora awoke with a start and felt drawn to the sixth level. She had no idea why, but this time she brought her Kodak Vigilant Junior Six-20 folding camera, intending to photograph whatever she might find there. She needed to be able to prove it to herself if the sightings were real. She waited until Ivan left for his daily pilgrimage to Central Park, where he would meet Shmuel, having finally formed a bond around their destroyed homeland and mutual grief.

She ascended the ramp, passing a myriad of blank faces and bodies, some supple, others stiff and halting, as they moved down the ramp with purpose or resignation. None of them smiling. The sixth ramp was empty and she assumed she'd passed the morning rush. But then a straggler approached her with an odd gait. He was wearing a white work suit. As he got closer she noticed he wasn't wearing any work boots. In fact, he didn't have any feet. The bottom cuffs of his work suit brushed the concrete ramp. He continued moving toward her as she raised her camera to photograph him. When she brought it up to eye level it pulled out of her grasp and floated about four feet above her head. The straggler stood in front of her gazing into her eyes, a face deeply weathered, benign and with a powerful presence. She noticed the name tag sewn on his suit pocket and shuddered: A. Sachiel. The Archangel Sachiel, a cherubim, "the covering of God," she recalled from her reading.

He stood before her for perhaps half a minute; she, frozen in place. Then he slowly raised his arm and turned his palm facing up toward the sky which split in half, one side night, full of swirling stars, the Milky Way like a thin slithering snake working through wispy clouds, and the other side bright day. Between the divisions a huge object appeared just outside of the ramp. It hovered there, rotating slowly. Davora recognized it immediately, Saturn with its rings of ice and rock. She felt as if the planet was pulling her in, drawing her into its immenseness, its density, until she felt unsteady on her feet. She began to move toward it and feared she would be engulfed into its mass and gone from her world forever—at least, the world she knew. She tried to scream but nothing came out.

Sachiel grasped her shoulders lightly, but with authority, and turned her so she was facing the seventh ramp, the highest level, the holiest of all—the home of God and his throne. There was a sound like the soft tinkling of glass that reminded her of the mobiles they sold at Woolworths, the ones from China, which she very much loved. Sarah had gotten her one for Purim. The sound increased quickly until it was almost earsplitting. A flood of crystals of multiple sizes and colors flowed down the ramp upon them, engulfing them up to their torsos. Behind the river of crystals a great light suddenly appeared, which Davora later realized was a single flame of the purest blue light she'd ever seen. A sudden blast of wind ended the vision and she found herself standing alone with her camera hanging on its strap from her shoulder. The wind continued, but not as intensely, blowing newspaper and candy wrappers around her feet. Her breath came harsh and loud. She'd perspired through her sweater and was shaking as she struggled to compose herself. Then she made her way back down the other levels, grasping the handrail with each uncertain step.

On his next visit to the park, Ivan brought pastrami sandwiches and seltzer to share with Shmuel. He'd packed them carefully and included a small container of mustard and two pieces of almond and honey havalah he'd gotten at Wasserman's bakery that morning. He felt good about this treat he would share with his friend. Anticipation was an alien feeling to him because previously what he'd anticipated he also dreaded. He kept looking toward the park's entrance to see Shmuel trudging in with his bags of nuts and bread for the creatures that dwelt in the trees, woods, and lake. There seemed to be a problem with the fountain pump. It spurted periodically instead of steadily and didn't shoot up in the air as high as it usually did, creating a meditative splashing sound upon its return. For some reason he found the malfunctioning of it disconcerting. He sat there for another twenty minutes and wondered if he should eat half of his sandwich.

The hotdog vendor opened the side door of his wagon and approached Ivan with a newspaper rolled up in one hand. "You waitin' for the squirrel guy?" Immediately this put Ivan off. He disliked being addressed by people he didn't know. "Well, you're gonna have a long wait, pal."

"What are you talking about?" Ivan snapped.

"Your friend took a dive."

"What are you saying?"

"Two nights ago, he hopped off the Western Gateway Bridge downtown. He's probably in New York harbor by now."

"No!" Ivan felt as if he'd been struck by a thunderbolt. "No, that can't be." But he knew very well that it was possible.

"Here, it's in the Gazette," the vendor said, handing him the newspaper.

Ivan read the obituary: Shmuel Krakoff, local resident, dead at sixty-five. What caught in Ivan's chest was: No known next of kin. Arrangements with M. Levine and Sons. Ivan thought, *I was kin to him...* He remembered Shmuel saying, 'I should not be alive. I wouldn't be if I had the courage.' *Was it courage for him to take his own life?* Ivan threw the newspaper and lunch items into the trash. He walked home in a depressed state, not paying attention to where he was going. Eventually, he found himself in an unfamiliar neighborhood at the far side of a huge cemetery known as Vale Park. He was lost and slightly panicked, and he resented having to ask a stranger for directions. The first person he saw was an elderly woman pushing, what he assumed, was all of her belongings in a shopping cart. He was reluctant, but he asked her for directions to Broadway. He noticed when she answered that she was almost toothless.

"Got yourself lost, sonny boy?"

"I need directions to Broadway."

"Through there," she pointed at the cemetery entrance.

He observed the entrance and the hundreds of stones, crosses, and markers fading into the distance, overshadowed by Cypress and Pine trees. "Is there another way?" he asked.

She threw her head back and laughed making her face an unpleasant toothless mask. "You don't have time to take that way unless you want to go swimming." She indicated the road stretching out behind them.

He thought for a moment to get a taxi, but the idea of wasting money on himself was completely alien. "How far?" he asked.

"Give me a dime and I'll tell you." He handed her a dime. "Twenty minutes. Follow the path through the cemetery until you reach the front gate. Turn right on State Street until you get to Crescent Park. You'll know when you get there." She cleared her throat and spat on the curb. "Give me another dime—I'll tell your fortune."

Ivan had never spent a dime frivolously. Money, for him, had come to mean safety, escape, and survival. But for some reason he handed her a dime. She looked in his face for a long moment then said: "Tell the girl she's playing with fire, hellfire. If she gets through it, she'll have her freedom. That's what the girl wants, freedom." She let out a piercing laugh, a witch's laugh that bounced off the tombstones.

Perplexed, annoyed, and anxious, Ivan entered the cemetery path quickly to get away from her. He turned back and shot a disapproving glance at the woman, but she was already gone. How had she disappeared like that? He walked on with a feeling of dread, unaware that he passed Josh's grave, where Mimi had had him unceremoniously buried. One of only a few Stars of David in the cemetery.

*

Rudy had put the ring on layaway and paid it off over a period of months. The Zales finance program of 'a penny down and a dollar a week' was no longer in force. He scraped hard and paid five dollars a week. At the end he brought home a 14K white gold, heart-shaped peridot with a diamond halo, an engagement ring, if she'd have it. He'd chosen a peridot because it was her birthstone and somehow the luminescent green color fit her personality. He didn't know that the Egyptians referred to the peridot as 'the gem of the sun.' They believed it had special healing powers.

It took Rudy two weeks to present the ring to Davora, who at first refused to open the ring box. She'd just come from the garage after servicing a Packard 148 touring limousine. She'd performed a major tune-up on its massive engine and her overalls and hands were covered with grease. There were smudges on her face as well. She pushed it back into his hand and told him he was making a mistake. That he had the wrong girl. "You're the greatest gal in the world and I'd do anything for you," he pleaded, pushing the ring box back into her hands. They stood there at an impasse for a few moments as the bells from St. Joseph's chimed five times.

Maybe it was the bells tolling, but something fluttered through her mind so quickly she couldn't glimpse it. She opened the box and gasped. "Is this real?"

He nodded and looked down. "It's real, alright. Just made the last payment. I thought... I'm asking... will you marry..." He couldn't get the last word out. Davora was deep in thought. The ring symbolized more than Rudy's affection for her.

"Davora, where are you?" She pushed her thoughts away and looked at him. He was on his knees. "Please, I have to have you. I don't know what I'll do if you say no."

She brushed his thinning hair as though he were a little boy. "You can't *have* me. You can't *own* me. We're not meant to be slaves." She took the ring out of the box and examined it. "It must have cost a fortune."

"You're worth more than a fortune, little bee. Look, just wear it for a few days. See how it feels. That's all I'm asking. Please..."

She slid it on to her finger and instantaneously felt the power of the gem. Rudy jumped up and kissed her soiled hands. "Yes, just wear it." He wanted to embrace her but didn't want to take a chance how that might go. He looked at her, scanned her face as if he were trying to memorize it. "You are not like any girl I've ever known before. You're not even like any *person* I've ever met before. You're...different."

"You don't know how different," she said with resignation. She felt the power of the ring move through her finger and up her arm and into her chest, warming it. *Was it wise to put on,* she wondered?

"Never... I'll always l-l-lov—," he choked on the word, "you." Rudy returned to his shop, elated and nervous. Would she really have him? Marry him? He thought that it would not perhaps be a normal marriage. *I don't care,* he said out loud. *I love her.*

Davora went into the house and stood at the window. She slid the ring off and looked inside at the shank and saw the stamp, 14K. It was in fact gold and she had no reason to believe the jewels weren't authentic. She held it up to the fading light. The glassy luster of the peridot was almost hypnotic and the diamond halo sparkled. Rudy had gone to great lengths to show his love. Could she let this man into her heart? Was there something she could love about him? Maybe it was the fact that he accepted her as she was. He would allow her to be herself, and wasn't that the greatest act of love you could show a person—to accept them as they are, and not try to shape them into an image of what you think they should be?

She slid the ring on her finger again and admired it. Peridot, a crystal of positive energy. A talisman for recognizing the creator's frequency of love. And used with right intent it expands one's ability to receive from the universe. Pitdah, the Hebrew word for peridot. She'd committed to memory much of what she'd read, including another fact: Moses' brother Aaron the priest wore a peridot when he went into battle. That fact unnerved her as she stared across the street at the ramp where a stream of workers entered the gaping opening as if being swallowed up into the next world. The street lights cast a muted glow on the structure causing it to look as though it pulsated. She made her decision. She would have to go in again—all the way up to the top this time.

She went into the kitchen and was shocked to see Jake at the kitchen table. He was spooning up a bowl of borscht as if he hadn't eaten in days. Sarah was at the counter slicing brisket into a dish for him. He immediately got up and embraced Davora. "Bisl bin," he said joyously. That was her nickname, used only in the family, Bisl Bin, Little Bee. He held her in an athletic grip that felt like he could crush her. She sat down at the table. Sarah brought the meat and Jake devoured it. She poured a glass of milk for Davora and put some hamantaschen on a napkin.

"What is that?" Sarah said, staring at her hand.

"Oh, it's from Rudy."

Sarah held her hands up to her cheeks. "He proposed?

Jake paused his voracious chewing. "You're getting married? My little Bisl Bin getting married?" He gave her another bear hug that almost caused her to spit out the pastry.

"Does your father know?" Sarah asked, visibly alarmed.

"Mama, it just happened."

Jake wiped his mouth on his sleeve. "Is he a good man?"

Davora studied her glass of milk for a few moments. "He's a good man. I just don't know if I..."

"This is not the old country," Sarah said. "I was given to your father by my father. I learned to love him because he's a good man. He saved our family." She turned away and rested her hands on the sink, her shoulders collapsing. "If you don't love Rudy don't marry him. Life's too short."

"Maybe I should have a chat with this Rudy fellow," Jake offered.

"No, Jake. I can take care of myself."

Davora noticed that Jake had lost weight since she'd last seen him. He needed a shave and his clothes were stained. She struggled to remember the name of the woman he lived with. "What about, what's her name?"

"It doesn't matter. I'm moving back in."

"Does Papa know this?"

"Yes, he told Ben to tell me to come back. He said he'd made a mistake."

It was the first time in their lives that Sarah and Davora had heard Ivan admit that he'd made a mistake. Then she remembered the letter she'd written to him. Had it really helped to change Ivan's mind? Either way, she was happy. Jake was home and Josh had been reborn, she hoped, from the Tree of Life, wherever he was.

Sarah looked at her children affectionately. "Some happiness maybe, for a change."

A few days later, Davora wandered down Broadway feeling restless and trapped by her surroundings. There was so much more to see in the world and she wanted to see it. Only the rich traveled with their steamer trunks and visited exotic places. She was also confused with the events that were spinning around her. She stopped in the stationery store and got a new journal. She'd already filled up seven of them and it was time for the next one. She drifted along looking in the shop windows. There were fresh pastries displayed in Wasserman's Bakery. She decided to get a box of mandelbrot and chocolate babka to bring home for Sunday dinner. It would save Sarah some extra work. She was busy making her special brisket, tzimmes, and lokshen kugel. The desert Davora got would go perfectly with it.

She left the bakery feeling a bit more settled because she'd gotten something her family would enjoy. She stopped to look in the window of Grobart's dress shop. She liked to follow the new styles and could replicate any dress she saw perfectly, to the last stitch. She prided herself on sewing her own clothes. Ivan had taught her well. She started back to the house, but heard something and involuntarily followed the sound. It was coming from the Three Aces. She crossed the street, which was quieter on a Sunday. The door was open and she peaked in and waited for her eyes to adjust to the darkness. The smell of beer and smoke filled her head. She saw him; Big Daddy Flanagan was sitting at the piano playing something beautiful and enthralling. She stepped inside the doorway to listen. A woman was wiping glasses at the bar and hanging them in a glass rack. She stopped and stared at Davora, squinting her eyes at the unwelcome intrusion. At first Davora cowered and backed away. *No*, she told herself. She squared her shoulders and walked up to the big man and stood next to the piano. He smiled at her, a deep open smile, and kept playing. She closed her eyes and tapped her fingers together to the rhythm. He finished the tune and laughed a loud thunderous laugh. "What was that?" she asked.

"Little Chickie, you finally made it in the door."

Suddenly embarrassed at her brazenness, she stammered, "I heard the music and I..."

"You like it?" he smiled. "No reason you shouldn't. Mr. Fats Waller. That's his Jitterbug Waltz."

She remembered the first time she'd met Rudy. He'd asked her if she was the girl in the Jitterbug dress. Was there some connection?
]

"I'm sorry, it's just so beautiful."

Flanagan closed his eyes and started playing again, something slow, quiet, and low. The woman at the bar tilted her head toward the entrance, signaling Davora that she should leave. The music held her there. His thick, stubby fingers struck the keys effortlessly. She could feel it in her stomach and chest. She listened; she drank in the music as if she'd been thirsty for a long time. Suddenly it was over with a last, sad, held chord. Then it was very quiet. Her eyes were wide and he intuited her question. "That, little Chickie, is the blues. 'Cause everybody gets 'em."

"Thank you," she whispered and left quickly. She heard the tune over and over in her head and marveled at how his large, powerful hands could make such precise, heartbreaking sounds. She felt sad, but uplifted at the same time. She wondered, *the blues, is that what I have?*

*

In preparation for what might be a marriage in the offing, Sarah insisted on taking Davora to Katz's in Albany. She had bought each of the girls a fur piece when they'd married. Davora thought it was a waste of money and resisted as long as she could. But the idea made Sarah happy so she finally gave in. They decided to make a day of it. They would take the Route 5 bus into Albany and walk up the hill to Katz's, then have lunch at Gershon's deli, see a movie, and come home on the seven o'clock bus. It turned out they missed that bus because they'd lingered at a soda fountain. Davora was delighted that Sarah could still, under the right circumstances, enjoy herself and laugh.

It was dark by the time they boarded the eight o'clock bus which was unusually empty. They sat toward the back on a bench seat still enjoying their time together. After a few blocks the bus stopped and picked up another passenger. At first glance he appeared to be a vagrant, perhaps a homeless person. He moved slowly, unsteadily, and carried a hiking stick or staff to help balance himself. He wore a thick robe of what looked like burlap and a diamond patterned black and white scarf over his head and around his neck which obscured his face. It was the kind of scarf she'd seen in pictures of Bedouins in the Sinai desert.

He sat directly across from them and leaned his staff against the window. There was a carved head on the top, possibly a lion or a panther with garnets set in the eyes. Suddenly the citrusy scent of Cyprus filled the air. Slowly he removed the scarf to reveal a face that looked like it had been carved out of granite. Davora immediately felt anxious. This was not some vagrant who'd used his last token to take a bus ride. Prominent among his features were his eyes, razor-focused blue orbs examining everything before them intently. He was staring at her hand, directly at her ring, the peridot. As he studied her ring his intense blue eyes watered and began to transform into a green luster. She pulled the muff from her handbag and slid her hands into it and whispered to Sarah, "He wants the ring."

"Who?" Sarah asked.

"Him," she said, her throat tightening. "That man."

"What man?" Sarah asked.

"That man, there," she said, her voice shrill.

Sarah looked up and down the aisle. "I don't see any man."

Davora stood quickly and pulled the cord, signaling the driver they were getting off at the next stop. She grabbed Sarah's arm and pulled. "We're getting off." When they got to the front of the bus the driver released the folding door, but it didn't open. They heard the whoosh sound of the rear door opening and looked back. No one was there. The door closed and then the front door opened. The driver got up and went to inspect the rear door. He checked all the seats in the back and returned.

"That's funny," he said. "Must be something wrong with the doors."

"There isn't anything wrong with them," Davora said. They sat down and rode the rest of the way home in silence. Sarah glanced at Davora nervously, afraid that something had taken over her child. Davora turned her head away and pretended she was looking out the window. She took deep breaths to calm herself.

*

At first Ivan refused to come out of his room and meet with the man. "He says he has an important matter to discuss with you," Ben said, who'd come to the house to help Sarah move some furniture in the living room.

"Tell him to go away." Ivan was still afflicted with the fear of speaking with any stranger. In Poland it was not safe to divulge anything about yourself, your family, or your business. You could be turned in to the Gestapo.

"It's something about a friend of yours...Shmuel. You know him?"

Ivan opened the door. "Shmuel?" he said "Shmuel?"

"I think that's it."

Ivan went to the front door and cracked it open. "What do you want?"

A short, stout, balding man in a wrinkled black suit, a stained white shirt, and a pale green tie stood before him. He held a valise under his arm. "I'm Guttmann of Guttmann, Guttmann, and Sachs."

"So?"

"Are you Ivan Rosensweig?"

The struggle came back—*always protect yourself.* "What if I am?"

"We did some work for your son, Josh, when he closed on his house."

"My son is dead."

"I know, please accept..."

"What do you want?" Ivan interrupted.

"Did you know Shmuel Krakoff?"

Ivan hesitated. "He's dead."

The man looked down feigning sadness. Ivan noticed his shoes, scuffed brown penny loafers with only one faded penny inserted in the left shoe. "I know, tragic. He never got over the loss of his family."

This angered Ivan, and he snapped, "Would you?"

"No, no, of course not. It's too much to bear. But he loved his furry creatures."

Losing patience, Ivan shouted, "What the hell do you want?"

"Have you ever heard of the ASPCA? It's the American Society for the Prevention of Cruelty to Animals."

"So what?"

Guttmann opened his valise and took out a piece of paper. "Well, he was very generous with that group in his will."

"What will? The man had nothing; dressed like a beggar."

"Looks are deceiving," Guttmann chuckled.

"And what is your point?"

Guttmann scanned the paper he was holding in his hand. "My point is, Mr. Rosenzweig, Shmuel was very fond of you. He included you in his will, an inheritance."

Ivan thought that this was some kind of scam that Guttmann was going to ask him for some money at any moment in order to release the inheritance.

Guttmann cleared his throat. "Quite an inheritance, I might add."

"What? A bag of nuts and some stale bread?"

Guttmann reached back into his valise and took out an envelope and handed it to Ivan. "A lot of nuts and bread. More than you'll ever need."

Ivan opened the envelope and looked at the check. "My God," he gasped "Oh my God."

Guttmann shoved a card at Ivan. "If you have any questions call our office." The little man backed away, bowing as if he were taking leave of a nobleman.

*

At the end of spring, summer burst upon the town with a blast of heat as if the GE plant had opened its massive doors and allowed the turbines to release their discharge into the air. Davora had just taken a cool shower and returned to her room to dress. She had a full day at the garage where she was scheduled to replace a clutch on an Oldsmobile with almost eighty thousand miles on it. Ben wouldn't let any of the other mechanics attempt it. One of them,

Leroy, would assist Davora, but she was to be in charge of the job. Leroy was Big Daddy Flanagan's nephew and she was especially fond of him. She made it a point to teach him everything she knew for when she'd finally *get out*. She wanted for him to have a solid job as a mechanic. He was a talented kid and played the alto sax in his uncle's band. She had convinced Ben to hire him. He was reluctant at first. Prejudice cut both ways. They had a heated discussion about hiring Leroy until Davora reminded Ben where they had come from and why they had to leave.

With Leroy helping, the job went smoothly. He stood nearby and knew exactly which tools to hand her as he cleaned up fluid spills and moved the lamp around so she could see well. They chatted while they worked, which Leroy seemed to enjoy very much. Almost none of the white women in the neighborhood would talk to a Black man. Davora thought that was silly; worse than that, it could lead to what was happening in Poland. She asked him about his childhood. He'd grown up in the neighborhood singing in the Living Truth Tabernacle and learning to read music as he studied the alto sax. Big Daddy Flanagan had been the choral conductor and organist as well.

"So you know this neighborhood really well."

"Like the back of my hand."

"Have you ever gone up there?" She tilted her head to the left to indicate the ramp.

"Oh, you mean up there? The Seven Heavens?"

She stopped working and lowered her wrench. "You call it the Seven Heavens?"

"Everybody knows that. My Aunt Grace says she saw the Lord up there sitting on his throne."

Davora was shocked. "She did?"

"Sure she did. She sees God everywhere. Saw the Virgin Mary in her Jell-O. Then she ate it."

Davora tried not to react and began working on the car again. "Give me the three-quarter inch, please." He already had it in his hand reaching out to her.

*

As summer came on in earnest, Rudy instituted a full-court press to convince Davora that he was the right man in her life. He was pushing for an early August wedding and a honeymoon in Florida where he wanted to take her to a magical place called the Everglades. He finally gave her an ultimatum: she could accept him or return the ring, the peridot with the diamond halo that he'd given her months before. He'd been patient, but now that he was doing well he wanted to get on with his life, a life he hoped to share with her. She acknowledged that it was a fair demand and asked him to be patient for just one more week. All Rudy understood about her was that he loved her and she was the most unusual person he'd ever met. But there was something she needed to settle for herself. Something she could not explain to him or to anyone else. She hadn't been into the ramp for sometime and she realized that she'd been avoiding it. When she accepted the fact that she was afraid, that was the impetus to make up her mind. She wouldn't give in to fear; she was going back in.

She decided it would be on the following Friday. She would wait until noon, between shifts at the plant, when she would be reasonably assured that Ivan would be on one of his walks. He would also attend Shabbat on the way home so there was no chance he would see her emerging from the ramp after...whatever might happen. She was intrigued and unnerved at what Leroy said about his Aunt Grace seeing God on his throne on the seventh level. Was it true? Davora had heard of instances of people seeing the Virgin Mary on cave walls and even pancakes. Was it just them longing to see such things? She had to find out. She'd read that the Seventh Heaven was the holiest of all—the home of God and his crystal throne, encircled by fire and angels.

She took a deep breath and started for the door when she noticed it. An envelope sticking out of her vanity drawer, a peach colored envelope, like the ones she used. She slid it out and opened it. There were two folded letters in it. She opened the first and gasped. There was two hundred and fifty dollars in it. And scribbled in Ivan's tight hand were just three words: *For nursing school.* She held the money in her hands and stared out the window. Suddenly the bills felt wet; she was crying on them. She sobbed into her pillow so no one would hear her. *Papa, you did this...* What had changed in him? He seemed so distant and lost in himself. *Oh papa, I love you so much.* And so much had changed for her, she thought. Did she even still want to become a nurse? With the money she'd saved working for Ben and this windfall she could put a down payment on her own apartment. That's what she wanted, she thought. Wasn't it? Or maybe she would travel. She'd dreamed of seeing the Pyramids. Was it possible for a young immigrant girl to do this? She didn't even know how to get a passport.

She put the money in her vanity drawer and slid the other letter out of the envelope. It was the one she'd written to Ivan weeks before, pleading with him to allow Jake back into the house. He'd returned it to her for some reason, maybe to let her know that he had given it some thought and changed his mind. She read the letter as it was her habit to read anything that came into her hands. *Dear Papa, I am so sorry if I offended you by going to Josh's funeral. I loved Josh very much, as I love you. I disobeyed and disrespected you, but I had no choice. I will never see my brother again and I miss him so much. (She couldn't tell Ivan that she had seen Josh and under what circumstances. He wouldn't believe her.) You still have Jake and Ben. Jake is a good man even if he is not up to your expectations. It's wrong to turn your back on your son. Once he told me that he wished he could have been as strong and decisive as you. Papa, what you did for our family was brave and wonderful. You saved us from the death camp and made a good life for us here. I want to be the girl you want me to be. But I also want to be free to live my own life and make my own choices. Isn't that why you saved us, so we could be free? So we could live without fear? I know how hard this has been for you. Please believe me that I will always love and respect you. Davora.*

Davora entered the ramp entrance at noon just as the whistle sounded at the plant. It was already eighty-five degrees, but it felt cooler in the shaded structure. She made her way up deliberately, acutely aware of any sounds or people who might be ahead of or behind her. There was a humming sound. Depending on how much wind there was and what velocity it was blowing at, there were often different pitched tones in the structure. Thus far she'd not seen anyone up to the fifth and sixth levels. Then she made the turn into the seventh incline and thought she heard music, but it seemed to be coming from below. She leaned over the railing and peered down and saw a Good Humor ice cream truck. It was the source of the music, but not the usual tinny song it played, recorded from a calliope. It sounded familiar, like something she'd heard many years ago. There were strings accompanying the song, which was not what you'd hear from an ice cream truck. Suddenly the words came to her, Oyfn Pripetchik, a sorrowful Yiddish song she'd heard in her childhood in Szemud. It had to do with giving someone, usually a child, a menorah, and the idea of maintaining the light of Torah study. The song caught in her throat and chest and she began to cry.

She cried for Ivan, for what he'd endured. She cried for Josh. And she cried for her homeland which she would never see again. How could anyone, the perpetrators or their victims, ever look each other in the eye again? She cried for Rudy also, realizing that she was perhaps someone who could never marry, never give up her independence. She had tasted freedom in the new world and she hungered for more of it. And all of it...what had brought her to this moment, about to enter the highest level, the Seventh Heaven, and see for herself if God was there on his throne, flanked by angels?

What could happen to her if she were to see such an awesome sight? She entered the seventh level and walked to the top. There was garbage strewn about, empty soup cans, crumpled bags, crusts of bread from sandwiches that had been discarded. And it smelled of urine. She concluded that perhaps a group of hoboes had spent the previous night there. There was nothing sacred or holy about the place. In some way she felt relieved. What she'd already seen in this place had upended her life, changed her permanently. And she had no one to share it with.

She began her descent as the intensity of the music increased, now with a woman's soprano singing the heartbreaking melody. No longer in the distance, the music surrounded her. Davora began to tear up again. When she got to the fifth level she saw two vagrants rounding the curve. One carried a crutch; the other looked as though he carried a book under his arm. She assumed that they were part of the hobo group returning to look for scraps or a place to relieve themselves. When she was within ten feet of them they stopped and waited for her to approach, which frightened her. They stood apart so she would have to pass between them. "What do you want?" she screamed. The one with the crutch, she suddenly realized, was instead carrying a staff with a carved head on the top, possibly a lion or a panther with garnets set in the eyes. The same staff that the vagrant had with him on the bus when she and Sarah had returned from Albany. It was the same fierce man in the burlap robe and sandals, but he was wearing a necklace, a thick silver chain with a perfectly round peridot the size of a walnut. It glowed with a greenish sheen and rotated like a miniature planet.

There was no choice but to pass between them, which she attempted to do but stopped involuntarily. Her legs weren't weak, but she couldn't move them. She willed herself to move forward, but she couldn't. The man faced her and removed the necklace and held it out to her. Slowly, without thought, she raised her hand and pressed her ring against his necklace. The two stones touched, creating a spark that ignited into a greenish-blue flame, which gave off heat without burning her hand. Suddenly she was overcome with feelings of grief and sorrow, deeper and more intense feelings than she'd ever experienced before. It was profound and shocking. She understood in that moment that she was suffering the loss of millions. The deprivation, the torture, millions gone into the flames. Her people and the others caught in the murderous web of the Third Reich. Only people without souls could perpetrate such crimes. She wept uncontrollably for the dead, the mothers, the fathers, the children.

The other "vagrant" touched her arm gently. She turned and looked into a deeply lined face, the face of the Black Hebrew Egyptian Prince. Not the White face lie that had been handed down for centuries. His crinkled beard disappeared into his robe. He slid the blue sapphire stone tablet from under his arm and took her hand gently and placed it upon it. She traced the tablet with her fingertips. She could feel the words carved into it. And she could hear the words: *Honor thy Father and Mother.* He released her hand and a swirling feeling came over her as if she were being drawn up into the air. The men backed away from her to either side of the railing. She stood equidistant between them, overcome with emotion. Then she became aware of an intense blue light. She looked about for the source of it and realized it was coming from herself. Rather, the men were projecting the light on to her from their chests, specifically from their hearts. She looked down at her torso and legs and saw that the light was entering her body—she was taking it in. It looked watery and reminded her of when she'd studied amoebas with a microscope. Her sorrow began to dissipate and she felt herself overtaken by an unimaginable sense of reverence, of love for her family and all the families that had perished. There was a brief disturbance like sheet lightning. She looked up and the men, the prophets, were gone. The music stopped with a final loud chord that startled her. She staggered to the railing and leaned over, gulping in the humid air. She thought: *I am changed.*

*

She ran through the neighborhood; she had to find Ivan. She entered the synagogue, quickly covering her head. Instead of going directly up to the balcony she disobeyed the mechitza law that men and women should be separated, and went straight to the main floor of the sanctuary and stood beside him. The other men, bent in prayer, made audible gasps and moved away from her. They stared disapprovingly. "You are not supposed to be here," Ivan whispered.

"Papa, I belong here as much as any of them," she said, referring to the affronted crowd that had gathered in the isle. "I came to pray with you." She pressed on and said the prayers and recitations with as much authority as any of the others, and in flawless Hebrew that astonished Ivan. He hadn't realized that she had retained so much. The men had stopped davening and the sanctuary became silent except for one voice. The rabbi turned to see where the female voice was coming from. Davora finished the prayer and waited in the silence. The rabbi's eyes widened. He spoke to the men in a hushed voice and then retreated to an anteroom where the worshipers followed him. Ivan and Davora remained seated. She noticed a tremor in his hands, his veins pulsating as he grasped the bench before him. His jaw was clenched. This was not what she'd intended. She had infuriated him. Finally, he stood and exited abruptly. She followed him for a few blocks, afraid to approach him. He stopped at Erie Boulevard and waited for the cars to pass, the late afternoon traffic, competitive and impatient. She caught up and stood beside him. He stood erect and unapproachable, his birdlike head movements glancing left and right at the traffic, waiting for a safe moment. He must have been livid with her. When it was time to cross the wide street she felt something touch her hand. It was his; he'd taken hold of her hand as he had when she was a little girl, walking home with him from shul. Without looking at her he continued to hold her hand firmly, but not too firm, as they walked back to the house. And in those moments her heart filled, he'd accepted her finally, as his child, his equal adult child—a gesture, an embrace, with just a hand, that would last her for a lifetime.

She was up most of that night, preparing, packing, praying, and crying. She wrote the letter and wrapped it around the ring box with the beautiful, now sanctified peridot inside. She crept down the stairs from the kitchen to the basement and left the letter and box on Rudy's workbench. Through her tears, she tried to console herself that Rudy was not a man who would go through life without a partner, and one day he would have children. Writing the note to Sarah was devastating, but she knew that somehow Sarah would understand. A mother knows the heart of her daughter. She slipped it into the pocket of Sarah's apron hung by the stove. For Ivan, she left her Hebrew school book with a message explaining where she was going and why. She promised that she would return to him after she'd accomplished something she needed to do, knowing that nothing is ever completely accomplished, and that survival was not necessarily guaranteed. She prayed that he would understand.

She left early that morning carrying a satchel and her backpack. The journals she'd filled up weighed on her shoulders, but she couldn't leave them behind. She hadn't realized until that moment that she'd written so much and that perhaps that's what she was, what she wanted to be: a writer. When she'd crossed the street she looked back at the house. It was the second time in her young life that she'd left her home. Once by Ivan's intuition and insistence; and this time by her own choice, a sense of urgency that forced her to go. As much as she loved her family she would lose the person she would become if she stayed—another death. In the predawn light the house looked transformed, listing to one side as if it had lost stability, uncertain on its foundation, the paint peeling from the pine siding, the windows cracked, and the shingles missing from the steep pitched roof. She tried to tell herself that she was imagining it. Behind the house in the distance, the ever watchful eye of the GE emblem faded in and out, flexing its corporate authority over those it ruled. She turned quickly and ran down the block until she reached The Three Aces. She peaked in the window, half hoping Big Daddy Flanagan might be there, but he wasn't. His piano stood at the ready, the cigarette burns on its ivory keys, waiting to be reanimated when the big man returned. She pressed her hand on the glass and pictured his stubby nimble fingers flying over the keys, his gold wedding band glinting in the neon glow of the beer sign. Then she walked steadily, determinedly, to the train station. The same one Rudy Stine had arrived at in the blizzard of 1940.

*

She bought a ticket for Empire Service which would take her to Penn Station in New York. From there she'd have to find her way downtown. She was surprised that the car was so packed that early in the morning. She walked down the aisle and couldn't find a seat. She made her way back up the aisle in case she'd missed one. An old man motioned to her. "You need a seat, miss? Here, take mine."

"Oh no, I couldn't. You need it." He looked unsteady and frail and she thought he needed the seat more than her before the train lurched forward. He smiled jovially. "Oh, I really don't need a seat. Here, you take it." He got up and stepped to the side so she could sit down. Once she was settled, he looked at her with a warm expression and said, "Good, you should be comfortable." She had never seen him before, yet there was something familiar about him.

When the train stopped in Poughkeepsie the woman next to Davora got up and exited. There were a few open seats and the man sat down next to her. "Sitting, standing, it's all the same to me," he chuckled. She hoped he wasn't going to be too talkative because she needed to think. Beyond getting to New York she was not sure how it would all work out. "Is this going to be your first time in the big city?" he asked.

"Yes...well, no. I stayed there for a week when my family first arrived."

"Oh, you came from the old country, perhaps?"

"Yes, Poland." She was starting to feel uncomfortable. She hoped he wouldn't turn out to be like some of the men who trolled through the ramps leering at young women.

He took out a small bag of nuts from his coat pocket and offered her some. "Do you have family in New York?"

She didn't want to be rude, but he was making her very uneasy. "Why are you asking me if I have family there?"

"Oh, I'm so sorry, just a nosy old man. You sure you won't have some peanuts?"

She answered coldly and firmly so he'd understand. "No."

He was quiet for a while. "Perhaps you're meeting an old friend?" How could he know she would be looking for Shana? She felt inside her purse for the crumpled piece of paper that Shana had written her address and phone number on so long ago. She decided that she would change her seat and started to get up.

"Please, don't go. I have something I'd like to tell you."

Just at that moment the train conductor came by to check on the passengers. She raised her hand to get his attention.

He whispered, "I know your father. I know Ivan."

The conductor stopped and she said, "How long is it until we get to Penn Station?"

He slipped his gold pocket watch out and said, "We'll be there in one hour and thirty-five minutes." He tipped his hat and continued down the aisle.

"How do you know my father?"

"We met in Central Park. Not the one in New York City."

She considered this for a few moments and then became alarmed again. "How do you know I'm his daughter? And who are you?"

He drew himself up a bit. "I'm Oliver Kent Crosswright," he chuckled, "Shmuel to my friends."

"I'm not your friend," she said forcefully.

"You're much like your father was when I first met him, fierce and suspicious—with good reason, where we come from. Anyway, I'll tell you what you need to know. Then I'll get out of your life. You won't see me again unless things change." He cleared his throat and said ironically, "Probably no one will see me again. But where I've been lately, it doesn't matter."

"Who are you? Tell me."

He answered quietly. "Someone who cares about you. OK, you got something to write with? Good, write this down, 421 Riverside Drive. It's by 81st Street."

"Why? What's it for?"

"You'll need it later...trust me." She wrote it down inside the cover of the most recent journal she'd been writing in. She tucked Shana's scribbled note with the address on Canal Street in with it. They sat in silence for a while. Finally he said, "I'm going to the club car. Do you want something to eat?"

"No, thank you." She was hungry, but she couldn't let him buy her food, whoever he was. He returned and ate his sandwich and drank an orange soda, and then he sank inside of himself as if he was meditating. He nodded his head in assent as if he were receiving instructions. When they reached 175th Street, the Bronx, he said, "OK, my stop, though I'm headed to 190th, my new assignment, not that it matters."

"That's where you live?" she asked.

His facial expression was serious but warm. "I'm still finding out where I live. I think you're gonna live here maybe." He touched her arm lightly and his fingers cracked. "Don't forget to visit your father; he's going to miss you." He got up and headed to the exit.

Whoever he was, she sensed he meant her no harm. Maybe he was trying to help her, guide her perhaps. "Thank you," she called out. "Goodbye, goodbye Shmuel." *Shmuel*...as his friends called him.

The cavernous Penn Station and huge crowd made her anxious. People bumped and jostled one another to get to their connecting trains and destinations. She ran up to the first ticket window she saw and tried to buy a ticket to Canal Street. She was directed to the subway below the station, which heightened her anxiety. After numerous inquiries she found a sympathetic booking clerk who sold her a token and gave directions to Canal Street. The train ride downtown both shocked and exhilarated her. People actually lived this way, with all the activity and noise, and acted as though it was completely normal. And there were so many different nationalities all traveling in the cramped car together.

She wandered around the neighborhood for a while, glancing at the address on the crumpled scrap of paper that Shana had pressed into her hand so long ago. She couldn't make sense of the building numbers. Finally, she asked a Chinese woman. She stared at the scrap and said something very quickly. Davora shrugged to show that she didn't understand. The woman pointed in the direction she'd been going in and gave her a little push. She'd remembered an imposing wood and brink single-family house, but what she found at 124 Canal Street was a bodega. She checked the address again and went in. A young Hispanic man greeted her. She showed him the scrap and asked him if it was the correct address. He said that it was. She asked him what had happened to the house that had been there. He said that ten years ago there had been a terrible fire in the neighborhood. The house she was looking for was one of the many destroyed in the blaze. "Did the people who lived here survive?" she asked.

"I don't know. It was very bad. Lots of people died." She looked around the shop and saw cans and jars of products she'd never seen before. She looked in the deli case and realized she hadn't eaten in about thirty-six hours. She was starving. The choices, especially the meats, did not look kosher. She ordered egg salad on a hard roll, a bag of potato chips, and a piece of flan. She'd heard of it, but never tasted it before. She felt distraught, without hope, but first she had to eat something, then she'd assess her situation. Outside, the street was hot and bright with sunlight. She sat down on a door stoop and devoured the sandwich and chips, as the traffic and pedestrians swirled around her. *I have never felt more alone,* she thought. Maybe she shouldn't have come to the city. Maybe she wasn't strong enough for this. The last thought got her on her feet and moving. She wouldn't give in to fear.

She didn't know how long or how far she walked, but she wound up at 12 Eldridge Street in front of an imposing building, a synagogue that had been erected in 1887. Instinctively, she went inside. She needed to rest, to sit down for a while and figure out her next move. She was amazed at the spectacle before her. It was a huge room with a high vaulted ceiling from which hung brilliant chandeliers. The pews were long, solid, and the wood reflected the warm light. She sat down in one and noticed the depressions in the floor where the worshipers had stood and prayed for decades. Sitting in the pew she viewed the monumental stained-glass windows. There was an extraordinary one in particular, high above the ark, a huge circular window of heavenly blue glass with stars depicting the constellations. She was mesmerized by its beauty.

She felt exhaustion overtaking her as she stared at the shimmering stained glass. She experienced a sensation of falling into it, swirling among the stars. She was suddenly a sky traveler comfortably moving between the massive bodies around her. It was a liberating and enjoyable experience as she floated and stared in awe. Slowly she lost altitude and drifted gently down until she was standing on the bimah, her back to the ark behind her. She looked out over the expanse of the synagogue toward the entrance, where a figure appeared and walked slowly and solemnly forward as if infirm. At the same moment she noticed on both sides of her peripheral vision two forms, one on her left, the other on her right. She knew at once who they were, the same beings she'd encountered on the fifth level, the prophets who bathed her in blue light. Everything seemed to freeze in place; she sensed it was a moment of great import. Her life was about to change again.

There was something familiar about the person approaching her. Words came to her: *in mourning.* In mourning for what, she wondered. She became aware of the sound of paper being torn. She turned around and saw that the ark had been opened and the Torah was on the table. The two men were standing on either side of the scripture, and one, the lawgiver whose name she could not bring herself to utter, tore bits of parchment from the holy document. The other touched his peridot necklace to each scrap, causing a spark to shoot out of it. Even in her trance or whatever power she was under, she looked on in horror at the act of desecrating the sacred scroll. At that moment she'd never feared God more in her life.

He, the lawgiver, the Black Hebrew Egyptian Prince, took her hand and placed a scrap in it and closed her fingers around it. The two descended the steps and received the man who made his way to the front of the synagogue and stood before them. She shuddered and began to weep as she looked upon Ivan whose visage was more ghostlike than human. Still, his quick birdlike gestures and sharp eyes took her in. The three entities began a metamorphosis as they pressed into each other, being absorbed into each other's bodies until they were one solid column of what looked like marble, but also a fountain of azure water, shooting up as high as the chandeliers, into the dazzling light. And then they were gone. Davora screamed with such volume that she thought she heard her voice echo throughout the cosmos.

She shook violently—or something shook her violently. "Miss, Miss, are you all right?"

She sat up and shrieked, "Papa, papa! Please God...not Papa!"

The woman shook her again. "How did you get in here? Miss? You're not supposed to be in here."

"I'm sorry...sorry, I didn't know."

"You're shaking. You're not well. Here, come with me," she said forcefully.

"Are you going to call the police?" The woman led Davora into a side office, an apartment. She lit a kettle on the stove and spooned out some Yemenite soup that was already heating. She cut a thick piece of Challah bread and placed it in front of Davora with some sweet butter.

"Eat; you look like you're starving." Davora didn't have to be told twice. She did pause for a moment. The bread tasted just like Sarah's. She glanced at her benefactor, thinking, after everything that had just happened, that it could be her. *Am I going crazy?* A chill rippled up her back as she thought of Ivan looking like a shade. *Was he all right?* She ate ravenously. The woman refilled her bowl before it was empty.

"What are you doing here?"

Davora sipped her tea; it was hot and strong. "I'm looking for a friend. Someone I knew a long time ago. She lived on Canal Street, but the house is gone."

"Do you mean the fire? It was horrible; people burned alive. Where is your friend now?"

"I don't know." Suddenly she remembered the address Shmeul had told her to write down. She pulled the journal out of her knapsack and opened the cover. The address was written inside. There also was the scrap of paper Shana had given her, and one more: the piece of parchment the lawgiver had pressed into her hand on the bimah. She examined and saw the letters IBAH and gasped. "Ivan, my God, Ivan. I don't know what's happening to me. I'm frightened."

"Of course, you're far away from home. You would be frightened." She set a small plate down with a piece of sponge cake on it. Davora ate it and drank the tea. "You are so kind. My body was starving."

The woman stood over her. "We all starved," she said, her voice dark like night dropping down hard.

"You were there?" Davora asked. "What is your name? Do you live in this shul?"

"I'm Katia. I'm a docent—I give tours of this place." She didn't answer the first question. Davora didn't ask again. "So what are your plans?"

"To find my friend. If she accepts me I may stay with her for a while...if she remembers me."

"Where is she?"

She looked at the inside cover of her journal again. "She might live at 421 Riverside Drive by 81st Street. But I don't know how that could be." She decided not to tell Katia about Shmuel. And if that was her address, how could Shmuel have known that?

"My mother lives on 96th Street, a few up from where you're going. I'm going to see her after work. If you can wait a little I'll ride up with you."

"Yes, thank you." She was relieved to have someone to take the subway with. It was too easy to get lost. And she didn't know what she'd do if she didn't find Shana. She might have to get a hotel room for the night and go home in the morning. But home to what? The thought depressed her.

When the train stopped Katia gave her directions from the 79th Street station to walk west from Broadway toward Riverside Drive, then north to 421. She gave her a fierce hug with tears in her eyes. Davora returned her affection. "You'll come back and see me?" Katia said. "I'll make us lunch."

"I promise I will." Davora found the building easily and entered the foyer. A doorman approached her quickly before she reached the wall of mailboxes and asked if he could help her. She explained she was trying to find a friend. The doorman, a tall, angular man, reminded her of a circus contortionist. He told her in an unfriendly tone that she'd have to leave. Only people who lived in the building could enter. She tried to explain, but he told her to get out. She left quickly, confused why he'd been so rude. Is that what people were like in the city? Katia wasn't.

She walked back to Broadway. Maybe she'd go into one of the cafes and have tea and something else to eat. She admitted to herself that she felt empty, hollow, and frightened. She didn't feel she was an equal match for the grinding traffic and people rushing through the streets. They all seemed to have a purpose, a need to get to where they were going as fast as possible. She felt that she had to get out of their way. *I don't belong here*. She passed a phone booth on a corner, ducked in and closed the door. It slightly diminished the din outside. She had never used a pay phone before. There was a phone book attached to a chain with endless names and addresses to search. When she got to it there was almost a whole page with the last name Coblentz and twelve with S for the first initial. And what if Shana had married and had changed her last name? It was impossible. She decided to go back to the apartment building and assert herself against the hostile doorman, though she knew it would probably be futile. There was something sinister about him.

She peeked into the lobby and didn't see him there. Maybe he was having his supper. Quickly she snuck in and scanned the mailboxes. There was an S. and R. Coblentz. She didn't remember if Shana had a middle name. She looked around to make sure it was safe and grabbed the receiver and dialed 7H. A woman answered and Davora stammered, "I don't know if you know me, but I'm looking for Shana. Are you Shana Coblentz?"

The woman sounded angry. "Who is this?"

"I'm Davora. My family stayed with you on Canal Street when we got here. It was a long time ago."

"I don't remember you."

Davora panicked. "Your father's name is Norm...no it's Noam. And your sister is Rima. That's it, Rima."

"Stay there," the woman snapped, "I'm coming down."

Davora replaced the receiver and turned to see the doorman approaching her. "What are you doing in here?" He'd come up from the basement and was carrying a tire iron.

"I found the right apartment. My friend lives here, 7H." He looked at her menacingly. She didn't think she could run past him. His long arms dangled at his sides, the tire iron grasped in his left hand, and he seemed to be lifting in height and twisting over her.

"I told you to get out. You disobeyed me." The elevator door opened and a woman stepped out quickly. She was a stout woman with short grayish hair and a ruddy complexion. She went straight to Davora and took her by the arm. She told the doorman dismissively, "She's with me. My guest, do you understand?"

When the elevator door closed, the woman said, "I'm Rima. Shana and I share the apartment."

Davora felt her shoulders loosen. The confrontation with the doorman had frightened her. "Thank you. I thought he was going to hit me."

"Him?" she gestured at the door disgustedly. "He's getting fired. Goddamn anti-Semite. Listen, I have to explain to you about Shana. She's not well."

"She's ill?"

Rima looked at her hands. "She's very ill," she paused. "She's dying," she said quietly.

The elevator door opened. They stood in front of 7H. "I don't know if she'll recognize you."

"I'm so sorry. What is it?"

"Cancer in her brain. It's been a year. And now..."

They entered the apartment. Davora set down her satchel and removed her backpack. Her shoulders ached from carrying it around so long. For the first time since she'd left home she felt safe, but terribly saddened. Rima told her to wait and went into Shana's bedroom. She returned after a few minutes and told Davora to go in and just stand next to her bed. "Don't try to remind her. If she recognizes you it may lift her spirits. If not, just play along."

Davora nodded that she understood and went into the room. The shades were down and it was dark. There was a medicine smell, a pall about the place—a sickroom. And there was music playing, a record player on low volume playing music that reminded Davora of Big Daddy Flanagan, but different. It was jazzy but more like from a show. A woman was singing something she didn't recognize. She had seen the show Oklahoma when it played at the theater in town and marveled at the skill of the singers and musicians. She stood next to the bed and waited. She ached to tell Shana her name, that she'd finally come back to see her. She noticed that Shana's hand rested on top of the sheet. She placed her hand lightly on hers. Shana opened her eyes and stared at Davora, a look of desperation that softened and then a look of surprise and delight. Her voice was faint but clear. "Sophia, my Sophia, is it you? My sister, you've come back to me." She pulled on Davora's hand until she was leaning over her. "Come," she pleaded.

Davora pressed her face to Shana's cheek. "Dear Shana, my dear Shana." Their tears combined.

Shana hugged Davora with more strength than she would have thought possible. "I have you back and you'll never go away again. Tell me, Sophia...you'll never go away."

It burned in Davora's soul that she couldn't be taken for who she was, but she saw an expression of hope on Shana's face. "I promise," Davora said, "I'll never leave you again."

Rima had been standing behind in the doorway. She came into the room and took a bottle off the nightstand. She poured some medicine into a small cup, held Shana's head up and pressed it to her lips. She motioned for Davora to leave. Shana called after her. Rima assured her that she'd be back shortly. A few minutes later Rima came out and went into the living room. Davora followed her, "She thinks I'm Sophia. Who is that?"

"Our younger sister. She died on the way here. She never saw New York harbor. She died of diphtheria. Shana has mourned her for years."

"I'm so sorry. I didn't know. I..."

"It's good she thinks you're Sophia. Maybe it gives her some peace."

Rima opened the curtains, revealing a stunning view of the Hudson River with the sun starting to set over New Jersey. The river sparkled and was active with ferries, tugs pulling and pushing huge barges of scrap metal and wheat, and sailboats on pleasure cruises. It was something that she thought she could look at forever.

Davora gasped, "It's so beautiful."

"Yes, it was more beautiful when we moved in, when Shana was still well. When she was still performing."

"She was an actress?"

"A singer and actress. The music in her room, that's her. She sang in a production of Lady Be Good and a lot more." Rima opened an oak cabinet that revealed many bottles and an array of different shaped cocktail glasses. Some with twisted stems of colored glass. She began making herself a drink. Davora took in the room and noticed the Broadway show posters displayed on the walls. On closer examination she saw that they listed Shana Cobb as a cast member. She'd probably picked that as her stage name instead of Coblentz. "You want a drink?"

"Oh, I don't think so. I've only had wine before." She remembered that day in Ballston Spa when Rudy had ordered them a bottle of wine by the lake. How he had tried so hard to court her, to win her over. He'd been so sweet. Had she made a mistake?

"There's white wine in the fridge if you want it."

"No, thank you. It looks like Shana had a good career. So many shows."

Rima took her drink up to the picture window, looked out and took a sip, her back to Davora. "She had the voice; she was a beauty, much admired." There was something about the tone in Rima's voice, a sense of resignation or even bitterness. "She had the talent and I..." she trailed off.

"What did you do? Did you perform also?"

"We studied music, theatre, dance; we took art classes, you name it. But me, I was the less talented one, the plain one. I worked as a stage manager for a while. And then I became my sister's assistant. I wrote her contracts. I looked out for her. I carried the costumes, hat boxes, and dance shoes." She took another sip. "I was her schlepper," she said with acidity. "And now..."

Davora stood next to her, scanning the streaks of reds, blues, and greens, as the sun reflected brilliantly on the river. "I'm sure she was grateful. She must love you very much."

Rima seemed to be withdrawing into herself, into her thoughts. "Nothing was really the same after the fire." She moved her hand in a circular motion and watched the ice cubes swish around. "In one hour we were orphaned. Everything, gone."

"I heard about the fire."

Rima went to the cabinet and refreshed her drink. "Our father's sister took us in. She had a dress factory on 37th Street off 6th Avenue. We worked for her. We didn't know about the will until later. He'd planned ahead; he always planned ahead. Gretchen, his sister, was going to take our money while we worked for...*soup*." She spit the word out.

"You finally got the money?" Davora asked.

"We sued her. The lawyer got a third, but there was enough left over for us. Shana's career took off early after a break—she stepped in for a leading lady who dropped dead a week before the show opened." She laughed and said in a sing-song voice, "Gretchen, that bitch." She sipped her drink. "Between the inheritance and Shana's success we survived. Actually we did quite well, up until now." She fell silent again. "What I'm saying is that we're OK for now. After Shana...well, of course she's not working anymore. Eventually they're going to raise the rent on this apartment, or even start trying to sell them to us. And I don't know what will happen. Real estate is changing in New York. Greedy bastards is what they are."

Davora was thinking about the fire, their mother and father. "Your parents...I'm so sorry."

"It's funny; they wound up in the fire anyway."

"Oh, don't say that."

"Why not? It's true. They escaped death there, but found it here."

There was a long pause. Davora observed Rima and took in her sorrow. Her face was a mask of suffering; she was a broken person. She'd lost everything and was about to lose her sister, about whom she had complex feelings. Shana had been the star, but her star was fading quickly. Again Davora felt empty and alone and embarrassed that she needed something to eat. "Do you mind..." she stammered? "I'm sorry to ask, but I'm so hungry...could I have something to eat? I have money. I'm happy to pay for it."

Rima stared at her for a while like she was seeing her for the first time. "Of course," she said. "Excuse me, I should have offered." She got up and Davora followed her to the kitchen. "I want you to do something for me."

"What is it?"

"She thinks you're Sophia. Anything that might help her...what I'm saying is will you stay here for a while and pretend you're Sophia for her until..."

"Yes, if I can do that for her...yes. I'll do it."

"It's for her," she said almost coldly, "Not for me. Here, look in the fridge and the pantry. There's plenty. I'm going to make another drink. There's wine in the fridge."

Davora moved into the spare bedroom, which to her delight had windows looking out over the river and the Jersey skyline. She moved the small oak pigeonhole desk to face out so she could see the river when she wrote in her journal. Sometimes she would just look out at the expanse and marvel at how her life had suddenly changed. She spent time every day with Shana, and became a second caregiver, which relieved some of Rima's stress. She had to be careful when Shana would ask her if she remembered certain things, picnics and trips their family had taken in Poland when it was still safe. Davora would say that she remembered. She also played the records everyday for Shana, from the shows she's starred in, or was part of the cast. Sometimes Shana would look confused and ask what song it was or who was singing. "It's you," Davora would answer, "it's your beautiful voice." She did this as she ached inside that Shana would never know it was her. The girl who'd escaped and stayed with Shana's family for just one week and had become so attached to Shana that she called her 'sister'. Everyday when Davora helped her eat or bathed her she would say, "I am Sophia, your sister."

Davora insisted on paying Rima five dollars a month for her room. Rima offered her a reduced rent if Davora would do a few chores for her as well. Davora agreed and Rima would make a weekly list: dry cleaning, though she rarely left the apartment, grocery shopping, specialties from Zabars, and the liquor store. She'd phone in her weekly orders and Davora would pick them up. Unlike when she'd arrived in the city, a frightened girl, lost and desperate, Davora began to appreciate the clamor and commotion, the circus-like atmosphere. She felt energized. The subway became a vehicle of discovery. It opened up a new world to her; she prided herself in mastering the various lines. She decided to make a pilgrimage to each of the boroughs to see what they had to offer. The idea of riding the train to endless and fascinating destinations was liberating. She would go on weekend excursions. One time she went to Coney Island, a magical place she'd seen pictures of. She rode the Wonder Wheel and wandered through Luna Park, marveling at the theatrical characters and the sites. Another time she took the train downtown to visit Katia on Eldridge Street, to have lunch with her at the historic synagogue. She'd begun to think that there was not a more exciting place in the world to live. *I'm becoming a New Yorker*, she thought.

Rima still liked to keep up with Broadway productions, so she kept her subscription to the New York Times. She read about all the new shows and plays but never went to see any. She said she didn't dare leave the apartment out of fear that if Shana...if it happened while she was gone, she'd never forgive herself. Davora had started looking through the Times Book Review and was amazed at the amount of books there were on varying subjects. She thought how wonderful it was to be a writer, to publish a book that might one day be well known. Was that her dream, to be a writer? One time she read an article about the Cloisters in Fort Tryon Park and decided she had to see the Gothic architecture and medieval art, especially the tapestries. She remembered once seeing some as a little girl, when she'd snuck into a church in Szemud. The caretaker of the church found her there and was pleasant enough. He allowed her to look at all of the artwork as he told her about the savior and how he would come back to gather the righteous. He called it the Rapture. He was kind, but when she left he said that he knew she was a Jewish girl from the village and that the Jews would burn in hell if they didn't accept the true Lord. She didn't understand but decided not to tell her parents. Ivan would be angry at her for going into a church.

On one of her Sunday explorations she took the train up to Fort Tryon Park to see the Cloisters. It was a cloudless day with a brilliant blue sky that enticed the gulls and pigeons to wheel about expansively. She wore a light sweater, but didn't need it by mid-morning. She was immediately taken with the place, the French monastery and chapel rooms. She was delighted to discover an exhibit called the Blessing of Unicorns. She followed a tour group around and listened from a distance to the tour guide, who explained everything. She also marveled at the stone sculptures. At one point she broke off and wandered through a cloister enjoying the solid coolness of the stone. It was like a fortress; she felt protect-ed. She came out into a medieval garden and took in the aroma of various flowers and herbs, lilies, fennel, and rosemary. She noticed someone sitting on a bench at the far end of the garden. He was slumped forward and was perhaps an elderly visitor resting for a while, or perhaps someone in an attitude of prayer. She worked her way along the bushes and stopped at the ornamental fountain. There were hundreds of coins on the bottom, reflecting the sun-light, under the rippling water. Some people had even thrown in silver dimes and quarters. They must have, she thought, desper-ately needed their prayers answered.

When she reached the end of the garden path she passed the bench where the man was sitting. She intended to avoid him and go back in to have another look at the tapestries. There was something heroic about them, something that attracted her. She glimpsed involuntarily at the man. He wore a stained trench coat; his hair was matted to his scalp, his trousers were shiny from wear, and his brown leather shoes, without laces, were scuffed and worn so she could see the outline of his toes inside of them. He was shelling peanuts and tossing them to several squirrels that scurried around his feet. She kept walking until he said, "What I love about this place is there's a vendor on almost every street corner. You don't run out of peanuts, right boys?" he said to the squirrels. It was the voice that stopped her, a voice she'd heard before.

"You were on the train."

"You've got a good memory, Missy. Say, did the address I gave you work out OK?"

He caught her off guard and she had to think for a moment. "Yes, it did. You were right. Their house on Canal Street burned down. I was lucky to find them."

"I know. It was tragic. So, how are you getting along?"

"You should know. You seem to know everything about me."

"That's because I'm in a rarefied condition."

She observed him for a few moments. He looked as though he was deteriorating, worse than he had been on the train. "Who are you? Tell me who you are. And why are you following me?" And then she wondered, *is he another phantom?*

"Are you satisfied with your living conditions?" he asked.

"You tell me."

"I think you are. You're maybe becoming a city girl, right?" She nodded; it was like he was reading her mind. He looked down, the smile leaving his face. "Look, ah, I have some news for you, not what I want to be telling you."

Immediately alarmed, she said, "What is it? Is it Ivan? Tell me."

"Yes, Ivan; you need to go to him now...in the next day or so."

"What is it? Is he sick? Please, tell me."

"I'm telling you, you need to go to your father."

She ran out of the Cloisters in a panic, her heart pounding, and hailed the first taxi she could find. *I've killed him,* she thought. *I've killed him.* When she got to her building she thrust some bills into the driver's hand and raced up to the apartment. She told Rima that she had to go home. Something was wrong with her father. She threw some clothes into her satchel. Rima tried to get details from Davora, but there weren't any. Rima seemed stricken at

Davora's sudden departure. She became accusatory, "What about Shana? You promised."

"Yes, I did. I'll come back to her. I have to go to my father now. I'll be back."

"She may be dead by then."

"What do you want me to do? Your father, would you have gone to him if you could have?"

Rima fell quiet and retreated to the liquor cabinet to fix herself a drink. "Please, don't be long. Shana needs you." Davora rushed out of the apartment, leaving her knapsack filled with journals under her desk.

Davora went into the Western Union office at Penn Station and sent a telegram to Ben saying when her train would arrive and asking if he'd please pick her up. But when she got there she couldn't find him. She called the gas station, but there was no answer. She took the bus to Broadway then ran up the stairs. She didn't notice Rudy watching her from the basement storefront. When she got inside the house the doctor was just entering Ivan's bedroom. Ben motioned to her from the hallway to come into the kitchen. He seemed irritated. Jake came to her and gave her a hug and kissed her forehead. Sarah was seated, leaning back on a chair with a compress on her forehead. Davora's sisters, Galena and Rose, stood protectively on either side. Hannah was not there and didn't return again, even after Sarah passed, a year and half later. Davora kneeled in front of her mother and took her hands in hers. "Mama, mama, it's me, your Bisl Bin." Sarah sat up slightly and looked at her without recognition. "Mama, it's me," she cried.

Galena was standing over her with an angry continuance as if defending Sarah from an evil force. "Mama doesn't need you anymore. None of us do." Davora observed her siblings. Save for Jake she could see she'd become persona non grata. Why? For trying to have her own life, for daring to have a dream? She still loved them all, couldn't they see that?

She got up and backed away, not wanting to incur more of Galena's wrath. The cellar door opened and a tall, slender woman stepped into the room. She was completely dressed in black, a close fitting black dress, stockings and shoes, and a string of black pearls around her very white, thin neck. She glared at Davora. Rudy entered behind her. He was even more dapper and expensively-dressed than the last time she'd seen him, no doubt reflecting the success of his business. He smiled at Davora, a broad, strained smile, his face cracking open in a display of false happiness, as his eyes devoured her with desire. The tall woman raised her hand to her mouth and touched her lip. Then Davora saw it, the peridot ring with the diamond halo, glowing as if it were radioactive. Davora stifled a gasp as she beheld the couple, as if they'd emerged from the depths of the underworld.

Words flashed in Davora's mind as her skin prickled: "The Dark Maid. O flyer in a dark chamber, go away at once, O Lili!" Rudy approached her as she backed up against the sink. He held out his arm toward the woman as if he was introducing a night club act. She could feel the strain in his body. "Davora, this is Lilith. Lilith, meet Davora." The woman seemed to rise up in her body like a venomous snake about to strike. Then Davora noticed the slight bulge of her stomach. She was pregnant. Pregnant with a child, certainly a girl, and Rudy would have no idea what was coming. Davora's chest constricted; she fought off an urge to run from the house and keep running all the way back to the train station.

And on it went for a week, Davora hiding in her old bedroom, creeping around the house, staying out of their way, her brother and sisters making it clear at each interaction that her presence wasn't needed. At one point Jake defended her and he and Ben almost got into a fist fight, which Jake would have easily won. Davora pushed herself between them. "No, don't do this. Think of papa; he wouldn't want this."

It was also unnerving that Rudy and Lilith were staying in the basement. They were waiting to close on their new home on Glenwood Boulevard, a neighborhood of venerable mansions, near the Ellis Hospital. Lilith insisted that every aspect and detail of their lives be first class, "exceptional value," as she called it. Davora had an uneasy feeling that Rudy might not live that long married to a woman like her. Her need for luxury was insatiable. But what could she do? She was there for Ivan and Sarah, if only Sarah would wake up from what had possessed her.

In the morning hours between 3 and 5 a.m., while the others slept, Davora would enter Ivan's room and sit with him. She prayed and spoke to him. She told him about her life in New York and why she had to leave. She suffered the triple grief of Sarah not recognizing her, the rejection by her siblings, and Ivan, whom the doctor said would not last much longer. She knew that she was losing her family, her childhood, and she would be left a young woman on her own. She would hold his hand. "Papa, papa, I love you. Can you hear me?" On the fifth and sixth nights she noticed more strength in his hand as he seemed to be squeezing hers. Her heart jumped; did she dare to hope for a recovery?

On the seventh morning at 5 a.m., he opened his eyes. "Papa, papa, do you see me?" His lips moved slightly but he couldn't speak. He lifted her hand and gently pulled it as if he were leading her someplace. Instantly she knew what he intended. He was taking her hand as he had the day they walked home from the synagogue. He was leading her into her life as he was leaving his. He was setting his little girl out into the world, which he could no longer inhabit. He was giving her the freedom she longed for. She understood. He took several final breaths, but kept looking at her, fierce and powerful in his death. He grasped her hand one last time and was gone.

Galena and Rose told Davora they didn't want her at Ivan's funeral. They'd heard from some of the congregants how she had disgraced Ivan by entering the section reserved for men in the synagogue. Galena's face was red and angry. "You've caused enough damage. You should go." Rose nodded in agreement. Davora felt helpless, but knew it would cause more pain if she insisted on being at the funeral. She didn't bother telling them about how Ivan had taken her hand on the way home that day. She felt like she was losing her past, the home that she'd had in that house. Everything she'd known since she was a child was being taken away from her with a harshness she couldn't bear.

The next day she stood outside of the iron gate at the cemetery with Jake as the others assembled around Ivan's grave. Jake refused to go in if Davora wasn't welcome. She mouthed the prayers with the rabbi and the men from the synagogue who shunned her. After the service, the others, including members of the congregation, went back to the house to sit shiva. Jake and Davora went to the bakery and had cake and coffee. Jake looked down at the table and slumped in his chair. "I wish you weren't going. I won't have anyone. The rest of them are...I don't know. Not like family to me."

"You're a good man, Jake. Papa was proud of you."

"He never told me that."

"He told me and I'm telling you."

"I just can't keep working for Ben. I'm getting nowhere. I've been saving up for my own truck. I could work for Star Furniture. I got offered a delivery job, but I need my own truck. I could deliver and set up beds and stuff. I've been saving for a while, but I'm short."

"How short?"

"A hundred."

Davora opened her purse and took out the envelope. "Here's a hundred and fifty."

"No, I won't take that."

She pushed the money into his hand. "Take it. Get the truck. You'll be your own man. Ben will get someone else to deliver oil for him."

"How are you going to live down there? Isn't it expensive?"

"I have a good situation; the woman I live with is very generous. And I'm going to find a job when I get back."

"Something else..."

"What, Jake, tell me?"

"The new bookkeeper Ben hired. She's quite a gal..."

"Yes, tell me more."

"Well, I've taken her to a couple of games. She loves baseball. I think she might be the one. She...likes me. But...but..."

Davora leaned over the table and whispered. "She's not Jewish?"

"How did you know?"

Davora could see the woman in her mind. She was a petite brunette, very pretty, and with lovely-shaped features. Most of all she looked thoughtful and sensitive. Davora said something that surprised both of them. "It doesn't matter what she is or isn't, Jake, as long as she's a good woman and cares for you."

"I think she's a very good woman." They sat there quietly for a while. Finally, he said. "I'll come see you."

"Yes, you will. You can stay with me." But she knew he wouldn't be visiting. He wouldn't be able to leave. She sensed that his life was finally just starting. She knew she wouldn't see any of them again. Jake gave her one more of his bone crushing hugs and she left. She would walk to the train station and take the train...*home*.

When she passed The Three Aces she automatically looked inside. He was sitting at the piano, but not playing it. She watched him; he seemed to be swaying slightly. *Should I just keep going? Would I be bothering him with his thoughts?* Then she tapped lightly on the window. He didn't move. She tapped a little harder. Then she tried the door handle. It was unlocked. She went in. He still didn't react. She came up to him. His eyes were red and puffy as if he'd been crying. She sat on the chair next to the piano. "What?" she asked. "What's wrong?"

"It's Leroy, he got stabbed."

"Is he...is he all right?"

"Don't know yet, pierced his lung."

"How, what happened?"

"A kid from one of the gangs. Drugs moving in here, the cops beating up on Black kids. Mobs coming up from the city, getting the kids hooked."

"Is Leroy OK?"

"He's out of surgery, sleeping. I'm heading back over there now."

"Do you want me to go with you?"

Flanagan gave her a long, thoughtful look, the sadness playing over his forehead, his wide nose and lips. "You're different than the rest of them...you don't care about color."

And then she said it, something she'd thought and felt deeply for a long time. "I don't care about color."

He placed his hand on top of hers, a powerful hand with a light touch, and arthritic knuckles from decades of working the keys. "You're a good girl, Davora. But you can't come with me to the hospital. It could cause trouble. You have your satchel, I see. Where are you going?"

"New York. I don't have a home here anymore."

He smiled knowingly, but sadly. "I think that might be the right town for you." He took out a pen and scratched out an address. "Check out this place. They got the music you like. It's in Harlem. Mention my name; you might get a free drink."

When she got back to the city she ran from the 79th Street station to the apartment. She was relieved to see that there was a new doorman in the lobby, a small Hispanic man, dressed in a tailored gray suit, a cap, and patent leather shoes. "Hello Miss, can I help you?"

"Yes, I'm staying with Rima Coblenz in 7H."

"Oh, they took her sister to the hospital yesterday. She's not back yet."

"Where? Do you know?"

"Sloan Kettering."

"Where is it?"

"It's on York. You want I should get you a cab?"

Two days later, after Shana's convulsions were under control, they released her from the hospital. The oncologist told Rima that she had maybe two weeks left. At the very most she wouldn't last the summer. But when she got home to her familiar surroundings she seemed to rally. She demanded more of Davora's time, asking her to play the show tunes and sing them with her, when she remembered them. Davora accommodated every request. She even slept in her room on a cot because it reminded Shana of their childhood when she and her sister Sophia shared a bed. To fill up more time Davora began making up stories to tell Shana, which she seemed to enjoy. She responded to them as if they were fairy tales. Davora would tell her stories about the magical Tatry Mountains in Rusinowa, near the five lakes, and the talking sheep that inhabited the area. Ivan used to take the family there in the summers when it was still safe to travel and they were welcome at the resorts. Afterward, Davora would write the stories down in her journal. Often she'd spend most of her nights making journal entries. Gradually, characters began to take shape, some of them painfully familiar. She felt compelled to write about them, and became a steady customer at Slone's Stationery on Broadway and 81st Street. It had changed for her; writing was now her passion.

Late one evening Rima knocked on her bedroom door. She was swaying a bit and slurred her words. She sat down on Davora's bed and leaned her back against the wall. "So whaddya gonna do?"

"What do you mean?"

"After...after...!" She turned away and sobbed.

Davora sat on the bed and rubbed her back, and said quietly, "What do you want me to do?"

"Why are you so...even, so OK with everything?" she asked bitterly.

"I'm not. My heart breaks for Shana. She is the sister I don't have anymore. I'll do anything for her. May I say something?"

"What?"

"I think it might be better for you and Shana if you didn't drink so much."

Suddenly Rima was up and angry, her face red and leaning into Davora. "This is my home. You won't tell me what to do. You can get out. Get out now! Go ahead. Take your things and get out," she screamed.

Shocked and frightened, Davora began to gather her things. The journals almost didn't fit into her backpack. Rima watched her coldly for a few moments and then went out to the living room. Davora knew there was a YWCA in the neighborhood near the park. She'd find it and spend the night there, and then...what? Maybe she could stay with Katia until she could get her own place. Now she would need a job immediately.

She walked through the living room, her heart pounding, and opened the door. She couldn't look back. The hallway was a dark and forbidding landscape about to swallow her into nothingness. She pressed the call button for the elevator.

Rima stood behind her in the doorway. "Don't go, please don't go. I'm sorry. I can't do this alone." Davora turned around and went back to her room and cried herself to sleep. That night she dreamed of Shmuel. He was sitting on the edge of her bed, transformed. He wore a double breasted sports jacket, a beige satin shirt, trousers, and what looked like a new pair of cordovan shoes with white socks. His hair, what there was of it, was pomaded back over his scalp, and he'd had a fresh shave. He reminded her of a Catskills hotel MC. He was chipper and upbeat, scanning the floor of her bedroom. "I know you're there. Where are you hiding?"

She sat up, astonished. "What are you doing here?"

"What I always do—feeding the squirrels."

"There aren't any squirrels here inside the apartment."

"That's because they aren't squirrels; they're souls."

"You should leave. Rima will be angry. She'll call the police."

"Don't you want to know about Ivan?"

"He's in the living room listening to the news cast."

He grimaced, "You know that's not true."

"It is," she cried, "he's my papa."

"And he always will be. He wants you to know that your sister and brother should not have hurt you." He looked up for a moment as if he was receiving the message he was giving her. "This is your home now. It will *be* your home." He began to fade until he was a form engulfed in mist, then he disappeared. But he spoke, "A blessing on your head. Sleep now, Little Bee."

She slept in much later than usual, until 9 a.m. When she awoke she only remembered a little of what Shmuel had said. She got up to look out the window, which she did every morning, hoping to see one of the big ships, and stepped on something that smashed under her foot. It was a cracked peanut shell with three perfectly formed golden peanuts in it.

Rima was vacuuming the living room and had washed the windows. She was in a more upbeat mood than usual. She asked Davora if she had slept well. She was much friendlier than the previous evening. Davora assumed she was trying to make it up to her. She appreciated that and asked Rima if there was anything she could pick up for her. It turned out there was. Shana had been asking for their mother's strudel. She didn't remember that her mother had died in the fire. There was a bakery on 86th Street, Cohen's, and they made delicious strudel, other pastries, and breads. It was on their sign: *Cohen's -- Home of Legendary Rugelach and More.*

Davora was pleased with the task. She loved walking around the city...*her* city.

First, she checked on Shana, who'd fallen back to sleep. She was somewhat agitated and talking. "Davora, where are you? You said you'd come back. Davora...I need you." Stunned, Davora stood looking at her, not sure what she should do. Would Shana remember when she woke up? Finally she took hold of her hand and kissed it once. *Oh Shana, I so want to be your Davora. You must know how much I love you.* Shana opened her eyes and starred at Davora for a good half a minute. "Sophie, I am so thirsty. Ask mama for some cold water, please." Davora went and got a glass of water. She held Shana's head up and helped her sip. "Sophie, I had such a strange dream about a little girl I knew so long ago."

"Yes," Davora said softly, "a dream, just a dream. I'm going to get something for Rima. When I get back we'll have strudel and I'll play Carousel for you, when you sang the part of Julie Jordan."

Shana turned her head away toward the window. "Who is Julie Jordan?"

She walked over to 86th Street by Amsterdam Avenue, taking her time, enjoying the various aromas of the ethnic restaurants. She passed a doorway and thought she heard a familiar song. She peeked inside. A young man with a guitar was sitting on a folding chair playing a tune she'd heard before. She walked in and was confronted by a big woman in fashionable clothes and her dog, a German Shepherd named Boss, who sniffed Davora up and down, wagged his tail, and slunk behind the bar. The woman wore a diamond necklace that spelled out her name, Helen.

"Are you looking for a job? Boss seems to like your smell. He doesn't like everyone. And neither do I."

Devora was taken by surprise and wasn't sure, but she said, "Maybe, no, yes, I am. What do you need?" She figured that this would cover her rent and any eventualities that might arise. Davora knew from the tune that this was a jazz club, as well as by the drum kit and upright piano on the small elevated stage. She thought about it, about how she had dreamed of being a nurse so long ago. Suddenly, the idea of being a waitress in a jazz club in this dynamic city seemed more exciting than anything else she could imagine. But she wouldn't neglect Shana, she couldn't. Usually, Shana was in and out of consciousness after dinner until she settled in for the night.

The woman leaned into her like she was taking her measure. "I just fired my last waitress. Can you bring a drink to a table and not talk too much—not flirt with the customers, you know what I mean?"

"Yes, I could do that. I'm no flirt, I promise." Then she remembered the song, Daddy Flanagan had played it for her.

"Good, can you just do Friday evenings for now? No guarantee; you're on probation. I'm trying you out, prep at 6:30."

Davora looked around the room; it was small and compact. It might not be that hard. And she'd get to hear the kind of music she'd heard at The Three Aces. "Yes," she said, "6:30 Friday."

"Fine," the woman turned abruptly, and ducked into an office with Boss close behind her.

Davora walked by the guitar player, who'd paused to re-tune his guitar. "The Jitterbug Waltz. It's a great tune."

The young man cradled the guitar on his lap and smiled at her. "Aren't you the sharp one? So who wrote it?"

"Fats," she couldn't remember his last name. "Fats...something."

"Waller," he offered. "You just get fifty percent. And I'll give you 25% more if you know what key it's in."

"Ah...I don't."

"E flat. But hey, that doesn't matter. I'll give you 100% 'cause you look like that kind of gal."

"One time a man played that song for me."

"Oh yeah? What man?" he asked, feigning jealousy.

"Big Daddy Flanagan."

"Daddy Flanagan?" his eyes widened. You gotta be kidding me."
"No, why?"

"He's a legend. They call him Mister Keys, you know, like piano keys. Where'd you see him?"

"Schenectady, where I'm from...actually I live here. I'm...a New Yorker."

"That's where he is? He used to live in Harlem, played with everybody, every cat up there and in the village too. He's a monster."

A monster? What did he mean by that? "I didn't know he was famous. He's a very kind man."

"Oh yeah, he made a great name for himself. Speaking of which, what's your name?"

She hesitated for a moment. "Davora."

His demeanor changed; he became serious. "Little Bee," he said quietly.

She felt her face flush. "How could you know that?"

"Ten years of Hebrew school. Where do you think I'm from? And my cousin's name is Davora." He chuckled, "Davora, the Queen of Orient Avenue. A real beauty, like yourself." He squinted his eyes. "She had seven suitors and wound up marrying a Hindu business man. Living a life of luxury in East Hampton. It was rough. Her folks sat shiva for her, sad. But I say, to each his own."
He was flirting with her; it was moving a bit fast. But she liked him; she could feel her female circuitry buzzing. It was different than with Rudy. "So how's life as a Little Bee?"

She thought about how much she'd seen already at her young age. She was still in mourning for Ivan, the rejection she suffered from her siblings, where she'd come from, the miracle that she was alive. "Life can be difficult, but interesting. Especially in the city," she said. "All in all I have a good life."

They were silent for a few moments. Then he said, "Well, I guess I'll see you Friday. I'll be here with Sam Shaffer and Tony Best.

You know those guys? Sam's the hottest Flugelhorn player on the continent. Came from the West Coast with that cool sound."

"No, but I guess I'll see them and hear them." She turned to leave, and then turned around. "You didn't tell me your name."

"David, David Isaac Menndel. But my professional name when I'm gigging is Dave Mann. Hey, think of it. David and Davora, D-a-v and D-a-v. We're a duo. It's on the beam." She smiled without answering him, but she felt some movement around her chest. She left quickly and almost forgot to pick up the strudel.

Davora was nervous at her first night waiting tables in the club. She didn't want to displease the owner, a bullish woman who seemed to enjoy firing waitstaff. But the music carried her through and she quickly loved the job. The idea that people could improvise as they did was fascinating; it all sounded authentic. The manager allowed the staff one shift drink at the end of the night. After a few shifts, she and David would sit at one of the café tables and talk for about an hour before she felt compelled to get back to Shana and Rima. David was eager to know every aspect about her life, her childhood in Poland, her new life in America. She was aware that he was also trying to court her. She felt an attraction for him, but thought she should take her time, move slowly. She felt that she had inherited some of Ivan's reluctance to talk about herself, but she trusted David; she believed that he was a good man, though she was a little nervous about where it might go.

The manager was happy with the trio not just because she was doing good business. Sam Shaffer was a draw. People came from all over the island and the boroughs. Jazz aficionados came down from Albany and Hartford to hear him as well. Sam was an iconic figure, considered to be a musical genius, but a tragic man, nearing the end of his career, brought on too early by alcohol and heroin. During the breaks he'd go out behind the club and shoot up. Davora was unaware of this, but knew from the first note he played that he was a tortured soul and all the grief, heartbreak, and sadness in the world, and what joy that could be reaped, came through his horn. It reminded her of when they'd blow the shofar at the end of Passover services. A call to something better, but of great sadness. Sam felt things at a deeper level than most people experienced. The trio was popular. Other fine musicians showed up, hoping to sit in with the guys. Tony the bass player filled in the sound with wonderful low tones that kept things moving as he held the bottom together. And David was an excellent musician. Watching him play she came to understand what it meant to accompany someone. He followed Sam wherever he went, with just the right chords. And when he took his solos the notes were like pure bell tones. People clapped and cheered.

Helen gave them an extended run because they consistently filled up the club. Davora was surprised at the amount of tips she made. It was more money than what she'd made repairing cars for Ben, which now seemed like a lifetime ago. Hoping, perhaps foolishly, that Shana would hang on for a while longer, she put an RCA Victor Radio Phonograph Victrola (610V1) on layaway. It would be a surprise for Shana and Rima as soon as it was paid off. She wanted Shana to hear how her voice would sound on a quality machine, assuming that she remembered that it was herself singing. Davora would somehow get her to remember. The old record player in Shana's bedroom lacked fidelity. The music sounded a bit fuzzy. Sometimes after Rima had a few cocktails she'd play records of shows she'd stage-managed, and tell Davora stories about the actors and their wild, lascivious episodes. Davora was slowly coming to realize that she was happy. Despite everything, she felt happy. *Do I have a right to be happy?*

A few times after the club closed, Sam would join her and David for a drink. She found his presence almost overwhelming, not just the way he expressed himself; he was a walking encyclopedia of jazz, and many other subjects. There was purity to his kindness. And his face; his face was deeply lined and craggy like a mythic hero who'd witnessed terrible rituals and seen much death. It was obvious that he liked Davora and took an interest in her. He asked questions and listened thoughtfully. He always asked what she was reading. He told her that he'd read everything by Hemingway and that was the guy to read to see how it's done. It was the first time she'd heard of Hemingway. She picked up a copy of *A Farewell to Arms* soon after and was amazed at how simple, but powerful and moving his language was. Sam also told her to check out W.B. Yeats, especially his poem, *The Second Coming*. "That cat really had it going on," Sam said, "a totally new language, like bebop." Sometimes he'd almost nod out as a result of the drugs and alcohol, but his interest was genuine. Usually, around 1:30 AM his ride would show up, a merlot-colored Studebaker Coupe. The driver was a woman, but that was all they could tell. She always wore a scarf over her head, a fur piece around her neck, and sunglasses, in winter or summer. David said they were headed up to Harlem, for a late night jam session and probably some more dope, as the musicians referred to it. "Why, why does he take dope?" she asked.

"Pain, it kills pain."

"Oh, did he have an accident?"

"Not to be highfalutin, but I'm talking about existential pain. Everybody feels it; some feel it more than others."

"Do you mean like the blues?"

"Yes, it's like that."

"When he plays...it's like you can hear wailing or sobbing, those long sustained notes, so sad, but so beautiful. Like when they play the shofar, the sound is supposed to mean repentance and sacrifice. I remember one time Daddy Flanagan played the blues for me. He said everybody gets them."

"I hope you're not feeling that way, blue."

"I've been very sad at times, but I feel OK now...with you."

David said, "You don't know how much that means to me. I want to ask you something. Would you go to Roseland with me?

The International Sweethearts of Rhythm are playing there next week. It's an all girl band. They're fantastic. We could dance and then hop a train downtown and go to Katz's for their famous pastrami sandwich on rye."

"You mean like a date?" she asked.

He answered nervously, "Well, we'd be there at the same place at the same time...together, if that's what you mean. Yeah, I guess it would be a date, unless you have something else..."

"No, it sounds like fun...except I don't know how to dance."

He smiled warmly, "Then we'll just sway. Please, it'll be fun."

"Yes, it'll be fun." She couldn't wait to get home and tell Rima, but she was passed out on the couch, a pink and green martini glass sitting on the coffee table. Obviously she had not been able to take Davora's advice that she should drink less. And the subject wouldn't be broached again. She needed Rima as much as Rima needed her, and she couldn't imagine not being with Shana for whatever time they might have left together. As usual, she went to Shana's room and kissed her good night on her forehead.

As late as it was, she felt energized to write down the entire evening in her journal, every detail, each exciting moment. She had just broken into a new one and loved the smell of the fresh paper. She wrote quickly, not wanting to forget anything. She looked out at the river and thought it must be a full moon. The choppy waves shimmered with shades of white: cream, eggshell, vanilla, snow, and more than she knew. On the other side, on the Jersey shore, the apartment windows, advertising lights, billboards, and moored vessels, added a multicolored border. The sum of it all was a magnificent canvas, dancing with life. Davora opened her window and leaned out to take in the air and the view. The breeze coming up off of the park was soft, warm and cool at the same time. Her thought was: *I am alive, very alive.*

She wrote a few more sentences about Sam Shaffer. He was such a compelling character that she wanted to get it just right. She thought for the first time: *I want to write a story about this man, this great musician.* She jotted down some notes quickly while they were fresh in her mind. She glanced out the window again to take in the magnificent nightscape. There was a disturbance in the middle of the river, some swirling and spouts shooting up dazzled by the moonlight. She studied the disturbance and thought she saw a form taking shape. It seemed to lift up out of the water in stages and was, she determined, a structure, a replica of the Seven Heavens with fire exploding out from each level and something else, shadows streaming out of the burning structure—*souls*, she thought. Souls being expelled, or fleeing from the conflagration. And just as mysteriously as it had formed, the structure sank into the turbulent water, extinguishing the flames, leaving a huge plume of smoke above a violent whirlpool. Gone!

Unnerved by the spectacle, she went into the living room to see if she could awaken Rima. If she couldn't bring herself to tell her about the frightening vision she'd just seen she'd at least have someone to be with. She was shaking. Rima was not there; she'd probably gone to bed. Davora sat down and noticed a cocktail shaker on the coffee table. It was cold; she opened it and drank the contents. It warmed her chest and made her cough several times. She needed to calm down and waited, trying to direct her thoughts elsewhere from what she'd just seen. And why did she see these things? Was she crazy? Was it that thing she'd heard of, second sight? What else could it be? The combination of the late hour and the remaining strong cocktail put her in a deep sleep within minutes.

Rima woke her up at 9:30 a.m. They'd both slept in. "I see you've taken up drink," she said.

Embarrassed, Davora picked up the cocktail shaker off the sofa and set it on the coffee table. "I had a nightmare. I was frightened and came to see if you were awake. The drink was there and I needed to calm down."

"You better stick with soda pop. This stuff is for big girls."

They heard a noise in Shana's room and then she cried out. She'd fallen out of her bed and was sprawled on the floor. They lifted her up carefully. "I have to go to the bathroom. No one was here."

"I'm so sorry. I should have been here." Davora rocked her gently. "Here, I'll help you." When they were finished, Davora gave her a warm sponge bath, dressed her in a fresh nightgown, and settled her back in bed. She made her a bowl of Cream of Wheat and some rye toast, while making a pot of strong coffee. She had a splitting headache from the Old Fashioned. That would be her first and last sampling of hard liquor.

As soon as it seemed appropriate, Davora told Rima she'd pick up her order at the butcher shop. She needed desperately to get outside and walk in the sun, in the healing light of day, and try to make sense of what she'd seen in the river. She thought that maybe, with the force of the vision, that it might be the culmination of her witnessing apparitions and visages, whatever they were. She wished them to be gone. She did not want to be the one to see things others didn't see. As she came back through the living room, Rima went to the liquor cabinet and opened a drawer and took out a key. She locked the cabinet and handed the key to Davora. Rima's eyes were red; she'd been crying, probably upset with herself for not having been there when Shana needed her. "Don't give me this key even if I beg for it or even if I threaten you. Do you understand?"

Davora became nervous again. "You won't throw me out? You promise that?"

"Shana needs you," she said, hesitantly. "I need you. You will still have your room here...after." Rima looked down. Davora embraced her.

Davora walked through the lobby, thinking, *We are three sisters. I have sisters again.* The doorman had just set a saucer of milk down on the sidewalk for a stray cat. He smiled at her. "I hope it's OK for you people." It was such a relief that he was in charge compared to the tire-iron-wielding fiend she'd first encountered.

She smiled at him, "Thank you, you're very kind."

He tipped his cap to her. "Most people are kind, Miss."

She didn't go directly to the butcher shop, but cut through the park to get a longer walk and clear her head. She was still shaken by the vision she'd had the previous night. She sat on a bench and stared out at the river. It was calm and everything looked normal. Perhaps, she thought, the intensity with which the Seven Heavens had sunk into the depths means it might be the last of it. She had no plans to ever see it again. *Please, no more of this.* She was somewhat cheered watching the children play, their laughter like music running up and down, reminded her of the scales she heard David practicing on his guitar. When was the last time she'd felt that free? For the rest of the week until she returned to the club on Friday, she woke up several times a night and looked out her window. Nothing; she began to feel comfortable again. *It's done with, maybe,* she hoped.

The next Friday, after the gig, David invited Davora to his parent's house for dinner. She wasn't surprised, but it made her nervous. Meeting his parents meant that he was serious about her, which she already knew, but still, it was another step. He offered to pick her up and ride the train to Brooklyn with her. She declined the offer and said she was comfortable taking the train by herself. It would be about an hour's ride. Whenever she went into a new neighborhood she enjoyed exploring it alone. She stopped at Cohen's that Sunday afternoon and got a box of famous assorted rugelach.

She found the house on Orient Avenue easily. It was an impressive three-story brick building with a well-kept front yard bordered by an ornate black metal fence. There were various bushes and ornamental trees and large flower pots with Mexican colors. The windows were huge and the architectural details of the house were striking. She realized as she lifted the handle on the gate that David came from a wealthy family, something she hadn't thought about. The heavy oak door opened as she climbed the steps. David must have been watching for her. He thanked her for coming, accepted the box of pastries, sniffed it and smiled, then led her through the entrance hall. She noticed the wood paneling and chandeliers in the rooms beyond, all light and sparkling even though it wasn't evening yet. The ceilings looked to be at least ten feet high. It was an expansive, tastefully decorated interior. She wondered for a moment if the dress and shoes she'd picked out for the occasion were good enough. Would she look like a peasant girl?

David's father came out of his office with a handful of magazines. He was a tall, well-built man with broad shoulders, possibly a former football tackle. He was dressed casually, but was smart in appearance. He wore a robin's egg blue sport shirt with four or five pens in the pocket. He stood directly in front of Davora. "So, you're the young lady David's been telling us all about."

Davora blushed. David said, "Please, Dad, she just got here."

"And she's quite welcome." He gave her a slight bow. "I'm just finishing up. I'll join you on the patio for a glass of wine before dinner. Your mother's out there fussing over the plants."

David led her through the library where she stopped to look around. There were brown leather sofas and chairs, reading lamps, fine glass sculptures and paintings, and a large ornate brass Egyptian vase filled with desert reeds. And more books than she'd ever seen in one place besides the library. Built-in shelves of books of all kinds. She scanned the spines of them and took in some titles. "So many books…"

"Yes, that's my dad's life, books."

"Is he, I'm sorry what's his name, is he a writer?"

"Yes, and an editor, and a translator. Oh, his name is Benjamin. It's OK to call him Ben."

"I think I'll call him Mr. Menndel. Do you mind if I look through the shelves? Not to be rude."

"You couldn't be rude if you tried. Not a gal like you."

"I'm a woman, David, not a gal."

"Of course you are, excuse me."

She stopped at one of the shelves and slid out a book. "I've read something by him, in Polish. Isaac Bashevis Singer."

"You hit the nail on the head. That's how I got my middle name. My dad's a fan of Mr. Singer. David Isaac Menndel. So you're really into books?"

She said what she'd been feeling for some time: "I want to be a writer. I'm just not sure exactly how to go about it."

"It's probably like the guitar. You practice forever. Then one day it comes. But you have to keep practicing. You should ask my dad; he loves talking about writing. Come on, I'll introduce you to my mother." He led her through the dining room, the kitchen, and out onto a huge, screened-in, expansive back porch. David's mother was examining the bacopa, lantan, and sweet potato vines. It was a green, lush, and comfortable environment. "Mom, I'd like you to meet Davora." The woman, elegantly dressed, as if she were going out to a formal affair instead of dinner at home, took Davora's hand and held it firmly for many uncomfortable moments. The mother's hand felt like ice. It was as if she was taking Davora's pulse, or rather, the measure of her character. Finally, she smiled, as if she'd determined something.

"Welcome to our home. I'm Leah."

"You have a beautiful home."

Leah looked at her but didn't answer, as if it would be obvious that she'd have a beautiful home. Davora was beginning to regret that she had accepted David's invitation. It was clear that Leah didn't approve of her, or thought that she was not suitable for David. What possible excuse could she make to get away?

David said nervously, "I'll pour us a glass of wine." He poured out four glasses into some beautiful crystal wine glasses.

Benjamin returned and swooped up a glass. "Let's toast to this fine young woman who has deigned to visit our humble abode." Leah was slow to raise her glass.

"Dad," David said, "you're so...formal."

"I'm delighted to have some new blood in here. Oh, when I breezed by the library, I noticed you scanning the collection. Are you a bibliophile?"

She wasn't certain what the word meant, but assumed it had to do with books. "I read a fair amount, and I'm interested in...writing," she said quietly.

"Splendid, you'll have to show me some of your work. I'm very good at helping young writers."

"Oh, I'm not very far along."

"Why don't you let me determine that?" She felt pressured and her chest was tightening. She was also shocked and put off when a Hispanic woman came out to the back porch and announced that dinner would be ready in fifteen minutes. Davora couldn't believe that they had hired help. Sarah had done every single chore and cooked every meal her entire life. She didn't think she'd be able to eat.

"Martina," Leah said, in a measured tone, and slowly, less she be misunderstood, "if you don't mind, just leave everything on the buffet. We'll serve ourselves."

Martina nodded. "Certainly." Davora could tell by the tone of their voices that the relationship between the two women was strictly employer and employee, and not necessarily pleasant.

As Martina retreated, Benjamin called out, "Martina, thank you so much." By this point David could tell that Davora was mortified. Benjamin raised his glass again and toasted, "Well here's to the literary life and aspiring writers." He clinked Davora's glass with his.

David joined in the toast, "I'll bet your writing's the cat's pajamas."

As soon as dinner was through, an agonizing hour later, Davora excused herself, saying she had a sister at home who was ill and she needed to get back to her. Benjamin made her promise she'd let him see some of her work. Leah's farewell felt like a dismissal. David insisted on walking her to the subway station.

Obviously uncomfortable with how the visit had gone, David struggled to make it right. "You have to forgive my parents. They're old school...uh...my mom can be a little...there are some circumstances that I'd rather not..."

"Obnoxious?"

David was stunned. "How could you call my mother that?"

Davora felt sick, like she might throw up on the sidewalk. "Because she is." She walked away from him as fast as she could. He started to follow her. She turned back. "Don't." Once the doors slid closed and the train rattled into the darkness, she shuddered and took some deep breaths. She was shocked at her behavior. She'd never been that direct and rude in her life. But she felt abused by Leah. The woman had made her feel like dirt. She meant what she said, but that was David's mother. Now what? How could she face him at the club next time? It would certainly be the end of any relationship they might have had. But what would it have been like anyway, with his mother looking down on her? And his father...*I won't do it. I have to take care of myself.*

Several days went by and David had not tried to contact her. On Friday morning she went to the lobby to get the mail. The doorman carried a box out of a side room. "Someone left this for you." It was solid and heavy. She opened it on the kitchen table in the apartment. It was a hard-shell, camel-brown leather case. She opened the case and gasped: a Smith Corona Clipper portable typewriter. There was a handwritten note in the roller: *I know you'll be a great writer. —David.* She rested her head on her forearm and closed her eyes.

When Davora got to the club that Friday night, Helen was sitting at a table with David and Tony, looking very serious and concerned. "What is it?" she asked.

David told her: "Sam overdosed last night. He's in Bellevue—they don't know if he's going to make it."

"That's horrible."

David noticed she was carrying the typewriter case. Embarrassed, she put it behind the bar. That conversation would have to wait. At eight o'clock, the time they usually started playing, it looked like it would just be a duo, David and Tony, but Lex Jay walked in, an accomplished young pianist, and graciously accepted the invitation to join them on stage. He'd come that evening, like many before him, to hear the stylings of the great Sam Shaffer. But that wasn't going to happen. The trio worked well together, even if the news about Sam took some of the joy of playing away from them. There was some murmuring in the audience as word got around about Sam. It was a difficult evening.

At the end of the night David timidly approached Davora. "Look, Manny's Typewriters and Business Machines don't take returns or give refunds. There's a big sign in the window that says it. So you may as well take that thing home and start writing."

Tears welled in her eyes. "I'm so sorry. I'm sorry about everything."

"Just so you know, they couldn't stop talking about you. Especially my dad. They thought you were swell...can't wait to see you again."

"But your mother was so..."

He lowered his voice. "She spent the last two years of the war in Buchenwald. What she saw...what happened to her... He lowered his voice almost to whisper. The commandant had a lieutenant who took a liking to my mother. I don't know if I can tell you this, if I should tell you this."

"You can tell me, David. I'll understand."

The words caught in his throat, "The bastard raped her. When she gave birth..."

"What?"

"They took the baby away. The bastards took it away. It's a miracle she got out alive. My father met her in Warsaw after the war. She wasn't always like this, the way you saw her at dinner. It comes and goes. She can't help it. My father told me..." He stopped, and then said, "It's late; I'm going downtown to see Sam."

"But what happened to the baby?"

"What they did with all Jewish babies, the bastards."

She couldn't hold her tears back any longer. "Oh, my God, David. I'm so sorry. I'm..." He took her in his arms and held her tenderly. "I should have told you before you came to the house. It's my fault. I'm sorry. I just wanted you to meet them. I wanted them to see how great you are." She continued to cry as he held her.

"I'm so sorry. How could I be so callous and stupid?"

"You're not, you're not. Don't say that." She couldn't remember the last time she'd been held like that. They held each other with all the strength of their young bodies. She was tired of having to be strong, but she didn't know any other way. She knew, and was certain now; he was a good man, a very good man...the man for her. She offered to go with him to Bellevue. "It's late, you should go home. If Sam makes it he'll be in rehab for a while."

That August, Shana took a bad turn. She was in and out of consciousness. Rima was beside herself and struggling with her addiction. She had started attending AA meetings. This made Davora the almost full-time caregiver. She had to ask Helen if it was OK with her to cut down to just one night on the weekends. Initially, Helen was not sympathetic, but hired another waitress and told Davora that it couldn't go on indefinitely. Sadly, Davora told her that it wouldn't. Rima went to her AA meeting on Friday night and Davora worked on Saturday night. She'd spend the entire evening with Shana, applying cool compresses to her forehead, giving her pain medicine and playing music she might be listening to. One night as Davora was leaving the room to get some coffee, Shana said, "Davora, stay with me. I feel like I'm leaving." Davora's heart pounded and her skin felt icy. Shana did know it was her after all! Or was she just remembering that it was her? She returned to the bed and held Shana's hand. Her eyes were closed and she didn't seem to be conscious.

"Oh God, no. Please..."

Shana spoke to her as if from a great distance. "Davora, stay with me. Stay." Then she called out, "Sophia, Sophia!" She was being pulled away. Davora could feel her leaving her body. She struggled not to cry out, not to do anything that might make it harder for Shana. The thought of Rima walking in at this moment was torture, yet she was so alone, so alone, but knew she would do whatever she had to do to help Shana cross over.

She took Shana's other hand. "I'm here, I love you. Can you hear me?"

"Yeeeeees...Davora." She took several shallow breaths and then stopped. She was still. Davora rested her head on Shana's chest and sobbed.

"My Shana, Shana. Oh God, why? Take me instead. Please God, help me. Shana, come back...please!" After some time, she didn't know how long, she went to the kitchen and called Weinstein's Memorial Chapel. Rima had left the number along with others on a pad next to the phone. Then she went back in and sat with Shana until the bell rang. She followed the attendants behind the gurney through the lobby. The Spanish doorman crossed himself and looked down. As they opened the back of the hearse, Rima ran toward them from the corner with a man following her. When she got to them, as the men began to slide Shana in the back of

the hearse, she collapsed. The man who had followed Rima helped
Davora lift Rima up and take her into the building. Her grief
was palpable and unnerving. She went into Shana's bedroom and
bundled her sheets and blanket in her arms and rocked back and
forth. Her wailing attracted the attention of some of the neighbors
who came to the apartment. Davora opened the door; they stood
just inside the entrance, some of the Jewish residents prayed, others
just stood silently and paid their respects. All they could do was
listen to Rima express her unbearable loss.

The funeral took place at Washington Cemetery in Mapleton,
Brooklyn, where Rima's and Shana's parent's ashes were interred.
The man who helped Davora bring Rima upstairs was named
Steve. He'd been attending the AA meetings for five years and
had befriended Rima. Davora did not realize to what extent he'd
befriended her, but she was glad for Rima to have support from
someone else in the program. Recently, Rima had begged Davora
for the key to the liquor cabinet, but stopped short of threatening her. As they lowered Shana down, Davora and Steve stood
on either side of Rima, holding her up. Her cries echoed off the
tombstones and mausoleums in the cemetery. Davora shook inside
with the pain of her loss, but attended to Rima. She knew that she
would be grieving alone, as she had for Ivan.

At first she hadn't noticed it, but as she looked around, she saw
that Katia was among the group standing around the grave. A
friend; she would make sure she kept in touch with her afterward.
Then Davora saw in the distance a figure moving in and out behind
the grave stones and trees. He wore a trench coat, was stooped
over, and carried a shopping bag. At one point he stopped and
held his hands together, faced the mourners and bobbed back
and forth. She could just make out the prayer book in his hands.
He was davening, saying the prayers for Shana. How he could be
there, why he kept coming, she didn't know. But he was there for
Shana...Shmuel.

As they walked back to the car a young man in a white medical attendant's uniform pushed a wheelchair along the path toward them. An elderly woman was hunched over in it, a shawl spread over her lap despite the August heat. The attendant stopped in the path as though he was waiting for their group to pass. He leaned over and whispered something to the woman in the wheelchair, who seemed to be asleep. She sat up and lifted her head and spoke, "I'm sorry for your loss."

Confused, Rima stared at her. "Who are you? Do I know you?"

The woman's voice was faint and they almost couldn't hear her with the traffic on the road. "Gretchen, I'm Gretchen." Rima stared blankly at her. "Your father's sister...Gretchen."

Rima's temper flared. "What are you doing here? You stole our money. You didn't do anything for us. And now Shana..."

The woman was agitated and tried to lift herself up from her wheelchair, but lacked the strength. She slid her hand under her shawl and took out an envelope. "Here," she held it out to Rima. "Here."

"What is it?"

"It's for you...I'm sorry."

After a few tense moments Rima took the envelope and handed it to Steve who put it in his suit jacket pocket. When they got to the parking lot Davora made a mental note of the name on the van that Gretchen must have traveled in: Haurwitz & Son, in case Rima would need to get in touch with her later on. When they got back to the apartment the doorman explained that a young man, the same one who'd dropped off the package a few weeks ago, came with some people to bring food to their apartment. "He's a good kid. I let him go in...all right with you?"

Davora thanked him. When they got upstairs to 7H there was a table set up by the door with a pitcher of water and a bowl. They each performed the shiva, the ritual hand washing. A few of the neighbors had prepared the seudat Havra'ah, the meal of consolation with the food David had dropped off. It consisted of traditional items: hard-boiled eggs, assorted breads, lentils, garbanzo beans, bagels, and some sweets. They had also covered the mirrors in each of the bedrooms and the bathroom. They'd even thought to bring two low stools for Rima and Davora to sit on. Davora explained that she couldn't accept the stool because she was not actually part of the family. Rima said, "Sit, and mourn your sister." One of the neighbors handed Davora a folded piece of paper: *Need anything - just call. D.*

After the seven days of shiva, Rima and Steve started attending AA meetings again. Davora cleaned out Shana's room, packed all her clothes into boxes and washed the sheets, pillow cases, and blankets. She sorted her records chronologically by the shows she'd been in and stored them in the closet. During the time she sat shiva she forgot to make the next payment on the RCA Victor Radio Phonograph Victrola. The store manager took it off layaway and refused to refund what Davora had already paid on it. She explained the circumstances of why she'd missed the payment, but they kept her money anyway. The manager showed her the layaway contract she'd signed. Davora ripped it in half and let the pieces flutter to the floor, and then she walked out.

With the week she had off before she returned to work at the club she began taking different subway lines, the 1 - 7. Her intention was to walk through each of the boroughs, losing herself in the neighborhoods, monuments, historic buildings and parks. And all the while studying people's faces, their physical presentations, and attitudes. While they all varied, there was a similarity about them that she couldn't quite express, but it had something to do with the human condition of being well-off or not, lacking the essential necessities for life, hunger and abundance. Striving, or just giving up. During this time, this wandering, she didn't feel alone. Her grief followed her and weighed heavily on her. But it was not a burden. She carried it, and therefore she carried Shana with her.

She knew that she would always carry her with her. She felt alert and strong as she made her way through the streets, crossed the bridges and marveled at the architectural masterpiece that each was. She stood on the shores of the island looking out at the Hudson and the East rivers, all the while embracing the heartache and a glimmer of hope that she held for her future. As she looked out from Battery Park at Liberty Island a memory came to her suddenly, with the force of a blow to her chest. They were coming into the harbor. She remembered Ivan picking her up in his arms and holding her out facing the statue. He had said...what was it? She remembered; it was one word: *freedom*.

She got to the club early that Friday, anxious to be back, to see David, to hear the music that had become *her* music—and Big Daddy Flanagan's music. The room was empty except for a solitary figure sitting at the bar. When her eyes adjusted to the darkness she was surprised to see that it was Sam. She thought he was supposed to be in rehab for sixty days. He was sipping what appeared to be a glass of seltzer in his left hand. In his right hand was his flugel-horn, his fingers working the keys in subtle movements. The horn was old and glowed softly under a hanging bar light. A venerable instrument, burnished brass, with a few dents in the bell. Davora didn't want to disturb him and quietly put her purse and backpack in the office. Boss, Helen's German Shepherd, leapt off the settee and greeted her profusely; slobbering so much on her hands that she grabbed a tissue to wipe them off.

When she returned Sam was holding the mouthpiece up to his lips, just blowing air through the leadpipe. Then a sound emerged from the instrument that stopped Davora from going behind the bar to prep. It was a hauntingly sad and evocative tune. He played deeply and with utter heartbreak. Though not an expert, she felt that she could identify the musical sentences and nuances he interjected in the lines he created. And his tone again reminded her of the sorrowful notes that came from the ram's horn at the end of services—a call to battle, and a call to the soul's existence—God's grace.

He finished and sat the instrument on the bar, his fingers still on the valves. He was completely still, as if in meditation. It was a profound moment of intimacy she'd witnessed. "That was beautiful. What's it called?"

Sam smiled, his lined and craggy face like chiseled stone. "Good to see you, Davora. How have you been? And that song, it's called 'Alone Together.'"

"I lost my father and sister since I last saw you. But I'm doing all right."

"I'm very sorry to hear that. Wish I'd been around."

"How are you feeling, Sam?"

"Better since I checked myself out of Bellevue. They were killing me, couldn't even go outside for a smoke. Too many rules."

"Are you sure, Sam? I've heard that addiction is really hard to get over."

He held up his horn. "This is my addiction and my salvation. You know what I mean?"

She nodded that she did. "Say, how are you and Dave doing? He told me you're the one, his one and only. Maybe I shouldn't have said that."

"Well, I met his parents and..."

At that moment Helen came in and headed straight for the office. She called back over her shoulder. "You're back, finally! Do a good set up; we're going to be busy tonight. Oh, I fired the other girl. She drank like a sponge."

"Sam, you're going to play tonight? That's wonderful." She hesitated, and said "I hope you'll take care of yourself."

Sam chuckled and looked at her thoughtfully. "You're a good girl, Davora. You got a special gift, you know that? Dave hit the jackpot with you."

She felt her face flush. She looked down and saw the glasses in the sink and started washing them. She hoped that he wasn't referring to the *special gift* she'd like to get rid of. But how could he possibly know? Still, he was a man of deep feelings and intuition.

The club was packed that night because word got around that Sam Shaffer was playing. Helen added more dates so that Sam's group played Thursday through Saturday nights, which resulted in more shifts for Davora and more money than she'd ever made. David led a jam session on Wednesday evenings, which was popular. The musicians were happy to play for free and try out new material, sometimes challenging each other. Sam always said, 'It doesn't matter how fast you can play. It's about what you have to say.' David was at the top of his game. A review in a local paper described his playing as "...stunning, rooted deep in the tradition, and with a melodic sense way beyond his tender age." She'd opened a savings account and had been diligent about saving. Up until then she'd stashed all of her tips in her desk until she was afraid to have so much money around, not that there was much crime in the neighborhood. She sensed that Rima and Steve might have their own plans for the apartment that would exclude her. She wasn't completely comfortable with Steve. There was something about him that went unsaid. Perhaps he was just naturally reserved. Was he the kind of person to take advantage of a woman like Rima? She was in mourning and not in full control of her faculties. Davora had to be prepared. Above all else, having a home was the most important thing there was.

It was a triumphant evening for Sam, who stunned everyone, including the musicians, with his sound and improvisational skills. She rushed home because she wanted to record the details of the evening in her journal. She was almost finished with her portrait of Sam and wanted to find out how she might submit it to a music magazine. She stopped at a newsstand and got a copy of *Down Beat*, the one the musicians subscribed to, and read it from cover to cover. She was certain that she wanted to write and she wanted to get published...if she was good enough. The only writer she knew was David's father, but she was reluctant to show him her work. What if he didn't approve of it?

A few days later, at the end of August, Davora woke up on a crisp morning that felt more like autumn, and went to the kitchen to make coffee. Rima and Steve were sitting at the kitchen table with a well-dressed man in a Brooks Brothers suit with a colorful handkerchief in his breast pocket. He wore thick-lens tortoise-shell glasses. There were papers spread over the table and two 14KT rolled-gold Cross pens. The man, who turned out to be a real estate lawyer, was explaining something to them. "If we do it this way," he said, "there will be fewer taxes when the time comes. The resale value, when and if you decided to sell it, would exceed your initial outlay by at least thirty-five percent. More than enough for a comfortable retirement."

Not wanting to interfere in what seemed like a private meeting, Davora started back to her room when Rima asked her to join them. "This is Mr. Solomon. He's helping us work out the details of the inheritance—what it all means, and buying, well, trying to buy this apartment, if we can swing it."

Davora sat down. "I don't know much about real estate." She felt a vague fear. Was she going to lose her home?

Mr. Solomon explained: "Well, Davora, it seems that Rima and Shanna's Aunt Gretchen, God rest her soul, was quite the recluse and miser."

Davora was shocked. "I didn't know she'd passed. When was that?"

"Two days after Shana, but listen to Mr. Solomon, he'll explain everything." It irked Davora that Rima and Mr. Solomon seemed to treat Gretchen's death as a minor detail.

Mr. Solomon continued: "You might know that she owned a dress factory on 37th Street off of 6th Avenue."

"Shana and I sweated our butts off in that place," Rima interjected.

Mr. Solomon went on: "Yes, well it's a large, imposing seven-sto-
ry brick building that produced dresses, shirts, and underwear.
The building is still in very good condition and after the factory
closed and Gretchen retired, she rented out the various rooms
to immigrant families and made even a larger fortune in doing
so. Gretchen lived in a cold water flat by the Lincoln Tunnel.
And boy was she a hoarder; newspapers, cardboard containers,
stationery—though she never wrote letters—and shoe laces, God
knows why."

Davora remembered the envelope Gretchen gave to Rima after
Shana's funeral. It must have contained the details of the dress
factory, and that she was leaving it to Rima, an inheritance. Still,
she wondered what Mr. Solomon was getting at. What did this
have to do with her?

Rima went on excitedly, "Mr. Solomon has put all the numbers
together for us. We're inheriting the old dress factory. The plan is
to make new apartments out of it, beautiful ones. People want to
live in that area now; it's up and coming. And this building here,
the owners have decided to sell the apartments as separate units.
We could buy this and have it for as long as we want it for a low
monthly maintenance fee."

"That's if we come up with some additional capital," Solomon
added. "I've calculated that we're short eleven hundred dollars.
Not a drop in the bucket." There was a brief pause as the three of
them gazed expectantly at Davora. She was utterly perplexed. What
was this all about?

Rima smiled, "We're offering for you to buy in, to be a part
owner."

"I don't understand; part owner of what?"

"This apartment, if we can get it." Steve put his hand on top of Rima's. At that moment Davora understood. They were definitely more than just friends from the AA meetings.

Mr. Solomon picked up one of the rolled-gold pens and scribbled something on a pad. He explained: "You would be a twelve and a half percent owner of this apartment. When and if it sold you would get your share of your investment from the purchase price. The profit would be substantially more than it would be now if you sold."

"I don't completely understand. But do you mean that I could still live here?"

For the first time Steve spoke. "Yes, you would have your room and the run of the place. You'd be like a caretaker."

"Would you be here as well?" she asked Rima.

Rima hesitated for a moment and said nervously, "Steve and I would take one of the renovated apartments in the dress factory. But don't worry, I'd be up here a lot to check in on you, make sure you're behaving yourself. Staying out of the liquor cabinet." With that remark she and Steve laughed nervously.

"Oh, but would I be forced to leave if you decided to sell?"

Mr. Solomon said, "You would have a right of first refusal, meaning you would have the chance to buy the apartment before anyone else. Also, we'd draw up an agreement stating that all parties, the three of you, would have to agree to sell. Lacking a mutual agreement we'd go into arbitration. And you'd still get your money when it did sell."

Now that she understood the arrangement, Davora said, "But I'm a small percent partner, couldn't I be out-voted, or whatever it is?"

Solomon chuckled, "You're a pretty sharp young lady. Ever thought about law school?"

Rima looked at Steve and then Davora. "Do you think I would do that to you after...all of this? What you did for Shana. Have some faith in me."

Davora desperately wanted to have faith in her. This is where she wanted to live. She would be almost independent. She was surprised as much as they were when she said, "I could go to the bank tomorrow."

Mr. Solomon's eyebrows rose. "You have that kind of money, eleven hundred?"

"I've been working since I was a little girl. As a seamstress, my papa taught me. I worked in a gas station pumping gas and repairing cars. I'm working as a waitress now making good money. I've been saving up for a long time. I've always wanted my own home."

Mr. Solomon chuckled, "You're some girl, Davora. But we wouldn't need it right away. Not until all the paperwork is finalized and we have a closing date. This deal is a bit complex, but doable." He looked around the table and smiled. "We'll meet again just as soon as I have all of our ducks lined up in a row."

After the meeting, Davora crossed Broadway in a dreamlike state. How could such good fortune have suddenly presented itself to her? It had seemingly come out of nowhere. She was completely astonished. Her life had changed dramatically in the course of a fifteen minute meeting. Was it luck? Was it preordained? A cab just missed her as she reached the other side of Broadway, its horn blaring. The driver yelled out the window, "Watch where ya goin', doll!" She laughed and ducked into La Maravilla and got a café con leche. She loved them; they were a bit stronger than regular coffee and she felt like the caffeine increased her mental acuity. In a giddy moment she thought maybe that's what writers drank. She wandered through Central Park and thought again: Was this really happening? Could she trust it? Would she have a permanent home, hopefully a permanent home, that she loved? Why would there be any hurry to sell it? Could she *trust* them? But then, Rima could have simply not told her about any of it. She would trust her; she didn't have an alternative.

It was a Wednesday and David would be leading the jam session that evening. She wondered if she should wait to tell him about it. She walked through the park and eventually found herself on the east side at Fifth Avenue, where she saw for the first time The Metropolitan Museum. She was amazed at the size and stateliness of the massive building. How had she missed it before today? She went inside and inquired if they had a collection of medieval tapestries. The young woman who handed her a ticket, smiled and said, "We have quite a collection of them." Davora spent the next two hours in the twelfth-century rooms viewing the most magnificent tapestries she'd ever seen. She was particularly attracted to the tapestries that depicted women standing in front of tents or castle entrances, or under trees with unicorns. She reflected on it as she hurried back through the park so she wouldn't be late to work: tents, castles, domestic scenes...*Home.*

When she got to the club Boss gave her his usual effusive greeting. Helen called him into the office. "He likes you more than me, for Christ's sake." As the evening progressed, Davora sensed a feeling of lightness, as if a great burden had been lifted from her shoulders. *Stability*, was that what she was feeling? David commented that she seemed to be on cloud nine. He asked her during the break if she'd have time to talk after the gig. Davora finished wiping down the tables and the bar and washing the glasses, then she sat down with David by the window where they could watch the activity on the busy street and take in the blinking lights. He was quiet for a while and obviously nervous. Finally, he said, "How about I buy us a glass of champagne?"

"What's the occasion?" she asked.

"Oh, I'm just feeling festive. It's going so well here. I'm getting offered gigs all over the place. Duke Jackson is looking for a guitar player to take with him on the road. But I don't know."

"Oh David, if it's an opportunity for you, grab it."

"Well, I'd be reluctant to leave you, I'd..."

"I want you to be who you are. I don't want to stop you from doing what you love."

She got them the champagne without mentioning that she was feeling rather festive herself. They toasted. "To you," he said. He took a big sip as if it were a soda, and stared into his glass. "Look, you know how I feel about you; you must know by now." Immediately the wine caught in her throat as it tightened. "I'm crazy about you. Never met a gal like you, ever!" She tried to just say thank you, but it didn't come out. "What I'm trying to say is...what I want to...ask you..." He stopped, and took a small velvet box out of his jacket pocket and slid it across the table to her. "Is this..." he finished. She stared at the box, the second of its kind she'd ever been offered before. She stared at it, her mind running like a racehorse. "Look inside." The tips of her fingers tingled on the soft velvet. She opened it. It was a star shaped peridot surrounded by diamonds in a yellow 14K gold setting. She gasped, and then slowly closed the box so it would not make a snapping sound and set it on the table. Alarmed, David said, "You don't like it? It's your birthstone, August twenty-first. You don't like it? I can get you something else...I thought..."

"It's beautiful," she said. "It's just that I... I..." She wouldn't be able to begin to tell him her experiences with that gem stone, the peridot, the fateful chrysolite that had impacted her so profoundly.

"Is there someone else? You have to tell me."

"No, there's no one else. You're a wonderful man. I just need a little time. I'm sorting some things out at the moment that will affect my life, my future, and I..."

"Just tell me and I'll go away."

"No, don't go away. Please don't do that. I'd be...heartbroken." She said it, and knew then that she meant it. "You won't go away, promise me."

"I'll promise you anything. I'll promise you my life if you'll just have me."

She lifted her glass, and he lifted his and they touched ever so gently. "Then let's drink to that for now. Just a little time is what I need."

He took their glasses and sat them on the bar. "I have to get down to Brooklyn. My mother is in one of her depressions." He left quickly as if to leave everything between them in place, at least for now. She sat for a few minutes just staring at the bandstand, her fingertips still slightly tingling. Finally, she got up, picked up the ring box and put it in her purse. She walked home in a soft rain, the colorful store lights blinking, the street vibrant with life, and the muted roar of the subway train coming up from the grates, all combining to sing to her: *You will never find another man like that.* 'I know,' she thought. 'I know.'

The deal Mr. Solomon was putting together was, he reported a few weeks later, moving along smoothly, actually a bit quicker than he thought it would take. Rima and Steve were spending a lot of time at the factory, meeting with architects and designers. They were energized and happy. Davora hoped it would stay that way. She'd heard that alcoholics sometimes fell off the wagon, with terrible consequences. Meanwhile, she was getting a lot of time alone and writing every day. She was making good use of the Smith Corona Clipper portable typewriter David had given her. Slone's Stationery shop carried ribbons for all models of machines and a choice of quality typing paper. Abe Slone, the owner, joked to her that she'd become such a good customer he was putting her on his Hanukkah card list. She had already gone through one ribbon and a half-box of typing paper. She found that she could get her thoughts down quicker than writing with a pen and paper. She'd taught herself to type in less than a week. She assumed that it had come quickly because of her ability with a scissors, needle, and thread, thanks to Ivan. By this point she had chronicled everything she remembered since she'd started waitressing at the club. The musicians, the patrons, some peculiar, some a little drunk and a little too friendly, Helen's imperial manner, and even Boss the ever vigilant canine with the sloppy tongue. She wished there was someone she could talk to about getting her writing published. How did writers do it?

Sometimes she would go into Shana's room and sit on her bed. She could easily recall and hear her beautiful voice, a voice stilled forever. She'd think about Ivan, Josh, and Shmuel, who'd given her so much guidance, and all the strange things she'd seen in the Seven Heavens. Why had she seen them and what did they mean? She thought about her life in New York, the club, David, and Sam and all the musicians who'd befriended her. She understood that in a strange and circuitous way the world had opened up for her. Something that wasn't in the cards from the beginning: the Polish immigrant girl who got out with her life. Was this what was supposed to be what people called the American Dream? If it was, she would embrace it with all her heart because it came at a high price.

At the end of September, just as the leaves we're beginning to change in Riverside Park, Mr. Solomon contacted everyone to let them know that the deal had gone through and that there would be a closing on the following Tuesday. And the deal included buying the apartment that Davora would call home. Solomon said that they'd got it for a good price and with what Rima would make off the new apartments, they would more than be able to make the payments. There was even some discussion about paying Davora a small salary for maintaining the place, which she gladly would have done for free. She went to the bank on Monday and withdrew eleven hundred dollars, leaving herself a cushion of five hundred dollars in case something came up. She was so nervous carrying that amount of cash that she ran home and hid it under her mattress, which probably would have been one of the first places a burglar would look for valuables. The closing went smoothly, but the bank lawyer's eyes widened as Davora counted out the money. Mr. Solomon chuckled, "You're not going to ask for a receipt?" A clerk wrote one out swiftly and slid it across the table to her. *My deed*, she thought.

After the closing, Mr. Solomon surprised them by insisting that he take them to Leibman's, a venerable deli, for a celebratory lunch. After all, he'd made out well for himself on the deal. He was proud of his business acumen and wasn't shy about it. The food brought back the memories Davora had of Sarah's wonderful cooking. She wondered how her sisters and Ben were doing. Did they ever think of her? Would they always despise her? She missed Jake and hoped somehow he would visit her some day. The thought faded and she ate ravenously. It seemed that no matter how much she ate, she always weighed in at one hundred and twenty-two pounds. She decided that it was time to tell David about the apartment. She hoped he'd be happy for her.

On Wednesday evening after the jam session she set two glasses of champagne on the table and joined David. She explained how the whole thing had come about. She described the deal and gave him a physical description of the apartment, especially her view of the Hudson River. He said he was happy for her, but looked troubled at the news. "So, you'll be living in your own place. I thought that...maybe."

"Did I say you wouldn't be welcome there?"

"No, but I thought maybe if you'd decided that we were getting...married...you'd..."

"David, whatever we do, we are equal partners. You have to understand that."

"What do you want? I'm not sure I can take more of this. Do you want me or not?"

"Yes, I want you. But I want us to be equal...free."

"I know what you're saying, but what do you mean?"

"What I mean is that I would never tell you to not be a musician. I would never ask you to be what I want you to be. I want you to be who you are. And I want that for myself as well. Is that asking too much?"

David laughed, "Well, if that's all you want, where do I sign? I'd never tell you what to do. I love you too much. I just want you to be happy, us to be happy. I understand, you're thinking of my mother and dad. Leah needs a caretaker because of what she's been through. Dad has to do that for her. She's fragile."

"I don't want a caretaker," she said firmly.

"You won't have one. By the way, did you pawn that ring I gave you? It's worth a lot of dough."

She took the ring box out of her purse and handed it to him. The place was empty now and quiet, except for Helen who emerged from the office with Boss on his leash. She walked by them brusquely, stopped and turned around, quite aware that it was an intimate moment for them. A very big moment. She smiled conspiratorially, "There's more champagne in the cooler. Goodnight, kids." He opened the box and took the ring out. It glowed like a tiny green candle with gold highlights. She thought for a moment she might tell him about her experience with peridots, but decided not to. Maybe another time, maybe never. It was something unique in her life that might be better left unsaid. He reached out and offered her the ring. She clasped and then unclasped her hands and then held her hand out. He slid the ring on her finger. "It fits perfectly. Like I said, DAV and DAV. We're a duo."

"An equal duo, David, remember that."

"May I...kiss you?"

*

It was a dazzling fall with wild winds, swirling leaves of red, purple, brown, orange and yellow. The sun had spotlighted the trees in September and rainfall has been plentiful, resulting in the vibrant colors. The river looked like a great wide blue channel for ocean-going vessels, pleasure crafts, and the Circle Line Ferry, delighting tourists with numerous and diverse views of Manhattan Island. The weather excited Davora and she walked briskly through Riverside Park every morning, enjoying the aroma of roasted chestnuts, the fluttering of pigeons, and the scurrying of squirrels. She liked to walk uptown to Grant's Tomb on 122nd Street by Morningside Heights. It was a forty-one block walk that she could do in an hour and a half. It was her exercise and meditation, all the while thinking what she would write about when she returned home.

She had a fair amount of time to herself as Rima and Steve were busy transforming the old factory into luxury dwellings and making plans for their future, she assumed. Though they hadn't announced it, it was clear that they were a couple. David was busy in the recording studio. Sam had told him that it was time he recorded his own record, and said he would play on it, which would help make it a success. Other notable musicians were glad to sign on and lend their talent to a promising young guitarist who was quickly becoming a fine composer of original jazz tunes, one of which was entitled "Davora's Waltz," a haunting and beautiful piece written in A-minor, with a Klezmer feeling to it. She would not hear it for a month or two until the record would be released. The project would take approximately three weeks. She would see David infrequently. They'd go up to the roof of her building, sometimes with a glass of champagne, and look out over the river. From there they could see the George Washington Bridge, an indelible creation, the longest steel suspension bridge in the world, gleaming silver with hundreds of beaconing lights, a stunning necklace that connected Fort Lee to Washington Heights in New York City. Their city, their place of opportunity, discovery, and hopefully eternal love.

The first few days of October were cool, and the leaves were peaking in a burst of colors, a stunning finale. It was a Sunday morning and she'd had breakfast at La Maravillas, her favorite

Spanish café, a fried egg on toasted bread with a splash of salsa, and café con leche. She walked uptown through the park with energy and a feeling of purpose. Something was formulating in her mind, something she needed to write about. She felt a sense of urgency; something was tugging at her. She reached Grant's Tomb in what felt like record time and started back just as quickly. The leaves were swirling around her and catching on her sweater, sticking in her hair, and pinging off her cheeks and forehead like pin pricks. The boat traffic on the river, with the autumn light, reminded her of a French impressionist painting she'd seen. About five blocks from the apartment she noticed two elderly men sitting on a park bench. One, stooped over, in a worn trench coat, was shabby looking but happily engaged. He tossed peanuts to squirrels. The other man wore a black suit. He sat upright, very aware of his surroundings, alert to any possible danger. His movements were quick and bird-like. The men were deep in an animated conversation. She stopped and watched them intently. She thought she could hear Ivan's voice through the wind. He was telling Shmuel that his daughter lived in the neighborhood and she was doing very well for herself, that she'd met a fine young man and was engaged. Shmuel smiled deeply. "A very good girl, indeed. You did well by her." Her tears came fast and blurred her vision. She leaned against a railing for support and cried from the center of her soul. She wiped her eyes with her sweater sleeve and began to run toward them. *Papa, Papa.* But they were gone.

When she got back to the apartment she called David, but he didn't answer. She knew that he was in the recording studio and she didn't want to bother him, but she needed to hear his voice. She put on some coffee and took a quick shower. She felt refreshed and was starting to calm down. *A blessing*, were the words that came to her mind. Yes, it had been a blessing to see them. They had come to bless her, to reassure the young girl they both loved. They came just for that purpose, and then they were gone...they were *free*, she thought...she knew that they were...*free*.

She sat down at her desk and sipped her coffee. She glanced out at the river, which looked completely still and serene, an endless expanse of flowing glass. She put a piece of paper in the typewriter and scrolled it up. She left some space at the top of the page because she didn't know what the title of the story would be.

She sipped more coffee, wiped a residual tear from the corner of her eye, and began typing:

It was once an imposing three-story home in a neighborhood that had long since seen its luster dimmed in the decades following the Second World War.

THE GAY SEVENTIES

K en often reflected on a line from a Simon and Garfunkel song: "How terribly strange to be seventy." *And stranger still to be seventy-four*, he thought. He and his buddies were careening through that precarious decade that often eliminates players by the dozen. Ken wrote in his journal: Death is an exacting referee who can sideline you permanently at any point in the game. *Even if you're winning.*

Ken and the guys met most Friday evenings at the local pub, Samoon's Oasis, formerly a rowdy bar called Golden Mugs & Sassy Shots, a favorite with the biker community until it was sold to a Jordanian woman named Sabah. Sabah's last name was Samoon. Hence, Samoon's Oasis. She switched up the burger, pulled pork, grilled cheese, fries, and onion rings menu and introduced items like Tofu Banh Mi and Mediterranean Chickpea Salad. She also added kombucha on tap, but fortunately kept a few good ales and IPAs in the beer lines. In retaliation, the bikers revved their engines in front of the place on the day of her grand opening, and then evaporated like a mirage. Word got back that they'd relocated a couple of towns away and held their "gatherings" at a venerable road house called Gayle's Bottom Feeder, aka *The Feedah*.

This worked out well for Ken and his gang as they were well past their chest-thumping days. Aggression didn't enter into their exchanges, though occasionally a few feathers got ruffled on a point of academic disagreement, or the exact sequence and details of some local event, usually of the outrageous kind. But it was always resolved in a good-natured manner. The meetings would begin with Sick Call: the announcement of new symptoms, the progress of various treatments and therapies, and the recital of verbatim conversations between patient and doctor. Ken preferred to keep his medical records private. He'd recently been discovered to have atrial fibrillation while he was being monitored during a colonoscopy. But his heart chugged along reliably at sixty-seven beats per minute. Doctor Cappelletti prescribed Eliquis and chirped, "No salt," as Ken left the examination room. But Ken had been known to lick the salt crystals off of a sourdough pretzel, and then sprinkle sea salt on it.

The camaraderie and beer helped to soothe the anxiety that accompanied the mortal matters they discussed. Ken mentioned one Friday evening that he'd recently read an article in Google News about a beer that was brewed in Israel with five thousand year old yeast discovered at the bottom of a clay pot. "It would be interesting to try it," he said.

Gary, who had recently sold his heating and cooling business and was on the other side of prostate cancer, according to Doctor Wadhwa, said, "I feel like I'm five thousand years old." He described his recent prostate biopsy as, "They put a tiny mechanical shark up your ass and it takes twelve little bites out of each neighborhood. Fun and games!" But he was grateful to be clear of cancer. He praised Doctor Wadhwa highly. "If you get prostate, he's the guy you want."

Richard, a retired Ancient Studies professor, responded to Gary's comments: "I'd say, without carbon dating, you don't look a day over four thousand years old." Laughs, clinking of pint glasses... followed by Denise, who brought the Sahara Platter to the table. It consisted of hummus, babaganoush, tabouli, feta cheese, grape leaves, Kalamata olives, figs, and toasted pita triangles, a generous portion. Denise always laid out a few teaspoons for the more fastidious gentlemen who preferred not to get the stuff on their fingers, but rather spoon it directly on to their pita bread. In addition, Sabah always sent out a basket of Pepperidge Farm Goldfish, the kind with a tiny eye and smile etched into them. She'd done her research and knew that they were one of the most famous snack crackers in the USA. The fish were always entirely consumed. The Sahara Platter amounted to a small feast and Sabah would swing by their table and say, "Enough? Eat boys, eat! Sihat jayidat! Good health!"

Arturo, an artist, who still showed his work at the local and college galleries, made his usual comment: "When the chips are down, you eat 'em." He always said that, whether chips were served or not. In the mid nineteen-sixties Arturo had enjoyed the distinction of having his work represented at an important gallery called Dane, on West 57th Street in Manhattan. He was considered to be one of the up-and-coming abstract artists of the period. A cranky, dismissive art critic, who rarely bestowed accolades on anyone's work, unless they were approaching their ninth decade, referred to Arturo as: "Not quite Jackson Pollack Jr., but mildly promising." Not exactly a full-throated endorsement, but it didn't deter buyers who couldn't approach Pollack's price range anyway. And wasn't the art world all about that: skewed economics, bad behavior, and vile competition?

For some reason—perhaps because Arturo's work was "Consciously indecipherable, but *catchy*," as a younger, more lenient critic pronounced it—young Wall Street types, upscale restaurants, and record company executives bought his paintings. His work cast them in a soft intellectual glow. Their clients would stare at the canvasses in their offices and studios. They would nod as if they understood what it was they were looking at, which gave the collectors leave to say, "Yes, I find his work quite fascinating." But Arturo maintained that all he'd been doing was playing with forms, colors, lines, and shapes, and gestural marks, blending them, and then throwing them onto the canvas willy-nilly. The same thing he'd been doing since third grade. "Jerking off with pigment," as he described it, yielding to his penchant for self-deprecation.

Ken justified his membership in the group, beside the fact that he liked the guys, with the fact that he was still working, still being productive. He was an active journalist and wrote every day. And he could at least say that he had a part time job in education. He was a permanently certified English teacher, grades seven through twelve. But now he did home teaching for the local school district. Before that he'd subbed for eighteen years. The day he received his state certification in the mail he decided that the last thing he wanted to do was be a teacher, so he became a permanent sub. His was an inner city school and the challenges were inherent, but he managed to negotiate the confrontations and occasional outbursts of violence by maintaining a laid back, sympathetic vibe that worked well with the students and the administration, whose policy on behavior and other troubling issues was: *Put a lid on it.*

The idea of retirement irked Ken. People liked to say, "Oh, so you're retired now?" Like they were lodging a formal complaint against him, classifying him as "out of the game." He didn't feel "retired," whatever that was supposed to mean...take up fly fishing, a Hawaiian dream vacation, or cooking classes? Screw all that! He worked and he wrote. He had two large wooden crates full of journals to show for it. Mostly they contained personal reflections, political commentary, op-eds, an occasional poem, or a paragraph of an abandoned essay. He kept his journals private, not because he hoped for his ruminations to be discovered and celebrated after his death, but just because. Lately, he wrote about life in its later stages and how it had been diminished to mulling over regrets and dodging medical bullets. There was, it seemed, unless he had missed the point entirely, no golden ring to grab hold of the last time around.

Another Friday night regular was Tony. He'd been a literature professor at a prestigious college and was an authority on an obscure Romanian poet as a result of having attended the School of International Letters and Culture at Arizona State University. It was not his first choice. He wanted to be a musician and played double bass in a band throughout college. Tony's father, Andrei, was adamant that their Romanian roots would live on in his son. The Dragavei clan had been proud farmers who'd lived off the land in Romania for hundreds of years. The name Dragavei was derived from curly dock, one of the staple crops they grew besides potatoes, sugar beets, and maize. Young Tony Dragavei was the victim of his father's obsession with their homeland and had no choice but to attend the Romanian Studies Program at Arizona State University unless he wanted to pay for his own tuition.

Tony and his writing/research partner, a graduate student at the University of Bucharest, had recently produced the definitive biography and critique of the poet's work, including his letters: George Bacovia, the Poet of Grayness. He was first classified as a Romanian Symbolist but his work developed into Modernism, and eventually Theater of the Absurd. He came to be considered a major figure in classic Romanian Literature. It started with a fluke: "Purple Twilight," a poem the young Bacovia wrote while accidentally locked up in a church tower overnight. Tony and his partner methodically analyzed Bacovia's body of work: the books *Plumb* and *Yellow Sparks*, and "Cogito," his 1950s poetical testament. Then came his poem "Autumn Notes:" *Silence...it is autumn in the borough.../Rain...and only rain says anything*. Lots of grayness. What really sold their scholarship was that they had access to Bacovia's letters because Tony's father's great uncle had lived in the same village as Bacovia and hung out with him at the local tavern. They drank and played darts. For some reason Bacovia handed off the letters to Boris, Tony's dad's great uncle, and instructed him to burn them. But he didn't. Based on that treasure trove, they got a publishing contract with the venerable Bloomsbury Press in London, which was a major coup. This resulted in Tony being invited to literary conferences in Europe, South America, and Romania, from which he would invariably return annoyed. He said, more than once, "I judge a city by how easy it is to navigate it on foot, the quality of its beers, and the firmness of the mattresses in the hotels. I was almost crippled sleeping in Craiova. I gave my friggin' talk with an icepack on my ass, tucked in my underwear." He rarely commented on the academic success of the book, which had initially retailed to universities, in hardcover, for two hundred and seventy-five dollars, except to say, "I'm so done with this shit it's not funny." He had been invited back to Marist to teach one or two courses at his discretion, but declined. He had a novel way of putting it when he found something undesirable or unacceptable: "Not my circus, not my monkey."

Ken appreciated Tony's offhandedness, his scholarship, and the manner in which he could succinctly explain and interpret complex forms of poetry and prose. He could dissect Pound with a chopstick; breakdown Pound's ideas on imagism, precision, economy of language, the foregoing of traditional rhyme and meter. And he could back it up with direct quotes from Eliot's *The Better Craftsman*. For fun, one afternoon when he was bored, he translated Sabah's menu into Hungarian, eschewing the Romanian language, which eighty-nine percent of the country spoke, in favor of Hungarian, which was spoken in Transylvania by only seven percent of the population. Tony chose Hungarian also because he was a Bram Stoker fan and had published a few papers on him as well. After he'd finished translating the menu he copied it out in calligraphy and presented it to Sabah who accepted it graciously with an expression of complete bewilderment. She placed it on her office desk and would look through it from time to time and marvel at the curlicues, the thick and thin lines in single strokes. Gradually it accumulated a layer of gooey knafeh drippings and coffee rings from her Al-Qahwa.

One time after Tony explained Pound's attraction to fascism, Gary snorted, "Pound, the guy was an anti-Semite. I wouldn't have fixed a ceiling fan for the bastard."

"Yeah," Tony nodded. "Dualism: you can be a great poet and an asshole at the same time."

"I need more *and*s and *the*s to make sense of that stuff," Gary said.

"Well, the guy is covering it all: ancient Greece and Rome, economics, politics; it's really the embodiment of literary history," Richard said. "He's got a lot of balls in the air."

Gary made a sour face. "Yeah, but only two of them count. And are you saying Pound is above my head? You calling me a mechanical?"

Richard laughed, "Not by a penny or a Pound."

Arturo took a long sip of his IPA. "A lot of balls in the air, huh. No need to get testicle."

"At any rate," Richard continued, "the Cantos are definitely not *Dick and Jane*."

Gary clinked Richard's glass. "Here's to balls, testicles, and Dick."

Arturo joined in and clinked his glass. "And to Jane as well. Without Jane, there'd be no Dick."

Ken laughed, "We shouldn't desecrate children's literature, don't you think?"

"What's with toasting anyway?" Gary said. "It's gotta come from the French. A dainty gesture, clinking glasses."

Tony lifted his glass. "It's medieval. Sometimes the wine was poisoned and concealed by the sediment. Clinking was a sign of trust and honesty. A toast to good health."

Arturo swished his glass around and stared at it suspiciously. "The bottom is cloudy. Did one of you guys poison me?"

Richard laughed. "You're drinking a New England style IPA. The action of the hops causes colloidal haze. That's why it's cloudy."

Gary snickered, "Colloidal haze, huh. I think I tripped on that once."

*

Lately, Ken's writing consisted of a special document he'd titled *Afternoon of the Gone*, with all due respect to Debussy's symphonic poem. It was intended for Trish, assuming he would predecease her as he was ten years her senior. Somehow she was never available, actually preferred not to be, to look over the documents she would need to have on hand when the time came. She simply resisted it, even in the presence of their lawyer, whom he'd dragged her to in order to sign their wills, power of attorney, DNR, Health Care Proxy Forms, etc. She kept her eyes closed as she scribbled her signature.

Trish despised paperwork, especially concerning their estate. She kept herself busy with yoga classes Monday through Thursday and Pilates on Fridays. In the summer months she kayaked, rode her bike on the rail trail, and took multiple walks and hikes with her cadre of girlfriends. In the winter she went snowshoeing and cross country skiing. With all that, she managed to log in about two hours per day of phone time with her mother and sister in Chicopee, parsing through their conflicting narratives and the psychic injuries they'd inflicted upon each other, real and imagined. Ken warned Trish that she risked getting cauliflower ear from the phone receiver.

When Trish wasn't consumed with other activities she worked on her meditation room, a long-term project. It was a comfortable open space for which she embroidered pillows and made silk curtains with Oriental themes. The room had French doors that opened out to an expansive deck overlooking the backyard. She had integrated blue solar LED string lights around the perimeter, which happily bordered a bird sanctuary. The lights added to the meditative vibe of the space. On occasion, when Ken stood on the back deck and reflectively enjoyed an American Spirit cigarette, which had been banned by Dr. Capaletti, he'd stare out at the ethereal blue lights and wonder about the possibility of attracting an extraterrestrial to their property. For a purpose that...who the hell knew? He was strict about his tobacco intake and only allowed himself one American Spirit every six days. Each time he inhaled he visualized Capaletti's small, disapproving Sicilian face, like a pouting Caravaggio angel, chastising him for sneaking a smoke. In private, Capaletti was a closet vaper, addicted to non-addicting "caramel apple." He'd take several hits off his vaping pipe between patients and then spray Lysol to conceal the aroma, which morphed into a bizarre eau de medical.

Ken got the supplies for his writing project at Staples, where he enjoyed a teachers' reward discount. He bought a three-ring binder, black vinyl with gold trim. It looked suitably official for his purposes. He also purchased a box of clear page protectors to insert the documents into. He still had his old college Swingline three-hole puncher, which would come in handy. (He was going to insert an essay he'd published in American Funeral Magazine called, *Death is Life's Homework*. But he decided it was superfluous and omitted it.) As he wandered around the aisles he noticed the colorful paper leaf decorations, corn stalks, and plastic pumpkins, which reminded him that it was fall, almost mid October. As a kid, Halloween had been his favorite holiday. He indulged himself and bought some Halloween-themed stickers and a small plastic glow-in-the-dark skeleton that he would glue on to the front of the binder. He was aware that he was courting some ironic morbidity, but it felt right for the project. Perhaps it was a bit of magical thinking, the warding off of imminent death by embracing it, at least with stickers and a glow-in-the-dark-skeleton, applied with a glue gun.

*

Denise appeared at the table and swept up the empty Sahara platter and took drink orders. The guys ordered their usual, except Arturo, who got a lager so he could see down into the bottom of the glass. Richard asked Denise how her coursework was going. She was finishing up a master's degree in political science and the guys were always interested to hear about her progress. They knew the professors at the college and had offered Denise advice on all aspects of navigating what could sometimes be unforeseen and gnarly academic hurdles. They'd also offered to write her letters of recommendation as well, as her intention was to earn a PhD. "Stay away from Gebbler," Richard always cautioned. "He's a bit too familiar with co-eds."

Denise smiled shyly, "He offered to help get me into Yale."

Tony snorted, "Gebbler didn't go to Yale. He got his degree out of a gumball machine."

"I installed the guy's central air system," Gary said. "It took him a light year to pay me off. Not like he didn't have it; he drives a Maserati MC 20."

"Well, he's retiring at the end of the semester anyway," Denise said.

Richard raised his glass in a salute. "You're kidding. The guy has been there forever. A regular vampire."

Tony raised his glass as well. "I spent a summer as a tour guide in Bran Castle."

"Really?" Gary asked. "Did you see Dracula?"

"No, but we hung out in there after hours. Me and Gabriela. She was a tour guide as well. We'd get drunk and sleep in the coffins...sometimes the same one," Tony laughed. "And that's not to leave this table. Besides, it was a century or two ago."

"Professor, I didn't know you were such a rake," Denise smiled.

"More like a snow shovel at this point."

Denise laughed. "I'll be right back with your beer. Anyone up for baklava?"

*

Ken finished his project, *Afternoon of the Gone*, just before Halloween and decided to give it to Trish on November first, The Day of the Dead. He would make chili and open a bottle of their favorite red wine. But she announced at the last minute that she was meeting with her girlfriends. One of them had hatched a plan to knit a thousand mittens and scarves for children in need throughout the state by Thanksgiving. She simply had to do her part. Miffed, Ken slid the binder into his desk drawer. He decided that he wasn't going to dine alone. He called Arturo because he knew that his wife Martina and their daughter Rosa were in Livorno visiting their relatives. Arturo showed up twenty minutes later with two bottles of Sangiovese and half a bottle of Sambuca without the cap on it. Ken sensed there was something off about him. He wasn't himself, usually bombastic and forceful; he seemed a bit skewed. And, Ken couldn't be sure, but either he'd dressed carelessly, or he'd slept in his clothes. Perhaps something not so unusual for a prolific artist.

They had a glass of Ken's wine. He put out some Trader Joe's Hot Pico De Gallo Salsa and corn chips. He slid the bowls onto the butcher block table and waited. Arturo didn't disappoint him and said his usual: "When the chips are down you eat 'em."

Ken lifted the top off of the crock pot and stirred the chili. An appetizing aromatic fog suffused the kitchen. "I knew you were going to say that...about the chips."

"What about the chips?"

"Nothing, how's the chili smell?"

"Molta approvazione!"

The timer sounded and Ken removed a tray of steaming cornbread from the oven. Arturo poured out more wine into their glasses and asked for a shot glass. He poured out the Sambuca. "It's good for digestion," he said. "Wait till you taste the Sangiovese—nectar of the gods."

"Let's go sit on the deck while the cornbread cools off," Ken suggested. It was a fairly mild evening, but it was already dark outside, so Ken switched on the ethereal blue lights and a porch light behind them so they could see well enough to avoid tripping over the flower pots.

They toasted; Arturo drank the shot down then swished his wine in his glass and examined it pensively, as if a clue or an answer to something was swirling in it.

"Don't worry, no poison," Ken chuckled. "So what do you think?"

"About what?"

"The end—the final curtain, you know, Frank Sinatra...'My W ay.'"

"You asking me that because I'm Italian?"

"Of course not. But don't you think about it? I'm seventy-four, you're seventy-one. Guys our age are popping off like flies."

"First of all flies don't pop off, they get stuck in the ointment. Or they get swatted. My mother is ninety-seven. She walks around her Queens senior housing complex like she owns the fucking place. The caregivers call her the Diva."

"I've been thinking a lot about it lately. I've dreamed a couple times that I died."

"You're not like, sick or anything, are you?"

"No, not at all. I've just dreamed about it."

"What's that like?"

"Well, it's like when you turn off a generator or a turbine. The motor winds down slowly until it stops, the sound modulates down, the humming fades. I feel like I'm falling into something. Then just darkness, nothing. I don't know, it's like you feel the motor of your life fades into nothing."

"All right, a free meal with philosophy," Arturo said with some bitterness.

"Really, you don't think about it? Guys younger than us check out."

"Everybody's checking out sooner or later and maybe it's a good thing. Look, I might die of starvation soon, you know what I mean?"

"Oh, I'm sorry. Let's eat. I didn't realize how hungry I was either. Must be the wine." For some reason it occurred to Ken that Arturo might not be eating regularly.

They sat down at the table and Arturo crumbled a piece of cornbread into his chili. "Got any cayenne?" Ken noticed that his fingers were stained, probably from paint. But he'd never noticed that detail before. Maybe he'd been working on his Moto Guzzi, which he rode infrequently, but kept in perfect tune. Ken had stood in Arturo's driveway and listened to him gun the engine. "Like music, a love song," Arturo always said. Maybe he'd forgotten to wash his hands.

"Of course. Trish ordered us some organic cayenne from Amazon. It actually tastes better than regular. And I won't affront you with anymore death talk. I've just been thinking about it. It's always there these days. Kind of like, I don't know, it's just there."

Arturo, paused and sat back for a moment. "There's all kinds of death, my friend. Even without dying."

"What do you mean?"

Arturo looked at the spoon in his hand. It was shaking. "Martina took Rosa to visit her folks in Livorno. I don't think she's coming back. Doesn't look like it."

Ken was shocked. "I'm sorry, I didn't know. I...."

Arturo slumped in his chair. "Said she'd had enough of me for a lifetime."

"Art, I'm so sorry. Look, she'll come back. She lives here, she has to."

"She shipped Rosa's piano over there. You don't take the piano on a family visit."

"No. She did that?"

"Yeah... she did."

"I'm so sorry. I don't know what to say."

"There's nothing to say. I wasn't going to mention it, but it's there... always... just like death. I've been... fuck it, let's have the Sangiovese."

Ken poured out the wine. "Let's toast to a quick resolution. She'll figure it out. She'll come back."

Arturo held his glass up and studied it for a moment, then took a sip. "That's the stuff. Tastes like home... like where she is... where I won't be."

"You have to go there. Apologize, do whatever you gotta do and bring her back."

Arturo considered that for a moment, nodded, and started eating voraciously. "You're a good friend, Ken. I appreciate it. But this isn't going to get fixed just like that. There's too much...fuck it, let's eat."

They ate in silence, Ken casting furtive glances at Arturo. He was, Ken realized, in a very bad way. At least he still had a good appetite. After, Ken made espresso and poured out some grappa in tulip-shaped glasses. "Let's have this out on the deck," he suggested.

"You're gonna get me drunk." He pushed up from the table. "Shit, I am drunk. You got anything to smoke, a cigar or something? Dried sheep dung? I don't care what."

"I've got some American Spirit. You want one?"

"May as well."

Ken went to his study and took out the cigarettes from behind his copy of *Leaves of Grass*. He thought, *I'm seventy-four, why am I still hiding them?* He opened his desk drawer and stared at the black binder; the miniature skeleton glowed eerily. The shape of its jawbone looked like it was smiling. It was ridiculous, a waste of time. Ken shoved the drawer closed. *Silly old man.*

When he walked back through the kitchen, Arturo wasn't there. "Art, where are you?" He heard water running and went down the hall. Arturo was coming out of the bathroom; his eyes were red and puffy. They stared at each other for a moment.

"What? It was the cayenne I sprinkled on my chili. I shouldn't have rubbed my eyes after," he said defensively.

Ken wasn't going to push it. The guy felt bad enough, having been cut adrift by Martina. And she'd taken his daughter with her as well. They sat on opposite ends of an outdoor sofa that Ken had bought recently for Trish's birthday. He slid two cigarettes out from the pack.

Ken took a deep drag and observed the smoke streaming from his nostrils out toward the blue lights. He noticed that they seemed to be flickering. Maybe they were supposed to, but he hadn't noticed it before. They could be defective. Not everything Trish ordered from Amazon was always of the highest quality.

Arturo leaned back and sunk into the cushions and exhaled a cloud of smoke. He grabbed at it and closed his hand into a fist. Then he opened his hand to reveal what he'd caught. "See? Nothing, not a fucking thing. That's what I've got, nothing."

"You've got your work," Ken said, struggling to say something positive. "You're a fantastic artist. Trish and I love the one you gave to us. It's in the living room."

"I stopped working after they left. She always said that was all I cared about anyway. Not them."

"Of course you cared about them."

"I was a selfish prick."

Ken looked out at the blue lights, which seemed to be brightening and strangely introducing a pinkish tint around the bulbs. Were they designed to do that and he hadn't noticed it before? He glanced at Arturo. Tears were streaming down his cheeks.

"Oh, man." He slid over and put his arm around him. "Artie, it's OK. It'll be all right." He could feel Arturo's trapezius muscles tightening as he sobbed. "Artie!" Slowly Arturo's head fell back on the cushion and he passed out. Ken noticed that he'd drained his wine glass and had drunk the grappa as well. He must have just chugged it down. Ken took the still burning cigarette from between Arturo's fingers and crushed it out. A wave of guilt sluiced through his stomach. He'd gotten Arturo drunk and now he was sleeping in his arms. It would be a sight for Trish to see them like this if she were to suddenly come home. But it was only eight fifteen and she probably wouldn't return for a while.

He covered Arturo with an afghan. His mouth was wide open and his breathing was loud and clutched from sleep apnea. Ken walked unsteadily to the stairs and leaned on the railing. He hadn't felt this intoxicated in a long time and was at a complete loss as to what he should do. He heard a humming sound, a low tone as if an electric motor was cut off, slowly fading out. *Like the motor of your life fading into nothing,* he thought. He tapped out another cigarette and fished the lighter out of his pocket. *OK, I'll have one more, then I'll make a double espresso and sober up. I'll tell Trish that Arturo showed up in a bad way, so I gave him dinner and had him lie down.* He listened to Arturo's unsteady breathing, which stopped for long worrisome moments. Then he'd snort percussively, gasp, and start breathing again. Ken wondered if he might also have atrial fibrillation, in which case he should see a cardiologist. He would mention it to him later on, after the present situation was resolved.

He finished his cigarette and, being more than a little drunk, uncharacteristically flicked it out into the yard. The red glow of the last bit of tobacco arced out like a miniature rocket and dropped down, then bounced back up shedding sparks as if it had struck a hard object. Immediately, the ethereal blue lights with their pink halos burst into harsh white lights, reminiscent of the clear garish bulbs that lit up car dealership lots he'd seen in the late sixties. *What the fuck is this?* He stared at the lights, then scanned the yard for... what, a used car, an alien spacecraft... what? Then he noticed it, a silver structure shaped like a bench glowing under the harsh glare toward the end of the lawn. Cautiously, he descended the stairs and approached the luminescent object. Now he could see that it was a tapered hexagon box, over six feet long. He shuddered: *It's a fucking coffin!*

He wanted to bolt for the garage and drive away as fast as possible. But he was mesmerized... drawn to the thing. When he got within a couple of yards, he determined that it was constructed of metal, possibly brushed aluminum, with four burnished gold handles, two near the head and two near the foot, convenient for carrying to the grave. Then he noticed the stickers, an array of colorful stickers evocative of the ones people used to apply to their luggage; Paris, London, Barcelona. He began to realize as he examined them that they were a compendium of the places he and Trish had visited on their cross-country trips. There was his high school sticker, with the wise owl, their football team mascot. There were other emblems of the colleges he'd attended, where he'd earned his master's and doctorate degrees. At the bottom of the coffin there was a plaque. He moved closer and saw that it was a weathered license plate. He stared at it until he realized that it was the same letters and numbers as his own license plate.

Terrified, he ran back and bolted up the deck stairs, tripping on the last one. He went down hard, knocking the wind out of himself. Dull pain quickly spread into agony throughout his body. He struggled for breath. Slowly he pushed up onto his hands and knees and gasped for air, each attempt setting off another wave of pain. When he could breathe comfortably again he stood, regained his balance, and saw that Arturo was gone, the afghan lying on the floor. How had he managed that? He'd been completely out of it, almost comatose. Ken limped to the railing and vomited over it, averting his eyes from the thing sitting in the yard. He staggered into the kitchen and drank some water, then started cleaning up, scraping the dishes, filling the washer, scrubbing the crock pot and putting it away. He dumped the empty bottles into the recycling bin. He was still shaking. *This can't be happening.* He made a strong espresso and drank it.

Cautiously, he approached the deck. The blue lights twinkled softly as they usually did. Everything seemed back to normal. The aluminum coffin was gone. He decided that the excessive amount of wine combined with the grappa, and the small shot of Sambuca Arturo insisted he'd have, for digestion, had caused him to experience a hallucination. What else could it have been? But Arturo's departure seemed inexplicable. The episode had frightened and disoriented him. He began to obsess that he might have a neurological disorder. He decided to make an appointment with his GP after the holidays and get a referral. He also decided he'd leave the black binder in his desk. Maybe he'd give it to her for Christmas. He could remove the skeleton and replace it with a miniature plastic snowman and peel the Halloween stickers off. He also decided not to mention the episode with Arturo to Trish.

*

The guys didn't meet up again at Samoon's until the second Friday in November after Veterans Day. As usual they reported new symptoms, treatments, and doctors' advice. Richard said that his dermatologist had discovered a patch of skin cancer on his neck and removed it. He'd have to be checked every three months from now on. Tony was struggling with a bout of sciatica and had brought a doughnut pillow to sit on. Gary was still in the clear for prostate cancer though his PSA numbers continued to fluctuate. "What I do is," he said, "I take the numbers and rearrange them and play PowerBall once a week."

Ken was reluctant to report his neurological scare, or psychic event, though he'd experienced no additional symptoms since the night Arturo had come for dinner. Instead, he described how his podiatrist, Doctor Kaiser, had painlessly operated on his ingrown toenails, though that had occurred months before. On the way to the bathroom Ken glanced out the window and saw Arturo dismounting from his Moto Guzzi in a pale white snow shower, the first of the season. Another motorcycle, a Harley-Davidson street bike, was parked next to his elegant Italian wheels, and dwarfed it. Both Arturo and the man next to him wore black leather jackets and silver helmets. As they approached, Ken could make out a red monogram on their leather jackets: RH&O Club. Apparently, Arturo had joined a biker club. Not the safest choice given his current mental condition. "We're going to have company," he reported to the guys.

Initially, Arturo took up a defensive stance in front of them as if he expected to be challenged. "This is Gino. He's the treasurer of the Ride Hard-On Club. They're the guys who used to come here before Samoon took over." Everyone greeted Gino like they'd missed him and anticipated his arrival. Always thoughtful and with deference for each other, no one asked Arturo how he'd wound up in the Ride Hard-On Club. Ken was pretty sure it was in reaction to Martina's leaving him.

Gino was a big grizzly bear of a man with a black beard streaked with gray that hung well down his chest. He wore a thick silver chain with an Irish cross on it around his neck, one of several. Denise set the Sahara Platter down and took more drink orders. Arturo got a pint and Gino ordered a pitcher of beer, remarking, "I don't like waiting for the next one." He eyed the platter with obvious interest. "Nice, I've had to go vegetarian for my cholesterol. Doc says I'm full of grease." This scored points with the guys. Gino's sharing his medical information made it easier to bond with him.

Denise collected the empty pint glasses. "I'll be right back."

"So, I didn't know that a motorcycle club needs a treasurer. Why is that?" Richard asked.

"We do fundraisers. Toys For Tots, Smile Train. Stuff like that. You have to keep clean records to participate. I was the obvious one, ex bond broker."

"Very cool," Gary said. "You guys do good work."

"Yeah, we do good work," Gino obviously was annoyed with Gary's comment.

"I always wanted to get a bike," Tony mused, "but Anna wouldn't let me."

Denise set their beers down and two baskets of goldfish on the table. "Cheers." Gino downed half a pint. "That's a sad thing. There's nothing like riding. By the way, isn't one of you supposed to be an authority on Bacovia?"

Tony looked shocked. "George Bacovia? Well yeah, I did research on him. A book actually. Why do you ask?"

"I did a bike tour through Romania years ago. I got drunk in Bucharest and woke up in Bacovia's garden behind his house. I didn't know it was a memorial museum. Next morning I pretended I was a tourist so I could use the bathroom. They were giving me the hairy eyeball so I got one of his books on the way out."

Tony leaned forward, "You're kidding, which one?"

Gino lifted his glass and studied the bubbles. "Let's see, I remember some of them. There was one about autumn."

"Yes, Monosyllables of Autumn. You read that one?" Tony was excited.

"*Hope will slowly fall into emptiness / all. / Will time ever be normal? / Autumn strikes the window with metal leaves.*"

"That's how the poem ends. You've got good recall."

"I like his stuff. He's a dark dude."

"The Poet of Grayness. That's what he was known as."

Gino recited: "*The world's gloom has grown. / I cannot forget the mad fiddler / and the piano player. / Life is a funeral song.*"

Tony was completely in awe of Gino. "That's the end of "Funeral March"! Wow! You really got it, Gino. Sorrow, sadness, a North Sea Landscape; gray, harsh, and nostalgic. He's the symbolist poet, a precursor of Romanian Modernism."

Gary broke in, "I could read this guy. He talks in sentences, not like Pound's Morse Code, whatever the hell that is. '*Life is a funeral song*,' heavy."

Richard broke in, "Well, I wouldn't belittle Pound; 'In a Station of the Metro.' Doesn't that confirm his genius?"

"You don't actually compare Bacovia to Pound. They're two different animals," Tony said.

"Well, which guy weighed more?" Gary asked.

Gino finished his beer and poured out another one. "You guys do this all the time? You'd be better off getting bikes."

The guys decided that they'd meet up again after Thanksgiving which would be the first week of December. When Denise approached the table with the check, Gino grabbed it. "I've got this." They protested his generosity and demanded to split the bill. Gino insisted, "I need the tax write-off if you don't mind." No one asked why, but they assumed that he'd done well as a bond broker, though they weren't exactly sure what that was. And they still wondered how Arturo had hooked up with the guy. When Denise came back with the credit slip for Gino to sign she wished them a happy Thanksgiving. Ken asked her if she had plans for the holiday. She hesitated, her usual cheeriness gone. "I'll be with my family in Plattsburgh." She hesitated again. "I'll be staying there a while."

Richard asked her if she'd heard about graduate school yet. "That's going to be on hold for now." Her voice broke, "I'm due in February... taking some time off." They congratulated her profusely—no questions.

Gino removed one of the thick silver chains with the Irish cross attached from around his neck. He held it out to Denise. "Bless you, miss, and bless your baby." Everyone was stunned. It glinted in the subdued light. She took it and slipped it over her head.

"Thank you. That's very kind."

The guys filed out into an active snowfall. Ken followed Arturo to the parking lot. Gino brushed snow off of his seat and windshield. Ken thought it was pretty much suicide to ride a bike in this weather. "So what's happening?" he asked Arturo. "Have you heard from her?"

Arturo wiped drops of melted snowflakes off of his glasses. "Martina? Yeah, she let me know, Rosa is coming back. She got into Purchase to study composition. She wants to be a composer. They're shipping the piano back to the states. I could have just burned the money."

"You must be happy about that. What about Martina?"

"Says she's thinking about it too. Livorno isn't quite home anymore. It's changed, or she has. Might want her own place here though. I don't know."

Ken sighed. "Maybe not. But everything feels so different. Impermanence, that's what it is... evanescent, transient."

Arturo mounted his Moto Gucci. The sound of both engines filled the parking lot, Gino's like a turbine, like an engine suddenly catching on after being stalled, then roaring like a prehistoric beast, burping gray exhaust. He made a salute to Arturo and gave a thumbs up. He rolled out slowly and then accelerated until his form became faint, just a silvery shadow as he disappeared into the curtain of snow. Arturo strapped on his helmet.

"Where are you going?"

"For a ride."

"Not a good idea in this weather," Ken warned.

"Tell me, what's a good idea?" He jerked the throttle back hard causing the back tire to spin out to the side. Arturo dragged his boot through the snow, which was about an inch and half deep by then, and powered ahead, turning tight, forming a circle as a shower plumed out from behind the back tire. He came around sliding and looped through it and did another circle, leaving Ken standing in the middle. A perfect figure eight. Then he followed Gino's tire tracks until he was swallowed up in a whiteout, mythic and surreal.

Ken listened until the sound of the engine faded. He stood still in the deafening quiet. The snowflakes, which had thickened and multiplied, pelted his face, and accumulated on his head and shoulders. He stood and waited, perplexed yet somehow amazed. He heard a voice, Gino's voice coming back to him: *"Life is a funeral song."*

Ken eyed his car at the end of the lot, a festive bloom of snow covering it. He became aware of his breathing and observed the soft clouds of vapor spreading out before him. Each one a yoga breath, slower and slower. They swelled and then burst and then vanished in the air like fragile balloons.

CONDIMENTS

G il promised himself after Marsha left that he would never run out of mayonnaise again. Under her culinary reign he'd been forced to hide small bottles of the stuff in the garage for his occasional egg salad or ham and cheese sandwiches. Marsha considered mayonnaise to be a carcinogen. Even as she packed the Prius with her luggage, yoga mat, exercise ball, lotions and conditioners, Gil slipped miserably through the back kitchen door and headed for the ShopRite. If Marsha had seen him pull out of the driveway, she might have been annoyed, or perhaps—after all of the bitterness and anger, and finally, the *decision*—she might have felt grief-stricken. It didn't matter though. As Gil often reminded Penny, their terrier, "Some things can't be fixed."

Given the circumstances, he tried to stroll leisurely through the cool aisles hoping to avoid any well-meaning but curious neighbors. When he reached the condiment shelves he placed two sixty-four ounce containers of Hellmann's Real Mayonnaise in his shopping cart. Though he didn't consider himself a consumer in the true sense of the word, he appreciated the outsized packaging and the bounty the store offered at discounted prices. He spotted the Hellmann's Ketchup, sweetened only with honey. He'd never noticed it before and was intrigued. Mustard was a no-brainer.

They were selling forty-eight ounce jars of Grey Poupon in packs of six, which seemed excessive. Fortunately someone, perhaps another victim of some marital calamity, had opened them up and taken just three jars. He placed the other three in his cart and moved on.

It was an early and unusually warm spring, so he'd decided to grill out on the deck most evenings now that Marsha wouldn't be there to manage their meals. Penny the terrier would be the recipient of choice bits of steak and barbecued chicken to assuage her bereavement over the absence of her mistress. He doubted that Penny would miss her mainstay meal: Fromm Gold Nutritionals Adult 33, at $67.90 per bag. He'd observed her eating the bits many times. She'd always pause and glance to either side of her bowl and then look up at her mistress to see if there was perhaps something else on the menu. He imagined her thinking, "This is what you want me to eat? This stuff, right?"

An additional perk for Gil was that he'd be able to enjoy his Pinot Grigio on the rocks, something Marsha could barely tolerate. "It just isn't done," she'd say. She often chided him about his dining preferences (he cut his meat, vegetables, and even pizza into little bite-sized pieces with a serrated knife—he liked them small). "People don't do that," she'd chide him. So what did people do? He read Google News every morning and saw that people did monstrous things, often for no good reason at all. He just liked ice in his wine. After they'd settled on the date of her departure, he'd ordered a set of two Cubette Mini Ice Cube Trays from Amazon. Half-inch cubettes; they froze faster and chilled more evenly.

Gil realized as he drifted through the aisles, taking in the aroma of fresh baked bread and rolls, eyeing colorful displays of cubed cheese samples and artisan crackers, and toying with kitchen gadgets, that he was just beating out time. Giving Marsha the last few minutes perhaps to walk through the house they'd shared for decades, the bedroom...the Ediline Wood Sleigh Bed. The bathroom with the acrylic slipper clawfoot tub with imperial feet and chrome deck mount. He'd gotten that for her for their fourth anniversary and she'd luxuriated in it up until...when? He couldn't remember. She used to like him to read the Times Regional News to her while she bathed. For a few years the bathroom had become their den, with comfortable chairs, books and newspapers, and the Bose tuned in to the classical station. She seemed most in her element in the tub, his water queen. He used to hold the towel up and wrap it regally around her. Sometimes, to his pleasure, she'd let it slide off her sturdy shoulders. But how long ago was that, at least a decade, maybe longer?

He flipped over a box of Squoodles—squash noodles—and scanned the ingredients. He couldn't imagine what sauce would taste good with them. It would probably require a stick of butter and lots of salt. Instead, he took two packages of Martelli's Spaghetti Pasta. He vaguely remembered having it once on a trip they'd taken to Tuscany. Even Marsha had enjoyed it with the wonderful garden-fresh marinara prepared at the table. He thought suddenly, if she were lingering in the house it wouldn't be decorous to return home too soon with bags of groceries that suggested he was planning a cookout or a picnic—a celebration of sorts. There was nothing to celebrate.

He paused by the lobster tank and rested his palm against the thick cold glass, and watched as they scuttled over one another with banded claws trying to find a comfortable place as they *waited*. He'd read in National Geographic that their claws were banded not just to protect the consumers' thumbs, but to protect them from each other. The article explained that lobsters were feisty, dominant creatures and would harm their own kind if possible. It went on to say that humans share a common evolutionary ancestor with lobsters. Both species exist in hierarchies fueled somehow by serotonin, a curious fact. They, the lobsters, pissed in each other's faces as a form of recognition—odor signaling.

Gil mused that he and Marsha had become crusty adversarial creatures, faulting each other over trifles, an old battling couple, clawing and snipping at each other's self-esteem, pissing on each other's shaken confidence, causing each of them to question if they were even good people anymore. And in the last year, the therapist sessions he so resented. How many times had he said, "Sarah is a nice young woman, but it offends me to my core to pay her to profit off of our misery." And he refused to discuss any of the sexual complaints Marsha still harbored from their earlier years, true or exaggerated, as viewed through the long lens of time. And certainly she wouldn't mention that she'd once allowed him to take her from behind while she was in the Downward-Facing Dog pose. Perhaps she'd forgotten that episode. But Gil remembered that pleasure distinctly. It happened while Penny the terrier was at the groomers. In the end, the therapeutic counseling service, *Mediate Don't Litigate,* saved him a bundle. Marsha had been right about that, and reasonable. But at one of their last meals together, when they tried to *talk*, have a respectful exit meeting as it were, she suddenly turned against celery as if it were laced with Novichok.

Gil loved celery, no longer as a natural alternative to Viagra, but for its flavor. He liked to soak it in ice water with a tablespoon of Himalayan Pink Salt. He rationalized that the excessive amount of salt wouldn't do him any harm because celery was also good for high blood pressure. And Dr. Goa had prescribed Zestoretic with LH1 anyway. Every six months he dutifully reported to his cardiologist who'd take his blood pressure, listen to his heart, examine his ankles and nod approval. "Stay on the Zestoretic, once a day. Stop at the desk...six months." He'd stopped asking how long he'd have to be on the drug. Dr. Goa, an ironic guy, answered one time, "For the duration." Gil would retreat to the parking lot and bite into an Extra Dark Pretzel Split, shot with diamond-like salt crystals—darker, crunchier, and bolder because of the "split" baking process. He'd chew thoughtfully and think, "For the duration."

He stood in front of the snack assortments for a full five minutes, not really considering the reduced-salt, whole wheat pretzels. His phone vibrated: *On way to Berkshires...now.* Marsha had told him that she'd planned a three day yoga retreat at Kripalu. He knew that, but she was just extending a courtesy, even after he'd avoided her departure, which he now regretted. It was rude. But what was he to do? The marriage was over, cooked. It wouldn't have changed anything if he'd waited. He realized that he just didn't want to be the one left standing there when she drove away, a discarded figure in her rearview mirror, the other half of their failure.

After her yoga intensive, Marsha planned to drive to her sister's goat dairy farm in Boulder. This was a bit of an undertaking for her as she had always preferred that Gil do the long distance driving, but this was her plan, her release into her new world. It was what she needed to do to initiate the next phase of her life—to get on with it. Marsha had shared that in their last session with Sarah. Gil suspected that Sarah thought that theirs was a successful outcome. A conclusion he did not agree with in the least. It was the dissolution of a long-term marriage, not a victory. There was no clear winner. And what did Sarah know about them anyway? She was just a young professional plying her trade for cash. He realized that was a harsh thought. But it riled him. What did therapy accomplish anyway? Getting on with one's life seemed to him just a pop psychology concept. He couldn't think of a single person he knew who'd gotten on with their life. It was just something people said to give the illusion that that's what was happening... *Getting on, getting older, and getting dead.* And he thought he'd detected a muted self-satisfaction emanating from the therapist's face. Or perhaps it was just a slightly pensive expression reflecting on the fact that the checks he wrote out to her each week were about to stop. The last check was already filled in, so he could just hand it over and make a quick departure at the end of the session. He had to avoid the obligatory warm feelings, thank-you's, and hugs. He'd leave that to Marsha and Sarah. It would have pushed him over the edge.

The goat thing, what was it? He recalled that Marsha had said if she enjoyed it out in Boulder she might join her sister's Go Go Goat Dairy Farm crew for a few months. Try something new. The one time he'd skipped off to the Jamaican place in town, he'd tried the curried goat and liked it, especially with their house jerk sauce, "Ya Mon." He bought a bottle of it and stored it in the tool drawer in the garage with the rest of his stash. At one point he thought about cataloging all the restaurants where he'd taken meals alone in the last year and a half. He'd call the file *The Solitary Diner*. But after brief consideration he decided it would be a sad commentary on their faded relationship. Where the hell had it gone, anyway? There were products in the ShopRite that had been available for more years than most marriages last. The Sunshine Oyster Crackers Gil liked with his tomato soup had been on the shelves since the 1800's. Marriage, it seemed, didn't have that long of a shelf life.

He avoided the checkout line for a few more minutes, as he detested the perky cashier girls. They always chatted him up, and if he'd forgotten an item a young runner would race back with winged feet and return with it, smiling brilliantly. "Hello, I'm Laney. I hope you enjoyed your ShopRite experience today." *Since when had grocery shopping become an experience*? He jabbed his debit card into the slot too quickly and had to do it over again. "Well, someone likes mayonnaise. Did you know that the third one was free?" He figured that the two containers totaling one hundred and twenty ounces would last him over four months. As much as he enjoyed mayonnaise, he didn't need one hundred and ninety two ounces, which would last half a year—that was assuming he consumed an ounce of mayonnaise every day. Dr. Goa would frown upon that kind of regimen.

"No, miss, it's fine. Thank you." Slightly anxious, needing the quiet intimacy of his car, he bumped the door guard with his basket, banging it hard before it opened automatically. He'd read online about Coles Grocery Stores in Australia. They'd instituted a special one-hour quiet shopping program designed for people with autism. It reduced noises, distractions, and store lighting by fifty percent. The cash registers and scanners were turned down to their lowest levels. And there were no animated store personnel popping up at you with trays of sliced pepperoni samples to try. No questions asked, no one in your face. Their staff had received training to be quiet and subdued in their movements. The only problem was that he wouldn't be traveling to Australia to grocery shop. *Anonymous, quiet shopping—a desperately needed innovation*, he thought. If it came to the states he'd be a loyal customer.

On the way home he stopped at Half Empty / Half Full to pick up the case of Pinot Grigio he'd ordered. Joyce always included a complimentary bottle of the week, usually a Chardonnay or Sauvignon Blanc from Oregon or Washington State. Gil noticed after a few times that she'd tied a yellow ribbon to the bottle neck. It was a nice touch. It also occurred to him that she'd stopped asking him how Marsha was some time ago. It was a small town and people gossiped. Joyce was recovering from breast cancer and a disastrous end to her marriage. Pete, her husband, had decamped just seven months earlier. He'd cashed in a large share of their investments, a substantial savings account, and most of their fine art collection, which included two works by George Inness and one by Frederic Edwin Church, each valued at over two hundred thousand. The private detectives had thus far been unable to locate him. It was as if he'd vanished. Compared to Gil and Marsha it was a horrible situation. At least they'd had a process, some finality, and *therapy*, for what it was worth. He truly felt sorry for Joyce. And everyone in their small suburb knew the story.

Despite all that, Joyce gave the appearance of someone who'd been relieved of an ugly and most unpleasant burden. She was upbeat, especially when she talked about wine. And she was solicitous to the point that Gil wondered if she might be interested in serving his other needs beyond his wine preferences. He couldn't imagine why she would be. And he couldn't imagine what his needs were anyway. It was too soon. Wouldn't she still be reeling from the shock of Pete's treachery? But she kept the shop going and was doing better than when Pete was involved in the business. People were supportive and she seemed to be rebuilding her life.

Joyce praised Gil on his choice of wine. The Pinot Grigio he'd selected was a Santa Margherita from Italy. She described it as bone-dry, and a wonderful flavor of golden delicious apple. There was also an aroma of honeysuckle, if you sniffed mindfully. The mention of honeysuckle caught Gil off guard and a strong reaction twittered through his chest and stomach, bringing a powerful memory of honeysuckle and Marsha. Suddenly, though dreading it, he was anxious to get home to his empty house. The sooner he faced it the better. Penny would need walking as she'd had a few accidents lately, urinating on the carpet. And he needed to settle himself on the deck and have a drink. He hoped that the deck would be a place of refuge for him in this new and difficult season. He'd ordered some comfortable chairs and a propane gas grill, the first one he'd ever owned. Marsha thought gas tanks were a fire hazard and the smoke from grilling meat was toxic. He slid his debit card out to pay. The wine went for thirteen dollars a bottle and would have cost about two hundred and twenty plus tax for the case. But she only charged him eleven dollars and fifty cents per bottle. He understood then that her interest in him was not just limited to retail. She'd looked at him earnestly and asked him how he was doing. He couldn't tell her that Marsha had left just about an hour and a half before. But he felt that she deserved a reply. "I'm doing..." he mumbled, "I'll know more how I'm doing in the next few days." When he signed the receipt, she placed her hand over his and said, "Take care of yourself." The shock of her hand on his caused the words to catch in his throat. His voice was husky, "You too."

I'm shaking, he thought as he sat in the car. *I'm actually shaking. Can't have this.* He needed desperately to get home, and it occurred to him that the new grill hadn't arrived yet and he didn't have any charcoal or lighter fluid for the old dented Weber. He'd have to make one last stop at Bernie's Hardware. He couldn't face the ShopRite again. "I see you're having a cookout," or "Are you going to set the world on fire? Hahaha." He felt exhaustion seeping into his body. It had suddenly become a marathon and he just wanted to get home, but if he didn't stick to his plan, cook out, treat Penny, drink wine, sink into the new chair, it would be worse. It would be...*unknown.* He would be set *adrift.*

He practiced his lie in the car. He'd tell Bernie that he was making a quick stop and had to be at the airport in half an hour to pick up Marsha who was flying back from her sister's in Boulder. That was plausible because Westchester Airport was a short drive away, and Bernie wouldn't want Gil to be late. But he was a talker, a pontificator on all things barbecue. He sold his own line of products which were displayed on the front counter. You couldn't leave his store with a Dewalt Cordless 20v Max drill without taking a bottle of his Smoked Chicken Palace Glaze or Bernie's Kamikaze Rib Dipping Sauce with a Hint of Vodka. Gil felt like his legs were about to give out, but he hustled in and grabbed a bag of Cowboy Charcoal and some odorless lighter fluid.

When he got back to the counter, Bernie was there beaming as usual. He winked, "Cookin' out, huh?" Gil hated it when he winked. People didn't wink anymore, or did they? Why should they? Quickly he recited his prepared lie and Bernie rang him out. "Whaddaya making?" This was the cue Bernie usually gave. Without answering, Gil grabbed a bottle of Bernie's Ginger-Mango Steak Plasma. "Nice choice. Remember, don't marinate it. Put it on while it's still sizzling on your plate." It worked; Gil was back in the car and just four blocks from the house. He felt momentarily panicked that somehow he wouldn't get there, he wouldn't make it home. Some unseen force would stop him. *This is silly. I'll be fine... just a period of adjustment.*

He parked the car in the garage and waited until the door had closed firmly behind him. He needed to shut something out so it wouldn't follow him into the house, though he didn't know what it was. He dropped the bags on the kitchen table, and went back for the case of wine, which he almost dropped as it seemed much heavier than when he'd carried it out of Joyce's shop. He whistled for Penny to come. Usually she was right there waiting to be fussed over. He grabbed the leash off the hook in the pantry and went into the living room. He called her a few times then went to the bottom of the stairs. My God, he thought, she took the dog with her? He heard whimpering and bounded up the stairs.

Penny was lying on Marsha's side of the bed. She'd peed all over the blankets and sheets. He lifted her front paws, placed her on his lap, and stroked her head gently. "Poor girl. I took too long. Poor girl. My fault." He felt something wet on his hand...tears? He knew that dogs whimpered or whined, but they didn't produce tears. They were his. He lowered his face and rested it in her fur and cried. He didn't remember the last time he'd cried. Maybe it was in college when his brother had unexpectedly died.

He let it out. "Marsha...I'm sorry...so sorry." He acknowledged to himself that much of it had been his fault. He'd just stopped trying. "So sorry." Penny lay still in his lap as he cried, willing to receive her master's grief. When he finally sat up, he glanced out the window. The sky had darkened. Perhaps it would rain and ruin his plans. A pang of fear jabbed at him. He had to avoid being set *adrift*. He stroked Penny a few more times, then he led her downstairs and out into the backyard. He couldn't take her out on the street and face any neighborly small talk or questions. It was a Saturday and some of them must have witnessed Marsha packing the car and leaving. He avoided the firethorn bushes, which he despised; he had already instructed the gardener to remove them. He led Penny to the rockery where she urinated for a good twenty seconds. "Poor girl, you really had to go." While he was walking around the yard he devised a clean-up plan, but it would have to wait until the next morning. He didn't have the energy to climb the stairs again. He'd strip the bed and put it all in the washer. He'd lean the mattress against the open window to dry it out. If it was soaked through, and ruined, he'd drag it out to the garage and put it on the curb for the next combustible trash day. He desperately needed a glass of wine.

Gil led Penny back up to the deck and settled her into one of the new chairs he'd bought. She seemed comfortable, but kept her eyes on him. He returned to the kitchen and uncorked a bottle of Pinot. He hadn't had a chance to put it in the refrigerator, so he dropped some Cubette Mini Ice Cubes into the glass. As advertised, it chilled quickly. He took out some boneless chicken thighs from the freezer and slid them into the microwave to thaw. Boneless meant that he wouldn't have to worry about Penny getting any sharp bones stuck in her throat. He practically collapsed into the chair next to her, exhaustion claiming his body. He inhaled the late afternoon air and took a full sip of the wine. It was cold and refreshing. Just as Joyce had said, bone-dry, and a wonderful flavor of golden delicious apple. And there was, he suddenly noticed, a faint aroma of honeysuckle. Again some static shot through his chest and stomach at the memory of honeysuckle. He placed the glass under his nose and took in the aroma.

Honeysuckle...he'd met Marsha just after the honeysuckle had bloomed next to the commuter train station parking lot. He'd watched her walk to the end of the lot and press her face into the bushes. Though completely out of character, he followed her and asked if she'd perhaps lost her keys, which he knew was a bit of a come-on, but believable given her behavior. Fortunately, it was a somewhat more gentle time, and she didn't automatically mace him or scream obscenities until a cop or some other rescuer came running. She told him she was smelling the honeysuckle, her favorite aroma. She did it every spring. She also pointed out that it was native honeysuckle, not an invasive species. Then she invited him to smell it as well. He was taken with her, that she'd do something so uncommon, not just rush to her car and drive away like the other commuters, as if they were escaping some natural disaster. And from that moment on he'd associated her with that fragrance...honeysuckle, for decades. Right up until...

After their meeting, he'd ordered several bars of honeysuckle soap from the New York Botanical Garden store and carried them in his briefcase until he'd hopefully run into her again. It was a full, frustrating two months before it happened. He spotted her ahead of him boarding and he hurried onto the train car and managed to sit next to her just as a woman passenger paused to scan the aisle for a better location. He squeezed in behind her and weathered a long dirty look. Marsha seemed distracted and he didn't think she remembered him from the flower-sniffing experience two months prior. He tried making small talk, but she seemed content to stare out the window. He took advantage of her staring off and slipped a bar of the soap into her handbag. He'd written his name and phone number on it. He got off in Dobbs Ferry, but not before he was able to scan her ticket: Irvington.

He started spending his weekends in Irvington, hoping he might run into her at the farmer's market, or the scenic riverside park. He wandered through the antique stores and the Stop & Shop. Early on, as a bachelor, he'd been a fan of Indian cuisine and had experimented preparing many types of curry. He was surprised at the choice of Indian condiments and products the store carried even before the foodie revolution of the 80s. He started shopping there regularly. It was on one of these forays into Irvington, where he was buying peach chutney and walnuts when his cell phone rang. It was her suggesting that they meet at the tea shop on Main Street sometime. He said that he just happened to be in Irvington and suggested they meet in fifteen minutes. He was too nervous to ask her name, and blurted, "I'm Gil," which she knew because he'd scribbled it on the wrapper of the bar of soap.

This is like a movie, he thought, as he sat there waiting for her. He stood when she arrived and they began an hour and a half animated conversation that included honeysuckle. She said that she loved the soap he'd slipped into her handbag and had bathed with it that morning. Surprisingly, she extended her hand and allowed him to sniff the underside of her wrist. *It's settled*, he thought. An hour later they were in his apartment making love. He considered his good fortune beyond anything he could have imagined. And she seemed to agree. They pressed their faces close.

"Yes?" he'd asked, "Are we...?"

"Yes," she'd answered. "We are."

"Yes," he'd said, "But how?"

"Shhh..." and she'd kissed him. It was better than a movie. It was real. And it stayed real for years...until...

Gil sat up suddenly, startled, his heart pounding. He'd been thinking and dozing; he couldn't tell if he'd been dreaming or remembering their beginning, the sweet time, the time of honey-suckle. Somehow he'd drunk three quarters of the bottle of wine. Penny was sitting up in her seat staring at him. An oppressive spring humidity had settled into the air. He stood and moved unsteadily to the Weber and prepared the fire. He couldn't make her wait any longer. The barbecued chicken would assure the dog that all would be well, that there would be good treats coming from her master. There would be...*stability*. He scratched Penny under her neck where she liked it, "Just a few minutes, girl," he promised. He poured out the remaining wine into his glass and shuffled into the kitchen.

He placed the thawed chicken thighs in a bowl and doused it with the Yeri Yeri Teriyaki Marinade Sauce, one of the *approved* products, in part because it was packaged in a BPA-free bottle. *Salad, need salad.* He opened the fridge and pulled out a bag of mixed greens from the drawer and was pleased to find tucked underneath it a bottle of Ken's Country French Dressing he'd secreted in there a while back, an *unapproved* product. "An entire meal," he muttered, "...not quite." He grabbed a bag of Cascadian Farms Crinkle Cut French Fries and threw them into the microwave. The fries would provide an opportunity to try out the Hellmann's Ketchup, sweetened only with honey, though he was a bit skeptical and in retrospect would have got the Heinz Ketchup 114-ounce bottle on sale. He opened another bottle of Pinot and filled his glass. There were still more than enough Cubette Mini Ice Cubes to chill the wine. Even if he ran out, there were regular ice cubes in the freezer he could smash with a hammer.

By the time he began grilling the chicken it was almost 9 p.m. He lit the tiki torches on each corner of the patio. He could have switched the floodlights on, but that would have been overwhelming; he didn't want to be on display. He needed the softness of the flames against the darkness that had ballooned in the sky, except for one remaining crimson streak of light, a jagged sword slicing the night in half. He found himself fixated on it with varying degrees of awe and discomfort. A *complete division, a final separation*, he thought.

Penny began whining again and he brought her back down on the lawn to pee, thinking perhaps he should take her to the vet and have her bladder checked out. As they returned to the steps a huge plume of flame and smoke shot up from the grill, blowing the top off. Penny leapt back and pulled the leash out of his hand, then ran whimpering into the bushes. Pieces of flaming chicken shot up about three feet into the air as if they were being juggled. The entire grill was fully engulfed in flames, both inside and out.

The black finish blistered and glowed red. Grease and sparks were spreading over the deck. Gil observed the spectacle dumbfounded. The next explosion caused the bottom of the kettle to drop out onto the wheels and the deck. He saw what appeared to be a molten square box and he thought he detected an aroma of rotten eggs, which seemed strange. He ran and grabbed the hose and began to douse the flames. At first it caused the fire to roar up again, but it gradually died down. He hoped none of the neighbors had noticed the smoke and called the volunteer fire department. When it felt safe enough, though still smoking, he rested the nozzle inside the kettle and let the water soak through. How could it have happened? Charcoal grills didn't just blow up.

He could hear Penny whimpering, but the yard, which abutted his neighbor's massive stockade fence, was pitch black. The daunting fence, which exceeded town code, was the result of an altercation Gil had had with the neighbors some years earlier. The Kossovers never really accepted Gil and Marsha as somehow being worthy to ascend to the elite neighborhood. Penny, as a playful pup, had scampered over to the Kossover's patio and peed on their herb garden. Lenny Kossover chased her back to Gil's yard with a rake and threatened to kill her if she did it again. Gil apologized, but made the mistake of suggesting that Lenny was overreacting. Lenny offered to show Gil his Springfield XD Mod 2 (9mm) handgun, which he would use next time to send Penny to "dog shit heaven." So much for neighborly potlucks. The next day, a crew arrived and dug deep holes for the towering fence posts. Gil could have reported the code violation to the town enforcement officer, but the fence provided a benefit; it would keep Lenny off of Gil's property as well.

Gil climbed the steps, keeping an eye on the grill in case it erupted again and reluctantly switched on the floodlights. A good half of the deck was trashed with glowing charcoal debris, burn holes, blackened chicken thighs, mixing in the water he'd sprayed on the fire. A plume of black smoke hovered about ten feet above the deck. The new chair closest to the grill was ruined, the cushions singed. He sighed miserably as he viewed the site. It reminded him, though on a much smaller scale, of terrorist attacks he'd seen on the news.

"Penny. Penny. Come here, girl," he called. She continued to whimper. From the sound he determined she'd crawled under the firethorn bush, which had filled in early due to the excessive warmth of the season. He got on his hands and knees and scanned the ground along the fence. He thought he could make out her ID tag glinting in the floodlights. But the light seemed to be coming from behind her, shining through the fence panels. He realized with dread that Lenny Kossover must have heard the explosion and come out to investigate. Judging from the movement of the flashlight beam, Lenny was working his way along the fence looking for a place where he could see into Gil's yard. Thank God for the fence, Gil thought. Lenny, unhinged and full of venom, might have just shot him and the dog without thinking. And of course, as was Lenny's practice, he'd report any untoward activity in the neighborhood, especially against Gil. "Come here, girl. Penny, come!" he whispered. She continued to whimper. The explosion had thoroughly spooked her. "Goddammit, I'm not crawling under there."

He began pushing himself under the bushes. The stiff branches bore many sharp thorns and he immediately felt them tearing his shirt open and sticking into his skin. "Goddammit, Penny!" He hated the idea of thorn bushes, but Marsha loved the small, showy white flowers that bloomed later in the season. They reminded her of ocean foam and waves. The branches were thick and dense, but he continued working his way toward the dog. One branch caught upon another, then released, snapping against his forehead. It stung sharply and he felt warm droplets of blood forming. "You can sleep here, goddammit," he growled. But he was close enough to grab her leash and drag her out in a more painful exit than was his entrance. Lenny had worked his way to the end of the property without gaining the surveillance he'd hoped for. "What the hell's going on over there?" He yelled.

Gil lay on his back trying to control his heaving breath so Lenny wouldn't hear him. It gave him some comfort that Lenny was denied access to the scene because he'd built the damn fence in the first place. Penny licked the blood from his forehead. He felt his shirt dampen with thorn punctures. "God...damn...it." As he lay there a pearlescent cloud slipped by and revealed a three-quarter moon with a cold ivory tint. In the craters and dark shadows he saw what resembled the face of a woman with something on her head, a basket of fruit perhaps. "Perfect," he muttered. "Fucking perfect."

It seemed to take all of his strength to get himself and the dog back up onto the deck. He took the ruined pillow from the chair, turned it upside down and commanded her to sit on it, then tied her leash to his chair. She immediately lunged for the chicken thighs and scarfed down the one closest to her. "Chew it for God sake. Wait, I'll cut some up for you." He stood in the kitchen looking around, slightly disoriented. He got a plate, a fork, a serrated knife, and another glass of wine, filled almost to the brim. "Bachelor party," he slurred as he returned to the deck. He turned off the floodlights and dropped into his chair. He noticed something glinting on top of the fence. He squinted at it but couldn't make anything out. It occurred to him that Lenny might have gotten an extension ladder and was spying on him with binoculars. *Fuck Lenny*. He leaned over and forked up one of the chicken thighs and began cutting it into small pieces. The aroma of rotten eggs caught his attention and he shot a look at the charred, square-shaped object which seemed to be oozing a sludge-like substance. Then he remembered: Hurricane Sandy. It was back in October of 2012.

While lower Manhattan, Staten Island, and Jersey bore the brunt of the storm, Westchester experienced high winds up to sixty miles or more per hour, causing extensive damage. Marsha went through the house taping large X's on the windows while Gil secured the lawn furniture and trash cans by moving them into the garage. For some reason the Weber grill, unused because of Marsha's concerns about toxicity, seemed less important. There was an old car battery in the garage that he hadn't gotten around to recycling yet. It weighed about forty pounds and he placed it in the grill hoping, though he actually didn't care, that it would help withstand the wind, keep the grill in place. The remaining chemicals in the battery were what caused the explosion and fire. The burning charcoals literally ignited the battery, hence the rotten egg smell.

He cut up a chicken thigh and held it up to his nose. It just smelled burnt and he thought it was safe for Penny to eat. It was gone before he set the plate on the floor. "Poor girl, you were starving." The microwave bell rang, but he stayed put and sipped his wine. He figured he'd have the French fries and a salad then drag himself and the dog into the guest room to sleep. He'd deal with the deck disaster and mattress in the morning, and probably a hangover as well. *Perfect way to start my new single life.*

He felt a vibration and glanced at the decimated grill, but it was his phone. Marsha had texted him: *Can't sleep. Twin bed uncomfortable.* He stared at the screen, bewildered. What was he supposed to do? What could he answer her? He figured that the beds at Kripalu for about $230 per night would be comfortable. *She's feeling it. That's what it is,* he thought. But now what? She'd reached out for whatever reason. He took another sip of wine and noticed the deck furnishings and tiki torches were spinning slightly. He texted back: *sorry.* He felt now that he'd have to monitor the phone, but he just wanted to sleep. Sleep and forget, at least until the morning. Maybe he'd call Servpro or someone to help with the clean up. She texted again: *Forgot a few things.* This text caught in his throat. He turned to Penny, to consult with her or something, but she was passed out in barbecued chicken happiness, her head resting on her paws. "She forgot a few things," he said to no one. He texted back: *I'll forward them to your sister's place.* When he pressed the send button a small shock wave went through his body as if he just entered a sweepstakes that could change the course of his life forever. And then came the payoff; she texted back: *I'll get them. You won't know where to look.* This got him out of his chair. It was quarter to eleven and he needed to sleep. It was too late for figuring and planning. He'd have to do that in the morning.

He woke Penny, who was reluctant to move, and dragged her into the house, into the guest bedroom. It was stuffy from the warm spring night, so he started the air conditioner and pulled the chain on the ceiling fan. The whirring sound was hypnotic. He practically fell into the bed and the dog pressed in snug against him. Gil thought he was already asleep when he flicked off the light. He had a dream that night that didn't seem at all related to the events of the day. He was back in his small hometown in the Adirondacks, fifteen years old, riding his Schwinn Black Phantom through the neighborhoods late at night. The feeling of exhilaration speeding down the hills through the dark unnoticed was liberating. He was the secret observer. No one knew he was out there. At times he felt a sense of delectable lightness, that he might command the bike to lift off the pavement above the trees and telephone lines, and fly over the town up to the mountain it was named for.

He'd ride on to the dock and stare out at the flickering lights of the cottages, homes, marinas, and businesses reflecting on the aching cold water. Then he'd light up the Newport he'd snuck out of his mother's pack and inhale deeply, enjoying the cool rush of menthol bracing his lungs. He'd exhale slowly through his nose and watch with satisfaction the vapor dissipate into the air. He knew that just about two hundred and thirty miles south of his home was a city that was so vibrant with light that it must look like a jewel embedded in the earth's surface from space. And he knew, he'd promised himself that one day he would live and work in that city of light. He would move beyond the mandatory autumnal deer hunt with the other boys, the breakneck snowmobile races through the woods, which had claimed the life of one of his friends before high school graduation. And, he'd solemnly promised himself, he'd refuse the ascension, the expectation his father held dearly, that he would take over his John Deere franchise.

He woke with a painful start. Penny had clawed his chest leaping out of the bed, and left red streaks on top of the burning pricks from the firethorn bushes. He rubbed his chest and didn't remember undressing the night before and sleeping in his boxer shorts, the novelty ones Marsha had got him in Provincetown, imprinted with starfish, clams, crabs and snails. They reminded him of a happier time. He noticed tiny red marks on the sheet where he'd continued to bleed from the thorns. His head throbbed. *Sunday hangover*, he thought. Penny clawed frantically at the bedroom door and he rushed to let her out before she urinated on the rug. As he strode through the kitchen he saw the two large plastic jars of mayonnaise on the table, wet with condensation. He distinctly remembered putting them in the refrigerator. He touched one and it was cold, causing his blood pressure to spike but remain under control thanks to the Zestoretic 10 mg. As he stepped out onto the deck, the shock took his breath away.

Chief Waryas from the volunteer fire department was there with an EMT and a police officer taking notes as they watched a technician in a white jumpsuit and a helmet with a visor kneeling next to the grill, scooping up samples of the goop beneath it. Another bomb technician then slid a thin plastic plate under the debris and removed it carefully, then placed it in a steel container and closed the top and bolted it. The technicians lifted the container by the handles and carried it slowly out of the yard. Once they'd secured it in the truck they returned and wrapped the grill in a plastic sheet and removed it as well. Waryas, who Gil remembered from the gym, when he used to go there, and from the Memorial Day Parade, gave him a doleful look. "Aren't you a bit mature to be playing with fireworks?" Gil took in the scene; the devastation looked worse in the bright early morning light, a certifiable crime scene. There were patches of burnt grass near the deck.

He tried to avoid her eyes, but there was Marsha staring at him in disbelief, shock, and an intense sadness that seemed somehow mitigating. When Penny had run out onto the deck she'd leapt into Marsha's arms and whimpered. Marsha held her protectively as if she'd been rescued from an abuser. Gil shuddered and was speechless. *All that's missing is a blood stained knife in my hand.* The two empty wine bottles on the stand next to his chair didn't help paint a picture of innocence. Nothing about it suggested that it could be explained away. But after all, it was a small town, an enclave of commuting humans with quirks and foibles, and sometimes inexplicable behavior. Waryas, assessing Gil in his sea-creature boxers, and sympathetic to Marsha's dismay, suggested that Gil stop by the police department first thing Monday morning and explain the situation to Chief Carbone. So, it's a police matter, Gil thought...an investigation. *Well, why not?*

After the chief and the others departed, Marsha continued to stare steadily at him. She took in the scratch marks and prick points on his chest and legs, and his utterly confused and compromised state. Finally, she asked quietly, and in a matter of fact way, if perhaps Gil had someone in the bedroom with him. It took a few moments for the synapses to fire in his brain through the hangover and make the connections. She was asking him, incredibly, if he had sought out a companion, or even a prostitute to comfort him on the first night of her absence. Or maybe someone he'd been seeing while they were still together. She actually seemed wounded by that prospect, which in turn wounded him. When the picture was complete and flashed over his consciousness, he broke up into fits of uncontrollable laughter; he howled. "Marsha, you think...?" He couldn't stop himself. He laughed until tears streamed down his face. The whole thing was beyond absurd, it was impossible, but it had happened. His plan for his post-marriage survival strategy had literally blown up in his face.

Marsha set Penny down and the dog followed her into the yard. Penny immediately relieved herself on the hose Gil had left on the lawn after dousing the flames that had engulfed the grill. Marsha wandered through the yard aimlessly, as if reacquainting herself with it, though it hadn't yet been twenty-four hours since her departure. The dog stayed at her heels. Gil itched terribly; he desperately needed a shower, some antibiotic cream, some Advil, and a fresh change of clothes. His humiliation was absolute, almost spectacular. But something about the way she moved through the yard touching some of the trees, kneeling to straighten out a ceramic elf in the stone work, reminded him of the beach house they'd rented in Truro many summers ago. Her routine each morning, after they'd had coffee on the porch, was to walk down the sandy path to the beach and swim. He'd watched her morning after morning, her lithe, yoga-toned body swaying slightly as she walked, her long brown hair that she liked to henna catching the sun as it flipped in the bay breeze. She'd return chilled and smiling, slightly embarrassed as if she'd done a silly thing, though of course she hadn't. He should have gone with her into the water and held her when she swam by, a captured mermaid. He'd hold the robe for her and she'd sit and sip warm coffee and shake the sand out of her hair. His...girl...the one who smelled of seaweed, salt, and...the honeysuckle soap she bathed in, the scent that would stay with him until...

He felt then that he was just a pair of eyes, a camera following her around the yard, watching her touch leaves and vines as if gaining nourishment or understanding from them, in this moment that was like an affecting video from long ago, sharp and wrenching with memory. She went to the firethorn bush, turned around and glanced at the deck to see if he was still standing there. He lifted his hand to wave furtively, but just pushed his hair back. She turned and focused on the bush with its vicious thorns. She touched one and pulled her hand away quickly, then pressed the tip of her finger to her lip. He wondered if perhaps she were thinking what he was, that later in the season, the small, showy white flowers would bloom. The ones that reminded her of ocean foam and waves.

REIVER'S RECEIPT

C hip, as he was affectionately known by his colleagues, and
some of his more enlightened students, walked the four
blocks briskly, or so he thought. The *new* briskly at any rate, which
meant not stopping to catch his breath or take the measure of his
balance. Falling had to be avoided at all costs. Falling hastened one's
decline. When he arrived, he took up his usual seat in Downing
Park near the sputtering fountain, known as the "Polly." From
there he viewed the pigeon-stained statuary awaiting the next power wash, and the neat row of Revolution-era brick homes lining the
block adjacent to the park. The late morning sun had warmed the
metal bench, soothing his lower back after a recent bout of sciatica.
He sipped black coffee and checked to see that his toasted hard roll
was still properly wrapped and invitingly warm. Then he offered
his face to a promising spring sky and repeated a familiar phrase,
Homeostasis, that's the ticket.

Chip and his wife, Sandra, had both recently experienced some
health scares, and were averaging five or six doctor's appointments
per month. So far, they'd managed to avoid any terminal consequences. All conditions held at bay for the moment. Sandra's
nagging arthritis seemed to be improving with the Qi Gong class
she'd started at the Y.

Not all of Chip's friends had been so lucky. Two days earlier he'd attended the funeral of his long-time colleague, Francois. They'd both taught at the SUNY Orange Community College for decades. Francois suffered a coronary from a heart condition that was being treated and "well under control," according to his cardiologist. He died while working out on his NordicTrack rowing machine. And not a month before that, Vince, a mathematics professor, had succumbed to prostate cancer that had metastasized to his liver and kidneys. Vince, with his ironic sensibility, had calculated his chances of survival at being one in three thousand.

Chip, Charles W. Gray, PhD, professor emeritus of American History, was well aware of the odds. At seventy-five, which he euphemistically referred to as three-fourths, he knew it wouldn't be that much longer before he'd be "shut up in the box," as Vince used to put it when they met for drinks at Garvin's. "Well, I'm not shut up in the box yet. So, drink up," Vince would say, licking the salt from the rim of his margarita glass. Vince was a salt addict. He salted his salted peanuts and carried a box of Maldon Sea Salt Flakes to sprinkle on his salads and entrées. "Why do you think the ancients called it white gold?" he'd say.

Chip stayed away from salt and credited his longevity to his mother's genes. His mom, Beatrice, had made it to eighty-six in relatively good health. A woman of cast-iron character, she believed in schedules. She lived out her days, each a replica of the previous one. From the time she awoke, took her black tea and oatmeal, and sat at her puzzle board, it was all according to schedule. She hated TV and refused to have one in her apartment. If she were some place where there was a TV, she'd say, "Look, when you're speaking to me, look at me, not at the damn screen." She was an avid fan of the Saturday radio broadcasts of the Metropolitan Opera and adored the Irish mezzo, Paula Murrihy, especially in her debut role of Stephano in *Romeo and Juliet*. Beatrice fiercely kept to herself and refused to play cards or share birthday cake or acknowledge any occasions in the common room with the other residents. She despised the elderly, a class of people she refused to identify with, especially the old men tottering around her retirement complex, looking puzzled and frail. She'd make pronouncements like, "He's good for another five yards or so. Ha!" She told Chip that if she ever wound up in the memory care wing of the residence, to bring a handgun with a silencer and discreetly shoot her.

In odd moments of confusion, a sudden twinge in his head, a brief pain in his stomach, or a tightening in his chest, he'd resist the symptom with a thought: *I, like my mother, will live well into my eighties.* He had recently given up on his stationary bike after he stumbled dismounting it. He'd decided walking would be a better alternative. Two feet on the ground at all times. Barring inclement weather, especially icy sidewalks—the bane of the elderly—he went to Downing Park every day to observe the sights, not the least of which was a curious, free-wheeling, young Jamaican man known as Reiver. Chip had come across the name before, which was also a term for a person who goes on plundering raids—a thief, in other words. He'd read, in some college library, years ago, about "border reivers" along the Anglo-Scottish border, active in the 13th to 17th centuries, clans who raided the border country. It surprised Chip that he remembered that bit of information. But this person, this man named Reiver, exuded gentleness; he had a forthright quality, the opposite of a violent marauder. For no reason he could imagine, Chip felt drawn to him. What could his life be about?

After the fact, Chip did some additional research and learned about the Scottish- Jamaican connection. There were in fact Jamaicans of Scottish descent, including some of European and mixed African and Asian descent, dating back to the earliest period of post-Spanish European colonization. Oliver Cromwell helped out in 1656 by banishing twelve hundred Scottish prisoners-of-war to Jamaica, the acquired English colony. This attracted Scottish immigrants, mostly indentured servants who worked alongside the slaves harvesting Jamaican sugar cane. So, that made it possible for someone to be tagged with the name Reiver. These days, Chip did his research with less rigor than when he was a graduate student. It was more of a hobby now, no longer for academic pursuit.

There were a number of individuals in Newburgh without homes, rifling through dumpsters and trash cans for useful items, or rattling collection cups at storefronts, some of them offering spoken-word or musical interludes; some spewing verbal assaults as they demanded spare change. They made their daily rounds from the homeless shelters, returning with the day's take at sunset. Some of them chose to sleep outside in doorways at the Catholic Charities Center, or in the riverfront park, in cardboard shelters on discarded mattresses. Reiver stood out from this group in several ways. First, his carriage; he was erect and precise in his movements. He walked with purpose. He'd scan a trash receptacle and instantaneously reject it if it wasn't promising. His bearing didn't suggest a homeless person down on his luck. Rather, an individual who was actively thinking, involved in a mental process that went beyond the task at hand. Occasionally he'd stop and tilt his head as if a sudden thought had come to him that required his attention. He carried a pad and would jot notes down. His overall presentation, despite his circumstances, was of a man who'd enjoyed the benefit of a privileged upbringing. He projected an almost regal quality. Had he consciously chosen this lifestyle, eschewing some higher existence?

One of the park maintenance men, who filled holes in the gravel pathways and scooped cigarette butts and liquor bottles from the fountain, filled Chip in on Reiver. Or at least the version he had of the man. He was the son of a Jamaican baker named Delroy Jefferson Johnstone, who'd immigrated to Newburgh with his family. He'd opened a shop on Water Street with his wife Irie, and

Reiver, who was fourteen at the time. Delroy's idea was to offer the community authentic Jamaican delicacies their island was famous for: meat pies, empanadas, fried plantains, and pastries: gizzada, grater cake, tamarind balls, toto, blue draws, peanut drops, and the famous Christmas Cake, a staple for the holidays, including birthdays, and any special occasion, graduations, and funerals as well.

Later, Chip learned more from Father Ken at Saint Mother Teresa of Calcutta church on Ann Street. As a little boy of six, back in Savanna-la-Mar, before the family left for America, Reiver watched his father make the meat pies and pastries and started imitating him. Delroy thought it was cute and folks got a kick out of seeing the "little baker" in the shop. It was good for business. Delroy decided to capitalize on it and outfitted Reiver with a small baker's jacket, black and white pants, and a toque, and set him up on a small platform where his patrons could watch him at work.

The "little baker" seemed possessed with creating the traditional island recipes, which he did with surprising accuracy and speed. Then something unexpected happened that shocked Delroy. He came downstairs one morning to open the shop to find Reiver sliding something out of the oven. At first, he scolded him because he wasn't supposed to be near the hot stove and sharp knives unless Delroy was there to supervise him. Delroy observed the item, a bit of gravy dripping from its pinched edge crust, which was perfectly golden brown. The aroma wafting up from it was intoxicating. "And what is this, little man?" Delroy asked.

"It's a Turkey Pot Pie," the boy announced proudly.

"And where did you learn to make such a thing?"

Reiver stared at his creation and then at his father, "I don't know, Papa. It just came to me."

"Where did you get the turkey?"

"At the market."

"How did you pay for it?"

Reiver fidgeted and looked down at his shoes. "I took it from the cash drawer."

"You stole it?"

The boy began to cry. "Please don't beat me."

"Have I ever laid a hand on you?" Delroy chuckled, cuffing the back of the boy's head. "Well, Let's see if it's worth you becoming a thief." He spooned out two portions of the pot pie for them to taste. It was steaming, and they held their spoons up and blew on them. Delroy didn't immediately chew, but let it sit on his tongue surveying the flavors. At once he was aware of the thyme, parsley, shallots, garlic, white onion, carrots, and white wine, salt and pepper, and heavy cream, all perfectly balanced. The tiny cubes of turkey were moist and juicy, having absorbed the ingredients. The puff pastry circles were perfect, crimped artistically at the edge of the bowl. Reiver looked at his father expectantly.

"Is it good, Papa?"

Delroy said, as he swallowed another bite, "It's...delicious."

"You really like it?"

"How did you know how to make it?"

The boy gently touched the top of the crust to see if it was satisfactory. "I don't know. I just did."

After that incident, there were others. Delroy would instruct Reiver to replenish some of the baked goods, dozens of each, plus blue draws and peanut drops, but would be presented with jumble cookies, pound cake, puddings, or apple dumplings with sauce. Delroy was both perplexed and a little anxious about where these recipes were coming from. It was as if the boy were channeling the recipes from some other time and place. He reprimanded Reiver and told him they were not the traditional sweets Jamaicans expected. Frustrated and concerned, and not wanting to waste the cost of ingredients, Delroy put the items in a side showcase as a special offering. After a few of his regular customers tried them, they sold out as quickly as they could be produced, with people clamoring for more.

But when the family arrived in Newburgh and rented the storefront for the bakery, Reiver abruptly stopped making the unexpected baked goods and would only turn out Jamaican treats. His demeanor seemed to change as well; he seemed sullen and distant. When Delroy asked him what was wrong, why he'd stopped making them, he said that he couldn't remember the recipes. They'd been washed from his memory. He felt that something was bearing down on him that stopped him from doing it, an unexplainable oppression. Something from a long time ago, but he couldn't remember what it was. But he made up for it by producing multiple Christmas Cakes that doubled their income between November and January. The fact was that Delroy had, for all his skill, never mastered the perfect Christmas Cake. Reiver could turn them out in his sleep, and every one of them was perfect. He knew the twenty-eight ingredients and thirteen steps in making the Jamaican Christmas Cake without consulting the recipe card. The fruit had to be prepared and combined well: dried dates, currents, pitted plums, cranberries, candied cherries, and mixed peel. And the alcohol, port wine and white rum, had to be measured judiciously. Getting it right required more skill than the average baker might have.

After five years of back-breaking work, the family was about to finally experience what Delroy skeptically referred to as *the deferred American Dream*. The one for *our people*, as he put it. He had made an offer, which was accepted, for a home on Union Avenue, a sturdy brick three-bedroom, two-bathroom house with a backyard large enough for a garden to supply the bakery with fresh vegetables. They would abandon their sub-standard apartment and finally live in a home of their own. But an unfortunate real estate deal ended their business and ultimately separated the family. The owner of the building would show up periodically from Brooklyn to inspect his property. He owned several adjoining structures beside the one the bakery was housed in, a half of a block in all. On one of his visits he was accompanied by several young men and a woman who meticulously toured the buildings taking pictures with their iPhones. Not long after that, the landlord informed Delroy that he was selling each of his buildings. The family would have to find a new storefront for the bakery. In place of the bakery, they heard from a customer, it would now be a sushi bar with organic sake.

Suddenly, it was as if the entire valley was besieged by New Yorkers traveling two hours north and buying property for chump change, compared to city prices. There was a misguided perception that these upstate towns would be the next Hamptons, which amounted to a death sentence for venerable establishments, mom and pop shops, and renters who were just getting by as it was. Delroy looked at multiple storefronts that might be appropriate for a bakery, but the rents had tripled and the landlords seemed reluctant to rent unless they were convinced the incoming business would be more than able to make the inflated payments. They wanted four months rent ahead of time. There was an undercurrent as well. Delroy noticed that the folks who wound up buying or renting the spaces were, to a person, young and white. That demographic was not lost on him. A familiar resentment rose from his stomach and soured his attitude. "I know what game this is," he remarked to the last landlord who turned him down, saying the place had already been rented, though it hadn't.

After the shop finally closed, Delroy fell into a depression and started drinking, something he'd stopped doing after Reiver was born. He and Irie got into nightly arguments, mostly about money. The disagreements escalated, despite Reiver's attempts to mediate them. After an almost violent episode, Irie announced that she was going to Newark to visit her cousin who'd recently come over from the island. She said that she'd be gone for a week or so.

After three weeks she called and told Reiver that she'd gotten a job and would soon have her own apartment. She said he could stay with her. He cried that night after refusing her invitation, sensing that his family was unraveling. But something was holding him back, keeping him in Newburgh.

Not long after that, Delroy was arrested at a bar for disorderly conduct after a fight with a fireman. Before the court hearing, which would mean more trouble, possibly jail time, he told Reiver that he'd decided to move back to Jamaica. Defeated and resentful, Delroy said, "White people are enjoying their privileges standing on soil baptized with the blood of Black and Red people." He tried to convince Reiver that they would be better off on their island where people treated each other with dignity.

But Reiver said he couldn't go back. Whatever life he was going to have it would be in the states. A month after that, at the age of nineteen, he found himself alone, the next recruit in the fast-growing army of the homeless. It seemed that the machine of Capitalism, a meat grinder, required a portion of society to flounder and despair, so a select group of citizens could flourish. The rest, the leftovers, were expendable; they were just pennies in a jar.

Thanks to St Mother Teresa of Calcutta, Reiver avoided having to beg for food. But he refused to eat for free. He insisted on giving back. At first, Father Ken, unaware of Reiver's talent, was skeptical about turning over the refectory kitchen to him, but finally relented. In return, Reiver unleashed his culinary skill and prepared enough nourishing meals for thirty homeless people for two days at a time, making him a celebrated person in the church community.

When he wasn't cooking, he collected items he found discarded in the neighborhoods and in trash cans along Broadway. He liked simple mechanical and electrical appliances and gadgets and could fix almost anything and sell it at a decent profit—enough to keep himself going. But his visibility on the street, his obvious deviation from what was considered to be a normal citizen, drew the attention of a few zealous law enforcement officers. There were some good cops who played fair. But there were also a few who were contaminated with the historic virus that plagues men with badges and batons. One in particular, Officer Karlmann, seemed to have it in for Reiver.

Karlmann's animosity stemmed from cornering Reiver for no reason one time. He questioned him, demanded to know his address. Reiver gave his address as 84 Liberty Street, in the city of Newburgh. Karlmann and his partner got a search warrant for that address to recover what they thought or hoped might be some stolen goods. But there were none, for two reasons. The first was that Reiver never stole anything. The other reason he couldn't be located at 84 Liberty Street was because anyone entering the premises would find themselves at George Washington's headquarters, Hasbrouck House, where the general had encamped for eighteen months while he fought the Revolutionary War. American History was apparently not on the curriculum at the police academy.

Reiver, for reasons he couldn't comprehend, despised General Washington. But he felt trapped, somehow entangled with him in a way that he could not identify. He was certain that there was a connection, a close one, as strange as that seemed. Night after night he found himself wandering around the property, as if he were haunting it. He had dreams, which at first, he only vaguely remembered. He managed to find an opening in one of the outbuildings and slept there several times. As repelled as he was by Washington, he was somehow joined to him.

The next time Chip saw Reiver was in Brew Crew 2, a high-end coffee shop that had taken over a bodega that had been in business for two decades. He found himself standing in line behind Reiver waiting to pay for his poppy seed roll and French Roast coffee.

Reiver was either nervous or excited, as he danced around a little. A heavy-set man in a patched trench coat and worn military tactical boots stood in line in front of Reiver. He turned to him and said, "Coffee over at Junie's place is half the price of this shit."

Reiver laughed, "Then why waste your time here? Junie's is waiting for you."

The man bristled, "Cuz that's all the way down the hill at the river. I hate walking back up. By then the coffee's cold."

Reiver said, "I drink it cold or hot, and with gratitude. It's good for the blood."

When Chip got up to the counter, he discovered that he'd neglected to put his wallet in his suit jacket pocket that morning. "This is extremely embarrassing, but I seem to have forgotten my wallet."

The counter person, a slender young woman dressed in black, her blond hair cut in a precise wave highlighted with green and blue streaks, said "I'll hold it for you if you'd like to come back later." She slid the coffee and roll off to the side behind the cash register.

"Of course, I'll certainly come back and pay for it," Chip stammered.

"See you then," she said dismissively. "Next."

"I got it." Reiver came over stirring sugar into his cup and placed a five-dollar bill on the counter. "No need to be discourteous," he said, smiling deeply. "The man forgot his wallet, that's all. Anyone could do that."

"*I* don't," she said, visibly irritated, "ever." She rang up the sale, placed the change, a dollar and forty-five cents, on top of the receipt and slid it across the counter, but just far enough so Reiver had to bend over to reach it.

Reiver took out a zipper pouch with an emblem on it that read I Love NY and placed the receipt in it. "My dad always said save the receipt 'case the man comes looking for you." Then he picked up the change and dropped it in the tip jar. "Have a nice day, miss."

Chip followed him outside. "Thank you for that. I'm so embarrassed. I will certainly reimburse you. How do I get in touch? I'm usually in the park most mornings."

Reiver observed Chip closely for a few moments. "Whataya do?"

"I teach at SUNY Orange. Well, I'm actually retired."

"You a professor?"

"I'm a history professor. I do research on the side."

"Research? Yeah, me too, down at the library over there. We're like in a historic town, right?"

"Quite right. Washington's headquarters is just down the road."

"I know all about that. And Hudson too. Read about him. He come tooling up that river down there, 1609. Only took seven years after that for the first ship to get to Virginia, 1616."

Chip knew what ship he was referring to, The White Lion. "Are you a history buff?"

"Maybe, I don't know. But I know how to count. You take 1609 and 1616 and just add the numbers individual, you get thirty, dirty thirty."

"Why do you add up the numbers? Why thirty?"

"For starters, thirty silver coins."

"I'm not following you," Chip said.

"That's what it took for Judas to turn on Jesus, just thirty,' he laughed. "And that ship come after Hudson, landed at Point Comfort...no comfort to those folks on board."

"Yes, the White Lion, of course. Docked in Point Comfort, Virginia." Chip added.

Reiver turned on his heel and started off. Chip called after him, "I'll pay you back."

Reiver yelled, "Pay it forward, bro."

Chip watched him walk jauntily down Broadway as the bells of Sacred Heart-St. Francis tolled ten times. *10 a.m.*, he thought. And he was sweating. It was an unusually warm spring. Maybe he was just heated up after the exchange with the barista in the shop. He stood there watching Reiver until he disappeared. As he turned to leave, he came face to face with a young woman with a guitar slung over her shoulder. She wore a rainbow-colored ankle-length dress without shoes. Her feet were stained and dirty from the gritty sidewalk. Her pearl-blond hair hung down to her waist. Her eyes were bloodshot. Chip smelled marijuana wafting from her clothes. "Would you have a bit of change, please?"

He observed her lined, aging young face. "I'm so sorry, I don't have my wallet with me." He regretted that he didn't have anything to give her.

She squeezed his hand. "That's OK. No worries. Bless you. And Happy Earth Day. Bless you and Mother Earth." He hadn't realized that it was Earth Day. She twirled away from him and skipped down the street. She seemed like an apparition or a foundling. He felt slightly spooked as he walked toward the park.

After the incident at the coffee shop Chip didn't see Reiver for almost a month. It was as if he'd vanished. On his morning walk, before going to the park, Chip would wander around Broadway and the side streets looking for him. Finally, in the last week of May, Chip was at his usual spot in the park when Reiver came through pushing his shopping cart, which was decorated with green, black, and yellow ribbons, Jamaica's colors. He called out, "Gadgets, 'lectercal items, CDs, and souvenirs. Satisfaction guaranteed." A few people walking through the park looked in his basket, picked up an item or two and handed him some cash. One woman grabbed a pink, retro-looking alarm clock and handed him some money. Chip approached him feeling relieved.

He handed Reiver a five-dollar bill and said, "Finally, debt paid." Reiver laughed, "No, prof, put it toward something useful."

"All right, what have you got there?"

Reiver pulled out an electric can opener, which was curious, because Sandra, Chip's wife, had asked him to pick one up. Her arthritic fingers suffered using the mechanical one. The *qi gong* had helped, but not completely relieved the pain.

"I'll take it, how much?"

"OK, the five and whatever you got in your wallet, minus twenty percent."

Chip laughed and handed him a ten-dollar bill. Reiver's breezy attitude and humor was refreshing. "Where have you been?" He didn't want to tell him he'd been looking for him.

"Newark, visit my mom."

"Oh, how is she?"

"Getting by, sells meat pies and stuff at the stadium. Still wants me to move in with her."

For some reason, Reiver reminded him of one of his students he'd had some years ago, LaShawn. He'd been raised in the projects, did well in high school, was a track star, and got himself into college. He wound up on Governor Cuomo's team by the time he was twenty-six.

"You ever think about going into politics?" Chip asked.

Reiver laughed. "None of that trash for me. What's the main purpose of politics? What's it used for?"

Chip answered, "Well, government, representation, public service for people."

"Serving them up, you mean. Look at England. They colonized the shit out of the world. Didn't do no good for the people they ruled."

"That's true. They also had a huge hand in creating democracy, the Magna Carta and all that."

"Democracy? Now that would be a love word if it was applied universal. Democracy for who?"

Chip thought a moment, and said quietly, "Yes, not everyone experienced the benefits of democracy."

"Still don't." Reiver reached in his pocket and took out a piece of paper, unfolded it and gave it to Chip. "You recognize this guy?"

The first thing Chip noticed was that the picture had been torn out of a book, page number 184. It was a painting, a color portrait of a Black man. He wore a white chef's outfit and was standing in front of a preparation table, looking out at the viewer. His expression was strong-willed and proud. His skin was milky brown. As Chip studied the face more closely, he saw a whimsical, knowing look, a bemused countenance that seemed to hold a secret. "Where'd you get this?" he asked.

"Library, I was doing research."

"You tore the page out of the book?" Chip asked.

Reiver gave him a strange look. "Of course, I did. Do you recognize that guy or not? A historic figure."

"Well, he looks colonial...judging by his clothing and surroundings. He's a chef, yes?"

Reiver snorted, "He's a chef all right. That's Hercules Posey, George Washington's chef and... his slave."

Chip knew that Washington kept slaves, and that he might have had a child with a slave woman, though it was unsubstantiated. But he'd somehow missed reading about Posey.

"Hercules Posey?"

"That's him, born 1754, had four children of his own. Took off from Philadelphia, 1797. Washington's birthday! Get this: served him and the missus dinner and was gone; just like that, walked away. Made it to New York City. They never found him. First American celebrity chef. Not some imported guy from Paris."

Chip continued to stare at the picture. He hoped the security camera at the library hadn't caught Reiver tearing the page out. "Why are you so interested in him?"

"Why? Look at me." He took off his mirrored sunglasses and rasta cap and stared straight at Chip. "Look at me." At first Chip didn't notice anything unusual, but like a distant object slowly coming into focus, he saw the whimsical, knowing look, the bemused countenance that seemed to hold a secret. He looked back and forth at the picture and Reiver's face, the milky brown complexion, the pride, and a survivor's fierceness. "See it?"

Chip looked again. "There is a remarkable resemblance...yes, I do see it."

Reiver sighed and sank back into the bench and exhaled forcefully as if he were releasing something toxic from his body. They were quiet for a while until a church bell tolled 1 p.m. Reiver took a basket out of his shopping cart and opened it. Immediately, an enticing aroma filled the air. "No sense starving to death," he said. He set two bowls and spoons on the bench. He filled the bowls with what looked like a thick corn chowder and cut up pieces of crispy bacon and dropped it in along with a dash of pepper. Then he sliced a few pieces of sourdough bread. He hummed as he did it. "*Al fresco*, that's the way to eat."

Chip stared at it, "Where did you get this?"

"I made it over at Mother Teresa. Father Ken turned the kitchen over to me," he laughed.

"Do you always bring enough for two people to eat?"

Reiver dipped a piece of bread into the chowder and put the whole piece in his mouth. "Lotta hungry people in this town."

Chip tried it. "It's delicious. What's that flavor I'm tasting...tangy? It makes it...I don't know, so good."

"Rosemary and a splash of white wine," Reiver winked. "But not too much."

After they'd eaten, Reiver wiped the bowls off with a paper towel and put them in the cart. Then he produced a thermos of coffee and two mugs. "How do you take it?"

"Black. Stronger the better, please."

"Me too. If you're gonna drink coffee, drink coffee, not cream," he chuckled.

The coffee was hot and bracing. Chip felt like he was with an old friend he hadn't seen in a long time. "I'm curious, what is it about Hercules Posey? You couldn't be related to him, could you?"

Reiver took a long sip and rested the cup on his leg. He looked off to the side at some pigeons vying for the remains of a Subway sandwich and potato chips someone had left on an adjacent bench. He stared into his cup and seemed to enter a meditative state. "Dreams, lots of 'em," he said, quietly.

"You dream about him?"

"Started right after we got here. I was in the library up at Washington's Headquarters, walking through a side room. I come face to face with his portrait hanging on the wall. Mr. Hercules Posey, chef. Stopped dead in my tracks. Got a very weird feeling. Dreams: the kitchen smoke, the meat sizzling, fish looking up at me with one eye. The vegetables hanging from baskets, the table spread out with bowls of sauces and seasonings, the pots, the fireplace blazing like the gate to hell. My boy chopping wood in the yard. It was not just a dream. I could smell it and taste it. It was like I was there, brought back 'gainst my will."

Chip observed him for a few moments, this curious man; generous, openhearted, wounded by the poison-tipped spear of racism. Everything moving around him, against him, past and present, he was somehow freer than Chip or any of his colleagues had been. No academic protocol or societal expectations to be met. Whatever he was, he was fully formed, a realized human with a marked degree of skill and talent.

Chip held his cup out as Reiver replenished it. "Are you talking about reincarnation? Do you actually think you were Hercules Posey in a past life?"

Reiver tapped a cigarette out of a pack and offered one to Chip, who was not a smoker, but accepted it anyway as an act of solidarity. Reiver lit both, and Chip held the cigarette between his fingers and tried not to let on that the smoke was making him nauseous. Reiver took a long pensive drag and expressed the smoke out of his nostrils and watched it dissipate before him as if it revealed something previously unknown. "I'm not exactly sure what I'm saying.

But I know ever single one of those recipes, the preparations, the spices, the sauces. The tricks of the trade. Watching the master eat from behind a cracked open door, seeing what pleased him and making more of it. I know Washington's palate like the back of my hand. Man ate more hoecakes than you've ever seen. Had to cook a lot of soft dishes for him. His teeth was fallin' out."

Chip didn't know what to make of Reiver's dreams. Maybe they were hallucinations? How could it possibly be true? Many of the homeless folks in the town presented behavior that suggested mental issues, or delusional behavior, but Reiver was not like that. He was lucid and direct. He was...just who he was.

Reiver flipped his half-smoked cigarette toward the fountain. "I hear his voice in my sleep. It had a kind of tremor to it. It was low and deep. I'd have to turn my ear toward him to make sure I got the orders right." Reiver closed his eyes and spoke; his voice changed. It was like he was channeling another voice: "Now, Mr. Posey, there will be a group of gentleman legislators here on Sunday and I'd like to offer them something special. Your braised fish, oyster stew, some pot roast, your fresh bread and an assortment of custards and puddings, and some Snow Eggs, I suggest, if you don't mind."

Chip was stunned. "Washington?" He'd once read a description of how the first president's voice sounded. Reiver's normal voice was so different in his choice of words and inflection. For a few moments they stared at the fountain with its irregular pulsating plumes of water. Chip was starting to feel uncomfortable. It was a bit eerie. Suddenly, the unattended cigarette between his fingers burned him. He dropped it and pressed his fingers to his mouth. They sat there for a while.

Finally, Reiver sprang up athletically and grabbed the handle of his shopping cart. Chip stood up, "You're going?"

"Recycling gets put out on Tuesdays. They don't know what they're giving away. I do. Enjoy the can opener, prof." Chip watched him wheel away. When he reached the corner, he stopped to check another trash can, then turned toward Broadway. A police cruiser rounded the corner, slowed down when they saw him, and followed Reiver from a distance so he wouldn't notice. Chip watched until they blended in with the traffic and pedestrians crossing the wide boulevard. The unnecessary surveillance irritated him. *Leave him alone.*

*

Chip's episode came on suddenly. He and Sandra had just returned from a retirement party at the college. One of his colleagues, Hunar, a biology professor, was calling it quits after thirty-seven years of teaching. Hunar's wife put together a memorable feast for the party: phall curry, laal maas, Andhra chilli chicken, rista, and paneer jalfrezi, each dish delicious and very spicy. Chip, who usually avoided spicy food as it gave him indigestion, couldn't help himself and partook of each offering and had seconds. She included wines from her home region, Hampi, in India. Chip wound up drinking a few more glasses of Grover Zampa La Reserve than he'd planned.

His stomach started acting up on the way home; a burning stream of acid filled his esophagus, and he began sweating profusely. Then his heart began beating erratically. Sandra swerved around a bus, made a u-turn, and got them to Montefiore St. Luke's Hospital in ten minutes. A team of doctors descended into the curtained space and worked him over, attaching sensors and instruments, while drawing blood. They ordered a reflux inhibitor and monitored his heart, which was beating wildly. He spent the night in the emergency room with Sandra dozing on and off in a recliner they brought in for her. By morning, the acid reflux abated, but his heart was still way off. A cardio specialist, Dr. Onderdonk, showed up at seven in t he morning, read the charts, and perused the various tests they'd performed. He listened to Chip's heart and nodded, "Atrial fibrillation. Did you know you had it? Probably for quite a while."

Sandra leaned over the other side of the bed. "Is it serious?"

"Only if it's not treated," Onderdonk smiled. "Your indigestion might have triggered the Afib, causing it to present itself, fortunately."

Sandra placed her hand on Chip's shoulder. "Does he have to have surgery?"

"Oh no, not at all." He turned to the nurse and asked her to have the pharmacy send up ten milligrams of Eliquis. "Eliquis will keep the blood from pooling in your heart. That will keep you from having a stroke. You'll take five milligrams twice a day and that should do it."

Chip asked, "Will it go away, the fibrillation?"

"Probably not. We can try a cardioversion, but it might come back. Best case scenario is the symptoms abate. Let's go with the Eliquis for now. It's an effective treatment."

Chip asked, "How long do I have to take it?"

Onderdonk paused. "From here on, twice a day, preferably at about the same time."

After that scare, Chip felt a bit fragile and spent more time at home, though he missed his daily jaunts to the park. A follow-up visit with Dr. Onderdonk concluded from the EKG that Chip still had Afib but was lucky that he didn't have symptoms he could feel. Chip decided to resume his visits to Downing Park. Also, he was wondering how Reiver was getting along.

He enjoyed the June warmth and watching the mothers play with their kids on the newly installed swings and slide. School was out and they had all summer to just be kids. But there was no sign of Reiver. Not for almost two weeks. Chip decided to do some reconnaissance. He began patrolling the neighborhoods, making it a point to stop by Washington's Headquarters at 84 Liberty Street. He'd peruse the grounds looking for Reiver. Early one morning he spotted a man making his way up the hill along Broadway. He looked familiar, but he couldn't quite place him. As he approached him, he heard the man mumbling to himself, repeating the word coffee. "Damn cold coffee, cold coffee."

Suddenly Chip remembered. He was the man in line in front of Reiver at Brew Crew 2 the day Chip had forgotten his wallet and Reiver paid for his coffee and roll, and then left the change as a tip for the impertinent young woman. "Excuse me," Chip said, "I think you know Reiver. Is that correct?" I was wondering if you've seen him lately."

"Reiver? His ass is in jail."

"When did that happen?"

"I don't know, a while back. Cops said he stole some stuff out of the hardware store."

"I don't think he'd do that," Chip said.

"Who knows what someone's gonna do."

"I don't believe it. Where is he?"

"In the jail, like I said. Waitin' for trial, rainment or somthin'."

Chip went to the library and signed in to use a computer. He looked up the recent police arrests. He found an article mentioning Reiver Johnstone, address unknown. Occupation, part time chef. He was charged with grand larceny, but it didn't specify what he'd stolen. He was scheduled to be in court the following Thursday, which was four days away, June 6 at 6 p.m. There were few details about the crime, which Chip thought was suspicious. The only concrete information was that the theft had taken place on April 22 at 9:45 a.m. And that there was a security video, purportedly, of Reiver walking through the store carrying a toolbox or something by a handle. This was according to Officer Karlmann, who made the arrest, several weeks after the robbery. The police still couldn't pin down where Reiver lived. His elusiveness spurred their zeal to capture him.

Something didn't seem right. He explained the circumstances to Sandra at dinner. She thought it was a difficult situation for Reiver if the police had a video of the time and date the theft took place. Chip worked through the details over and over. Was there something he'd missed or had forgotten? This went on for two days; it clawed at him. He Googled Officer Karlmann and learned that he'd been disciplined several times before for misconduct, but there wasn't any specific information. Chip was also consumed with self-doubt. Who was he in this situation? A liberal college professor standing up for a homeless Jamaican man. Is that how he would look if he showed up at Reiver's arraignment? Would it look like cultural appropriation? It could be embarrassing. Maybe he was becoming senile. He'd wind up looking like a silly old man. Maybe he already was. But damn it, he was going anyway. To hell what people thought of him. He'd stand up for the guy. He believed that he knew Reiver well enough. He had a lively personality and might even appear to be quirky. But his integrity and kindness were palpable. He could not be a thief.

The night before Reiver's court appearance, Chip had a dream that unnerved him. He was back at CUNY, as a young man, defending his doctoral thesis before a group of professors. Responding to the first query questioning his premise, his front tooth fell out onto the desk the men were sitting at. No one noticed it. He snatched it off the table and put it in his pocket. Another man, one whose course he had failed, questioned the validity of his line of reasoning. Chip soiled his pants. When he looked down, he saw that he was wearing a diaper. This went unnoticed as well. Part of his conscious mind was aware that he had earned a PhD, but he was trapped in a dream, a nightmare. As the dissertation committee whispered back and forth, a few of them laughed out loud. Chip's left arm slipped out of his suit jacket and fell on the floor. The gold Mondaine Swiss Railways Classic wristwatch his parents had given him as a graduation present glinted eerily. When he picked up his arm to reattach it, his left hand grasped his throat and squeezed violently. This too was unnoticed as the men continued to consult and laugh.

He awoke shaking and had sweated through his pajamas. He dressed quickly and left the house to distance himself from the dream. He stopped at Brew Crew 2. Even if one of the staff could be testy, they did have the best coffee. He was relieved to see a new face behind the counter. A young Hispanic woman with raven black hair corralled in a large charmeuse scrunchie and full red lips the color of late summer tomatoes. She wore several rings, amethyst, garnet, and a carved silver band, and silver bangle earrings. She smiled and spoke in a sing-song voice to everyone lined up in the shop. "I've got you, babies. Steamin' and creamin' here. Get your morning fix. Drink that Joe and off you go." Chip tipped her excessively and shoved the receipt and hard roll into his pocket. He felt a strange feeling on his lips. He was smiling. He must not have smiled for a long time. On the way out he passed the manager stocking espresso cups and spoons on a glass shelf. "She's a keeper," he said. It seemed that the coffee shop management had figured out that an upscale business model was not necessarily an exact fit for a down home town like Newburgh.

He was annoyed when he got to the park and saw that all the benches were taken up with grade school kids, backpacks, and lunch boxes. There were also tall leaf bags, rakes, and shovels. The kids were cleaning up the park as their teachers walked around pointing out debris and cheering them on. "Five cents per soda bottle," one of them yelled.

Lacking a bench seat, Chip entered the playground and sat down on the bottom of the slide. He sipped his coffee and ruminated. He watched the kids cleaning up the park and marveled at their enthusiasm. He took his hard roll out of his pocket and started to unwrap it. The receipt was stuck to it. He began to crumple it up, then stopped and read the printout: June 6, 2019 - 9:30 a.m. "Earth Day! It was on Earth Day. The girl told me."

"Excuse me." A woman was standing a few feet away from him. "Sir, excuse me. My son is waiting to slide down."

Chip turned and looked up and saw the child, a little boy sitting on top of the steep incline, waving at him. "Oh, so sorry." He stepped away from the slide. "Earth Day," he repeated.

"That was last month," the woman corrected him.

"Yes, the waif told me it was Earth Day."

The woman observed him with concern. Her son came careening down the slide and fell face down on the rubber mulch and began screaming. The woman scooped him up and ran off. She shot a frantic look back over her shoulder to make sure Chip wasn't pursuing her. He called out, "Sorry, I'm so sorry." He wandered back into the park and found a new bench that had been placed beside the fountain. Either it was new, or he hadn't noticed it before. He sat down and weathered a brief storm of anxiety. *It wasn't my fault. It was an accident. She thought I was a crazy old man. Am I?* The event, besides the dream, left him feeling jittery and unsure of himself.

He went home and took a nap. Sandra woke him at 4:30 p.m. and reminded him that she was meeting her friends at Pam's house for their annual gardening group to plan their gardens and talk seeds and best practices. Sandra observed him, "Are you alright? You look a bit...confused. Are you? I don't need to go."

"No, I'm fine. You go ahead. Really, I'm fine."

She kissed him on the forehead and told him there was meatloaf, potatoes, and salad on the kitchen counter. He dressed in one of his finer suits and his favorite tie, an Italian blue silk with lilac and white polka dots, that Sandra had given him the Christmas before he'd retired. Then he left for the courthouse. He was nervous and had no appetite. When he arrived, he waited in line to get in. An officer had everyone sign in and another officer ran a handheld metal detector meticulously over each of them. Chip took a seat in the front row where he'd be sure to hear the proceedings clearly. The bailiff immediately called out: "All rise." Judge Chu, a small Asian-American woman, entered from a door behind the bench.

It looked like her black robe was a little too big for her. She took her seat and everyone else was instructed to do the same.

A door opened to her left and an officer led a group of nine men and two women to a long bench and motioned for them to sit down. Reiver was the third man in. Chip wondered if they'd go in the same order as they'd entered the room. Judge Chu welcomed everyone, spectators and defendants alike. "Let me be clear, I tolerate no outbursts or interruptions. If anyone has managed to sneak a cell phone in here, it will be confiscated. And the result will be worse if anyone attempts to photograph the proceedings. We understand each other, I'm sure. Mr. Sheehan, you may proceed."

DA Sheehan stood for a moment, glanced at the defendant, and stepped forward, his body language oozing contempt. The woman stared back icily. She was being charged with having used a credit card, which she said she found on a bus. She'd charged up four hundred and eighty dollars worth of food, cigarettes, and alcohol. Sheehan launched into an explanation on why she should be prosecuted, given the serious nature of the crime. Sentencing for a crime like hers could see her in lockup for three years, which he intended to recommend.

"Thank you, I know the sentencing guidelines, Mr. Sheehan." The DA looked visibly annoyed. "Doreen, is that your name?"

"It's Doreen. But they call me Dor."

"I understand that you have a court appointed attorney. Is that correct?"

"I don't have a fuckin' lawyer."

"Watch your mouth. You should have been given one."

"I don't have a freakin' lawyer."

"Are you willing to proceed without an attorney now?"

"Sure, what the hell, you're gonna screw me anyway."

"OK, Mr. Sheehan, I'm converting this to a settlement conference—in the interest of justice."

Sheehan scratched his protruding stomach. "I'm not sure I agree with this."

"You want to be here all night?"

Judge Chu looked around the court at the officers. "Anyone know anything about this?" No one answered. "OK, Doreen, Dor, this is your lucky day. The credit card company canceled the cardholder's debt you ran up. And the cardholder, the victim, has decided not to press charges. That said, I suggest less alcohol and cigarettes. They did cancel the card?" she asked the court clerk. "Is that correct?"

"Yes, your honor. That's correct."

"Dor, do you have a job?"

"I cut hair."

"Which salon do you work in?"

"I do it freelance at home. And I provide enhanced services, massage, and stuff."

"Don't tell me about that," Chu snapped. "How come you don't work in a salon?"

There was a long pause. "Cause I don't have a license."

"Do you have fifty dollars with you?"

"Well...yeah, but I need it." She slumped.

Judge Chu nodded. "Fifty is your ticket out of here. The court fine is usually two hundred and fifty. It's a nominal fee, and more than fair, in satisfaction of all charges. To satisfy the People," she said, with a slightly maniacal grin aimed at Sheehan.

"Yeah, I guess so..."

"One last question, Dor; what are you going to do next time you find a credit card that isn't yours?"

She thought for a moment. "Cut it up."

"That's the right answer. Hearing no opposition, the court accepts this resolution. Case dismissed. Pay the bailiff over there. You're two hundred dollars ahead of the game."

Sheehan walked toward the bench, "Your honor, I am opposed to this resolution... I have to say...."

Chu flashed her palm at him in a motion to stop. "I said case dismissed. Next." And so it went. There was obviously some bad blood between the DA and the judge. It gave Chip some reason to hope it would turn out the same for Reiver. In most of the cases, Chu meted out minimum sentences unless violence was involved. And if there was, she offered reduced time if the perpetrator agreed to take an anger management class or agree to have therapy. She was clearly a believer in restorative justice and Sheehan was obviously not.

Finally, it was Reiver's turn. Just as he got up to face the judge, a young man, who looked about twenty years old, rushed in from the hallway swinging his briefcase wildly and stood next to Reiver. He wore a rumpled suit and his hair was an uncontrollable tangle of brown and blond tufts. Chip thought that the man looked familiar. He'd seen him somewhere before but couldn't recall where. Chu looked him over and smiled. "Ah, Mr. Rose, nice of you to join us."

"I apologize, your honor, there was construction on 87. It was crawling." He glanced at the remaining line of prisoners waiting their turn. "Is Ms. Doreen Maroni here? I'm also her public defense lawyer."

"Well, Mr. Rose, Ms. Maroni's case was just dismissed. That's one down." She cast a wary eye at Sheehan and said, "You may proceed."

Chip thought that Sheehan seemed a bit too eager on this one, a bloodhound hot on the trail. He read the police report enthusiastically verbatim and asked to show the court the video taken in the hardware store. The bailiff played it on a six by eight-foot screen. Everyone watched intently, Chip even more so. The date and time ticked along the bottom of the video. The image was somewhat clouded, but visible. The man walking through the aisle with whatever object he carried, moved with difficulty. He appeared smaller, shorter, and older than Reiver and he wore a thick gold necklace. Chip had never seen Reiver wearing one. At one point the thief turned so that the camera caught his face head on. "That's not him," Chip heard himself say. He looked around to see if anyone had heard him. He struggled to piece his thoughts together. If they'd arrested Reiver the day after the crime, how could they be certain it was him? Did they really bother to match up the video with the thief? Or did they just want to arrest someone? It didn't matter who. Just get it over with so it looked like they did their job.

After the video, Sheehan said, "Your honor, there shouldn't be any question here about this case. Obviously…"

Chip stood and said, loud enough for everyone to hear, "That's not him."

Judge Chu looked Chip over, with some annoyance, but not disdain. "Do you remember what I said about interruptions?"

Chip's voice was shaky, but he continued. "I apologize, your honor. But he didn't do it. That's not him in the video."

"Are you saying that you wish to be heard on behalf of the defendant?" Chu asked.

"Yes, your honor… ah… I apologize."

Attorney Rose turned and looked at Chip and was surprised. "Professor Gray. Do you remember me? Your honor, this is Professor Gray, my American History professor from Orange County Community College. I got an A in that course."

"That's a touching reminiscence. But let's not lose sight of the appropriate procedure. You, Mr. Gray, rather Professor Gray, can't just interrupt. You have to have permission from the attorneys to ask the court to hear you. Understand?"

"Your honor," Chip stammered, "I have evidence. Ah, I think I have evidence. Some evidence…" Now he was shaking and feared that he might pass out. He also felt a strong urge to urinate. He was afraid that he couldn't go on.

"Not another word. The defendant's counsel and Mr. Sheehan need to agree that I hear this gentleman before we proceed."

"I absolutely agree, your honor," Rose said. We should hear from Professor Gray."

"Any objection from the People?" Chu asked.

Sheehan raised his arms and clapped them against his thighs in frustration. "Yes, I object; who knows what this man's motivation might be?"

Chu flashed a devilish smile at Sheehan. "Don't you want to hear what the man has to say, in the interest of justice?"

"*You* obviously do," he said. Sheehan stepped close to Chip and whispered in a harsh tone: "All right, Clarence Darrow, let's see what you've got." Sheehan's remark made him more nervous. He might be getting himself into trouble. Chip cleared his throat; he felt like he was losing his voice. "May I ask the defendant a question?"

"Ask," Chu snapped. "I have five more cases to get through."

"Reiver, do you have your zipper pouch with you, the one with the I Love NY emblem on it?"

Reiver stared at Chip for a few moments. He seemed confused, as if he didn't understand the question. Chip wondered if they'd mistreated him since he was in custody. Had he been somehow compromised?

Judge Chu snapped again. "Mr. Johnstone, the world is turning. It's getting late. These good people need to go home and have their supper."

Chip thought maybe his Afib was acting up. He took a few deep breaths. Slowly, a smile spread over Reiver's mouth. He slid his hand inside his shirt and pulled it out, the zipper pouch. Two officers immediately pounced on him and took the pouch and cuffed his hands behind his back. Apparently, they'd missed the pouch when they'd taken his other possessions after he'd been arrested.

"Open it," Chu instructed one of the officers. He did cautiously, as if it might be contaminated with fentanyl. "Well?" Chu was getting agitated.

"It's just papers with printing on them."

"They're receipts," Chip said.

"And...?"

"One of them, your honor, is going to be for the Brew Crew 2, dated April 22 before 10 a.m."

"How do you know that?" she asked.

"I was standing with Mr. Johnstone in front of the coffee shop on that day. It was 10 a.m. I heard the bells of Sacred Heart-St. Francis toll ten times. Mr. Johnstone could not have been recorded on the hardware store security video at 9:45 a.m. I was standing with him."

"Give them to the clerk," she ordered.

The clerk went through the receipts slowly, meticulously.

"Well?" Chu tapped her pen on her desk.

"I'm looking, your honor. They're a little sticky." She went through a few more of them, stopped, and held one up over her head like a small white flag." The bailiff plucked it from her hand and gave it to Chu.

"Hmm, April 22, 9:45 a.m. Mr. Johnstone, you save your receipts? That's a good business practice."

Reiver did a little jump in place. "Always save the receipt 'case the man comes looking for you."

Sheehan approached the bench. "I'd like to see that receipt, your honor."

She handed it to the bailiff and said, "Make a copy of this and give it to Mr. Sheehan."

"I'd like to see it, your honor," he pressed.

"You're getting a copy of it. It stays with the court."

Visibly angry, Sheehan retreated to his seat, glaring at Chip as he passed by him. Chip smiled apologetically; he didn't know what else to do.

"Looks like a short workday for you, Mr. Rose. Well," she addressed the officers, "take the cuffs off." They did, reluctantly. "And by the way, where's Officer Karlmann? He made the arrest. Where is he? I have questions about that video." A deafening silence followed. Chu banged her gavel on the sound block. "Case dismissed."

Chip waited outside in front of the courthouse for Reiver. He figured it would take them a while to return his belongings and provide him with the accompanying documents for his dismissal. The police had confiscated his shopping cart, but it was scheduled to be returned the following day. After about twenty minutes Chip decided to go home. Reiver had probably left from the back entrance of the courthouse where the sheriff's van was parked. The prisoners' entrance. Chip figured he'd see him at Downing Park. The main thing was, he was free, charges dismissed. Sheehan didn't get to nail the wrong man. And whatever video Karlmann was peddling, with obvious inconsistencies, he'd have to take that up with his chief. Chip took another deep breath and started walking north on Broadway. As he walked, his steps felt unencumbered. There was almost a bounce to his step. He felt lighter. He had a warm sensation in his chest, not constriction or pain. His mouth felt funny once again. He was smiling. He greeted people as he passed by them, folks sitting on their door stoops, taking in the spring air. "Evening. Good evening. A warm spring, don't you think?"

He passed the Brew Crew 2, stopped, and decided to go in. A celebratory espresso seemed like a good idea, even if it would keep him up half of the night. He ordered an almond croissant and sat at a little table next to an open window. A slight breeze added to his comfort. He heard a guitar chord and looked across the room.

They'd set up a little stage and a singer-songwriter was sitting there tuning up. Chip felt like he was being taken back to a time in his youth when he and Sandra frequented little bohemian cafés in Greenwich Village and listened to music and poetry. He had tried his hand at a few poems, usually dedicated to Sandra for her birthday and Valentine's Day. She was always gracious about them, though he knew they were more of the Hallmark variety.

The performer, it turned out, was the waif girl who'd asked him for money and wished him a happy Earth Day even though he had none to give her. It was the same day Reiver had paid for Chip's coffee and saved the receipt. She looked a bit more put together this time. She wore a white peasant blouse with colorful, embroidered flowers and peace signs, above a long, gauzy black and white chenille skirt featuring cardinals. She'd covered her feet with pink ballet slippers. She also wore an array of silver jewelry, hoop earrings, bangle bracelets, and necklaces with small colored stones peeking out. All in all, Chip thought, she was a little homeless girl, acting grown up.

"Hi everyone, I'm Delcie and I'd like to sing some songs for you." She winked at the small audience, who were not paying much attention as they were busy chatting or looking at their laptop screens. She began with a John Denver song, "Take Me Home, Country Roads." Her guitar playing was not conservatory level, but full and steady enough to accompany her voice and carry the lyrics, which she delivered in an emotionally convincing soprano. Chip thought it was rather pleasant and wished people would settle down and listen to her. At the end of the song, there was a smattering of applause. She lowered her head and graciously thanked everyone and the management of Brew Crew 2 for inviting her to perform.

Gradually, people started to listen. She sang a Joni Mitchell tune, "Both Sides Now." It occurred to Chip that some of the young folks in the audience might have never heard these songs before.

Delcie, as young as she was, was channeling the sixties with sincerity and the purity of her interpretations. She wasn't just another singer-songwriter. People dropped bills in the large cappuccino cup placed on the stage floor. A few of them even closed their laptops.

When it was time, Delcie said she was going to finish up with a Leonard Cohen song called "Suzanne." Chip noticed an older couple nodding. They'd heard the song before. As she sang, the lyrics, in her fine soprano, captured even the most jaded heart in the room. A few of them dabbed at their eyes. In this time and place, in the great real estate grab, in the time of social media and the mania of accumulating, it was a bit of a miracle, an unexpected gift. When she finished, the last chord still ringing in the aromatic roasted coffee bean air, there was just the sound of breathing, and then uproarious applause, given the small crowd. People approached her, shook her hand, asked her where she'd be performing next, and dropped more money into the cup.

Chip stood outside the shop collecting his thoughts. The songs brought back memories of himself and Sandra when they were a new couple. The apartments, the rooms they'd made love in, that never produced a child. The life they accepted that way still managed to be full. The devotion through the years. The flowers he'd bring her. His memory carried him back so poignantly that his chest heaved slightly as he teared up.

"Hello." Delcie approached him. "I hope you liked the songs."

"Yes, I loved them. You're a wonderful singer."

She curtsied, and said, "Thank you, sir. The songs are food for me, especially when I have no money. But everyone here was so generous."

"Tell me," Chis asked, "Where do you stay? Do you have a room?"

She looked down at her pink ballet slippers and wiggled her toes. "I stay by the river," she giggled, "like the girl in the song."

"It's not the safest place," Chip said.

"A man down there lets me sleep in a room in his warehouse. But I prefer to sleep outside in the nice weather."

"Why do you sleep outside?"

"Because that's where I can see the barges and cruise ships and the trains on the other side of the river. But especially, I can see the stars."

"Please," he said, "take this." He offered her a ten-dollar bill.

"No, I have more than I need now."

She smiled and started walking down Broadway. He watched her until she was gone, vanished practically, a small vulnerable being. He wished her well and that she'd be safe. He headed toward the park. It was quite dark now. When he reached the fountain, he saw that they'd installed lights; plumes of red, yellow, and blue water shot up and splashed soothingly, with the faint smell of chlorine. He watched it for some time, the hypnotic repetition of water arcing and splashing, illuminated with spotlights. He reflected on the day's events, the child on the slide, the mother who ran away from him, Reiver's court hearing, Judge Chu's feisty responses meting out justice. And Delcie's performance that had brought up so many memories, so much nostalgia, sweet and aching, so far away, never to be recaptured.

Chip heard what sounded like wings beating. Suddenly, something whooshed by his left side, close enough so he could feel the displaced air. He saw what he thought was a large owl careening above the streetlight. Something dropped from its claws and fell toward the fountain. It was a mouse. Instantly, the owl was there, at a fierce angle, not more than a foot away from Chip's head. It snatched up the creature just before it hit the water, then lifted above into the dark like a feathered rocket and was gone. Chip felt unnerved and wished he were home already.

Sandra got home just after him. She'd had a lively evening with "the girls." Pam had made mimosas. Sandra had planned out their garden, which was just off their enclosed patio, their favorite place to sit in the warm months. Climbing roses surrounded their pergola, providing privacy from the neighbors or anyone passing by. Years before, after they'd moved in, they'd shared intimate moments there.

Sandra fell asleep, snoring lightly, something he always found endearing. Chip woke up at four-thirty and went to the kitchen for some water. It was still dark, but the sun would rise soon, beginning at 5:15 a.m. He went out to the patio and sat on the small sofa. The roses and plants surrounding the pergola glowed with dew. They looked like miniature Christmas lights. He looked up; there was no discernible moon, but a sky blazing with stars, and shooting stars. The raiment on full display—Venus like a spotlight. Delcie's words came back to him, 'But especially I can see the stars.'

The screen door banged shut. Sandra approached him in her silver nightgown. "What are you doing out here?"

He smiled, "Looking at the stars."

She looked at him quizzically for a few moments and then sat down beside him. He put his arm around her, and she leaned her head on his shoulder. "We used to look at the stars from here. We had a telescope—I don't know where it went."

"It's probably in the attic with everything else. I don't want to face that mess, but I suppose I should start clearing it out." He remembered one time, he'd seen the Half Moon, a replica of Henry Hudson's ship, from the attic window. It's bowed sides and colorful railings, and full sails. It was making its way upriver to Kingston for a centennial celebration. It was around 2009, he recalled. He recalled Reiver's words: *Only took seven years after that for the first ship to get to Virginia, 1616.*

"Oh, I didn't get to tell you," he said.

"What?"

"Reiver's charges were dismissed."

"The young man from the hardware store?"

"Yes, the judge dismissed the case."

"Why?"

"Well, the video the police claimed was him was most certainly not him."

"How did his lawyer prove that?"

"He had some help from an elderly Perry Mason."

"I'm glad that your friend was acquitted, but I still worry about you hanging out there in midtown. It's not safe."

Chip answered quietly, "It engages me, makes me feel vibrant. Gives me a sense of purpose...life."

"We have a life together. Remember?"

"Of course, I do." He kissed her gently on her cheek. "I just like to get out and see people, see what they're doing, how they get by...I don't know."

Chip lay down thinking he'd just rest for an hour or so, then he'd walk into town and see if Reiver might be in the park or at one of his haunts on Broadway. In minutes he was in REM sleep. The chandeliers blazed with candles reflecting off the dishes and pewter mugs on the tables. He passed by servants carrying trays of roasted veal, turkeys, ducks, fowl, and oyster stew. There was a long sideboard with bowls of pottages, puddings, jellies, oranges, nuts, figs, and raisins. And a selection of fruit pies. The aroma was intoxicating.

Chip entered the tavern room and was inundated with lively conversations and spirited discussions. Men in waistcoats, vests, lace collars, cravats, breeches and stockings, some smoking pipes, were animated as they debated. He approached the bar and took the one remaining seat next to a well-dressed, large, muscular-looking man. As he sat down, the man reached for his gold-headed cane and placed it between his knees for safe keeping. But not before Chip noticed the letters H P engraved on it. In his right hand he held a sturdy two-quart beer mug filled with porter. He took a long draft and exhaled contentedly. Before him was a large bowl of West

Indies pepperpot soup, some cornmeal fried oysters, and a small loaf of Sally Lunn bread.

Chip glanced furtively at the man's face trying to decipher exactly who he was. The man finished his oysters and took another long draft of porter and turned on his barstool and looked penetratingly at Chip. "No need to stress your eyes, mister. This is what I look like."

Chip saw the expression, strong-willed and proud, milky brown skin. The whimsical, knowing look, a bemused countenance that seemed to hold a secret. "I'm sorry, I didn't mean to stare. You look like someone I know."

"You know me, prof, and I know you," he smiled.

The bartender leaned over the bar protectively. "Do you need anything, Mr. Posey?" He glanced suspiciously at Chip. "Is everything all right?"

"Quite all right," the big man said. "Just catching up with an old friend."

Chip felt confused. "I didn't mean to interrupt you, Mr. Posey. But you do know Reiver, don't you? I mean, are you somehow related to him?"

"We both know him. And we know where he came from."

Suddenly, everyone in the room became instantly quiet, then stood up. A nervous ripple snaked through the crowd. The servers lined up at the entrance. Two revolutionary soldiers entered the tavern and scanned the room. "It's him," someone whispered, "the President, he's in the dining room."

Posey bristled and stood as well. "Can't get a damn break from that man." He downed the rest of his porter and motioned to the bartender, who extended his hand eagerly, shook Posey's hand, and said, *Good evening, sir.* Then he slid a receipt across the bar for him to sign. His signature was florid. It was the signature of a gentleman, a man who would soon live on his own terms, freedom.

"If you'll excuse me," he said to Chip. He headed toward the kitchen, avoiding the dining room. One of the servers held the door open for him. Chip figured he was exiting from the kitchen. When the bartender wasn't looking, Chip peeked at the receipt. He read the date and the final two words.

Chip woke with a start, his heart pounding. He grabbed a pen and a pad and quickly jotted down every detail from the dream that he could remember, even as it began to recede from his memory. *Damn it, remember!* It was fading quickly. But the last part left an indelible message in his mind. He'd remember the words for the rest of his life: *Philadelphia City Tavern, April 22, 1797. President's chef. NO CHARGE.*

A FACTOTUM IN THE LAND OF PALMS

I realized much later that it was the universe trying to get my attention. That's why I lost the most lucrative job of my lifetime. Here in Florida, sitting on top of the Nom de Plume Basin, we were enjoying a real estate boom like none other in the country. I had been fortunate to be a top sales rep for the Ray Shaft Wanger Real Estate Agency here in the Sunshine State. I had closed deals on seventeen homes in our new enclave, Elite Estates: *Where comfort and security thrive and exclusivity reigns.* In private, we agents referred to the place as Seersucker Acres—bring your wading boots, y'all. Four of the homes I've sold have already sunk several inches into the 'nonexistent' swamp. But hey, not my problem—*caveat emptor.* I just sell 'em, I don't guarantee they'll float. I very much regret that cavalier attitude now, after having experienced a severe financial downturn and multiple hardships, some of them of a bizarre and nightmarish nature. I've learned a serious lesson in humility. At least I got to keep my vintage forest-green MG Midget, only because it was already paid for and it gets good gas mileage. But eventually I parted with it as well.

The end came suddenly when a fleet of black SUVs encircled our office complex and commenced a raid. Federal officers led Ray S. Wanger, with his laptop, and crates of documents, out of the building, and hustled him into the back of one of their units. Ray lifted his handcuffed hands and gave us thumbs up and a reassuring smile as we watched from the windows. Releasing a deep sigh, I slipped off my custom brass name tag, glanced at it—R.B. Zoitner / Sales Rep—and dropped it into the trash, certain that I'd have no further use for it. After I'd moved out west, I read online that Ray was serving twenty-three years for trafficking. That explained the cadre of fetching young South American house cleaners, nannies, and dog walkers who hung out in the office and at Ray's swimming pool when the staff was invited for barbecues.

Some of the scenes I witnessed there could have filled a graphic novel. My participation in a few of the episodes was mild—I was mainly a spectator, compared to other associates, visiting corporate execs, and contractors. I assuaged my guilt by slipping the girls envelopes of cash, which some of them used to escape Ray's dominion. They either returned home or settled in with relatives here in the states. But it was something to watch, a bizarre entertainment; corpulent, graying Ray sauntering around the pool to the bar in his white satin robe with the state animal, the Florida Panther, emblazoned on the back, and his fire engine red flip-flops rhythmically slapping the bluestone. He fancied himself to be The Wolf of Wall Street, but he was more of a conniving swamp puppy.

Fast forward six weeks after the Feds' devastating visit, I am now living in Solana Beach, California, just off the Avenue with Everything, as it's called. Solana means sunny spot, and it is—Warby Parker sunglasses are a necessity. An old college friend, well, sort of a friend, a bit of a creep really, Bart, talked me into moving out here and renting his spare bedroom. He and his girlfriend, Saradonna, a massage therapist / singer-songwriter, who also waits tables part time at the Belly Up Tavern, have the master bedroom.

My "bedroom," it turned out, is the size of a modest broom closet, with a gamey smell lingering in the air. I found out later that the previous tenant kept hamsters and rats in there, lots of them, with treadmills that kicked up debris. And he was lax about cleaning their cages. Eventually, I discovered where the stink was coming from. There were piles of wood shavings and rodent droppings under my creaking futon frame. At least there's a window that allows a view of the resplendent Pacific Ocean. The waves lull me to sleep most nights, especially after a couple cans of the fine local craft brew.

The draw for me to come out here, besides my being done with Florida, and the shame of my conduct there, was supposed to be that Bart was going to hook me up with his landlord, who was a "big SoCal real estate guy," or so he said. Gizzard, which was his handle, turned out to be a trailer park slumlord. I met him in a disheveled, poorly-lit, storefront office in Oceanside, a locale that spawns trailer parks, a famous fishing pier, brew pubs, surfboards displayed as art, army surplus stores, and a somber cast of people without homes, pushing their belongings around in shopping carts—paradisiacal destinations being ripe for camping out in the open, so it would seem.

Gizzard's office smelled of marijuana and leftover Taco Tower take-out. It irked me that everyone in SoCal seemed to have stage names: Saradonna, Gizzard. What was that about? Bart, I noticed, when I picked up the mail to bring to the apartment, had for some reason rearranged the letters of his first name, so it read Tarb Vidovich, which I surmised had something to do with not being tracked down if he stopped paying his bills. It was like everything around me had a slippery coating on it, including all the doorknobs in the apartment, which might have been because Saradonna was constantly trying out various massage oils on her clients. She had a theory about matching up the intensity of the oil with the intensity of the client she was treating at the moment. It made me feel like I needed to take a dip in the sea and purge myself in salt water—a reverse King Richard II thing—to wash away the unwelcome balm. But at this point there was nothing regal about my status; serfdom was swiftly taking up residence in my affairs.

Gizzard received me with a vacant expression and offered me a flimsy metal folding chair, while his assistant, Pretty Flemish Cat, brewed us espressos. He seemed uncertain about why I was there. I reminded him that it was for an interview. I recited my resume, which he had misplaced under a pile of papers on his desk, some of which were invoices stamped red: *Thirty Days Overdue*. He listened to me with mildly stoned interest, as if I were a false prophet come from the East to enlighten him. Then he cracked up and laughed so hard he had to steady himself in his chair. Flemish Cat laughed in solidarity, which caused her back to arch, and her straw-colored hair to splay out like a cat's. I said, "What's so funny?"

"Reciprocity," he laughed. "Dude, your license is from Florida. Florida and California don't have reciprocity for real estate licenses. Dude, you can't work here. You're in the wrong state, dude." I was stunned at this realization and embarrassed that he was laughing at my misfortune. And how could I have overlooked such an obvious detail before moving here? I'd neglected to do my homework. Angry and humiliated, I got up and left without a word. I had to flee the freak show of the two of them, my stomach already quaking from the espresso. It was blinding bright outside and I shoved my sunglasses on, wondering if maybe I should have bought welding goggles instead. My MG Midget was thoroughly baked, waves of heat rising off the roof. Pretty Flemish Cat ran after me, "Here, he found your resume." She shoved the page in my hand. "Maybe you'll need it, I guess." It was stained with coffee rings and something sticky that smelled like molé sauce.

"Sorry it didn't work out, ya know."

I stared at her for a moment. "Is your name really Pretty Flemish Cat?"

She giggled. "Well, no, not really. I do movies, ya know? Like not for kids, ya know? Gizzard's my agent." I watched her slink back into the office. She did move like a cat. She turned back and called out convincingly, "Me...ow!" Which I think was her way of declaring, "I am."

That evening I sat on the side deck of the property with Bart, drinking the beer he had asked me to pick up on the way home. He seemed to be preternaturally out of cash. He had already borrowed seventy-five dollars against the rent money, which wasn't due yet, from me. The sun was setting on the Pacific, the waves rolling in like blue flames, as they crashed on the shore; a spectacular visual. I marveled that people out here got to see this most every day—California Dreamin'.

Bart seemed to be engaged in a compelling thought process, which caused him to frown and smirk simultaneously. I interrupted him: "I wish that you'd been a little more straight up about your situation here. It doesn't feel quite right."

"I know, Saradonna thinks you're weird—overly serious, constantly questioning reality."

"I'm weird?" I said, surprised. That was news to me. Nothing had been said prior to that. And what did *questioning reality* mean? I had already begun to doubt Bart's connection to reality.

"Well Bart, she's a bit unusual herself."

"She's an artist—high strung."

"What's that have to do with it?"

"Nothing. Anyway, it doesn't matter. I'm moving up to Oregon at the end of the month. Gonna help out some friends on a hemp farm. Let the weed times roll, brother," he chuckled.

"Are you kidding? I came all of the way out here to live in an animal hutch and you're leaving?"

"You can take over the apartment. It's only nine hundred fifty. Get another roommate."

"I'm paying you five hundred and fifty a month, and I don't have a job. I can't work here. There's no reciprocal agreement with Florida. And what about Saradonna, does she know you're taking off?"

"I haven't told her yet. She's a big girl, she'll figure it out."

I stared at him, the guy I knew in college. The *angle man* as he was known because he was the self-proclaimed master at zeroing in on what benefited himself the most at any given moment. At least he did when he wasn't drunk and hurling partially digested pizza and beer on the monuments in the quad. He liked to say, 'If it's good for me, it's good for you.' He was, I already knew, but was beyond certain at that moment, nothing but a scam artist. "And what's with Tarb? What's that about? What happened to Bart?"

He downed the rest of his beer. I'd bought sixteen-ounce cans of Swami, a fine local IPA brewed by the folks at the Pizza Port, where I'd soon find myself cleaning toilets in order to survive until I could come up with something better. I was determined that my relocation to the Golden State should not be a complete failure. But I'd definitely made an error in judgment moving out here, as beautiful as the weather was. Aside from that, embarrassingly, quite painfully, I was lately overcome with a J. Alfred Prufrock kind of malaise, as I observed the young ladies, mostly blond, and with toned muscular bodies, playing volleyball on the beach, their bikini bottoms lifting up with them as they spiked the ball over the net, exposing milky cheeks of delight. The result of which was an overwhelming loneliness, attended by the "eternal footman," and all that stuff. "You didn't answer me," I said. "What's with Tarb?"

He popped open another Swami and took a long, greedy pull off it, a bit of foam dripping down his weak, unshaven chin. "Did you only buy one pack?"

"Two, there's another one in the fridge."

He stared out above the surf and tracked a helicopter, one of many per day patrolling the coast from Fort Pendleton to San Diego and back. He formed a gun shape with his forefinger and thumb and pointed it at the helicopter and said "pow." I wondered why there was still a need to patrol the coast; World War II was over more than a century ago. "Tarb, it's short for Tarbosaurus," he said. He smiled, revealing candy corn-colored teeth, in need of serious prophylactic care.

"Tarbosaurus? What the fuck are you talking about? Whose Tarb Vidovich?"

"*Tarbosaurus bataar* of the Cretaceous period. I am a carnivore with a body mass of 1,650 kilograms."

I studied him for a few moments, his facial features shifting around a bit as he tried to assume the persona of a dinosaur. He looked more rodential and pathetic than ferocious.

He repeated, "1,650 kilograms. You know how many pounds that is?"

"I don't care," I said.

"That's 3,637 point 727 pounds." He shouted, "*Tarbosaurus bataar*. I am the alarming lizard!"

Alarming loser, I thought. Sometimes I think in pictures instead of thoughts. This one was a triptych: me packing up my stuff, me tiptoeing through the apartment, and me driving away in the dark, to anywhere but there. And never mind that I hadn't given him the rent check for the month I would soon owe. Tarb, aka Bart Vidovich, self-proclaimed prehistoric asshole, deserved little or nothing after the hosing I'd taken.

I waited until he fell asleep in the living room in front of the wide screen, a necklace of beer cans surrounding him. The final catastrophic scenes of Fallen Kingdom, the last Jurassic World movie, all bellows and roars, exploded out of the surround-sound.

Back out on the 101, windows wide open, gulping ocean air, away from the stench of rodent poop, massage oil, and dinosaur psychosis, I felt relieved, even though I had no idea what I was going to do next. A sign caught my eye: The Belly Up Tavern. I was hungry and I wanted a drink to celebrate my escape. I read the sign; it was singer-songwriter night, featuring among others, *Our Very Own Saradonna Monserrat.* I sat at the bar, with a good view of the stage, and ordered a Brie Burger and some Cajun French Fries. I ate ravenously and ordered a pint of San Diego Magic. San Diego is to beer what Tiffany is to glass. Both sparkle and are perfect examples of their class.

I scanned motels on my cell, figuring I'd buy myself at least two nights off the street to assess my situation. Meanwhile, the singer-songwriters offered up the standard fare; unrequited love, endless road trips, almost always at least five hundred miles, venerable guitars they'd owned and lost, and all with various degrees of skill. Some failed at attempted guitar flash, or produced a sequence of chords that didn't seem to resolve satisfactorily. But I didn't care; I was out of that disgusting apartment and done with Bart, enjoying the buzz of a fine craft brew, which imbued me with hope for the future. I ordered another one.

The MC, Vondisha Royal Tree, a tall (...tree?), slender woman with streaked orange hair and long, silver, dropped earrings, in a black leotard and tiger striped high heels, offered a bit of stand up between acts. Her humor was inscrutable; no one laughed. Finally, she introduced Saradonna, praising her songwriting skills profusely. Saradonna sat perched on a stool with her blue Stratocaster guitar, adorned with stenciled planets and stars, at the ready. Vondisha Royal Tree exited the stage, squeezing Saradonna's arm familiarly, and yelling over her shoulder, "Go get 'em, girl."

Saradonna violently attacked the strings with a strident E chord, a favorite rock key. Her amplifier must have been turned up to eight or nine. I could feel the vibration on my pint glass. Everyone at the bar turned around to watch her. She threw her head back, shooting her chestnut hair out like a halo. She'd applied a thick black and white makeup scheme that reminded me of the guys in Kiss. She screamed more than she sang: "I am paint. I am soap. I am hope. I am dope. / You can pick me up. But don't you fuck me up. / I am man. / I am child. / I am woman hot and wild. / Set your clock on my rock. / I'm the tick on your cock. / You can lick me up. / But don't you lock me up." It went on from there—a sort of notice to would-be trespassers. It was interesting, the juxtaposition of her funky and edgy lyrics, with her new age massage business.

Her performance seemed to speak to some of the women in attendance. They approached the stage, nodding with approval, dropping a few dollars in the tip jar. Perhaps I was missing something. I guessed that the lyrics were her poetry that she'd set to music. There was one about the life of a crustacean, which is short and hard. In it, she encouraged them to come out of their shells, comparing it to coming out of the closet. Another song, one in blank verse, was called "Billy the Cod," a humorous cowboy/fish song. She seemed to go for seafood themes. There was an anthem of sorts, kind of a tip of the hat to the play *The Vagina Monologues*, celebrating the importance and magnitude of the vagina. And finally, a curious, indecipherable one called "How I Think is Not Up to You, Motherfucker," which I determined to be her manifesto of sorts; but I would be at a loss to explain it as an actual series of corresponding, connected concepts. She concluded the song with some spoken word, no guitar. It sounded like a poem in a Native American language. The words, which I didn't understand, were soothing and sounded ancient, and she offered them with heart and authenticity. It was actually quite moving and folks were quiet for a few moments after she'd finished. Someone whispered, "That was beautiful."

By then, I'd selected the least seedy looking motel in downtown Oceanside, The Sleepy Seagull. I needed to rest and hit the job search early in the morning. I was feeling a bit drunk and ordered a coffee before I drove Mission Avenue. "So, what'd you think?" It was Saradonna; she sat down next to me. "Bart says I have a voice like a pterodactyl. Do you think so?"

Well," I said, cautiously, trying not to affront any of the political positions she'd just expressed, "I didn't know pterodactyls could sing." She let out a primal screech that drew startled glances from around the room. The bartender smiled and poured out a shot of Wild Turkey and a short beer, her after-gig toss off, I assumed. She took a sip of the beer and downed the shot, then coughed violently into her sleeve. "Bart, he's a fuckin' monster, you know that?"

"Well, he thinks he is."

"We're all monsters, isn't that true?" she said dejectedly and sipped her beer. "Are you one?"

I stared at my empty coffee cup. "I hope not. I try not to be." The bartender sat another San Diego Magic in front of me. "Thanks, but I didn't order that."

"She did," he said. I hadn't noticed; maybe she'd given him a hand signal. I sipped it slowly.

"The asshole probably doesn't even know I'm gone."

"Gone, what do you mean?"

"I left a day ago. He wouldn't have noticed. He's too busy getting hammered and thinking he's some big thing...I don't know."

"Like a Tarbosaurus?"

"Whatever he is he's fuckin' history. Look, you wanna get out of here?"

I was surprised, this coming from a woman who said I was weird and overly serious, unless she hadn't said that at all, and it was more of Bart's dissembling. Still, I felt like a net was being thrown over my head. I knew it was probably best to gratefully decline her offer. "I packed up and left tonight," I said. "I'm staying at a motel...looking for work."

"Why waste the money? I'm sharing a bungalow near the mission."

"There's a mission around here?"

"Yeah, San Luis Rey de Francia, old as shit. They used to shoot Zorro episodes there, or something."

"You rented a bungalow? Isn't that expensive?"

"It's not mine. I'm staying with a friend, a relative, sort of."

"How do you know it'd be OK with your friend, I mean relative?"

"We come from the same tribe. She's full Tongva or Gabrielino, the ancient people from Santa Catalina Island. I'm her adopted daughter, spiritually speaking, so I have rights as a Tongva."

That information made me nervous. A friend? The Tongva tribe? I'd never heard of them. But I didn't really want to stay in a motel, and the money saved would buy me more time. "I could pay you," I offered.

The bartender poured her another one, which she tossed down quickly. Then she shoved her tongue in the shot glass, swished it around dexterously and licked up the last drops of Wild Turkey. "We'll work something out, don't worry."

*

We passed the mission on the way to her place. When I read the pamphlet a few days later I learned that out of all the twenty-one missions in the system, San Luis Rey was known as King of the Missions. I could see why. It was an impressive structure featuring a long corridor with thirty-two Roman arches. It was also the last remaining church laid out in cruciform plan. It was said to be a pristine example of a Spanish mission church complex. The place was lit up, glowing eerily white against the fading dark blue streaked sky. One thing I did like about living near the beach was watching the constantly shifting atmosphere. In the morning, the solid wide gray wall of the marine layer would float on top of the ocean's surface and then slowly dissipate by noon, revealing an endless expanse of rolling water.

Her friend's bungalow was brown stucco with creamy red trim. Two prolific lemon trees dominated the front yard. I noticed there was another car parked in the driveway, a venerable, dust laden, gray Jeep with bumper stickers: Joshua Tree and another that read, Indigenous People of the Los Angeles Basin Onboard. She directed me to park on the street. I decided not to bring my bag inside in case I needed to leave quickly.

The first thing I noticed was the unmistakable aroma of essential oils, a byproduct of Saradonna's massage therapy practice. An assortment of candles for every occasion, along with a collection of ornate dreamcatchers. The living room was cozy with a worn purple, sink-in sofa and mismatched pillows, and two plump arm-chairs. A retro Bohemian beaded curtain hung over the entrance to the kitchen, where I saw someone carrying a steaming pot and setting it down on a table. I assumed that was her friend or relative. There was a jungle of plants suspended from thin silver chains and many more in large yellow and avocado clay pots, the vines reaching up and climbing over the windows, causing them to be smudged. A huge Day of the Dead poster hung on an opposite wall. There was also a foot-pedal pump organ in one corner that looked like an antique with a sheaf of music displaying JS Bach in large letters. An interesting opposition to Saradonna's compositional style I'd just witnessed at the Belly Up. All in all, it felt like being encased in a cocoon of Rain Forest, Mexicali, and native splendor. Still, a better situation than the Sleepy Seagull, where I'd have to rest with one eye open. Then again, I might have to sleep with two eyes open here.

The hanging beads parted, and an elderly woman strode purposefully into the room and stood in front of me. She was resolute and self-contained. Saradonna said, "This is ..." She stared at me realizing that she'd forgotten my name or didn't even know it in the first place.

"R.B. Zoitner," I said.

The woman extended her hand and I took it. Her grip was surprisingly firm. "I am Toypurina." She quickly added, "Don't say it unless you say it right. Toi-poor-ee-nah."

I said her name and she seemed satisfied. She did not look as elderly as I first thought. Her braided hair was mostly gray with streaks of red and black. Her face was weather-worn as if she'd spent much time outdoors farming or gardening. She was dressed in a pink, button-down Oxford shirt and jeans. She wore beaded moccasins and was obviously Native American. After the fact, I was quite taken with her presence and I bowed slightly out of respect. "What does R.B. stand for?" she asked.

"My name...R.B., Robin Bell Zoitner."

Her brown eyes widened as she considered this. "That is not the name of a warrior," she said, smiling coyly.

"I'm not a warrior," I said, in an unwarrior-like tone. My mother had insisted that part of my name would be Robin after Cristopher Robin. She was an avid fan of A.A. Milne and insisted that his books were better written than the Bible, which she didn't believe in anyway.

"He's a real estate agent," Saradonna offered.

"Not in California," I replied, which reminded me I'd be up early in the morning responding to the ad for a maintenance person at the Pizza Port in Carlsbad.

"Real estate? Like the Spaniards who came for our land and poisoned us with their white men's disease?" Toypurina said.

"No," I said, "just houses and condos...that kind of stuff. But I'm actually thinking I don't want to do it anymore."

She laughed, "That's more like warrior thinking." We all stood there for a few moments, a strange tableau of disparate characters without an apparent reason for our gathering. Finally, she said, "What do you need, R.B. Zoitner?"

Her directness was startling. "Just a place to sleep for one or two nights until I get a job."

"OK, let's smoke." By this point I was exhausted and just wanted to lay down and sleep. But I was a guest, a supplicant; I had to be compliant.

We went outside onto a flagstone terrace attached to the bungalow. It overlooked the back of the mission. The spotlights on it caused the structure to glow and create a haze in the immediate night sky above. The omnipresent sweet smell of palms, the small coast oak trees, and the floral citrus notes of Bird of Paradise flowers filled the air. I would have, at that moment, been satisfied to breathe in that essence instead of some marijuana, or whatever Toypurina was fishing out of her pouch and filling her pipe with. I had a history of bad reactions and behavior to pot and would have welcomed another beer if it was offered. Still, there was a prophetic feeling about the moment, something magical churning in the air as the stars began to populate the heavens. There was an impressive view of the three-story, domed bell tower with the cross on top. I found out later that it housed four bells that sounded transcendent when they tolled. I was quite attracted to the place.

I grew up in an atheistic household by the Jersey shore; my parents were unaffiliated with any of the local synagogues. My father was the son of a steel welder Trotskyite from Brooklyn. My mother saw and rejected God at the Woodstock festival because he'd manifested as a man. She rejected the idea that God was a male, given the Women's Suffrage Movement and the ongoing struggle for legal abortion. When the Christian caravans would stop by our house, with Bibles and pamphlets in hand, my father would tell them politely that he (we) didn't believe in God, but did the right thing anyway, without thought of a reward here or in the afterlife. Consequently, I was a sucker for Christmas lights, decorations, and nativity scenes. I was intrigued by the pomp, symbolism, and mystery of the Catholic Church and studied photos of medieval cathedrals from all over Europe. I bought a set of Autumn Rainbow colored rosary beads and kept them hidden in my room. I played with them like other kids played with marbles.

Toypurina struck a wooden match against the stone, held it up above her head and waved it, and then lit the pipe. She took two hits and inhaled deeply, then handed it off to Saradonna, who took three hits. I hoped they weren't expecting me to take four. The mixture smelled of jasmine, sage, and a hint of Wild Turkey, some residue from Saradonna's shots. The smoke was not harsh and was easy on my throat. I took one real hit, waited, took a half a hit, and then blew lightly into the pipe so the grass glowed in the bowl and looked like I was having another one, just to be hospitable.

We were quiet for a while like we were waiting for a message that would be whispered in the dark. Finally, Toypurina stretched out her arms and began to undulate them up and down like bird's wings. I heard a low tone, something that sounded like a bassoon. She was doing a bit of throat singing. Saradonna began waving her arms slowly as well. The Kiss themed makeup she'd applied for the show had melted. White and black streaks dripped down her face and made it resemble a skull. Toypurina called out: "*Miyiiha, miyiiha*! Then she pivoted forty-five degrees and called out again. She repeated the call to each of the four directions.

Saradonna performed the same movements and calls. When she faced me again, she said, "*Miyiiha*, it's Tongva for hello." At that moment my psyche, stretched and exhausted, collided with the contents of the pipe, which must have been laced with a hallucinogenic, because I was detaching from my body, a clumsy, unfit vessel drifting off course into unchartered waters. Suddenly, I found myself back in Florida in one of the mansions at Elite Estates. The structure was rocking wildly back and forth. I looked out of the custom cathedral window and saw mud, lots of mud. There was a loud sucking sound. I ran to the front door and tried to pull it open, but it wouldn't budge. Mud was oozing in rapidly under the threshold. Horrified, I realized that the house was sinking into the swamp, the house I'd sold to some unsuspecting retiree was tanking into the Nom de Plume Basin. Terrified, I ran to the side of the house that was tilting upward. It was gradually assuming the position a ship takes just before it sinks beneath the waves.

Then the girls came running in screaming from the upstairs bedrooms and the rec room. The young women Ray Shaft Wanger had enticed from their homes in Columbia, Peru, Chile, and Ecuador, with promises of an easy life with rich husbands in the States—the bastard. The girls were transformed into their younger selves. They wore rags and were shoeless, their faces dirt stained, and their hair tangled and unwashed. They had reverted back to the neglected children they once were, begging on the streets of their villages and thronged capitals. They yelled at me with clenched fists; their terrified faces close to mine: "You do this. You do this to us! We die...we die now!"

Suddenly, with a horrific sound that made my ears pop, as if the air was being sucked out of the house, everything went black, as we dropped down into the depths of the swamp. The girls screamed as I prayed, begging God not to let us go this way. I screamed: "OK, I did this. Take me. Let them go. They didn't do anything. Take me!" Then I started convulsing. It felt like my body was shaking apart, shaking violently. When I opened my eyes, I saw Saradonna hovering over me. "Wake up. Wake up! You're dreaming." I sat up and stared at her blankly. I was in a fog, completely disoriented. I hadn't had anxiety like this since college. I was trembling and drooling.

"Take it easy. I'll get you some coffee." I looked around and realized I was on the purple sofa. I had no idea how I'd gotten there. I struggled fiercely, trying to orient myself. I had difficulty focusing my eyes. I continued to tremble and felt like I'd vomit. She handed me a mug and the smell of the coffee—fresh, hot, black coffee—was, at that moment, the best thing that could have happened. Coffee is reality. Coffee is confirmation of existence.

I breathed in the aroma and sipped it, hot and stabilizing. After about ten minutes, and another cup, I was starting to recover but was still quite shaken from the dream. I realized I had no idea how I'd wound up on the sofa. Did they carry me in?

"What happened? Did I pass out on the patio last night?"

"You were actually quite entertaining. Did you know that you can fly?"

"Fly, what do you mean, fly?"

"You tried to. You kept jumping up and down and flapping your arms. It was funny."

"Funny? Not funny to me."

"Toypurina said that you revealed your totem...the crow. Do you ever dream of crows?"

My anxiety spiked again and I shot up off the sofa and was shocked to see that I was completely naked. I cupped my hands over my crouch. "Where the hell are my clothes?"

"There," she pointed at a pile next to the sofa.

"Did you do that...take my clothes off?"

She laughed. "You did. You put on quite a floor show."

I dressed hurriedly as she drifted over to the pump organ and sat down. She turned a few pages and started playing. I recognized the piece: "Jesu, Joy of Man's Desiring." She played it skillfully, with feeling, and even in my disordered state I was moved. I listened for a few moments, but it was time to go, time to get out. She paused, letting a chord drift in the air, and said, "It was the wisdom of crows that brought down fire from heaven. That's what Toypurina acknowledged with the flame of her match when she held it up to the sky." I had no recollection of a match or anything else. I closed the front door softly and stood outside, taking several deep cleansing breaths. I listened to her play, trying to reconcile the beauty of that music with the discordant and embarrassing experience I'd just endured. I noticed that Toypurina's Jeep was not in the driveway. I picked a plump lemon from the tree and palmed it in my hands like a baseball. It helped to ground me. Then I got into my car and drove away quite certain that I would never see either of them again.

*

I lasted six days at the Pizza Port. I accepted it as a penitence for previous sins of peddling crappy real estate and not being more proactive to defend Ray Shaft Wanger's handmaids. The volume of business the Pizza Port did was staggering, which resulted in repulsive bathroom presentations from unflushed toilets, urine spills, soggy feminine hygiene products, gooey floors (I tied plastic bags over my shoes), and changing tables with soiled diapers hot off the press. Human waste is an unfortunate byproduct of human life—the sludge factor. I had a constant urge to vomit. I just needed to make enough to buy gas, food, and a few nights sleep on the road to get back east—not southeast to Florida. And then what? I didn't know, but I was pretty sure that my degree in English Literature, with a minor in Philosophy, wouldn't result in a job that could support me. Besides, I really didn't like writing that much. I found it daunting. After I'd get a sentence or two written down, then came the anxiety of what comes next? Where were the words coming from? What mystical gate did they have to pass through to take up residence on the page, only to be deemed inadequate and require revision? Writing, I decided, required fearlessness, a quality I lacked in huge proportions.

It was on my last shift, just before I told the manager I was quitting, when I found the wallet in one of the stalls. I cleaned it off meticulously with an alcohol wipe and saw that it was a Shenola men's wallet, light brown leather, with a slim billfold. Ray Wanger supposedly had one, but he'd only flash it at you furtively. One of the house-cleaner girls, Esperanza, told me it was stamped on the back: Made in Hong Kong. After I thoroughly cleaned the wallet, I examined the contents. The guy, whoever he was, Cristo Sid Polizacio, had every high-end credit card one could qualify for, including a Platinum American Express. The picture on his license was exotic. Cristo wore a turban; he had thick tortoise eyeglasses, and he sported a flat gold chain with an amulet, a Tunisian gold coin. Cristo Sid Polizacio—what a bizarre name! Some kind of Arab sheik with Mafia ties? There were also sixteen brand new one-hundred-dollar bills pressed tight together, and a shiny card from a club called The Cage, which featured a crisscrossed chain and whip. It read: *Have you been a naughty boy?* I tucked the wallet in my pocket. The manager, Drayko Spawn, a local surfing hero, accepted my resignation with resignation. "We go through a lot of maintenance guys," he said. He paid me for the six days and boxed up a pie with mushrooms, green peppers, and olives, my favorite, which made my heart pulse with gratitude. I thanked him profusely and promised that if I ever got the smell of excrement out of my nose, I'd work for him again.

I decided, for no particular reason, I'd drive down to La Jolla and deliver the wallet to Cristo Sid Polizacio in person, ignorant that this off-the-cuff decision would be a turning point in my life—almost an end to my life. I decided that I'd splurge on an ocean front motel and a nice meal for my last night; I love fried clams with extra tartar sauce, a holdover from my teenage years on the Jersey shore. I'd leave for home in the morning, wherever that would be. I was no match for California, and I knew it. Even the seals who barked at me on my beach walks knew it.

La Jolla was an eye opener. I'd heard it was fancy but I wasn't prepared for how plush and opulent it was. Cristo's house was not a house, but an exquisite Muirlands trophy estate, sited gracefully with a two hundred-eighty-degree view of the ocean world. It made Elite Estates look like a fifties Adirondack campground with black flies and mosquitoes swarming.

To access the gate bell, I had to put my hand in a cement lion's mouth and press the button. Nothing happened. I thought, momentarily, that I should just toss the wallet over the gate and get on with my evening. Then a covering in the wall next to the gate slid open, revealing a screen. A striking looking woman, seated at a desk with a bank of security screens shifting behind her, stared at me as if I were a toxic lab slide about to be put under a microscope. "Do you have business here?" she asked. I noticed a camera lens aimed down at my license plate.

"Is this Mr. Polizacio's home?" It felt funny to use the word home. Kingdom would have been more appropriate.

"Why are you here, Mr. Zoitner?" Their intel was fast. It took less than ten seconds after scanning my license plate. She seemed to be typing something into her laptop. Then a bank of LED lights lit up the gate like Legoland at night.

"I have something for him."

She whispered into a microphone clipped on the collar of her sheer black blouse. A moment later something huge and ominous was lumbering toward the gate. As it advanced, I saw that it was a Hummer. There was a dome on top of the roof with something that seemed to be rotating around inside of it, maybe radar. As it closed in, I realized that someone was standing in it. It looked like a machine gun turret. Slowly, the gate began to slide open. My instinct was to back away and get the hell out of there as fast as possible—I should have. But I froze, staring at it.

Two guys in paramilitary uniforms hopped out and walked around my car. One had a scanner that he swished over the exterior. The other one shoved an under-vehicle inspection mirror beneath the frame. Then each one stood on either side of the front windows and shined flashlights on the interior, including myself, down to my feet and between my legs. "Follow us in," one of them commanded, in a thick accent.

"I think I have the wrong address," I said weakly. "Sorry."

"Follow us in," he said. It was a forceful invitation. I wanted to flee, but I didn't know what they would do. I looked into the rearview mirror and thought; I should not have come here. I should have left his wallet with Drayko at the Pizza Port and let him sort it out. He was very good with handling tough customers.

I followed them slowly up to the massive marble columned portico and we parked underneath it. Off to the side was a squat two-story building of stone and glass, a small fortress, with various length antennas spiking up in the air. About six or seven more guys in military uniforms hung out, some on their phones, others smoking. Next to the building were parked several more Hummers and a few Mercedes-Benz Sprinter Passenger Vans. Obviously, transportation was intrinsic to whatever operation was going on here. We got out and approached the massive oak doors which yawned open automatically. Each door displayed a carved crescent moon and star. One of the soldiers—maybe they were security guards—turned around and pointed at my car. He said something in Arabic with some English mixed in: "Can crusher." The other guy laughed.

We entered a great hall and marched along a maroon carpet that went on and on past large side rooms, a library, and some museum-quality art and vintage furniture. When we reached the elevator, just one of them accompanied me in, the bigger one. He pressed number four. I made a bit of small talk. "It's quite a place you've got here." He didn't look at me; he just grunted and patted the bulge under his jacket where I saw the tip of the holster resting snug against his thick leg. The door slid open to a massive conference room. There was a long table with ten chairs set around it. At the first seat next to the head of the table sat a diminutive figure that looked very much like a child, a young girl perhaps. I was directed to sit across from this person. Immediately, a servant entered the room with tea and a plate of assorted mid-eastern pastries.

I calmed down a bit and realized that this beautiful young person was not a girl, but a young man of perhaps nineteen or so. He wore a simple Cubavera linen shirt with a banded collar. His hair was jet black and shined with oil that smelled of jojoba. The only adornment he wore was a Rolex Yacht Master wristwatch. I recognized it because Ray Shaft Wanger wore one proudly. He always turned his wrist when he shook hands with you so you couldn't miss it. It was an item that cost about $16,500, but rumor had it that his was a fake, Bolivian knockoff.

The young man stood and offered me his soft hand; he was obviously not someone who performed manual labor. "I am Naeem Rahman Polizacio," he said cordially. "You have something for me, I believe?"

"Well, it's actually for Cristo Sid Polizacio."

"Yes," he nodded, "my father. I am conducting business for him as he is traveling out of the country."

If he was out of the country, how did his wallet wind up in a bathroom at the Pizza Port in Carlsbad, I wondered? Not an auspicious beginning, the mysterious separation of the man and his wallet. "Oh, he's not here," I said, to give myself a moment to think. He stared at me; his almond-toned skin translucent. For all his good looks and charm, there was something delicate about him, a certain vulnerability. He had the look of a person who was recovering from a childhood illness. I took the wallet out of my backpack and slid it over to him. He smiled and opened it. He examined the contents thoroughly, removed the credit cards and dropped them into a paper shredder under the table.

"That's a lot of credit you're shredding there," I said.

"They're fake, it doesn't matter."

"Fake? Why?" I felt suddenly that I'd fallen into a scam, some kind of grand manipulation. But what could they want from a poor schmo like me? I had nothing to offer.

He didn't answer. He took the crisp hundred dollar bills out and placed them on the table. "How many, Mr. Zoitner?"

A trick question, I thought. I answered directly, "Sixteen."

He counted them and smiled. "Yes, sixteen. You weren't tempted to keep them?"

"I wouldn't be here if I was."

"Then why are you here?" His playful eyes shone like lapis lazuli.

"I'm just returning something I found."

"What are your plans?" he asked.

"I'm heading home tomorrow...east."

"I see." He took the business card out for The Cage and glanced at it, chuckled, and fed it into the shredder. I was, by this point, more than ready to leave. I'd have to get myself and my car out of the front gate, which seemed formidable given the squad out there.

I took a nervous breath and said, "You're welcome...I'll be leaving now. Very good to meet you."

"Of course, and with much thanks for your honesty. My father would be impressed with a man like you. Perhaps," he paused for a few seconds, "you might be interested in some short-term employment. It pays quite well."

I'd just gotten out of a bizarre situation with Saradonna and Toypurina. I was decidedly not up for any more adventure. I deflected the offer by saying, "You don't even know me. Why would you hire someone without checking their references?"

"You've been vetted already," he said, offering me another pastry, which I declined.

"I don't understand."

"You returned the wallet with all of the money. That's what an honest man would do. A trustworthy soul," he added congenially. He was too smooth.

I wasn't feeling particularly trustworthy at the moment. I was more suspicious and anxious to get away. I wanted to be done with people with strange names—done with California, as intoxicating as it was.

He smiled again. "Five hundred per day, cash. No taxes."

I would need more money to get home, but what would I have to do to make that kind of money, I wondered? And who were these people anyway? Arab, Italian mafia millionaires? Probably billionaires. "I'm afraid I'm a bit out of my league here," I said.

"You shouldn't sell yourself short. I'm sure you have more talent and skills than you're even aware of."

"Thank you, but I'm anxious to get home. I..."

"Have you ever had any experience with royalty? A person of high stature, a titled individual?"

I'd once sold a house to a family named King, some mattress and bedding magnates from Buffalo. But I didn't tell him that. "May I use the bathroom?" I asked. I needed a think break.

"Of course." He indicated a door at the end of the long conference table. I peed and then glanced at my cell phone. My cell was dead, which surprised me. I knew I had fully charged it earlier. Fear gripped my shoulders and squeezed hard. They must have been blocking my service. The woman in the black blouse had probably read my emails and downloaded all my contacts by now. Was I being detained? Anxiety reared its fearsome head. I forced myself to breathe and not panic. When I opened the door, she was there, showing Polizacio Junior a document. It was probably a printout of my cell phone contacts. What the fuck was going on?

I stopped about ten feet away and said, "I'm leaving now."

He smiled and said, "May I introduce you to my sister. This is Syeeda Johre Polizacio." It was the same woman who'd greeted me on the screen from the security office. In person she was as stunningly beautiful as any woman I had ever seen: raven black hair, almond shaped eyes, skin the color of cocoa fused with milk, and her full claret red lips poised in a frowning grimace.

She turned her head slightly in recognition of me. "Yes, Mr. Zoitner. Welcome to Qasr Fakhm Polizacio," she said with an edge in her voice.

Naeem gave her a slightly disapproving look. "Dear sister, we should not allow ourselves to resort to cynicism." Later, when I got service back on my phone, I looked it up on my Pimsleur Language

App that Qasr Fakhm was Arabic for "opulent mansion." Apparently, Syeeda was telegraphing some resentment about the place, and perhaps her situation in it. Maybe some family issues. How could there not be? The place smelled of patriarchal dominance. And where was the matriarch, I wondered? Traveling with Cristo Sid, or perhaps locked up in a tower? Prominent, on Syeeda's ring finger, was a reddish carnelian stone the size of a pregnant chickpea, set in a gold setting. It glowed when she gestured with her hand.

She gave her brother a meaningful nod and whispered something to him, then brusquely left the room. Then came his offer. "Good, she approves of you. What I need, Mr. Zoitner, is a driver to chauffeur her around, a civilian as it were, to take her to various places of her liking."

"Why can't your people drive her around? There's a whole fleet parked outside. Those guys," I almost said *thugs*, "who brought me in here, they seem capable enough to drive her around anywhere she wants to go."

He got quiet for a few moments. I could see that he was trying to figure out how to best bend me to his will. "The situation is more delicate than that." He folded his hands and stared at the table. "Mr. Zoitner, I'm going to take you into my confidence, if I may."

I needed to assert myself. "I can't get involved with this. I...have a dinner engagement, and I'm going to be late."

He smiled and gave me a penetrating look. I'm a lousy liar. "Let's say $800 per diem." That got my attention. With that kind of money, I could take the car train back east and stay in a sleeper and order room service. He lowered his voice. His expression changed; he looked somewhat pained. "We, as you may have construed, are a royal family. Syeeda is betrothed, or rather hopefully almost betrothed, to a young man, a prince from another royal family—if she will acquiesce and accept his proposal, which she hasn't as yet. It is my father's sincere wish that she will agree to take the young man for her husband. I won't go into more detail about our families, though I suspect you'd be familiar with the name of the prince's family. And," he said, with a coy expression, "don't believe everything you read in the press. Politics are always in play, especially with...well, I'm sure you understand. I'll just say that my father is keen to create this connection, this alliance if you will."

I didn't like what I was hearing. It irritated me. "And she has no say in it? An arranged marriage? What's that about?"

For the first time he seemed ruffled. "It's not arranged. We don't do that anymore. My father thinks that it's a good match. But Syeeda, though she was born in our country and lived there until she was sixteen, and then came to the states for college, well, she has different ideas about things."

"She should," I said. It sounded like an arranged marriage to me—a giveaway to benefit the family, whatever they were about. "What is it you're really asking me to do?"

"I need someone, an American in particular, such as yourself, to accompany her—to be her driver and escort. To take her mind off of family business."

"Like selling her off to the highest bidder?"

His face turned red with anger, but he controlled himself. "I've made you a very generous offer. She approves of you. All you have to do is drive her anywhere she wants to go, except out of California, not Mexico, that's off limits. She can shop, go to museums, have lunch...whatever. She has an unlimited credit card. You won't have to pay for anything. You get eight hundred a day, free and clear. No strings attached, as they say."

I was parsing it out in my head; the person of high stature, the titled individual, was Syeeda. It occurred to me that there might be security issues driving her around. There could be some serious strings attached. "OK, she's royalty. How am I supposed to guarantee her safety?"

"Yes, she is a princess...and...she could be more than that if affairs go well. We'll provide security. There will be a detail following you in an unmarked vehicle two car lengths away at all times. You won't even notice it—you don't have to worry." He waited a few moments, "You will be less obvious driving...whatever that is."

I filled in the blank, "It's an MG Midget." His promise that I wouldn't have to worry made me worry. There was something off about this whole arrangement. It felt outside the parameters of reality. But all of my experiences here on the West Coast had pretty much been that anyway.

He laced his fingers together. "Exactly, you'll look like locals," he said with a bit of distaste.

"How long will this go on for?" I asked.

"Until all the arrangements are made," he let it slip.

"Until what arrangements are made?"

"Contracts, etc. International considerations. Until the time comes when she goes back," he said, quietly.

So that was the deal. I was to entertain her until they married her off to some prince to boost the family stature and pocketbook. They were just going to use her—send her into a bad situation, most likely ship her off to Saudi Arabia, or some place in the Middle East against her wishes.

He slid the cash, sixteen hundred, across the table. "Here, eight hundred per diem. This is for the first two days. You drive a hard bargain, Mr. Zoitner," he chuckled a bit nervously, perhaps because he'd revealed more than he'd intended. "And if you want a place to stay, we have plenty of room in our humble abode," he added in an ironic tone.

That sounded like a captivating offer. "No thanks, I'll get my own place. I want to be by the ocean."

"You can see the ocean from here. We have beautiful views."

I resisted his arm twisting by not answering him. He stood and extended his hand. "Well, I'm delighted you've accepted my offer."

I nodded, shook his hand and left wondering if I'd made a mistake, going for the money like that. Was that all I really cared about? What about Syeeda? I didn't want to be an accomplice to her future misery—maybe even slavery. It irked me that her freedom might be at stake. But what was I doing? Did I imagine that there was some way I could help her? What if I tried and it went wrong? I could wind up dead with this crew. He called after me, "Tomorrow at nine," he said cheerfully.

*

I checked into The Diamond Head Inn Motel and got a room with an ocean view, just a few steps away from the beach. At one hundred and forty-nine dollars per night, I was in good shape with an eight hundred per diem paycheck—cash no less. I picked up some San Diego Magic IPA's and a Taco Tower Steak Burrito with the works, and settled into my room. It was late and I didn't think I could sleep after the unexpected events of the day. I needed to think, and drink. I sat down on my private deck and listened to the waves rolling in, gentle and quiet at the moment. I noticed a blue-green glowing light as the waves splashed gently on the beach. It was as if a neon sign was placed just under the water. I couldn't stop looking at it. I found out later, when I asked Patchen, the motel manager, if she'd noticed anything like I'd seen. "Sea sparkle, it's bioluminescent plankton. The waves stir it up and it causes a chemical reaction. You get an automatic light show." She added that the first time she saw it was off of Malibu, she was tripping and swimming naked. "I kept biting at it trying to eat the light...I wanted to be full of light. I almost drowned. But it's good you saw it. Supposed to be good luck."

I retired to my room to get some rest before my new chauffeuring job in the morning. I sat on my deck with another beer. The air was bracing. The moon offered a luminous wide path across the great expanse of ocean. I felt that I could float over it. Even if everything wasn't turning out the way I thought it would, I had to acknowledge that this was a beautiful corner of the American landscape. Gradually, thoughts came to me. I was beginning to understand that I'm an outlier, a nervous errand boy; worse, maybe a fall guy. I was missing the relaxed vibe, the laid-back gene that folks seemed to possess in ample supply out here. It also occurred to me that I'd never felt like I was completely attached to the places I'd lived in: Jersey, Florida, my college in Worcester. I never felt quite at home, nor was I completely at ease. I'd not found anything to attach to. The true question, the overwhelming question that presented itself to me was: Who am I? And what is it I'm supposed to be doing? "Who are you?" I whispered. The ocean answered with more sparkle and hissing foam sliding over the beach.

Then it hit me. What the fuck was I doing? How had I managed to let Naeem Rahman Polizacio manipulate me like he had? He'd reeled me in like a dimwitted salmon. It wasn't just the money he was dangling; he was tempting me with his sister, the princess. Ego, vanity, lust, and cash; he'd wrapped them all up in a little gold Pandora's Box to-go and offered it to me. And I took the bait, swallowed the hook. And given the players, I could wind up maimed or worse. And what the hell would someone like Syeeda want riding around with me? It didn't add up. I made a decision, a hard one, one that would not financially benefit me. I'd return the money to Naeem in the morning. I'd be out the motel, dinner, and beer bill, but it didn't matter. I'd refund him and walk, assuming I could walk out of there. I couldn't just disappear. They'd find me and probably make sure that no one would ever see me again.

I don't know why I didn't hear my cell alarm, but I overslept. I panicked, got dressed, and drove to the compound. She was standing on the steps leading up to the massive front door. I noticed a few of the guards observing us as I parked and got out of the car. She stared at me; her expression was one of anger and abandonment. She got in and said, "You're late. How could you be late?" I started to apologize and explain that I wasn't going to be her driver, that I was going to return the money to her brother and go home. She didn't want to hear it. "Drive," she ordered. She seemed desperate, so I did. She directed me to a secret exit out to the street behind the mansion. Apparently, they'd purchased the house there, modest by any standards, compared to their place. I could access the property and exit from the driveway onto a side street, giving the impression that we lived there like normal people, not in the citadel towering behind us.

In short order I abandoned my plan to return the money to Naeem and bail. Instead, I showed up every day at 9 a.m. The itinerary was—wherever she wanted to go. She sat next to me with her silk scarf trailing in the wind, her hair tied in a pony-tail, and three-figure sunglasses, like a 1940s movie star. I'd notice men craning their necks to get a look at her when we passed by or stopped at a light. Here, in the land of make-believe, where stunningly gorgeous women are plentiful as seashells, she was a standout, an exceptional beauty. I felt a bit shabby at times sitting next to her. I'm decent looking, so I've been told, but definitely not a leading man. My people emigrated from Eastern Europe, rather they escaped from there, and none of us contained a drop of royal blood. It seemed satirical that Syeeda was being chauffeured around by a second-generation peasant in what some people described as a clown car. But wasn't that what America was supposed to be all about?

We were supposed to look like the perfect couple, at leisure, out to shop, dine, and enjoy the best there was to be had in SoCal. At first, she just wanted me to drive along the coast, the spectacular 101. She'd turn her head from side to side taking in the view, inhaling hungrily, filling her lungs with the sun-tinged salt air. It seemed as though she was eating the air as nutrition, such was her desire to breathe it in. She said to me one time, "Do you know what it means to be free?" I glanced at her, but before I could formulate a response, she said, "That's all I want, that's all there is really." She was free financially speaking, but she was trapped in a patriarchal family she couldn't escape, despite her struggles to do so. I smiled to hide my shame that I'd perhaps misunderstood my freedom, squandered away something of incalculable value, just to make a living without any meaningful direction. What was, or had been, my goal? I didn't know. What I also didn't know was that Polizacio Junior had his guys equipped my car with a miniature camera focused on both the driver and passenger seats. They could watch and listen in to our conversations. They'd performed this task during my initial interview with Naeem. How could he have been so confident that I'd sign on?

When she'd had her fill of driving up and down the coast, she decided one morning that she'd like to do some shopping. "I want to support the local economy." She laughed, a full-throated laugh that suggested defiance, liberation, and a playful nature she was starting to reveal, which was absolutely charming. Following her direction, I plugged Rodeo Drive into my phone and off we went. I'd seen a certain level of opulence in Florida, but this was a whole other thing. And she could shop like a demon, with abandon and detachment; sandals, dresses, hats, multiple pairs of jeans and a dozen thongs. And she didn't bother to try anything on. We walked through Bulgari, Dolce & Gabbana, Escada, Loro Piana, and Vera Wang, to name a few. In each establishment they assigned an associate to follow her around. She'd simply point at something and they put it in her cart. Despite the monstrous purchases, the obscene desire for acquisition, the store personnel were accustomed to witnessing, there were still a few eyebrows raised. When she was done, I followed her, my hands cramping around eight stuffed shopping bags, accompanied by a clerk with six more. It reminded me of a Chevy Chase movie. With my small car stuffed like Santa's sleigh, and the challenge of putting on seat belts, we headed back to La Jolla.

But when we reached Oceanside, she decided that we should take a detour and maybe walk out on the iconic pier. She remembered when she was a little girl *back there*—she always referred to her country as *back there*—her grandfather, with whom she was very close, used to take her fishing. It wasn't something that most young royal family girls did; but she loved it. She hadn't fished for many years now, but she liked to watch. The pier was lined with anglers, reeling in mackerel, bonito, and halibut. I watched her; she was genuinely excited to be around the action. She seemed happy, at least for the moment, and that made me happy. I had to remind myself that I was just her driver, her servant, really, nothing more.

After we left the pier, we drove around the town. She was hungry. For a woman with a Greek figure, she could eat copious amounts of food. As we drove over North Cleveland Street, she spotted a wine tasting room called Orfila and told me to stop. She recognized the name and recalled that Mr. Orfila, Alejandro Orfila, a winemaker, had also been the Argentine ambassador to the US, Japan, and the Soviet Union.

"How do you know that?" I asked. She remembered his name because she'd been with her father years ago at a meeting, or some reception of The Arab League in Washington and she was introduced to him.

"You've got some memory."

"He was the only diplomat who spoke to me, asked me questions like I was an adult. He was very sweet. Let's have some wine." We sat down on the patio and perused the wine list. She kind of peeked over the menu. "He knew Nixon and Carter."

"Really, Mr. Orfila?"

"Yes. I saw a picture of him dancing with Jackie Kennedy. Do you think I'm as pretty as she was?" She said this playfully and it caught me off guard, a little flirtatious. Before I could answer that she was prettier, a shadow spread over the table. I looked up. He was smiling, a full toothed smile—great teeth, a young man, maybe about thirty. He was toned and tanned, like a bodybuilder. Blue eyes and a square jaw—a friendly Viking vibe.

"Thanks for stopping in. I'm Kule." Kule, I thought, like Cool, another quirky name. I'd yet to meet a Bill, Frank, or Steve out here. I looked at his nametag: Kule Rodsey, Executive Chef, Orfila Winery. Syeeda offered her hand and he took it. "I'm Syeeda. I've heard of your vineyard."

He chuckled amicably. "Oh, I'm not the vintner. I'm the chef."

She gazed at him with obvious appreciation. He was definitely a looker. When it was my turn, I shook his hand and said, "Kule, is that a Swedish name?"

"It's German origin. My mother named me that. It means like a hollow or a depression in the earth. German families liked to choose names after land features by their homes. We must have lived near a hollow," he explained. *Hmm, hollow*, I thought.

"Where in Germany are you from?" Syeeda asked.

"I'm not from there. I'm a San Francisco boy, born and raised. Look, let me get you a couple of wines to taste. The rosé is new; it's really dry, fruity, and excellent. Be right back."

Syeeda said we should try some appetizers since Kule was so gracious. I agreed, but had an unpleasant wave of jealousy came over me. She was taken with him. How couldn't she be? It engaged my long-term sense of insecurity. Here I was sitting with the most beautiful woman I'd ever seen, being served by an Executive Chef who looked like he just stepped out of an Arnold Schwarzenegger movie.

He was gone for a few minutes, more than I thought it would take to pour two glasses of wine. He returned and served us the wine and a plate of his crispy Brussels sprouts and a small cheese platter with grapes and toasted pieces of baguette. "Here, have a snack with it."

I thanked him and said I hoped we weren't taking up too much of his time. He explained that it was the lull between lunch and dinner and he'd done all of his prep work already. The staff was on a break that they usually took at this time. "You guys are great, I'm happy to offer you something." He said "you guys," but he was talking to Syeeda. "Here," he handed her his card. "Let me know when you're coming this way again and what you might like to have. You should try my local Baja Halibut with roasted red pota-toes and seared asparagus with a light butter, garlic, white wine sauce. No one has sent it back yet," he laughed. The connection between them was obvious. And the wine was great. He went back to the kitchen to answer the phone. "Duty calls," he laughed. You had to love the guy, he was a ray of all-American sunshine. Even so, I sat up erect in my chair and tried to look more substantial.

Syeeda sipped the wine and then offered her glass to me for a toast. "I hope you're enjoying yourself. I am."

I didn't want to be bitter, and jealous of all things. "I'm having a great time...with you," I said with mixed emotions. I thought: *This girl is going to break my heart unless one of Cristo's gorillas breaks my neck first.* Perhaps both would happen.

We took a leisurely drive back to La Jolla. On the way Syeeda spotted a sign: Women's Resource Center. She had me stop there. It was a small, discreet building. She went inside while I waited. I looked the place up on my phone. It was a safehouse for women escaping domestic violence. What could she possibly want with them? Finally, she came out trailed by two other women. "Help me get the bags." We methodically emptied the car of all her pur-chases, carried them into the place, and left them in an alcove. The director, Concepcion, was ecstatic if not a bit shocked at the haul they'd taken in. She began writing out a receipt for Syeeda's taxes. Syeeda said not to worry about a receipt. Concepcion followed us out to the car. The two women hugged. We drove for a while without speaking. I glanced at her from time to time. She seemed to be deep in thought, tentative and vulnerable. She was staring out the window as if she was looking for something in particular. "What is it you see out there?" I asked.

"Women, thousands of them, safe from violence, without restraint, free of antiquated restrictions, living their lives as they wish, beyond authority—living fearless lives. Can you see that?"

She didn't notice me wipe my eyes with the back of my hand. "Yes, I can see it," I said, with much regret for any harm I might have caused in the past or been witness to without acting as I should have—sins of omission perhaps being worse than the more damning cardinal sins. "I see it clearly," I said.

After that outing, I didn't see her for a few days. My services weren't needed. Something was brewing at the compound. I missed her terribly and was relieved when I got the text: *Tomorrow morning, nine AM, sharp.* I got there early. She slipped into the car, all jaunty and in a good mood. "Driver," she said, "The Getty, please."

"The Getty Museum? That's probably an hour and forty minutes, maybe more."

"Aren't you getting paid by the mile?" she said in a teasing manner. This was only our second time out exploring, but I already felt committed to her. I would have continued driving her for much less, maybe just gas and meals. I realized that my developing attachment to her was imprudent at the very least, and quite possibly suicidal. This was no casual arrangement. I was driving a royal personage around from a globally connected family. I'd done a bit of research on the Polazacio clan and learned, while they were not at the very top of the food chain, they shared close connections to the Al Khalifa family in Bahrain. Based on that information, I determined that it was probably young Prince Wahid Al Khalifa who'd taken a fancy to Syeeda, or so her father hoped. A little further investigation at The Friends of The Arab American National Museum explained the ties between the two royal families. After some extended reading, with the help of a kind curator, I discovered a newspaper article about a one-of-a-kind pricey jewel delivered by courier to a certain Princess, Syeeda Johre Polizacio, a reddish carnelian stone engagement ring. And why would she wear it, I wondered? Too appease her father? To buy more time? She had a highly developed aesthetic. Maybe she just liked jewelry. It seemed that everything about this family was mysterious. How could I know the truth about them? Another painful thought stabbed at me; could I really trust her if it came down to it? Was I some part of an elaborate plan of hers? Was I just being played? But why? What could she possibly need from me?

We were greeted lavishly at the Getty. A guide was waiting for us when we got to the main entrance to accompany us through the exhibits Syeeda wanted to see. Either she or someone from the compound had called ahead to pave the way for us. And it was paved generously; the guide, Mahrosh, brought us to a cozy out-door café overlooking the Los Angeles skyline. It was an unusually clear day, the sky cerulean blue, and the buildings shimmering in the sunlight. Mahrosh served us coffee—Qahwa Arabiya and tiny star-shaped honey and nut pastries. She and Syeeda commenced a lively conversation, I assumed about the art we were about to see. It sounded like a different dialect than I'd heard Syeeda or her brother speaking. At one point Mahrosh looked at me and said something that made Syeeda laugh. "She wants to know if you're an expert on antiquities. She thinks she might have seen your picture in the Smithsonian Magazine."

"Did you tell her I'm just the driver?"

She gave me a look, one of those incalculable female expressions, slightly vulnerable but with an edge. "You're not just my driver." I didn't respond to that but wondered what she meant. Was I her confidant, her friend, something more? That couldn't possibly be.

We spent the next two hours viewing two installations: *Assyria: Palace Art of Ancient Iraq*, and *Mesopotamia: Civilization Begins*. Syeeda explained everything we were seeing to me in vivid detail. She was fluent about various styles, dates, stories and legends surrounding the various wall hangings and sculptures. It wasn't until we were leaving that I learned that she and Mahrosh had both attended the Stanford University program of Art & Art History. That explained the special treatment we'd received. The two women embraced and Mahrosh offered me her hand. "Be careful with the LA traffic, you're driving a very important person around."

"I'm starving," she said as we drove down Westwood Boulevard. "There's a place called Sunnin Lebanese Café. It's the best one. My father used to take me there after we visited the mosque on Vermont Street. He provided scholarships to a lot of the young men who went there."

"Sounds like he's a very generous man."

Her expression soured. "Generous, if you see things his way. Unfortunately, I don't."

"You mean like about marriage?"

"Do you really think I don't know what's going on?" She was angry now. "And you're participating in this? How could you?"

"I don't agree with your father. I think you should marry who-ever you want or not at all if you don't want to." As I said that I felt an ache in my chest. "I think," I added, "maybe you should get away from the family."

"Where the hell in the world could I go?" she yelled. "They'd find me. You don't know who you're dealing with."

We sat there in front of the café for a while. She dabbed at her eyes. Finally, I said, "Let's go in. Come on, my treat this time." She looked at me and laughed in my face, a loud, harsh, and dismissive laugh. It was as if a bucket of ice had been dumped on top of my head. The disparity between us, the obvious difference of our lives and class was like a chasm I was falling into. She, a royal princess, an educated art historian, and a woman whose face could have been rendered by Raphael, a woman who was never denied anything she desired. And me, a floundering ex-real estate agent, lacking any meaningful direction in life, who was already approaching the middle years. I sat there holding the steering wheel, staring out at the palm trees.

She leaned over and put her hand on my arm and squeezed it softly. "I'm sorry. I shouldn't have done that. It was cruel. I don't want to be cruel."

I suppressed an urge to cry, which would have been complete and utter humiliation. "It's all right," I said. "We come from different worlds...we..."

She slid her hand up my arm and pressed her palm against my cheek, gently, causing an electrical current to run through my body. "Come, let's eat. Their food is wonderful."

When we entered the café, the manager, Ahmed, bowed to Syeeda and told her it gave him great joy to see her again. He inquired about her father's health, and that he hoped Cristo was well. He sat us in a curtained booth with plump cushions and retreated, but not before I caught his quizzical glance at me. The waiter immediately placed two Moroccan Champagne Cocktails on the table, and welcomed Syeeda extravagantly. And the food was wonderful. The best hummus I'd ever had with pitch-perfect pita to dip it with. We shared the mixed grill plate and the waiter kept bringing out little side dishes that the manager insisted we try. He also treated us to a Marrakech Mule, a heady concoction. For dessert we had Shaabiyat and Maatouk Lebanese Coffee with cardamom, plus a little shot of something on the side. When the waiter brought the check, he bowed and handed her a large to-go box and said it was for her dinner—a gift from Ahmed. He bowed to her, then slightly to me with a look that suggested she'd brought her dog into the café by mistake.

We were both tipsy when we got back into the car. "Thank you, that was great," I said.

She didn't answer me and was quiet for a few moments. "Where are you staying?" she asked.

"The Diamond Head Inn Motel," I answered, suddenly nervous.

"Let's go there."

"That might not be the best thing to do," I said, my stomach knotting up.

"Why? Are you afraid of me?"

"I'm afraid of the situation. It's not like we're..."

"You're supposed to take me wherever I want to go," she said in her commanding princess voice. "Isn't that the deal?"

We were quiet for the rest of the drive. When we got there, I showed her the private deck off of my room. The ocean was riled up, waves crashing on the shore with an explosive impact. A three-quarter moon appeared between jagged clouds. We sat there uncomfortably for a while. Finally, I asked her if she'd like some tea. She asked if there was anything else. "Just beer," I said.

"I've only had 3 percent beer. Is it good?"

"Yes, well, if you like the taste of it. It's a 7 percent IPA."

"I'll have one," she said.

I went to the mini bar and grabbed two cans and glasses. What am I doing? I thought. This is insane. I stopped in the bathroom and looked in the mirror. *Take her home,* I commanded myself. *I can't...* When I went back out; she wasn't there. I looked at the path to see if she might be walking down to the beach. "Syeeda, where are you?"

"Here," she said quietly, almost in a whisper. I looked in the room and saw the glow of the fractured moonlight in the window intersecting her body. I stifled a gasp as I stared at her—a real life Botticelli. How had I walked by her and not noticed she was lying on the bed? "I'm here," she said again, in a tone I can't describe, but as a direction, an imploration. I stood at the foot of the bed, breathless at the sight of her naked beauty, and then slowly, I knelt down on my knees and kissed the soles of her feet.

*

We got back to the compound around nine o'clock that evening. They were waiting for us. The Hummers were lined up on either side of the parking area with their lights on like a landing strip. They were flanked by ten guards in full gear, five on each side. I noticed some vehicles I hadn't seen before. Five large tan units with the usual bells and whistles attached. They all bore the same insignia on the vehicle doors; the flag of Bahrain, symbolizing the five pillars of Islam. It would have taken a McDonnell Douglas YC-15 transport plane to ship them here. They didn't just drive over the ocean. Their presence spoke of government manipulation—calling in some favors the public didn't know about. The sight of them sent a distinct chill up my back. Syeeda unbuckled her seatbelt, "Oh, no."

They hurriedly waved me up to the portico. One of them leaned into my window. "He wants to see you." It sounded like an ominous invitation. An older woman, rather distinguished looking, perhaps an assistant or an official of some sort, was waiting for Syeeda. She approached her urgently and whispered something in her ear, which further alarmed Syeeda. They bolted into the building and disappeared down the long hallway. I was escorted, not too gently, inside and into the elevator, then up to the fourth floor, accompanied by another guard. When the elevator door opened, I saw that it wasn't going to be a one-on-one meeting. They had company. Naeem was in his usual seat and appeared to be nervous. At the head of the table was an imposing figure, a huge man in a turban with tortoise shell glasses, wearing a flat gold chain displaying a Tunisian amulet—a gold coin. He wore a white thawb, a loose-fitting robe. Here, finally, was Cristo Sid Polizacio, the man whose wallet I may or may not have returned, reality being at a premium at this point. As all of the seats were taken, I positioned myself off to the side next to a table adorned with an ornate flower display and an extravagant fruit and nut platter. I was grateful not to be seated amongst them.

The other chairs were occupied by military men in full regalia, metals and tassels, and several in matching suits. Three of the men had dossiers before them and were, I conjectured, secretaries or ministers. It looked like a meeting of the UN. I noticed that seated next to Naeem was a young man about his age. I guessed that he was Prince Wahid Khalifa, come from Bahrain to claim his bride. He was dressed impeccably in a William Westmancott Ultimate Bespoke suit, a $102,000 outfit. Ray Shaft Wanger supposedly had one, but it was rumored to be a Korean knockoff for $500. I'd seen him in it once at an award ceremony for the National Association of Realtors. Ray was being honored for selling the most homes that quarter. He was, indeed, the king of sinking mansions. This was about six months before the raid on his business and his arrest. After a jury of his peers found him guilty of trafficking, he was placed in a 6x9x12-foot piece of real estate at the Raiford Prison in Bradford County, Florida.

No one said a word; there was an eerie silence pervading the room. They were waiting for Cristo, who was perusing a multi-page document, his expression changing as he read. Mostly he frowned. The whole thing felt like a military tribunal, or rather, a trial. He crossed out sentences and drew lines through some of the paragraphs, then he slid it to Naeem who nodded solemnly. Naeem studied the changes and then handed it off to Prince Khalifa. He glanced at it and seemed to become suddenly agitated. He handed it to one of the ministers sitting next to him, who began shaking his head. He spoke in English, "No, this is not possible." Tension flashed through the room. I guessed that the document contained the provisions for the marriage agreement. And it was not satisfactory to Polizacio senior, nor anyone else apparently.

I didn't understand why I had to be a witness to this. They could have just sent me on my way. But I also realized that Syeeda's immediate future was about to be decided by a room full of men. Men who were used to having things turn out the way they wanted it to—no matter what it cost anyone else. Cristo spoke in a measured tone; his English was impeccable, reflecting the Ivy League school he'd attended. "This document does not reflect the agreement we made early last spring."

"The world changes," one of the ministers sagaciously observed.

"The world works on promises kept, especially those made by people like us." Cristo said this cordially, but the threat was implicit. I felt something touch my hand; it was a drop of sweat from my forehead. *This is not going to turn out well*, I thought. I ran my tongue over my lips, which were very dry. I resisted a shiver as I realized I could still taste her in my mouth. I thought for a moment that I was going to pass out. Could any of them possibly know what happened?

The minister cleared his throat nervously and said: "The financials are not exactly as they were initially represented to be."

Cristo leaned forward in his chair, emphasizing the animal bulk of his frame. His tone changed as he stared fiercely at the men—a few of them flinched. "Are you suggesting that there was some insincerity in the figures we presented? Is that what you're saying?"

A long, deadly pause hung in the air. The prince glanced at his entourage beseechingly. Another minister spoke, his voice quivering, "We are not able to proceed with the agreement unless certain adjustments are made. We believe that with some negotiation, just a few minor changes, we can reach an accord that is acceptable to both honorable families."

Cristo answered quietly, his baritone dropping even lower, "We had an agreement. Unless, of course, the Princess Syeeda is no longer foremost in your thoughts and affection." He said this directly to Prince Khalifa who winced as if he'd been struck with a pipe.

"Cristo, we must be reasonable," one of the ministers pleaded. "I beg you to reconsider the situation. It should be a fair arrangement for all of us. Think of the multitudes that will be affected when the arrangements are finalized and announced at home."

At that moment a side door opened and Syeeda entered, followed by the woman who had received her upon our return. The older woman was elegantly dressed and wore a tiara with blue and yellow jewels. Obviously, she was not just an official. Immediately, all the men stood and acknowledged the women. I could see from some of their expressions that they were not immune to Syeeda's overwhelming beauty. I noticed that the prince's lip twitched. The princess wore an aqua thawb and silver slippers. A diamond tiara sparkled in her hair. She nodded and the men sat down. Another uncomfortable pause ensued. The prince remained standing, his eyes and entire body in a posture of adoration. Syeeda bowed to her father and then to the prince. I noticed a subtle change in Polizacio's demeanor as he observed his daughter. He was completely enamored of her; his pride was obvious. So why was he about to bargain her away? Though it seemed like, and I sincerely hoped, the deal was about to go south.

Syeeda approached the table and placed a velvet ring box next to the prince. "I am sorry, but I cannot accept your proposal for marriage." There was a simultaneous loud gasp as if an air hose had suddenly ruptured and was flailing wildly in the room. This was unheard of in their culture. Women were supposed to do what they were told to do. It was the kind of disobedience that could lead to an honor killing. And as if on cue, the elevator door opened and two guys, the security detail that had been following us around, entered and approached Cristo tentatively. One of them handed him a note. I felt myself starting to collapse as my chest jolted in shock. My heart may have actually stopped. I steadied myself on the side table and scanned the exits. I actually could feel the cold vice-grip of death closing around my throat. I thought fleetingly, that there could be a distinct advantage to being dead at that moment.

Polizacio read the note and his large pale head turned the color of persimmon as the veins swelled. He looked around the room, located me; his expression was...death. If I had been a marble column, I would have crumbled into dust on the spot. Had the security guys managed to set up reconnaissance in my room at the Diamond Head Inn? Had they managed to observe us through the window or the open door of the deck? That would be worse than damning. Is that what the note said? Was that scribbled document that Cristo shoved angrily into his pocket a signed decree for a double honor killing? An honor I'd prefer to eschew on both counts. Was this, finally, my comeuppance? My payback for getting into situations I had no business getting into, from Ray Wanger to...this? I promised myself, and the God I didn't believe in, that if I somehow managed to walk away from this unscathed, I would return home and embrace a quiet life, even one of singular desperation.

Prince Khalifa stared at Syeeda in disbelief and shock that what he thought was a done deal was indeed not done at all. He'd been rejected by the woman he'd chosen to elevate. Nobody dared to move an inch. At that moment, sirens erupted ominously from a nearby firehouse. Whatever was burning couldn't have been as intense as the heat in the conference room at that moment. Conflagration seemed imminent. Slowly, as if in a dramatic act of finality in an *opera seria*, Khalifa picked up the ring box and slipped it into his jacket pocket. "I have offered you the world, and it is not good enough for you, Princess." I didn't like the way he said Princess; he kind of spit it out.

Syeeda answered directly, "The world I choose for myself is one of freedom. I am not a commodity to be exchanged for something else. There is no genuine value in that."

The prince puffed up and leaned menacingly over the table. "You have humiliated me and dishonored our families." His tone was harsh; and the previous look of adoration was replaced suddenly by a mask of detestation. I'd never seen such a frighteningly fast transformation before, maybe just in a vampire movie.

"I have dishonored no one," she said. "And I have not humiliated you. You choose to feel humiliated. A feeling many women must bear each day of their lives—and worse. I only wore the ring because my father asked me to as a personal favor to him. It was a courtesy to my father to acknowledge the gift of the ring. And yes, it is beautiful, and will still be so on the hand of another."

I couldn't believe her courage. I'd never seen anything like it before in my life. The prince turned to Cristo and yelled angrily: "Do you hear her, old man? How dare she speak like that to me. She has dishonored us...this...bitch!" He was suggesting something horrible. Did he actually think that Polizacio would pop his daughter off on the spot? Through bared teeth, the prince threatened: "You will remember this day with sorrow. You will pay for this, all of you."

Cristo shot out of his chair and grabbed Khalifa by his expensive lapels and lifted him about two feet into the air. "Bitch? You call her bitch? You are garbage. You are not worthy of her."

The prince yelled a command in Arabic. Suddenly, the military guys stood up and drew an array of weapons, mostly handguns of different makes and calibers, and pointed them at Cristo, Naeem, Syeeda, and me. A ridiculous thought flashed through my head: this is going to be the OK Corral, mideastern style. But there was nothing silly about it. These were real soldiers with real guns. Would they actually shoot us?

Cristo let go of Khalifa, who fell unceremoniously into his chair with a painful yelp. Then he shouted: *"Taeal alan!"* All of the side doors burst open and his crew surrounded the table, pointing their weapons at Khalifa and his soldiers and ministers. And they had the advantage of being positioned behind them. Also, there was, which I hadn't noticed before, a balcony above the far side of the room, in front of a huge stained-glass window, decorated with blood lilies and cemetery irises, and more of Cristo's men aiming semi-automatic weapons down at Khalifa's people. So much for mutual trust and cooperation. Khalifa's guys were definitely outnumbered. It would have been more than a twenty-one-gun salute; it would have been a total blood bath. Incredibly, no one fired a shot. That was because the command wasn't given to fire—military discipline. That only could have come from Polizacio or Prince Khalifa.

The firetrucks that were responding to the alarm raced past the compound, then down toward the shore, their sirens fading. I felt frozen in place, incapable of movement, yet I began to walk slowly around the table. It was like I was watching myself walk around the table. As I did, I heard their weapons lock and load. It sounded like a field of steel crickets. The barrels of the guns followed me as I walked. All that was needed was a simple command. My thoughts were a jumbled mess. They were something like: OK, here is the moment in my life where I have to stand for something. I have to do this, and not just as an empty gesture. I could no longer live with myself if I didn't take action. I was, I thought vaguely, giving up who I'd been for so many years. It was time to be someone else...or no one at all. When I got to Syeeda, I turned around and stood directly in front of her, shielding her. *I will stand here*, I thought. *I will not move.*

There was some confusion followed by whispering between the two factions, back and forth. They'd switched their language to Arabic again and spoke in hushed, but frantic tones. I could sense

Syeeda behind me. I thought I could feel her very life force, her soul struggling to be free. Then it was quiet. Finally, Cristo, Naeem, and Prince Khalifa bowed stiffly to one another. The guns were withdrawn into holsters and robes. It took about ten minutes to clear the room. Some of Khalifa's people took the elevator. Others were led down a staircase by Polizacio's men. I continued standing where I was. The woman who'd accompanied Syeeda grabbed her hand and pulled her away. Syeeda glanced at me as the door closed—a look that revealed her fear for my life. I was left alone with Cristo and two of his men. When the elevator door opened again, he said something. The force with which they threw me against the interior wall knocked me out.

*

I don't know how long I was unconscious. But when I came to, I almost passed out again from the pain. I was in a large basement with about twelve-foot-high barred windows. Light showed through on to the concrete floor I was lying on. I guessed it must have been midmorning. I felt my head, which was covered with dried blood. There were blood stains on the floor. My face, though I couldn't see it, felt swollen and was no doubt very bruised. I tried to get up, but my legs wouldn't support me. They must have worked them over as well. The only thought I could formulate was that the beating was meant to be terminal. I lay there falling in and out of consciousness, needing water and medical attention, which I was pretty sure wasn't forthcoming. I'd taken a stand for once in my life. I realized that my action incriminated me in Polizacio's judgment. I'd crossed a line that he wouldn't tolerate—a common er...with his daughter, even if it was also her choice. But something had prompted me to act. I'd made a gesture; I'd walked around the table and stood in front of Syeeda to protect her. *Take my life, not hers.* I did it without any thought of the future, a future that was receding quickly before me as I passed out again.

The dream was vivid: a gentle waterfall, dappled with sunlit pastels. I was sitting on a rock, the water running over me, cool and soothing. I opened my mouth to catch some as I looked through the liquid curtain it created. There was a figure on the other side, a woman looking in at me. She held her hand out and I did the same; we pressed our palms together and interlaced our fingers. She stepped through the softly cascading water. "Look at me, I'm here," she said. We were naked in a garden of water. She knelt and we embraced, falling back, and then entwining.

I opened my eyes and cried out in pain. Syeeda held my head in her lap and the older woman I'd seen before wrung out a washcloth ~~with~~ so the cool water fell on my face. "Shh, be still."

"Syeeda..."

"Do you think you can stand?"

"Not so well right now...water, please." She held the cup up to my lips and I drank until I coughed.

I could see that she was shocked looking at my face. "You don't look so good," she said, worried.

"I didn't look that great before."

They reached under my arms and helped me to my feet. At first, I thought that my legs might be broken as we walked toward a huge metal door. I would have fallen if they let go. I was disoriented and thought I would pass out again.

"Who are you?" I asked the older woman.

Syeeda answered: "This is Balqees, my mother."

"Oh, I'm sorry to meet you under..." Just then the metal door, which was partially open, drew back fast and with such force that it banged against the stone wall on the other side. Cristo and two of his men stood there with weapons drawn, blocking the doorway. Syeeda and Balqees moved toward them with determination. I stumbled along between them.

Syeeda spoke firmly, "Let us pass."

Cristo bristled, "Since when do you give orders to your father?"

Balqees tightened her grip on my arm. "A worthy father respects his daughter's wishes."

Syeeda spoke again: "Let us pass. You almost killed him."

There was a long silence. Cristo's jaw was twitching, or I think it was. My vision was blurred, which alarmed me. Was I permanently damaged? The two men remained where they were, but one of them slowly lowered his weapon toward the floor.

Syeeda said: "Let us pass or you'll never see me again, by my hand or yours." This sent a chill through me and it made an obvious impression on her father. He stood there a few more moments, then gave an order and weapons were shouldered. I was suddenly being carried out by the two guards, gently this time. When we got to the courtyard, Polizacio yelled something and another guy jumped into a Mercedes-Benz passenger van and brought it over. Carefully, they laid me down on the wide back bench seat. The guy sat behind the wheel. Balqees had some brusque words with Cristo and he called out another order. The guy got out of the van and Balqees took over. Syeeda sat in the back with me and I was out again before we exited the gate.

I woke up to pre-dawn light, alone in a room. There were lights blinking and machines beeping and several tubes inserted in my body. At first, I thought I was dead, viewing myself from a few feet above the bed. I saw a nurse call button and pressed it. Her name tag read: B. Nidjah. She checked my vitals and the IV bag. "I think you're going to need one more, perhaps not. I'll ask Dr. Arif."

"He's my doctor?"

"Yes, and a good choice. You have some serious injuries. He'll be in this afternoon." I soon learned that two days had passed since my rescue, and I was in an expensive private room in Cedars-Sinai Hospital.

About an hour later, Syeeda and her mother arrived. My vision had cleared up, but I was still worried about my legs. Could I stand up and support myself?

"I want to apologize for what happened to you, Mr. Zoitner," Balqees said, as she served me some lentil soup.

I didn't know what she knew about Syeeda and me, but I answered, "Thank you. It's certainly not your fault." Then I lied: "I'm feeling much better." I wanted to put a good face on my situation, as much as for them as myself. Syeeda looked away to avoid eye contact with me. That made me nervous. Had she come to say goodbye?

Balqees' cell phone rang. "Excuse me, I have to take this." She left the room, but not before smiling kindly at me.

Syeeda sat on a chair next to my bed looking down in her lap. "I never should have gotten you into this. I never should have..." Her voice trailed off. "I almost got you killed."

"What happened with us...between us...was...I'll never forget."

"Forget? You mean that's all? That's all you wanted from me?"

"No, I don't mean that. Look, it's impossible for us. You're..."

"I know who I am and where I come from," she said defiantly.

"You're much more than that. I can't..." I was choking up.

"I'll see you if I want to see you."

"Your father..."

"My father is a powerful man. He lost something he wanted and his pride has suffered a harsh blow. But he is not of a mind that he would do without his wife and daughter so easily. And, we are not *back there*, where I would have no choice. I would probably have been executed by now."

The bastards, I thought. Nurse Nidjah came back and adjusted my medicine port. Sadly, I watched Syeeda's beautiful face fade into darkness. Perhaps I'd never see it again. Nothing was certain. Three days later, Dr. Arif discharged me with some more medication and a prescription for physical therapy. He said he thought I'd recover almost completely, but I might have a slight limp due to the damage on my right thigh muscle. They must have hit it with a blunt object. But it could also heal over time with therapy.

I'd undergone severe trauma and it would take a while. He offered me his hand and I shook it with both of my hands, squeezing tight with gratitude. "Thank you, so much. You got me through this," I said.

He bowed slightly and smiled. "God gives me my skill. And it was not your time."

*

I stood outside the hospital with the support of the HoneyBull Walking Cane (freestanding and foldable). After lying for days in bed, I felt shaky. The pain pill hadn't fully taken effect. I was also sensitive to the intense afternoon sunlight. My sunglasses had been misplaced and I was squinting at the landscape, the flowers, the endless traffic, the concrete buildings, taking in the thrumming vibration of LA. I felt small and inconsequential, and very much alone. Abandoned, actually. As I looked around, a great uncertainty and a knifing anxiety overtook me. I trembled violently with the realization that I was intensely alone. I thought Syeeda and her mother would have been there to pick me up. Dr. Arif would have notified them. He was a family friend, one of the young men from the mosque. Cristo had helped pay his way through medical school. Their absence increased my anxiety and the feeling of helplessness.

The black Mercedes passenger van pulled up ominously to the curb. I was still loopy from the drugs and my injuries and misread the license plate: FATWA - CA, which resulted in an anxiety attack. My mind raced: Death had courteously come for Emily Dickinson in a carriage. Mine was a black van driven by a thug. One of Cristo's goons motioned for me to get in. No greeting, no "how are you?" I didn't want any more of their hospitality and I said, "No."

He observed me with a mixture of malice and superiority that seemed to satisfy him deeply. "You want to walk back to your place, you cripple?" I tried to think... I didn't even know where my car was. Lacking any other option, I climbed in with difficulty, maybe for the last ride, the fatwa express. There was no choice. When we got back to the Diamond Head Inn, I noticed my MG Midget parked in the lot in front of my room. I had no idea how it got there. The driver was in a hurry and gave me a bit of a rough exit out of the van. Then he shoved an envelope at me.

"Where's Syeeda, why didn't she come?" I asked. "Is she alright?" He got in and sped away, showering me with stinging crushed seashells. I got myself inside and opened a San Diego Magic and went out onto the deck. I took a long draft and sat there for a while. Finally, the beer linked up with the pain pill and gave me some relief. I opened the envelope. There were fifty one-hundred-dollar bills in there and a sticky note that said: GO HOME. DON'T COME BACK. I probably should have done that a long time ago.

The next few days were a depressing blur. I called and texted Syeeda repeatedly, despite the risk of giving my location away to any would-be assassin. But I was desperate to reach her. No answer. I couldn't imagine what had happened to her. Had she come to her senses and resumed her role as an obedient princess? Given the person she was, or I thought she was, that would have been impossible. Had she been spirited away? Perhaps she and Balqees had fled the compound and gone into hiding. I was pretty sure that Cristo would not take revenge on them. So, what was it about? I spent a few more days on pain pills and beer, ordering pizza, sitting on the deck, swaying with the ocean, and reviewing my errant life. I think I hallucinated a few times, a result of getting cracked on the head. Finally, I decided that it was time to go. It was over, way over. She didn't even dump me in person. She was just gone. There would never be another Syeeda for me. How could I have been so vain and arrogant to think that a woman like that...?

I was in less pain than when I'd returned to the motel, but I was stiff and moving slowly. I could walk, and when I realized that I wasn't limping, I smiled broadly, but no one was there to see it. I sent a silent thank you, a blessing of sorts, to Dr. Arif. He'd saved my directionless life. And my vision had cleared up as well. I knew I should be thankful, but I was crushed knowing I'd never see Syeeda again. I also knew I was in no shape to drive two thousand eight hundred miles to Jersey, or wherever I'd wind up. I could just scrap the car and fly back. But something was holding me here. I had an idea of what it was, but couldn't put words to it. I settled my bill in the office, in cash, which seemed to please Patchen. She'd just made coffee and offered me some. "Where you headed?"

"LA, on business," I lied. I didn't want to tell her I had no idea where I was going.

"I'm going to a party after work. Wanna come?"

"Thanks, but I need to get on the road."

"It's gonna be fun...lick the toad."

"I'm sorry, I don't know what that is." It didn't sound like something I wanted to do.

And I wasn't up for any new adventure that involved amphibians.

"You haven't heard of it? This shaman we know comes from the Sonoran Desert with

toad venom. He gets it off of the toad's back and reduces it to a smokable dust form. It's a powerful psychedelic—a religious trip. But you have to be careful, you can white out. The shaman guides us. It's two hundred a pop."

I tried to be enthusiastic. "Sounds great. Maybe next time I'm coming this way."

I drove north on the Five for no other reason than I'd come to La Jolla that way. I passed Solana Beach with no intention of stopping. Suddenly, a large seagull dive-bombed past my open window, made eye contact with me, and let out a dreadful prehistoric shriek that unnerved me. I thought, irrationally, it was Bart aka Tarb, stoned and transformed up in Oregon, sending me a greeting. I had been hit in the head pretty hard a couple of times by Cristo's guys.

Perhaps there was some residual confusion left over. Maybe I'd just imagined that I saw the threatening bird. I drove through Oceanside along Mission Avenue and passed Gizzard's office. It looked dark and shut down. Maybe the unpaid invoices had finally caught up with him. Or perhaps he was on location with Pretty Flemish Cat, shooting another skin flick. His deprecating nasal voice came back to me, this time as an echo: "Dude, you can't work here. You're in the wrong state, dude."

I drove past the pier and thought how delighted Syeeda had been watching the people fish. That magical day and evening we'd spent there...together. And later...in my room. I sat in the car sinking into myself, into a depressing hole I didn't think I could climb out of. Finally, a cop tapped on the door. "You OK?" I managed to nod, yes, that I was. "You're in a no parking zone—just pedestrians. You mind moving?"

"Yes, sorry." I drove up through the main shopping area and saw a sign for the Stone Brewing Tap Room on Tremont Street. I convinced myself that a beer and a pain pill might snap me out of my funk. I knew that was a lie, but went in anyway. I also knew that washing pills down with alcohol, the Hank Williams practice I'd once read about, was not the road to success. The tap room had been retrofitted from a pottery shop and was a thickly shaded oasis of huge boulders, walkways, and vegetation. Their tap beer selection was bountiful. The server was ecstatic about their product and directed me to try the Scorpion Bowl, a brisk 7.5% alcohol content IPA, because it was new and people loved it.

I took my pint to a quiet corner on the patio and sat under a palm tree. There was an ocean breeze drifting in from the shore, which enhanced the experience. I was in just enough pain to justify the medication, but it was the psychic pain bringing me down. All I could think of was Syeeda. I popped the pill and sipped. It definitely lived up to its reputation in Beer Advocate: "Hoppy forward, medium bodied, high carbonation, and reasonably boozy." Just what the doctor ordered, I told myself. When I finished the third pint, I was sufficiently numb and should have sat there for a while and sobered up. I think I had a blackout in the car because I didn't remember driving to the Mission San Luis Rey. I arrived there on automatic pilot, and there was nothing self-congratulatory about it. I could have killed someone and myself. That realization made me shudder. Was that what I was about now, self-annihilation?

I wandered around the cemetery for a while reading some of the headstones and the columbarium walls. Some were in Spanish and I couldn't decipher them. I found a bench and dozed off for a while. Just before I fell asleep, I thought, *I'm going full vagrant.* All I needed was a shopping cart. I couldn't remember the last time I had a bath or shaved. I felt a hand on my shoulder and jumped. It was one of the friars. "Are you feeling well?" he asked, kindly. "Are you hungry?" I assured him that I was all right and wandered out under the arch toward the parking lot. I noticed that the church doors were open. I went in. It was cool and smelled of incense, and maybe pine. There was a receptionist sitting at a small desk. She greeted me and asked me if I'd like to buy a candle to light. Impulsively, I bought three. I walked through the nave toward the altar and slid into a pew and stared at the giant crucifix, surrounded by figures of saints. The mission was beautiful: Revival style, stucco walls, deep windows and door openings, and red clay tile. It calmed me down a bit, but the melancholy was omnipresent. I felt the votive candles in my hands, ivory and smooth, waiting to be dedicated. I stared at them. I heard words: *What do you want with us?* I was, I think, at that moment of two minds: my standard mind—serious, misguided, easily manipulated—and the one I was rapidly going out of. The last thought I had, as I stood and bowed to the figure on the cross was, *It's time for an intervention.*

I turned in the transverse aisle and entered a side room through another arch. There was a metal votive stand with two shelves, with a locking offering box at the bottom. The stand looked like it held about eighty candles, dozens of them flickering. It had been a busy day for the faithful. Then I noticed the statue, a large life-like rendering of the Virgin placed on a pedestal against the wall, about two feet above the tiled floor. Her skin and hair were translucent in the candle light. Her dark eyes, mournful and soft, seemed to follow me as I bent to light the first candle. Not really schooled in the religion, just a fan, I made up my own prayer: "This is for Syeeda. Please, may she always be safe and happy, and free...most of all free. May she know...I loved...love her." My tears almost doused out the flame as I placed it on the shelf.

I looked at the Virgin again. I'd seen representations of her in churches in the past, but this one was remarkable for its life-like expression. Her arms were extended with her palms open. A stream of light seemed to emanate from them. "This one's for you," I said to her. "And all the mothers in the world." I lit the votive and placed it on the shelf. She tilted her head slightly and nodded, or at least I thought she did. Her arms opened wider as if she were beckoning me. I felt compelled to kneel before her, but a voice said—one of many I was hearing at that precarious moment—: *If that's not at least inappropriate, it might be considered a grave transgression*. I'd read somewhere about Marian Devotions, but I knew that mine might be more pathologically centered. I lit the last votive and placed it with the others. I said out loud, "This is for the rest of you poor bastards like me."

I took out one of Polizacio's crisp one-hundred-dollar bills and slid it into the offering box. Then I walked around the votive stand and approached her. As I did, her face transfigured slowly, the features shifting until it formed into the most beautiful face I'd ever seen—Syeeda. She whispered: "Here, I'm here."

"I thought you'd left me...I'd never see you again."

"I wouldn't do that. I couldn't come before. Now I'm free and so are you."

Slowly, I sank down on my knees and kissed her feet. They were not the hard texture of a glossy statue, but the soft living flesh of a woman, an eternal being that gave hope to my soul. The woman who'd resurrected the havoc and ruin of my broken body. That I might be made whole again.

Their hands were strong, but not forceful. They guided me away from the alcove to a private room behind the altar. The two friars stood on either side of me. They sat me in a chair and poured a glass of ice water. "Here, drink; you're not well."

"I'm sorry," I cried. I shouldn't have…"

"You caused no harm, but you need help. You're not well."

"I know…I know."

"Who is Syeeda?" one of them asked. "You kept saying her name."

"She is everything…everything to me."

"We need to take you to a hospital. Are you alright with that?"

*

The Tri-City Medical Center Inpatient Health Services in Vista was a sprawling building located between a Denny's and a huge Ford dealership. It was a pleasant enough place, for a nut house. The friars, who were beyond kind, brought me there in my own car, followed by the San Luis Rey Mission van. The intake staff greeted them warmly. Apparently, they'd dropped off other wack-os before me. I thanked the friars profusely and promised them I'd be better behaved next time I visited the mission. They blessed me and left.

The intake questions mainly centered around confirming that I was not a threat to myself or anyone else. The more they asked me, the more effort I made to convince them that I wasn't really a crazy person. I'd just fallen on some bad luck. They were also very interested in what my relationship to reality was. Did I know the difference between reality and unreality? I told them that my relationship with reality, of late, had been so real and painful, that it had broken my heart.

They were also keen to know if I wanted revenge against anyone in particular. Cristo Sid Polizacio and his thugs who beat the shit out of me came to mind. What would I do to him if I had the chance? I'd take Syeeda away and he'd never see her again. That thought caused my spirits to sink. I said that I was not up for revenge, just getting my shit together and going home.

Addiction, of course, played a big role in their line of work. They rattled off a list of drugs for me to claim a relationship with. When they got to alcohol I hesitated. I had to present something, and why lie about it. I told them that I was very fond of beer, especially microbrews like San Diego Magic, and Stone Scorpion Bowl. And how many did I drink at a time? The most I'd ever had was five, I said. That stamped me as an alcoholic. Finally, they had something concrete, or rather liquid, to classify me with. I'd be getting counseling for my alcoholism, and whatever underlying condition that caused me to act out like a Yellow-billed Loon at the mission, they said.

Other than that, they seemed satisfied with my responses and showed me to a room with a view of the parking lot. I could smell the exhaust fans from Denny's and it made me hungry. They said I would see Dr. Van Tragen, a psychiatrist, at eleven the next morning. Then they urged me to take a sedative to help me sleep. Sleep would be good. I dozed off remembering a line from a high school play I'd been in many years ago: "Sleep that knits up the raveled sleeve of care." *Macbeth*. I'd played the Servant, of course.

At our communal breakfast, featuring granola, fresh fruit, and avocados, Thirteen, formerly a member of an outlaw motorcycle club, set his tray down next to mine and smiled. The kind of manic smile that informs you that you two will be the best of friends, whether you want to or not. He was an emaciated, copiously tattooed person, shaped like a straw, bent at the top for easy sipping. And a fast talker. Dr. Luna Case Van Tragen was, he said, among other things, a highly rated women's kickboxing competitor, ranked third in the state of California. Thirteen said he was there when Van Tragen took out a two-hundred-and-fifty-pound schizophrenic from Pasadena. "You know man, like the song: 'The Little Old Lady from Pasadena.' Go granny, go. The motherfucker was raging on meth, my former muse. He threw two attendants against a foam wall and left their impressions in it. Then he ripped the reception desk out of the floor, out of the fucking floor. Motherfucker was raging! Dr. Luna took him out from behind. Didn't know what hit 'im. Then one fist to the side of his head and he was out. Cold-cocked the motherfucker. Three days of screaming his meth head off in the recovery room. It was not music."

I thanked Thirteen for the information and spooned some raisins and yogurt into my granola and stared hard into my bowl, thinking he might go away. He had an adhesive quality. "You remind me of one of the guys who rode with us, Rose, he was a Jewish guy. You Jewish? Anyway, this Rose was as gay as a tulip, or something. Let me tell you, we accepted that guy, rainbow handlebar tassels and all. If a guy rode with us, paid his dues on time, he was in. Are you gay? Because I don't care. I accept you, bro. I accept everyone. See what I mean?"

I excused myself and went back to my room with my breakfast. I sat at the window and ate. I realized that if I got close to the screen and craned my neck to the left, I could see Denny's. I was a fan of their Loaded Veggie Omelet with Hash Browns—catsup's *raison d'etre*. Syeeda and I had lunched at a Denny's one time. She'd had the Cran-Apple Chicken Salad. She was a good sport about it but insisted that a middle-eastern diet would help Americans live longer. That was the only time she said something about Americans, and she was right. Thinking of her depressed me again. The thought that I would probably have to stop thinking of her entirely, and how was I going to do that, depressed me even more.

At eleven, someone knocked on my door. She was about six feet tall, athletically proportioned, her black hair pulled back and tied off with a gold ribbon. She didn't look like she could take out a two-hundred-and-fifty-pound schizophrenic. Maybe Thirteen imagined that she had. "I'm Dr. Van Tragen." She extended her hand and I shook it. She had a vice-like grip and a warm, reassuring presence. "Mr. Zoitner, you are feeling perhaps better this morning?" I detected a German accent and hoped to God she wasn't a Freudian analyst. I said I felt much better, having decided that I'd like to get out of this place as soon as possible. "Do you have time for a little chat?" Why was she asking me that, I wondered? That's what I was there for.

I followed her down the hallway, but instead of entering her office, she brought me out to a patio behind the building away from the noise of the traffic. There was a compact refrigerator which she opened and offered me a drink. We each had an iced tea. She sat across from me and opened a file folder, no doubt my intake interview. She seemed completely at ease, comfortable with her body, almost lounging in her chair. "I see that you're a fan of the Virgin Mary." She smiled, an engaging and pleasant smile, which immediately put me at ease.

"I'm afraid I had a bit of an episode."

"Episodes are us," she chuckled. This threw me off. Why would she make light of my behavior, or rather, her job of parsing out strange behavior? "What you did," she said seriously, "doesn't matter. It's where it came from. Something unresolved, I'd guess. It usually is unless it's psychosis or schizophrenia. And you don't present as either of those. Not from your intake responses or my observation of you at this moment." She was a quick study.

"Thank you so much. I don't want to be. I just got hit in the head a little too hard. Physically and emotionally."

"So, tell me, what happened?"

"It's a long story. It started in Florida, but I think it started a long time before that by not really making the effort to know who I am."

"Most people don't know who they are. I've known perhaps six people who actually might know who they are, a few in the desert, a couple in Europe. And still, you can't be sure. You're not alone, Mr. Zoitner."

I realized that I was in the presence of a very unusual being, maybe another Toypurina, but without the smoke. I was all about reality at the moment. That's how I was going to matriculate out of there. The last thing I wanted was to be stuck as Thirteen's sidekick. I viewed Dr. Van Tragen with a bit of awe.

"Are you, doctor...do you feel that you're a realized person. I mean, do you know who you are?"

"I know my profession and I'm damn good at it. I know my physical capability. I've kicked ass on Muscle Beach a few times. I know what satisfies me. But who I am, where I came from, beyond the obvious biological and sociological facts, who knows? I like to make an analogy to canines."

"What do you mean?"

"I mean this: you go to the pound and adopt a rescue. You bring it home frightened. In a few days, he's wagging his tale, licking your face, playing outside. He adjusts. He doesn't stay up at night howling because he doesn't understand his place in the world. In short, he adjusts. People have no choice but to adjust. It is what it is, Mr. Zoitner."

I was stunned by this. She was, at least, an original thinker, perhaps brilliant, or just another quirky character I'd encountered on my wobbly sojourn through California. She was quiet for a while. She stared at me as if she was waiting for a response.

I wanted to sound smart, to make her think I understood what she was saying. But all I could come up with was: "Dogs...I think I've been too much of a puppy, and that's been part of my problem. Not growing up."

She smiled, revealing a perfect set of teeth with slightly pronounced canines. "I'd say I'm more of a Dobermann Pinscher." She waited a few moments while I digested the fact of her superiority, and wondered what brand of therapy she was practicing. "Mr. Zointer, I'm going to make short work of this. You are not crazy. You are hurt and lonely like many of our human family. You've been manipulated and abused. You've hidden from your personal power. Let me ask you this: have you ever seen something you've wanted and said to yourself, 'I'm going to have that? No matter what, I will have it.'

It was like she was telling my fortune, like she knew my secrets. "I, well, there is a woman who I would very much..."

"Then go tell her that," she interrupted forcefully.

"It's impossible, I mean she's from a royal family, she's...I almost got..."

"Find her and tell her. Do it. Break through. Reclaim yourself."

We fell silent for a while, then I began talking and she listened. Finally, she scribbled a couple of notes in my file and closed it. I'd told her everything, from my difficulties in Solana Beach living with a guy who thought he was a prehistoric monster to how I met Syeeda at the compound in La Jolla, our day trips and the intimacy that grew out of them. I didn't provide details of our joining, but just said that we were close. Or I thought we were. But I still felt that the situation was impossible.

"It always seems impossible until it's done," she said.

"I've heard that phrase before."

"Yes, Nelson Mandela. That's an example of a man who knew who he was. So much so, that he gave his life for it."

I nodded agreement. "How long will I have to stay here?"

"You can sign yourself out today if you want to."

"What about alcohol counseling?"

"Drink less." She stood up and offered me her hand. I shook it firmly. I wanted to tell her that I thought she was an extraordinary person with an amazing gift of insight. But I couldn't say it. How she'd made the whole thing like we were just friends talking. The few times I'd consulted a therapist in the past; it was nothing like this. I thanked her, and made a little bow, an obsequious habit I have. "Let me know what you decide," she said. I watched her walk back inside, a full portion of admiration lifting me up. And then the usual cloud of indecision, uncertainty, and anxiety moved back in over my head like a pending thunderstorm.

I decided to give it one more night to make sure I really wasn't crazy. If anything happened, another episode, whatever, at least I'd have support; I was still shaky. I just needed to tamp down the synapses firing off indiscriminately in my head. My plan was to leave the following morning. I'd cut my losses and start the drive back east. I'd certainly mourn the loss of Syeeda, but I couldn't ride the psychic rollercoaster any longer. California would be in the rearview mirror and I'd try to apply some of the good advice Dr. Van Tragen had dispensed. But I doubted that I'd ever know who I really was. I'd spent so many years wallowing in the unknown. Just making a living, getting by, following foolish pursuits without any real direction. What had I learned here? What was my takeaway? I'd weaved through a crowd of odd personalities, shamans, international royalty. I'd fallen in love and gotten my ass kicked. Almost been killed. And I'd leave it at that and go home, wherever that would be at this point.

That evening, the communal dining room was serving tofu cutlets, braised with ginger-scallion sauce and sweet potato fries, and the usual full salad bar. They'd installed a fresh kombucha tap, for those who could stand the vomit-like taste of it. I scanned the room to see where Thirteen was so I could avoid him. He was yucking it up loudly with some guys at a corner table. There was something up with him. He was gesticulating madly, his angular body striking acrobatic poses. He looked like he could twist himself into a pretzel. An attendant was standing nearby, keeping an eye out for trouble. I sat at the opposite end of the room near a woman with an array of evenly proportioned hair, brown at the bottom, yellow in the middle, and orange at the top, ending in the shape of a wick. It seemed designed to resemble a candle flame. She wore a tight-fitting silver lamé jumpsuit with an emblem sewn on that said, *Bike Bitch*. She said, under her breath, without lifting her eyes from her tray: "Are you the fucking man of the hour?"

I said no and tasted the tofu cutlet. I decided not to risk Thirteen spotting me going back for the ketchup. I ate quickly and reconsidered my plan to leave in the morning. I wished I'd left already. Four bites in, and he was standing at the end of the table, hovering unsteadily on his toes. Over the years, when I'd been accosted by street people, some with Tourette Syndrome, I noticed that they tended to walk on the balls of their feet, which gives the impression that they're bearing down on you. "Rose, where ya been. I missed ya." His eyes were like spin-art kids make at county fairs. They were wide and pulsating. He must have found a meth cookie jar somewhere and feasted on it. And his presence was obviously inciting the flame-headed woman. Her arms and torso were twitching. She was murmuring something that sounded like a chant.

"I'm not Rose," I said. He had me confused with his gay riding buddy.

He came closer, within striking distance. "Give it up, Rose."

"Give what up?" I said.

"You know what...the shabu, the glass, the ice, crank, chicken feed."

I wasn't steeped in drug slang vocabulary, but I assumed he was referring to meth. I repeated, quietly, "I'm not Rose."

"The fuck you ain't Rose—you pussy, kike, faggot." I got up and headed for the exit, just as my dining companion looked up from her plate and shocked me. Sometimes, when you observe a painting, like something from post WWII, you spot a face that seems entirely devoid of humanity, perhaps due to the horrors of war, a visceral reaction to what they'd seen. That was the face she presented. Before I reached the exit, I heard a scream. I looked back. *Bike Bitch* had stuck her fork in his thigh and was pummeling him violently with her dinner tray. Blood was spreading over his pant leg. The attendants rushed over and were frantically trying to separate them. When I got back to my room, I pushed the bureau in front of the door since there were no locks. I decided that I'd leave first thing in the morning—early.

I slept fitfully, but dreamed off and on. We were sitting together in the back of a limousine on our way to some glitzy event, an art opening at the Getty, a fundraiser, something. I was dressed in a tuxedo with a red gem, perhaps a garnet, in my lapel. Syeeda wore traditional clothing and exuded quintessential royal beauty. I said it was nice to have someone chauffeuring us instead of me driving her around for a change. She leaned over and kissed me. "Let's not get home too late, right?"

I kissed her. "Yes, darling, early." We seemed to be driving through LA, but then the scenery changed. The sign read: Welcome to Elite Estates. We rode through the neighborhood, staring at roof tops, chimneys, and satellite dishes peaking just above the swamp line. The whole place was submerged. Suddenly, the limo went out of control, swerving left and right, the tires spinning. The windows were dripping sludge and blackening.

The driver, one of Polizacio's thugs, called back through the intercom: "Welcome home, Zoitner." I shoved the door open as hard as I could and a rush of mud and slime filled the car instantly. Somebody screamed.

I awoke screaming. Dr. Van Tragen was shaking me. "Wake up, you're dreaming." I was panting as well, completely out of breath. I looked around the room wildly. She'd pushed open the door with such force that the bureau lay on its side with the wood split in half on top. She was wearing a running outfit and a sweatband around her forehead. "Are you alright?"

It took me a few moments. Her outfit, not clinical, was throwing me off. I was staring at her, hoping it was her and that I wasn't still dreaming. She told me that sometimes she jogged to work from her home. She asked me if I was still planning on leaving. I said I was. She asked if I witnessed the incident in the dining room. I said I had. "All right, let's have coffee before you go. I'll be in my office." I thought that was a strange invitation, but I accepted it. A send-off from her would at least be something, a marker...I didn't know what.

Her office door was slightly ajar. I knocked. "Come in." I sat down before a steaming mug of black coffee, taking in the brewed fragrance of French Roast. She'd changed into her clinical uniform. "That was maybe a significant nightmare you had. Want to talk about it?" I described it to her in detail. She thought for a few moments and changed the subject. "We had to have Thirteen hospitalized. And his ex as well."

"That was his ex, the Bike Bitch?"

"Yes, well, for a month or so. They shouldn't have been in there at the same time. Somebody screwed up and we're going to be investigated, MHL."

"What's that?"

"Mental Health Licensing, California. Worst case scenario, they can fine us. It'll probably be a fine. And they'll want someone fired, maybe me."

"But it wasn't your fault. You weren't here."

"That's not how it works. I'm the physician in charge."

"I'm sorry. If there's anything I can do, testify, whatever?"

"No, better for you to be out of here, especially now. And..." She handed me a copy of the San Diego Union-Tribune. "I don't want to complicate your departure, but there's an article in there you should probably see." She'd left it opened and folded to the page. It read: *Cristo Sid Polizacio and son Naeem, of La Jolla, in Federal Custody. Deportation anticipated. Unspecified crimes. But drugs and weapons sales suspected.* Holy shit, so that was the family business. That's how the cash was flowing in. But what about Syeeda and her mother, I wondered? Would they be implicated?

Dr. T. topped off my mug. "I felt that you should know. If you'd just left, there would be no chance of resolution."

"Resolution?" I said. "How could there possibly be resolution? This is like a tsunami."

"That would be worse. You won't know unless you call her...about resolution that is. Wouldn't it be better to know one way or the other?"

My mind was racing. I took a few moments to observe her, a really quite attractive woman, amazingly capable. I knew she could crack someone's femur bone as easily as you could snap a pencil. "Why," I asked, "are you so solicitous, so caring about me?"

"It's what I do for a living," she said breezily. She laughed: "There's something in you that you should confront. You're a much stronger person than you think you are. I encourage you to take the journey. Come into your own power and authority. It's there, you just have to open up to it. Quite likely, you're a brave person."

I was astonished. "I don't feel very brave. But I wouldn't mind a dose of power and authority."

"You don't answer it. It's not like a doorbell. It's something you just do, as you would step over a threshold. Don't mind the alligators." She stood and offered me her hand. "Forgive me but I've a mess to clean up, if it can be cleaned up."

I took her hand and returned the firmness and resolve of her grip. "I'll try...thank you."

"I've enjoyed our time together," she said.

I sat in the parking lot for maybe forty-five minutes obsessing, checking my phone. Afraid to make the call. I replayed her words: *I encourage you to take the journey. Come into your own power and authority...you're a brave person.* Brave? If I were filling out a personality survey that's not a word I would circle. But I knew if I just started for home, I'd never be able to get my tail out from between my legs. I'd just be a pathetic done-with. Another sad ghost haunting parks and super markets, and bars, probably never finding love again. She'd have to tell me; no one else could. She either wanted me or not. My hand trembling, I touched her number.

It rang once. "Where the hell have you been? Do you know what's going on?"

"What do you mean? I've been trying to reach you since I got out of the hospital. Are you alright?"

"It's chaos here. Federal agents are occupying the compound. I haven't been able to go anywhere. They've arrested my father and brother."

"I know, I saw the paper. Are you and your mother alright?"

"We can't leave. We're being held upstairs in the living quarters. They just gave me my phone back after I don't know how many days. I would have called you if I could. I don't know where my father and brother are. Naeem is not well. I don't know if he has access to a doctor."

That's why I hadn't heard from her. And why she wasn't there when I got out of Cedar- Sinai. The raid must have happened right after Cristo's guys brought me back to the Diamond Head. "What's wrong with him?"

"He has diabetes; he's on medication. He can't miss it. I'm worried sick about him."

"I didn't know. I'm so sorry."

"They've arrested the entire security staff and have taken them to FCI, Terminal Island."

"How did they do this?"

"They came in on military helicopters, smashed through the gate with, I don't know, something. They're all over the place. They have a forensic team going over the conference room."

"OK, I'm coming."

"You can't come here. They'll arrest you. You were my driver. I'm sure they're looking for you. Where are you?"

I figured they were listening to our call. "I probably shouldn't give my location." But they'd know my location from my cell. There was no getting away from these guys. It occurred to me that I should have gone on Google Maps and accessed 'Location: Allow Location Access.' I could have set it on 'Never.' Too late for that, if it would even work.

"Don't come...you should go home, it's over for us. It's over for my family." Suddenly the cell went dead. The bastards were listening—they cut her off. Or she cut me off.

It was a forty-four-minute drive from Vista to La Jolla. Not enough time to think about what I was doing. And what did I think I could do? Any vestige of the *power and authority* that Dr. Van Tragen saw in me had melted in sweat on the car seat. It was dripping down my forehead into my eyes and distorting my vision. The only thought I could formulate was that Syeeda was there, she was in trouble—and that's where I was going. I don't know how, maybe I touched the tuner inadvertently, but the radio popped on mid-song, a 70's station: "Plenty of room at the Hotel California / Any time of year / Any time of year / You can find it here." I was too far gone to appreciate the irony.

The gate was open, rather, smashed open, twisted steel rebar jutting out, jagged like a metal web. The cement lion's head bell was broken in pieces. There were two fully-equipped GI Joes on either side and guys in suits milling around the grounds. I stopped and waited. One of the suits strolled up to my window. He was rather overweight for what I imagined these athletic guys to be like. His face was red and splotchy. His dark brown eyes sank into doughy cheeks, the way raisins sink into a warm pastry. And he was panting like he'd just run a fifty-yard dash. He placed a meaty hand on my door and said, "This way, Zoitner." He took me into the two-story building of stone and glass, the small fortress where I'd seen Polizacio's security guys hanging out the first time I'd visited. Two more guys in suits with short-cropped hair and sunglasses stood on either side of the entrance. Inside, the electronics were impressive. They'd installed a communications center and a small café with an impressive cappuccino machine. It smelled like a Starbucks, but it wasn't about leisurely web surfing, lattés, and trying to look like you're writing an award-winning novel.

He led me into a small side room where a secretary sat in front of a computer. A microphone was placed on the desk. There was also a camera lens pointed at the chair where I'd be sitting. A muscular German Shepherd sat on a mat in a corner of the room; he lifted his weighty head as I approached, his eyes following my slightest movement. "I'm Agent Kates. This is Miss Blatter." I wasn't about to say, "pleased to meet you." I nodded.

Kates slid his sprawling stomach tight against the desk, which made his neck bulge, and took out a pocket recorder. Apparently, one wasn't enough. "You've been keeping some bad company, Zoitner. You should have stayed with real estate."

I still had no adequate response. I just said, "Uh huh."

Kates smiled and slid a Mont Blanc pen out of his shirt pocket. He tapped it on the desk and then pointed it at me. "Let me make an analogy. The pot is simmering with a cast of characters. It's loaded with ingredients. Which one are you?"

I stared at the guy for a few seconds, confused by his mixed metaphor, or whatever it was.

"I don't know. If I was an ingredient, I'd be like...oregano."

"I would have taken you for cinnamon," he said. Miss Blatter tittered as she typed.

I ignored the spice insult.

"Anyway, Zoitner, the pot is about to boil over and there's going to be some serious scalding, if you follow me."

"I'm not a scientist, but I get it." It was like the guy was doing standup, except he was sitting at his desk, twirling his Mont Blanc like a miniature baton.

I struggled to put something together to present, to start making a case for Syeeda and her mother, if there was even a case to be made. "Listen, whatever those guys did, Syeeda knows nothing about it. I spent a lot of time with her. She never said a word about anything, drugs, weapon sales, not a word."

"Who said anything about drugs and guns? Where'd you hear that?"

"I read it in the paper, that it might be."

"What paper?"

"The Union-Tribune."

"That's a lot of tossed salad." Another allusion to food. What was with this guy?

"Then, what is it?" I asked.

"You ever heard of Habibi Imports—PSC?"

"No, why would I?"

"PSC? Come on, you look like a bright boy, a regular cracker-jack."

"Oh, Cristo Sid Palizacio backwards." Then a light clicked on. I remembered that in every Middle Eastern café and eatery Syeeda and I stopped at, the proprietors always asked about her father, wishing him prosperity and good health. I figured that he'd frequented those places and sent them lots of business, such were his connections.

"He's the biggest importer of Middle Eastern food products to the Western states, particularly California. He has a virtual monopoly on LA. And he's made a fortune doing it. He didn't need to trade in drugs and guns. Hummus is addictive enough."

"Isn't that good news for him? There's nothing illegal about the import business."

"No, nothing, except you still have to pay your taxes. You can't hide the pita in your pocket, if you get what I mean."

"Oh, taxes...tax evasion?"

"Just like Capone, that spicy meatball. He offed all the guys he wanted to, but in the end, it was the taxes that bit him in the derriere."

I couldn't wait any longer. "I want to see her. Syeeda and her mother. I need to know they're alright. Can I see them, please?"

"You're in no position to be asking for favors."

At that moment, another suit came in and handed Kates a document. His eyes widened as he read it. Miss Blatter leaned over to get a peak, but he shielded it from her. "OK, I'm going to need a few minutes here. The fax machine started spitting out pages. I want you to escort Mr. Zoitner upstairs to the living quarters to see the princess. Stay with him at all times."

I stood and thanked him. I cast a quick glance at the document on his desk. Printed at the top of the page in bold letters, it said, Khalifa Family, Bahrain. He swiveled around and called to the dog lying on his mat in the corner: "Bieben, beachtung!" The shepherd stood immediately at attention, his head slightly cocked to the side, waiting for orders. Standing, he was a good four feet tall. His paws were the size of ciabatta rolls. "Bieben will accompany you." Then, to the suit, "Be back here in twenty-five minutes tops. The chickens just might be coming home to roost."

We walked across the wide patio toward the mansion. I noticed lights and a TV crew parked just outside of the smashed gate. Six Joes stood there blocking the entrance. The dog followed close behind me. If I'd been wearing shorts, I would have felt his breath on my legs. "Bieben, is that his name?"

"It's German."

"I figured that. Bieben, what's that mean?"

"It means bite, as in bite your ass."

It turned out Bieben didn't like elevators, an interesting reaction for an attack dog. He curled up and whimpered as we rose to the fifth floor, the residence. I tried to give him a pat to comfort him, but he snarled at me. We exited one floor above the fourth-floor conference room, where I'd first been engaged by Naeem, and later had the shit kicked out of me. We walked along a corridor where some very pricey-looking Egyptian art graced the walls, obviously Syeeda's curating. There was another Joe seated at a small desk with a notebook, keeping watch. The suit stopped and knocked softly. Balqees answered. She nodded and held the door back for him, gracious even under the current circumstances. The suit was very polite. "I apologize for disturbing you."

"Come in."

Syeeda was sitting at a desk in front of a computer. She stood and gave me the faintest of smiles, which unnerved me, then motioned for me to sit on the sofa. She addressed the suit forcefully. "Where are my father and brother? Where have you taken them?"

"I don't know. I'm not part of command or any decision making. I'm sorry." Syeeda returned to the computer and typed fiercely then signed off. She crossed the room, full of what must be a fortune in antiquities, and sat down on a Silk Abrianna Flared sofa.

Balqees assessed the situation—Syeeda and I needed to be alone to talk. "Here, you will have some tea and pastry," she offered, indicating a table by a window with curtains. Not just any curtains, but La Palais Royale Panel Pair, blue with white leaf design on the sides. The suit accepted her hospitality and sat down with her. It was easy to see where Syeeda had inherited her elegance and beauty as I watched Balqees bend the suit to her will. I approached Syeeda as she held me steadily in her gaze, which I interpreted as: *exactly what is it you think you can do about this, really?* She had told me not to come, but I had to. She looked exhausted, worn out from the assault on her family, the precarious situation her father and

brother were in. I approached her and took a seat at the opposite
end of the sofa. Bieben sat near the doorway watching me closely.
One command from the suit and he'd rip my throat out, ruining
the sofa upholstery, and the Persian Rug as well.

"Are you recovered?" she asked.

"Yes, it took a while...and there was another..." I decided to leave
out that part of my brief stay at The Tri-City Medical Center, and
my encounter with Freddy Krueger, the motorcycle gang guy. And
the insightful, kickboxing Dr. Van Tragen.

"It's good to see you," she said cordially. Her greeting felt chilling
and distant. No sign of the intimacy we'd shared, her face devoid
of any emotion. But of course, she was mainly concerned about
her father and brother. It was not the time for me to be licking
my wounds. I had an obligation to do whatever I could for her, no
matter what the outcome. Meanwhile she was scribbling on a pad.
She checked to see if the suit was engaged with Balqees. He was
laughing at one of her stories. She tore off the sheet and gave it to
me: *Do you know anything? What's happening?*

I took the pad and wrote: *something may be going down
now—Khalifa!* She scribbled something else and gave it to me: *Are
you really going back east? I didn't mean to tell you to go home.* I took
the pad and pen and wrote: *Not if you want me here.* She nodded,
"Yes."

I took the pad and was about to write *WHY ME?* in upper case
letters, but the time was up. A fast twenty-five minutes. But useful
if it gave her some hope. The suit was thanking Balqees for her
hospitality. They were about the same age and he seemed quite
taken with her. Given the nature of international intrigue, maybe,
when this episode was over, he could wind up stealing her away
from Cristo and disappearing into the Levant.

As we walked back across the grounds, I felt Bieben nose my calf,
which made me walk faster. I was briefly ecstatic. She had said yes,
she didn't want me to leave. I had to focus on: what could I do

to help Syeeda and her mother? When we entered Kates' office, he was reading through some paperwork intently. I noticed that Miss Blatter wasn't there. "How's the princess? She OK?"

"She's very worried about her father and her brother. Naeem has to have his medication for diabetes."

Kates gave me a withering look. "We're not monsters, you know. And...there might be some good news for the Polizacio clan."

He placed his Mont Blanc on top of the pile of papers. "This is privileged information. I don't know the exact extent of your involvement with the family. Maybe you're a bad apple, maybe not. Maybe you're a candy apple." His laugh was high-pitched like when you release air from a balloon pulling the sides apart so it squeaks.

"I was just Syeeda's driver. Naeem hired me so she could get out of this place for some day trips. She wouldn't ride in the limos with his guys."

"And in the course of your chauffeuring her...you became...attached. Is that right?"

Before I could stop myself, I said, "That's none of your fucking business."

"Yes, attached," he mused. "And that may have come back to haunt you in a mortal way, if you follow me.

That sounded ominous. "What do you mean?"

"I'll get to that." He drummed on the pile of papers with his Mont Blanc. "Have you ever heard of the Khalifa family, or rather I should say cartel?"

He was obviously setting a trap for me. How could he not know that I was at the fateful meeting when Syeeda refused Khalifa's marriage proposal, he and his crowd with their military vehicles. There was no way out of this one. I just said, "Yes, I've heard of them." I hoped he'd leave it at that.

He gave me a gotcha look and asked: "Have you ever been in the same room with him, the prince?"

Checkmate, I cleared my throat, "Yes."

"Good choice, you didn't lie. Have you ever heard of SolarWinds or FireEye?"

"I don't think so. Should I?"

Russia used it, SolarWinds, to hack Microsoft. As well as the Treasury and Commerce Departments. And Equifax, the credit company."

"What's this have to do with me?'

"Ostensibly, nada, but Prince Khalifa had a bone to pick with the princess, Cristo, his son, and...you, if you follow me? She rejected his proposal. Sent a third of the Middle East into a tizzy. The figs were dropping dead off the trees."

Then I remembered Khalifa's threat and repeated it to Kates. "He threatened all of us. He said, *You will remember this day with sorrow. You will pay for this, all of you.*"

"That's very helpful, significant. It adds up, tops off the scenario.

"Good, but where's all this going?"

"Let me give you an analogy. Both families are important—world players. But compared to the Khalifa clan, the Polizacios are small potatoes. The Khalifas got their fingers in more pies than you can count. And our pal, Prince Wahid Al Khalifa, has friends in high and low places, and a special relationship with the Russians. In particular, Russian hackers, the cream of the crop."

"And the point is?"

"The point is, the Prince had his Russian hacker friends hack into the IRS files and do a number on Polizacio's taxes. They made it look like he'd been scamming on his taxes for years. How, the IRS people wondered, had they missed it? Because these guys are so good at it: malign code, supply chain attack, moonlight maze, Titan Rain, you name it, the whole enchilada. They're flawless. It's like they replace reality with a more convincing reality."

"OK, if I got this right, Polizacio and son are off the hook, or will be. But why did he have a small army here at the compound if everything was on the up and up?"

"Two reasons: we live in a dangerous world; you might have noticed. If you have a lot of eggs in your basket, someone might want to take some of them from you, Easter or not. You saw the art up there in the mansion. Reason number two, he's a paranoid whack job. He's got more security around this place than the treasury, almost anyway. Plus, it can be a nice tax write-off. Ha-ha."

"OK, so after the father and son are released, what about me?"

"That, my friend, is not so simple. The prince is not a very forgiving guy. This is confidential: after the fact, when they got home, he had one of his ministers executed for blowing the marriage deal. He blamed the minister for it. Can you believe that?"

"What the fuck?"

"He threatened to get even with Polizacio, Naeem, and anyone else involved who contributed to his unhappiness, as he saw it. Unfortunately, he zeroed in on you, the driver and whatever else you may have been to her, if you get what I'm saying."

"How could he possibly know about...us? And it's none of his fucking business."

"How could he know? I just gave you a list of the technology these guys use. Forget your cell phone. You make calls with it, but it's a tracking device. And didn't Cristo have a security detail following you two around? "

"Yeah, those guys. And I did turn off Google Maps. Look, what's the bottom line; am I in trouble?"

"You're not a tech guy, are you? You turned off Google maps. Great, you don't know where you're going. Every cell tower out there picks up your phone, Google Maps or not. You're tracked by the signal connections. The whole world knows where you are. Personally, I couldn't do without Doordash." He thought that was very funny. He got quiet for a few seconds and looked down at his desk. "Well, the bottom line is, and this is a bit sticky— he put a *fatwa* out on you."

"What the hell is that?"

"You know like...you ever watch The Sopranos?"

"I don't watch much TV."

"Well, a fatwa is like a hit, when they put a contract out on someone...to take them out."

"How could he do that? He's like eight thousand miles from here."

"First of all, don't relocate to Bahrain. But there are airplanes, and people travel."

"You mean someone would come that far just to kill me?"

"Not all Bahraini people live in Bahrain. And...there's some chatter we've been monitoring since this came in."

"What chatter? What are you talking about?"

"We're constantly monitoring the web, specific sites, cell phones, you know. There was something about a possible acolyte coming this way from Phoenix."

"What for? To kill me? Is that what you're saying?"

At that moment, Miss Blatter returned with two big Burger King bags. Agent Kates looked pleased, almost gleeful. "Finally, supper."

I yelled at him. "Are you saying that some fanatic is on his way from Phoenix to kill me?"

"Don't worry, if Mr. Phoenix is on his way, he won't make it across the border into California. We'll track him."

"So that's it?" I said. "What's my government going to do for me? Am I going to get any help, protection?"

He pulled his Whopper out of the bag and unwrapped it with child-like anticipation as if it was a Christmas present. "Well, we could look into the witness protection program."

"Fuck that. Look, can I leave? You need anything else from me?"

He paused for a moment, a thin line of catsup and beef juice dripping down the side of his mouth. "Actually, we don't. You're free to go. We'll find you if we need to. Anyone can be found these days. And, I'd keep a low profile if I was you." He swallowed his mouthful with a sip of soda. "But you shouldn't worry too much. There's bound to be another incident, some international catastrophe out there soon enough to take Khalifa's mind off of things. I see this stuff all the time. And really, taking you out would be like swatting a fly when there's so many others at the picnic, if you follow me."

"*Bon appetit,*" I said, slamming the door with a definitive bang. Biebin clawed at the door behind me and barked ferociously in retaliation. I ran to my car and jumped in and headed for the gate, but it felt like it hesitated shifting into second gear. The news crew had been cleared out, but the Joes still blocked the exit. One stood directly in front of me, his legs spread apart, boots planted firmly on the ground, and pointed his handgun at the windshield. In my frantic fatwa hysteria, I thought, irrationally, that he was the guy, come from Phoenix, disguised as one of the soldiers, to execute me. Another one of them called out. "Where do you think you're going?" They made a quick call to Kates, and then waved me off. "He's good to go." I had only one motive, and that was to lead any would-be assassin as far away from Syeeda and her mother as I could. If that would be my last mortal act of unselfishness on earth, then so be it.

Lacking a cogent plan, as usual, I drove back up the Five because I didn't know where else to go. Meanwhile, my MG Midget engine was starting to sound like a meat grinder. I had 136,000 miles on the odometer and the car was supposed to be good for about 140,000 miles, tops. And repairs, just to keep it going, would be excessive. What was I thinking? The car probably wouldn't have made it back to the east coast anyway. I tried not to listen to the engine devouring itself. It gave me a sinking feeling.

Syeeda called. "Where are you?"

"I just left, heading back up the Five."

"Why? What happened?"

I outlined the information I'd learned from Kates. I told her everything, how Khalifa had set her father up with the IRS, all of his cyber witchcraft. That I'd also reported the threat the Prince had made against us. And that it looked like her father and brother were off the hook and should be home soon.

"Then they're going to be released?" she asked hopefully.

"Well, yes, it'll probably take a few days, maybe a week at the most. You know, bureaucracy. It'll have to go through their headquarters in DC, whoever the hell these guys are."

"Where are you going now?"

"Back up to Carlsbad. I need money...and my car is dying."

"We have cars, lots of cars."

"Those are your cars, not mine." I choked, but made myself say it anyway. "Syeeda, I can't have you taking care of me."

There was a very long pause, in which my hands sweated so much they almost slipped off the steering wheel. "I respect your self-sufficiency, but you don't want to see me?"

"Of course I want to see you. I want nothing more than that. But you can't pay for me."

"Do you know how much you saved him in legal fees? It would have been drawn out and cost thousands of dollars with the lawyers. And if it went bad and they had been deported it would have cost even more. It can be dangerous over there as well. He has enemies. He wouldn't want the publicity. He'll be grateful to you. He owes you and I'm going to make sure he pays up."

"Your father? I remember his gratitude whenever my thigh aches."

"Who do you think I'm talking about? And my brother. He has his own doctor here to manage his diabetes. His sugar count fluctuates." Then she got angry. "What's going on? This doesn't sound like you."

There was no way around it. I had to tell her. I couldn't have her thinking I didn't want to see her, though I had no idea how we could have an actual relationship under the glaring public light of a royal family. "He put a fatwa out on me. I can't risk being there with you and Balqees if some fanatic shows up to kill me. Kates said there's been chatter."

"Khalifa did that? The bastard."

"I don't know how real it is, but I can't take a chance with you and your mother. I shouldn't even be using my cell. They can track me. I didn't know that."

"What are you going to do?"

"I've been advised to lay low for a while. Wait until the next Middle East crisis happens. I don't know."

"I'm going to make some calls."

"What do you mean?"

"Don't ask."

"We just got your father and brother out of a situation. Let's leave well enough alone."

"My mother wants to tell you something."

"Mr. Zoitner, you are a better man than he is, that dictator. His nobility is false. It is bought and paid for. Yours is genuine. I will remember your act of bravery."

I said goodbye to Syeeda. "Maybe you should put the security guys on increased alert, just in case. I'll call you."

"Let me know where you are."

"I will if I can."

*

I passed the Pizza Port in Carlsbad, but I couldn't bring myself to go in and ask Drayko for my job back. Also, I thought I should find work somewhere else as part of my "lying low" plan. I continued into Oceanside and stopped in front of the Sleepy Seagull Motel.

I could afford it for at least a few nights while I figured out a more long-term strategy. Someone behind me was flashing their lights at me as if I was in the way. I didn't know what their problem was; I was parked by the curb. Finally, she got out of her car and came up to my window. "How have you been, Mr. Crow?" It was Toypurina.

"I didn't think I'd see you again," I said, not meaning to be rude.

"The turtle and the crow cross paths many times in a lifetime. Are you still in Oceanside?"

I assumed her totem was the turtle. The last thing I felt like was a crow, maybe the Scarecrow. "I've been back a few times. I...it's a long story."

"Why are you parked in front of the motel?"

"Checking in for the night."

"You're welcome in my home. Some people complain of bed-bugs at this place."

"Really? I didn't know. I don't want to impose."

"There is much room. Saradonna has moved to Oregon to join Bart. She, for all her fierceness, is a mouse. She will mature slowly."

We passed the Mission San Luis Rey on the way up to her bungalow, which caused a range of emotions in me, mostly anxiety. I still didn't trust myself completely after my bizarre episode there. I was determined to maintain my stability. Also, I had to be on the lookout for strangers bearing fatwas. It pissed me off that after all was said and done, I was the person they wanted to take out. I parked my dying MG next to Toypurina's dusty gray Jeep and went in.

The place had changed. All the furniture, including the pump organ in the front room was gone. But the dream catchers remained, and there was a collection of stone and shell tools, pottery, basketry, jewelry, and beadwork. There was also a medium-sized reed canoe where the blue sofa had been. "You've decided to make a museum here?" I asked.

"It's for a departure—all that is required."

I thought that sounded dark. Was she planning her own funeral?

"Are you hungry?"

I followed her into the kitchen where spooned out two large helpings of acorn soup. It was mushy and cold, which surprised me. She set a bottle of chianti on the table; the Italian kind that comes wrapped in a tight straw basket. "Do you like wine?" I thanked her and didn't mention that I like wine only in the absence of beer. She poured out two generous portions. The cold soup was delicious. She explained that it was a Tongvan recipe, her native tribe. She had made cornbread to dip in it as well. I glanced at her as we ate. A slender woman the first time I'd seen her, she might have lost some weight. She did look somewhat haggard; fatigue had set in upon her. Yet she was also centered and strong. I asked her if she was feeling well. She suggested we take our wine out to the patio.

It was almost dark, and there was a steady fog moving in from the ocean, causing the surroundings to glow eerily. From our perch above I could make out the bell tower at the mission below. The moment I looked at it the bells tolled—sustained, somber tones, the pitches combining to call forth the faithful. It was a soothing sound. "What do you hear?" she asked. I explained how the music of the bells was uplifting, yet, there was a feeling of sadness.

"I hear the screaming of my people, the domination, whippings, the soldiers raping our women, the destruction of our land and culture. I hear the words, the prayers, they forced into our mouths and made us recite. Not *our* words or prayers."

"Yes, of course, I know...I'm sorry."

She looked closely at me for a few moments. "You are perhaps more of a warrior than the last time we sat together."

"I've suffered, I guess. But I may have had it coming."

"You didn't," she said quietly. "Do you know who I am?"

"Toypurina."

"I am the descendant of Toypurina. I carry her name with honor. She was known as California's Joan of Arc. She was a medicine woman whose magic could overcome padres and soldiers. She led her people in the rebellion of Mission San Carlos Borromeo in Carmel. But the Spaniards got news of the attack and our people were defeated. Toypurina was exiled. She died on May 22, 1799. It is now only the beginning of April, but soon, I will cross the Owl's Bridge and join her and the others of my tribe who perished at the hands of the Spaniards."

"Are you...sick?" I asked.

"Only my body is, with one of the diseases the Europeans brought to us—their gift to indigenous people. That and slavery." She took a few moments to fill a long pipe with beads and feathers fastened to it. She lit it and inhaled, then held it out to me.

"I don't really..."

"When our elders would die, the padres forbade us to return to our villages and dance for our dead and smoke the pipe. You won't deny me the pipe, please."

I took it in my hands, felt the smoothness of the carved cherry wood, the warmth of the glowing bowl, and then I took a long pull from it and inhaled deeply, as I began to realize that I was in the presence of someone who knew, in truth, who they were; the rare meeting of a person with self-knowledge. The kind of entity that Dr. Van Tragen had spoken of to me. "But are you...who will help you...when...it's time?"

"My people will come. They will know. Everything is in place."

"What can I do for you?"

"You have eaten my food and listened to my story. You have smoked the pipe with me."

She stood and stretched her arms out as she had the last time when Saradonna was still there. She moved slowly and rhythmically, to the left and then to the right. She lifted her feet and patted her moccasins on the stone patio. I followed her, clumsily, but did my best to imitate her movements. Again, she faced the four directions. I followed. When she stopped, I stopped. Something caught my eye. Standing just off to the right were two Tongvan people, a man and a woman, dressed as their totems, a fox and a hawk. Their eyes glistened in the dark; their copper skin, translucent. They began to rise into the air slowly until they were engulfed in the fog that was dropping down thicker now, a cool, damp spray falling upon us. I heard her singing, but I couldn't see her. Staring into the fog it was as if I were looking through one of those ViewMaster toys I had as a child. Suddenly, it was in my hands with a reel in it. I slid from picture to picture. I saw Toypurina's village, the woman cooking and caring for infants. The reel changed by itself from scene to scene. There were the men, preparing to hunt in their ceremonial clothes. Then the Spaniards intruding upon them with their frightening muskets. The people being led away in yokes like oxen. The last one I saw was of two women, a bursting blue sky behind them as if they were no longer earthbound, but beyond gravity, eagles and doves circling around them. Their arms entwined, they held hands and gazed out peacefully. Two sisters, Toypurina and Syeeda. I heard words: *There is no separation. In nature we are fixed between the earth and the sky. We leave and we return. As spring returns from winter. As dawn is born from night. There is no death.*

I awoke with a start; there was a thumping or vibration on my chest. I slapped my palm over the movement thinking I was having a heart attack. It was my phone. I was in a room with nothing in it but a bed and a window shaded by an ornamental vine growing around it. I sat up and checked my left arm for pain. The phone slid down my shirt. "Hello." Ironically, it was a robocall offering to extend the warranty on my vehicle. I got up and realized I must have fallen asleep in Saradonna's room. The telltale aroma of rosemary massage oil gave it away. I smelled coffee and found a pot in the kitchen, still warm. I took some and sat down at the table. I was grateful that the tobacco, and whatever else might have been in it, did not result in a bad trip this time. It was quite emotional, but not frightening. More like something I was supposed to see and take in. I thought it might be what the native Americans called a vision quest.

I noticed an envelope fastened to the refrigerator with a sunburst magnet. I took it out to the patio. Her printing was small and neat: *Robin Crow Man is the name I give you. If you should ever encounter Tongvan people you will give that name. They will understand. I have gone to San Fernando to meet my cousin Nicolas. He and his wife and nine children live in one of the poor communities my people have settled in. He is the director of the food giveaway program and after-school childcare at the Pukúu Cultural Community Services center. His wife had made me a sterling silver ring with inlaid garnets and amethysts. I have collected canned and dried foods to bring to him and the community. No one takes everything for himself. It is always shared. I stayed awake last night and meditated. What you saw in the fog was there for you to see. You have learned much. You are welcome to stay at my home as you like. But there is more for you to do further south. Go with an open heart. Believe in the strength you've earned. Believe what you saw and experienced. It is different now. Remember me, —Toypurina.*

I placed the page on the warming stone and put some pebbles on it, as it was wet with my tears and I intended to keep it with me always. I went back to the kitchen and heated the coffee. I would drink all of it that was left, what she'd left me. Then I would leave. She was right; it was time for me to go. I returned to the patio and the page was gone. There was no breeze, just the warming morning sun. The pebbles sat in a small pile, as if they'd been arranged that way. I looked in the bushes and the perimeter. Nothing. It was gone. An image of the Cowardly Lion came to me. He didn't need the unknown liquid the wizard gave him to drink to find courage. I finished the coffee, looked up into the sky to see if perhaps the page was gliding in the air. I set the lock on her door and went to my car. In the cup holder was a large pale-yellow lemon. I remembered the last time I'd left Toypurina's house, I'd picked a lemon from her tree and palmed it to steady my nerves. I also remembered that she was not there that morning and couldn't have seen me pick the lemon from the tree. Yet, here was a lemon, another gift of unknown origin. And I laughed when I thought about my car. It was turning out to be a lemon. But it wouldn't be funny when I'd find myself walking along the shoulder of the freeway.

As I drove by the Pizza Port, the aggressive stench of the restrooms came back viscerally to me. I covered my nose and mouth with my hand. I couldn't do it. Drayko had treated me decently, but the bathrooms hadn't. Of course, I never would have met Syeeda if I hadn't found Cristo's wallet next to a commode. And why was it there in the first place? How did it get there? Was it really his wallet? Was it planted there to lure some unfortunate fool into their web? I sensed that my thinking had started to take a turn away from Western reality to Eastern mysticism, the reality of the *other*. By chance I was driving by the Self-Realization Fellowship in Encinitas while I was having this mini-satori, and then it happened. The engine light came on and my car lurched forward. The tires squealed, there was a loud mechanical stuttering noise, and then it sputtered to a stop. Plumes of smoke engulfed the hood and blocked the windshield. I got out and started pushing it. A teenager skateboarded up to me and offered to help push the car to the side of the iconic 101, if I'd lend him ten dollars. We got it off the road and he rolled off with a more reliable vehicle than mine. Why had I waited? What did I think was going to happen?

I leaned against the door and looked out over the ornamental gardens of the Fellowship property, out to the vast expanse of the sea. The Golden Lotus Temple shimmered in the sunlight. It was truly a magical place of intense beauty. Who wouldn't want to live out here, despite the real estate prices, utilities, gas, and groceries?

I kind of tranced out staring at the horizon. For some reason, probably because of Toiporina, I thought about the indigenous people who lived peacefully along this shore before the European conquerors came to claim it for themselves in the name of God.

"Is this your car?" An imposing looking woman in a denim work-shirt stood a few feet away. Bright orange logos stitched on the shirt pockets read Gal's Towing on one side, and Val on the other.

"How'd you know I needed towing?"

"There's smoke pouring out of the hood."

"Yeah, I think it died."

"Want me to take a look?"

I nodded. She put some work gloves on and popped the hood. A plume of toxic smelling smoke shot up, causing her to step back. Then she looked in. "Oh, man. Not good. The engine is like melted. All the parts are stuck together, the belts, the radiator, it's like in one piece, a sculpture or something. Sorry." I looked; the engine had turned into modern art. "I can tow it for scrap. No charge. But I get the scrap money—not that much. OK with you?" I agreed, and watched her attach the chain under the front bumper and haul it up onto the flatbed. A few minutes later she handed me the license plates and reminded me to cancel the insurance policy which I wouldn't need anymore. "At least you won't have to reregister it again," she said. I shoved the plates into my backpack and thanked her. "It's a bummer, man, no wheels. Whattaya gonna do?"

"I'm going to walk," I said, mindlessly.

"Where to?"

"I don't know. I think maybe it's just time for me to walk."

"Have you been spending time in that place?" She jabbed her thumb at the Fellowship temple. "They got some real nutjobs in there, let me tell you."

"No, I just broke down in front of it."

"Well," and I could see she wasn't sure she wanted to offer but she did, "you need a ride somewhere? Where do you live?"

"I was living in Florida, but I'm from Jersey, one of the shore towns."

Her face lit up. "The shore, no shit, I'm from Spring Lake. Moved out here when I was twenty."

"I've been here..." I went blank. It seemed like a lifetime, but it couldn't have been more than six or seven months.

"Well, do you need a lift?"

At that moment her question carried all the weight of a Japanese Koan. "I don't really have any place to go to at the moment."

"Oh, I see. You're between homes. There's a men's shelter here in town I could take you to. I know guys who've stayed there. It's alright."

So, it's come to this, I thought. A homeless shelter—pathetic. Was I pathetic? "Do I seem pathetic to you?" I asked.

"Look, I'm just trying to help out. I don't have all day."

"I'm sorry, you've been very kind, but I don't need a ride, thank you."

She got exasperated. "Well, what are you going to do?"

"I'm going to wait until it's safe to see the Princess."

Her expression changed to one of pity, acknowledging that I was a head case. "Oh, I see," she said, backing away. "Well, good luck with that." She hopped into the truck and was gone with my oldest friend, my forest green MG Midget. As her truck disappeared in traffic, I realized that I had forgotten to grab Toypurina's lemon from the cup holder. It was a gift; I wanted to keep it. Then, a strange thought: *I am a man without a compass, much less a ballast. And which one would be more useful?*

I don't know how far or how long I walked. It might have been a couple hours. I followed the path above the beach. There was no humidity, but the sun was hot. I stopped at a food truck and got a bottle of water. I kept walking. The beach, like an endless moonscape, was on my right, packed with surfers, sun worshipers, volleyball teams, kite fliers, gymnasts, treasure hunters, dogs and walkers. I saw them in passing as I ran a rough-cut film through my head of my experiences since I'd arrived. I walked into the next town and was surprised, jarred actually, to see the sign: Welcome to Solana Beach. Well...I'd come full circle. Back in Solana Beach. Now what? On a side street next to a florist, I found a small park with a lot of shaded vegetation. I sat down on a bench to cool off. My cell rang; it was Syeeda. "Are you alright?"

"I think so. How are you?"

"Relieved; my father and Naeem are home. The IRS backed off. No prosecution. Kates wasn't lying."

"That's good news. I'm happy for you."

"What's going on? You sound strange."

"My car died, and I just took a long walk. I'm tired."

"Where are you? We can pick you up. My father wants to apologize to you, in person."

I thought a moment and answered quickly. "I don't want to see your father. I accept his apology, but I won't in person."

There was a long pause. "I see. I understand how you feel. It's difficult."

"Yes, it feels that way."

"I have other news that might be more to your liking," she said. "Do you remember my friend, Marosh, at the Getty? She's off to Iraq for three months to help classify some new discoveries. It's an exciting find. She's invited me to fill in for her at the Getty. The board has approved it. I'll be staying at her apartment in the neighborhood, Westwood Village. There's plenty of room," she added quietly.

"That's great. You deserve it."

"That's all? You don't sound enthusiastic. What is it?"

"It's just that I don't know what I would do there. I'd be walking around the neighborhood, doing I'm not sure what."

"You'd be with me." Her tone was slightly angry. "Isn't that what you wanted?"

"Of course, yes. I'm sorry. I've been through something. It's been...a lot. The fatwa and everything."

"Oh, the fake fatwa," she laughed. "Kates told me before he left the compound, that their intel found out that Khalifa had neglected to consult the palace mufti, who happened to be in Paris at the time getting his prostate biopsy. There was never a legitimate fatwa."

"The bastard. I thought I was going to buy it. Jesus Christ, why didn't you tell me?"

"Well, where the hell have you been? Why didn't you call? Are we still...or what?

"I was afraid they'd come after you and your mother. I was...trying to protect you. What the hell? You've got a squad looking out for you. I've got..."

"Nothing? Really?" Her voice softened. "Look, I'll be moving into her apartment on Tuesday. Can you meet me there? I'll text you the address." She added, "I'll explain to my father. He'll have to understand. Tuesday?"

"Yes." I looked around and assessed my situation. It was Sunday. I had two days to go and would need a place to stay. I had checked my wallet a few hours earlier and was alarmed at the lack of money in it. I still had a hundred and seventy-five dollars. I could find a cheap room with a shower for two nights, I hoped. But there was nothing to be had for less than seventy-five dollars per night. If I did two nights, I wouldn't have enough for a ticket on the Amtrak Surfliner to LA. I made a strategic decision. I decided that I'd sleep one night on the beach. How bad could it be? I went to the Dollar Store and bought two lightweight flannel blankets. One to lie on the sand, the other to cover myself with. I'd use my backpack for a pillow. I could be a beach bum for one night. Around seven thirty the sky started to darken, and some clouds rolled in. I didn't worry about it because it hardly ever rains here.

I was starting to feel vague and realized I'd hadn't eaten all day. I did a phone search and located Tito's Timely Tacos. It was nearby and delicious. I got the Three Amigos Taco Special and a can of Sculpin IPA, which featured a mean-looking determined fish with poisonous spikes on the label. I found out later that the Sculpin is also called a sea scorpion and can give a nasty sting. I bought a few extra cans and put them in my backpack for later. I figured they'd make a good nightcap before my beach sleep. I decided that I wouldn't go down to the shore until at least eleven. I wasn't completely comfortable with the idea now that the time was getting closer. I also didn't want the cops to find me there. I knew it was illegal. An arrest could postpone my arrival in LA.

I accessed the beach at Fletcher Cove. It was deserted when I got there. I looked around and found a pile of planks with some pieces of twisted metal that might have washed in off a wrecked boat. I set up next to it so I'd at least be hidden on the entrance side. I spread out the blanket and sat down. The clouds had dissipated, leaving a brilliant sky thrumming with stars. The full moon was bright enough for me to read the ingredients off of the beer can I'd popped open. All in all, I was pretty comfortable. The waves rolled in rhythmically, then sluiced back in with a pleasant sizzling melody. Faintly, just above the waves, I heard mockingbirds chirping. I covered myself with the other blanket and rested my head on my backpack and let the elements lull me to sleep.

I dreamed that I was swimming. I was moving quickly through the water, as if I was being assisted with battery powered swim fins. It felt effortless and refreshing. The salt water was like a balm cleansing my body. I was releasing all of the stress and anxiety I'd carried with me for so long. I sensed that something was swimming along beside me, a friendly porpoise perhaps. As I continued, the surroundings became darker and the current was slowing me down. The texture of the water changed and felt slimy. Suddenly, I was swimming in mud and losing buoyancy; I was being pulled down with a force I couldn't resist. The creature swimming beside me darted ahead and whipped around and presented a horrific face. It was a huge Sculpin, maybe six feet long. It spoke: "Last stop in Elite Estates, Zoitner." Then everything went black.

I woke up screaming. A dense fog had rolled in overnight and I was barely able to see in front of me. A slight gleam shone through the fog. It might have been daybreak. I grabbed my backpack and the blankets and started walking, trying to locate the path back to the street. Suddenly, I was standing in water and realized I was walking toward the ocean. I turned and hurried back the way I'd come, or thought I had. My shin banged into one of the planks in the pile I'd slept next to. And then, excruciating pain. I had stepped on something sharp, a shard of metal or a nail. I felt it penetrate. I fell on the sand and grasped my foot with my hands. They were sticky with blood. I couldn't find anything to pull out. Where was it? I didn't know how deep the wound was, but the pain was intense. I tore the sheet in half, and kept tearing it until I had a strip that I could tie around my foot. Once I secured it, I struggled to get up and made my way toward a dim street light that would lead to the path. The effort to walk on the wound was unbearable; I was hobbled. The faint light fractured into rays and geometric shapes. It was like I was trapped in a maze of lines and blocks of pearlescent light caused by the fog. My anxiety accelerated to code red. When I finally located the walkway, I half-dragged myself up using the handrail. I could feel the blood soaking through the strip of flannel. I thought I might pass out from the pain. It was a bad wound.

When I made it back to the street, I collapsed on a bench. I could see a glimmer—the sun lifting to begin its trek above the ocean. Shortly after, it was more visible, but the fog still lingered. There was not much traffic and I didn't see any taxis. I needed a doctor. I checked my cell; there was an emergency care walk-in clinic about six blocks away. I didn't think I could make it that far. I called them. It rang for a long time. I figured they weren't open yet. The answering service picked up. I explained my situation. They told me to hold on. I waited; my foot was throbbing. They got back on and took down my location. It turned out one of the doctors was on her way in to work and could pick me up. "You'd do that?" I asked surprised.

"Not usually, but she's coming that way and said she would. Are you high? On any drugs?"

"No, absolutely not. Thank you so much."

About ten minutes later a silver Porsche Cayenne pulled up to the curb. She wore a laboratory coat and silver slacks, and what looked like Prada high heels, also silver, to match the car, I thought. A stethoscope was draped around her neck. "I'm Dr. Esmerelda Cruz Ruiz. Who are you?"

I wasn't prepared for such a formal introduction. I paused for a moment. I almost said, "I'm Robin Crow Man." *What was that about?* "I'm Zoitner," I said.

What's the extent of your injury?"

"I stepped on a piece of metal, a nail or something on the beach."

She slipped on some surgical gloves, unwrapped my foot, and chucked the strip of flannel into the trash. She took a close look, then wrapped the rest of the blanket around the wound and helped get me into her car. I noticed that there was a large gold cross hanging from her rearview mirror. She saw me looking at it and swatted it so it swung back and forth tapping the windshield. "I'm a Charismatic Christian, you got a problem with that? Otherwise, I wouldn't have picked you up. I'm your miracle today. So, be thankful, and don't you dare bleed in my new car," she said. I couldn't tell if she was joking.

"How bad is it?"

"I think there's a piece of metal in there that's going to have to come out. It'll have to be thoroughly sterilized. You don't want to lose your foot, right? Do you have any kind of health insurance?" She laughed, "Why am I asking? And when's the last time you took a shower?"

"I used to have complete coverage when I was in Florida, everything, even dental. To answer your other question, I'm checking into a room today that has a shower."

Obviously, she thought I was a vagrant, a certified street person, what the cops referred to as a skell. And, as I thought about it, I was. I'd finally graduated. How easy it is to slip into an alternate sociological category and then be categorized as that individual. All it takes is a couple of downturns, a little misfortune, your car dying, being the target of a fatwa, being out of work. And with the wound on my foot, I might even be losing mobility for a while. Despite all of that I knew I didn't have a right to feel sorry for myself.

The clinic, Solana Emergency Care Walk-in, was in a strip mall. Dr. Ruiz and Nurse Cleo helped me in and up onto an exam table. The pain in my foot was shooting up to my thigh and my leg felt hot. Nurse Cleo began placing surgical supplies on a cart next to me. Ruiz focused a light on my foot and spread the wound open with her thumbs, which sent a lightning bolt through my leg. "OK, definitely a piece of metal in there. We're going fishing. Listen up, I'm going to give you two injections of Dilaudid and it's going to hurt like hell. No way around it. After it takes effect, you won't feel a thing, but you'll be numb up to your knee for about two and half hours."

Nurse Cleo prepared the injections and handed the first to Ruiz. Then she leaned over my torso with her full weight, which was considerable. I screamed and bucked up so hard I lifted Cleo up with my chest and the needle went in further. It took all of the nurse's strength to hold me down. Ruiz decided to wait a few minutes to give the second shot. It wasn't much better than the first. Ten minutes later I couldn't feel anything. Nurse Cleo doused my foot with iodine or some antiseptic, then handed Ruiz a forceps. She quickly removed half of a thick, broken ring shank nail, the kind used in boat construction. She dropped it into a tray and showed it to me. It had a jagged edge and was thicker than a standard carpentry nail. "You're lucky, just a minor crucifixion. Imagine what the real thing was like. I'm going to give you an injection in your arm, a very strong antibiotic. I'm prescribing antibiotic tablets and painkillers. You're going to need them. Take them like your life depends on it. *Comprendo*?"

I swore I'd follow her directions. I wasn't about to sustain any more losses, physical or mental. But I had no idea how I was going to walk out of there. In fact, I wasn't, not just yet. They moved me into a side room and laid me down on a cot. I explained again that I intended to rent a room for the night and was going to LA in the morning. She looked at my foot. It was already bleeding through the bandage, despite the stitches. She told Nurse Cleo to change the dressing. "I doubt you're going to LA tomorrow unless it's in a cab. You won't be walking on that foot for at least two days so it can start to heal. And praise God that you'll even be able to walk."

They left me in a side room with water, pain relievers, a banana and some oranges. Dr. Ruiz returned at 4:30, closing time. "How are you doing?"

"All right, I guess. A little groggy. My foot is still numb. I suppose you want me out of here."

"That is a bit of an issue. Our lease doesn't allow overnights. Where is the room you're renting?"

"It's at the Roost on Barbara Avenue. It's an SRO. I didn't make a reservation. I should have."

"Always good to plan ahead, right? OK, let's go. I'll drop you there on my way to the gym."

Nurse Cleo brought in a pair of crutches and adjusted them to my height. "Try to only put minimal weight on your foot."

Ruiz tossed her keys up in the air and caught them with her other hand behind her back. "Let's go, I've got a personal trainer waiting for me."

It was a short drive over to Barbara Street. I didn't need to get out of the car. The place was boarded up and the sign was legible from the car: Board of Health, etc.

"OK, change of plans," she said.

"This is too much; it's not fair. I'll just get out here."

"And do what? The next twenty-four-plus hours are crucial. You have to take care of that foot. Really, you could wind up losing it if it gets infected. I should look at it before you leave for LA. OK, here's the plan. I don't want to miss my gym time. There's a café there, you can wait for me, only an hour. They have a killer latte. I have an Airbnb on my property. You can stay there tonight. I'll take you to the clinic in the morning, check out your foot, put on a new dressing, then you can think about LA., if you feel well enough to go. I advise you to take it easy."

"Why are you doing this for me? You don't even know me."

"I told you, I'm a Christian. Real Christians perform acts of kindness in their daily lives. Christians are Us." She released a manic laugh. "You came to me for a reason. I am blessed to have a personal savior. I am also blessed to have a personal trainer. And I'm late. Wait for me in the café. Do you need money?"

"No, thank you."

I called Syeeda from the café. "I can't get there until Wednesday, maybe Thursday."

"Why? What's going on with you? I'll be in meetings both of those days. Are you coming or not?"

"I am, I just had an accident and had to have surgery. I'm OK, and I am coming."

"What happened?"

"I stepped on a nail."

There was a long pause. "I don't know if I believe you."

"Why wouldn't you?"

"Something has changed. You're not the same."

"I don't know...I..." And she was gone, hung up on me. Was that it? Had she broken it off with me? Did I cause that to happen? The suffocating feeling of being drowned in mud overtook me again.

My cell rang. "Something happened with the phone. I lost service. We need to talk. When you get there, I'm leaving the key with the concierge. Just go to the lobby and tell him you're there. You have to show him your ID, they're very...careful about visitors. I get home about six."

I felt like I was answering her from inside a grave of mud. "OK, I'll do that."

Dr. Ruiz's home was situated on a heavily wooded private road. There were Hispanic gardeners and maintenance men working on almost every house in the neighborhood. She had a two-car garage. In the shadows I got a glimpse of her other car, a silver Mercedes. She showed me to the Airbnb cottage. It was more than utilitarian; it was luxurious. I took the rest of the money out of my wallet and handed it to her. She laughed and pushed my hand away. "I don't need that. You'll need it for the train and whatever. She gestured toward the house and the cars and swept her hand in an inclusive gesture. "How do you think I have all of this? Where do you think it comes from?"

"Well, you're a doctor."

"Yes, I am. Working in a corporate-owned walk-in clinic. Treating people who have next to nothing. It's not even gas and grocery money. That's not why I do it. It's from God; everything I have is from God allowing me to experience miracles in my life. Manifesting in the here and now. Not at some vague time in the future. Screw stocks and bonds; you need God. If you believe it, God makes it happen."

I didn't know what to say. The Charismatic Christian thing didn't really speak to me, but I wasn't going to insult someone who'd been so generous to me and possibly saved my life. "You're a very good person. You deserve it," I said.

"I'm having some friends over this evening, a little prayer session. You're welcome to stop by. You could use a miracle infusion. You just have to open yourself up for it. God's gifts are endless for those who believe."

"I'm a little wiped out from the surgery and the pain pills. Let me see how I feel after a nap."

"Don't miss out on it. Could be a gamechanger." I watched her sprint effortlessly up to her house, which was a three-story monument to the highest quality wood and stone design, with an array of geometric windows at all points. A roof walk with a silver turret crowned the structure. There was also, covered and tied off, what I guessed was a telescope for star or neighbor gazing.

I looked around the cottage. It had a queen-sized bed and what looked like all brand-new furniture, and all of it comfortable. There was a patio off the kitchen door with a rock garden and a fountain with a statue of the sea shell goddess, but not spouting water at the moment. I checked the kitchen pantry and it was completely stocked with microwave and canned products. My foot was throbbing so I took a painkiller and an antibiotic and lay down on the sofa. I was out in a minute. When I woke up it was dark. I grabbed my crutches and limped outside.

Ruiz's house was lit up with colorful hand blown glass light fixtures. I heard singing. I had no idea how I recognized the music: Hildegard Von Bingen, *Canticles of Ecstasy*. It must have been from when I snuck into one of the churches in Jersey at Christmas time, a curious teenager. I definitely would not have heard it at my house or any synagogue. What was it about? Another strange offshoot of my psyche—a religious agnostic. I stood by the French doors and peeked in. Unlike the visionary Hildegard, it looked like a prayer episode of Lifestyles of the Rich and Famous. I'd only seen just a bit of the show in a bar once in Orlando, but I remembered the phrase, "Champagne wishes, and caviar dreams." We had been at the bar, the entire sales crew celebrating another milestone for the Ray Shaft Wanger Real Estate Company. We'd been voted most reliable agency in Florida—irony to the nines—and with most homes sold again that year. It was a garish event, which included young women pole dancing. Ray had arranged for an open bar and all the clams you could eat. He strutted around the place, toasting everyone, slapping backs and making crude references to clams, not just the mollusk kind. I was finally ashamed enough to leave early, but not before I'd had too many beers and threw up in the parking lot.

As I continued taking in the prayer gathering, I saw a lot of cocktail dresses, diamond necklaces, earrings, and ankle bracelets, and much-cared-for spa-white skin. The men wore an array of leisurely fashions, many in loose cream-tinted shirts with the obligatory white and gold chains, most of them with crucifixes embedded with jewels. They all looked like they were in miracle mode, receiving God's bounty, as if seraphim were shoveling cash in through the doors. But the folks who needed it most were out there tonight pushing shopping carts through the parks, alleyways, and high crime neighborhoods of the coastal and inner cities of America. And I was beginning to think I had more in common with them than the people I watched at the moment, who already had everything they'd ever need.

There was a person who seemed to be directing the prayer service, a priestess of sorts. In contrast to the worshipers, she was dressed in plain brown chino pants, an embroidered peasant blouse and sandals. The only adornment she wore was a small silver cross. She was standing with her eyes closed and her arms stretched out above her head as if she were receiving divine transformation. The congregation moved in a circular pattern, each stopping before the woman, who upon a closer look was diminutive, and definitely not spa-certified, and placed their palms on her head, chest, stomach, and thighs. It was as if she were a holy relic, or at least a good luck charm. Her lips were moving in prayer and she didn't seem to notice how or where they touched her. She was, apparently, the conduit of their good fortune.

I decided not to take advantage of Dr. Ruiz's invitation to join the group and receive material blessings. I hobbled back to the cottage, microwaved a package of macaroni and cheese, then looked in the bar. There was an assortment of liquors and some wine. I checked the fridge and discovered a treasure trove of local brews, all IPAs, my personal holy water. I took my food and beer out to the patio and sat near Venus so I'd have some company. Looking at her, one of thousands of commercial copies of manufactured beauty, I felt how lonely I was. It seemed that despite all the people I'd had interacted with, good and bad, I was bereft of companionship. Of course, there was Syeeda, and what a price I'd paid to be with her. And the fact of her royalty, her place in the world...her family! How could this possibly work? I didn't know if I could live as a male Cinderella. My size four-and-a-half glass slipper was actually a ten-and-a-half Nike with a nasty wound in my foot. What an incredible blessing it was just to be able to walk unencumbered. *The small things*, I thought, *be grateful!*

When morning came, I was more than ready to head back to the clinic. Have her check my foot and catch the train. I was done with this part of SoCal. Ruiz whistled while she drove.

"How was your gathering last night, good?"

"God's miracles and riches were heaped upon us. You should have come over." She slipped into the passing lane and opened up the Porsche. She passed about twelve cars on the freeway. "I love this thing. You know what I grew up with?"

"What?"

"A Toyota Sonoma and a tractor in the Central Valley. We were a dirt-poor farm family. My mother sold eggs and honey door to door. My father worked himself to death producing lettuce, grapes, and lemons. We ate what we grew when we weren't starving. I promised myself I would do better than that. And I did. I worked like a dog, dragged myself through medical school. But it was God who made it happen. Do you see that?"

I just said, "yes."

Nurse Cleo had everything set us for us when we arrived at the clinic. She quickly unwrapped the bandage and stood back, astonished. "It's gone, healed...what the fuck?"

Dr. Ruiz entered in her surgical gown. "What's gone?" She checked out my foot, nodding her head, a knowing smile spreading across her lips. "We know why, don't we, Zoitner? Last night, God's love filled my house and everything around it. You, my friend, are the recipient of God's healing grace." I couldn't think of anything to say. At the moment, I wasn't having any pain, but I assume that was because I'd taken a pain pill before we left her house. "Do you think you can stand on it with full weight?"

I slid off the table and stood. Nothing, no pain. "It feels much better. Good doctoring."

Ruiz laughed, "I'm the technician, God's the physician."

At noon, Nurse Cleo gave me a ride to the train station. "You mind if I smoke a joint, just a couple of tokes?"

"Sure, go ahead." She offered me a hit and I declined. "I never know how it's going to hit me."

"I always know, and I like it. Life's a shit show sometimes."

"It can be." I agreed. "Why do you think my foot healed so quickly?"

"It happens. I've seen it before, usually with athletes. But it's always a surprise. You an athlete?"

"I'm kind of a mental athlete. But I am very grateful to Dr. Ruiz. She's a unique individual—very generous."

"She is all that and she's also out of her friggin' mind."

"You mean all the God stuff? She really believes that's where she gets her wealth from."

"Yeah, and it helps that her ex is an HBO VP, pulling in two million plus a year. Alimony, God's little helper."

"Wow, I didn't know that."

"But she's good to me, passes over her old clothes, practically new, and shoes I could never afford; we're almost the same size. I have to squeeze into some of them. She also talked the corporate clinic creeps into covering my health insurance. I have no complaints."

When we got to the station, I handed her a ten-dollar bill. She started to refuse, so I stuffed it in the cup holder. "Take it, please, I would have had to pay for a cab. And thank you for taking care of me."

"I'd still finish the course of antibiotics, just to play it safe." I promised her that I would and headed for the ticket machine. I turned back and waved goodbye. She'd relit her joint and blew some smoke and words out of the window: "*Bueno y buena suerte.*"

I boarded the train and took a seat on the ocean side, so I could have a view. An elderly woman struggled up the aisle with two stuffed trash bags, probably all of her earthly goods. She dropped down in her seat across from me and sighed heavily. Her face was deeply wrinkled, and her mouth was toothless, but she was chewing a fat wad of gum like a major league pitcher. Her eyes expressed a mischievous twinkle. As the air brakes released and we eased forward, she leaned over and said to me, "Get ready for the City of Angels, Mister."

It was a smooth ride. I stared at the ocean and thought of a line from a Billy Joel song: *Man, what are you doing here?* I still didn't know. All this time out here in the West and I still had no idea what I was supposed to do. I got off the train and waited for the old woman in case she needed a hand with her bags. She'd been behind me in the queue, bumping me with her bags. I waited until the door slid closed. She was gone, vanished. That caused me to feel slightly unsettled. But as I walked through Union Station, which I'd never seen before, I was struck by the architecture: Art Deco, Streamline Moderne, and Mission Revival. It was like arriving at a museum. On the way out of the station, I caught a glimpse of myself in a mirror and averted my eyes to avoid the unkempt, unshaven street guy, who hadn't showered in days. The soiled knapsack completed the picture. Not exactly a Portrait of Dorian Gray. I caught the Metro bus and after an hour and twenty minutes I arrived across the street from Westwood Village, the luxury apartment building Syeeda's friend had set her up with. Suddenly, my hands were sweaty, and my chest was tight.

I don't know for sure what my hesitation was about, but when I crossed the street, I felt that I was crossing a divide that would result in a life-changing situation. As I reached the entrance, a young woman was just returning from jogging. She flashed her ID card at the scanner and the imposing glass door swung open. I followed her in, realizing that if the door had closed, I would have not gotten in. The young woman disappeared into an elevator. I approached the marble reception counter, which displayed vases of fresh cut flowers. On the wall behind the reception desk was a large photo-mural of Westwood Village and the immediate neighborhood, taken probably from a helicopter. The concierge strode around the counter and blocked my approach. He wore a canary-yellow sports jacket, brown pants, and loafers. A gold chain with a gold pineapple attached to it hung from his thick neck. He was over six feet tall with a wide torso, tapering down to a thin waist like a prize fighter. His name tag, in script, read: G. Bwana. He carried himself in a relaxed manner, a confident person who could handle any situation, with words or brute force. His teeth were perfect when he smiled, gleaming white against his midnight skin. "I think you're in the wrong place, my friend," he said softly.

I interpreted that to mean, *you don't belong here.* I started to say, 'I'm Zoitner,' but it didn't come out. He hooked his arm in mine and started to escort me toward the door, without force, but with muscular intention. "Please, I will see you out."

"You're East African," I said.

He seemed slightly surprised, but kept steering me toward the exit. "How would you know that?"

"I had a friend in Florida, Radhi. We were in the same real estate firm. Same accent as yours. I worked with Radhi for five years. He could sell you a house, a car, or whatever, even if you didn't want it."

"Sounds like a talented man," Bwana smiled. By then he'd hustled me out to the sidewalk. People stepped around us, just another vagrant being shuffled off. I finally got her name out of my mouth. "Look, Syeeda Polizacio is expecting me. She said you would know. Syeeda? You must know her."

"This is my third day here. No one left me any message about you, Mr..."

"Zoitner. I'm Zoitner."

He released my arm. "Look, my friend, you know that you don't belong here. Maybe you're confused. Here," he slipped a twenty out of his pocket and held it out to me. His words reverberated in my head, ...*you know that you don't belong here.*

I stared at the twenty-dollar bill and said, mechanically, as if it were a mantra, "I don't belong here." I turned and walked away. I waited for the green icon to appear and crossed the street, the divide, deep and wide, closing behind me. I knew that I would never be able to go back. My only direction, my only hope, if I could call it that, was to move forward. It felt like something was falling away from me as I crossed the wide avenue. It was like I was shedding a layer of skin as a snake does. Discarding what was no longer needed and taking on a new covering. It was at once frightening and liberating. I was beginning to understand, though it hadn't become completely clear yet, that nothing would be the

same in my life again. I'd moved beyond myself, as it were. And I
would soon meet the new person I'd become.

I returned to the bus shelter and sat down. I stared across
the street at the Westwood, an impenetrable fortress I could not
breach. Bwana's words came back to me again: ...*you know that you
don't belong here*. I didn't and I finally knew it. As I sat there, the
old woman ambled by, hauling her overstuffed garbage bags. She
stopped at the bus shelter. I was going to ask her why she didn't
get off the train with the rest of us. She had the same mad twinkle
in her eye. She pulled the wad of gum out of her mouth and stuck
it on the bus schedule sign. Her voice was thin and raspy, but I
heard her: "Get the 306." She took hold of her bags and continued
down the street. I watched her until she was swallowed up by the
crowd. I looked at the schedule and the map. Bus 306 went north
up Route 405 to San Fernando where Toypurina's cousin Nicolas
and his family lived. I remembered that Nicolas worked at the
Pukúu Cultural Community Services center. He coordinated the
food giveaway program and after-school childcare.

It was an hour and a half bus trip going north on Route 405. I
was very low on cash at this point, but had enough for the ride.
By the time we arrived in San Fernando I was starving and felt
dehydrated. I'd already covered a lot of miles by train and bus. I
knew that the community center was on Second Street. I might
have found it sooner if I wasn't so burnt out. Finally, I stumbled on
1019 Second Street # 2. It was a neat square white stucco building
with green awnings and black wrought-iron railings and window
guards. It had the type of orange tile roof that was ubiquitous to
the area.

My fatigue, and state of mind, was such that the building seemed
to recede as I approached it. It was cool inside, a relief from the
heat. And there was a water fountain that I made use of, gulping
mouthfuls of water. The inner room was open and expansive.
Tables and chairs, sofas, and computer stations. It was obviously

set up for community service. At the front of the room was a long table. A towering man in jeans, a gray tea shirt with a falcon imprinted on it, and an LA Dodgers cap, was hoisting up crates of fresh vegetables, canned and dried goods, and personal care products onto the table. He cast a quick glance at me and kept working. He worked effortlessly until the table was filled. When he was finished, he drank from a half gallon plastic jug of water. He set it down and stared at me. He said nothing and waited for me to approach him. "Nicolas?"

His eyes widened, dark, thoughtful, and pained. "How do you know my name?"

"Your cousin told me. She said you lived here with your family—nine children."

"Toypurina?"

"Yes, she told me that she would pass soon. Do you know if she's still alive?"

"She is alive and was here not long ago. Who are you?"

"I'm..." I hesitated. There was a line here I didn't think I should cross, didn't have a right to cross. Of all my acknowledged sins, I didn't want to add that one to the damning list—just another white guy usurping a minority's traditions for self-enhancement. "I'm Zoitner, but Toypurina called me, well, she said after she meditated, that I was Robin Crow Man." He stared at me for a while and nodded his head slowly as if he was considering the veracity of that name. Was it deserved? He didn't look quite convinced.

There was a commotion at the entrance to the building. I could see cars pulling in and people getting out with boxes and shopping bags. "Are you busy right now?" he asked.

"No...I uh, have nowhere to go."

"Can you help load groceries and carry them out to the cars, especially for the elders?"

"Yes, I'll do that." For the next hour and fifteen minutes we packed boxes and bags and followed folks out and loaded them in. And every single one of them was grateful. They thanked me. A couple times I started to explain it wasn't me providing this, but then gave that up and just kept packing and loading. Just as we finished with the food giveaway, a school bus pulled up and released about thirty-five middle schoolers, who came running in.

"OK, snack time." I followed Nicolas back to the long table in the front of the room. Two women emerged from the kitchen with large trays with cups of soup, bologna and cheese sandwiches, potato chips, and oranges and peaches. Nicolas yelled to get their attention: "Listen up! Take a seat at one of the tables. No seat, no snack," he laughed. We went around with the trays and set the food in front of the kids. They went at it like they hadn't eaten all day, and maybe some of them hadn't. Nicolas called out again: "Who do you thank?"

The kids answered in unison, "We thank our mothers and fathers." One kid yelled out after that, "We thank Mr Nick." The big man came up behind the child and cuffed him gently on the back of his head, then pulled him into his side and gave him a hug.

He yelled out one more time: "You went to school today. You learned. You will learn more and more every day, and you will grow up to be smart; you will be leaders in our community. Do you hear me?" The kids cheered.

Around five, some parents started to arrive to pick up their kids. The rest of them boarded the bus to be dropped off at home once their parents were home from work. The woman started clearing off the tables, wiping up spilled soup and crumbs. I joined in and helped carry the trays to the kitchen. We scraped, loaded the dishwasher, and filled a couple of trash bags. The dumpster was beside the back door. I took the trash out and returned to the dining room where Nicolas was sweeping the floor vigorously. I grabbed the dustpan and kneeled down in front of the pile he'd collected. I dumped it in the trash.

"You like this kind of work," he observed.

"It's more satisfying than some I've had—it's honest."

"You said before you have nowhere to go. If that's the case, we have work here. It doesn't pay much."

His offer was kind of like a thunderbolt. I hadn't anticipated it. "I could do that for now," I said, almost inaudibly, shrinking into myself with uncertainty.

"Are you OK with shared housing? We provide meals."

"Yes, I'm OK with that." Maybe, I thought, I could get a part time job to supplement what they'd pay me.

"OK, my family will be here at six-thirty, as will other community leaders. We'll have dinner here as we have our planning session. A representative from the mayor's office is supposed to show up, finally, and talk about supporting the Tongvan community, especially enhanced educational services for our kids. It's like a lot of them don't even know we live here. We're the invisible people."

"Thank you...very much."

He observed me for a few moments as if he was taking the measure of my authenticity. "I think she was right."

"Who?"

"Toypurina, about your name."

"She was very good to me."

"Do you know who she is?"

"I think I do...there was so much to her."

My immediate agreement to sign on to what Nicolas had offered both surprised and didn't surprise me. I actually had nowhere to go at the moment, no resources, no money. Well, fifteen dollars. I could make the impossible call to Syeeda, who'd be getting home about six, and arrange to have her send money or send a limo to pick me up, but the idea seemed like it could only exist in a past life. When I'd crossed the street back to the bus shelter, I'd left that part of my life behind. I knew it couldn't be resurrected. But still, I owed her an explanation, at least a respectful goodbye.

I passed through the kitchen on the way to the parking lot, looking for some solitude. The women were busy at the commercial Garland Range cooking dinner. They talked and laughed. Their friendship and ease with each other were uplifting. We nodded and smiled. They were preparing savory stuffed pumpkin infused with herbs and ancient grains with black sage and tempeh sausage stuffing. There was also a large pot of corn soup brimming with three kinds of beans and pork. The mixture of aromas was more than enticing. It was intoxicating. They were making special dishes because, in the interim, they'd heard that the mayor himself was coming. They wanted him to not just experience their culture, but to taste it. I was still very hungry, but I didn't ask them for anything. I'd wait and eat with everyone else. The idea of a large group dinner seemed daunting at the moment. I needed some time alone to adjust to my new circumstances. I was light years away from being a high-rolling, crooked real estate agent in Florida to what I was now. *And what am I now?* I wondered.

There were a couple of folding chairs leaning against the side wall. I sat and looked at the neighborhood. The street lights were just coming on, illuminating the humble two-story apartment building beyond the back fence. I could see figures moving in the windows, a woman cooking dinner, another carrying a baby. I procrastinated as long as I could, then finally called Syeeda. It rang once and immediately went to her voice mail. That had never happened before. I called her again and got the same response, straight to her voice mail. She'd always answered me before; it seemed that I was blocked. I knew that the next thing would be a test, a final one. I texted her and got an answer immediately, but not from Syeeda: "Your text messages will go through as usual; they just won't be delivered to the Android user." I stared at it for a few moments. So that was it. She'd had enough of my excuses, my disappearance, my going AWOL. My sloppy transformation into something else. And I couldn't blame her. But it was abrupt. No closure. No, as lame as it sounds, "I'll never forget you." No nothing. Just a cold slap in the face via social media technology. I'd been deleted. And did it hurt her to do it? I'd never know. Unfortunately, I had no more pain pills, and would have welcomed one if I had. But there's no real medicine, no effective cure for heartbreak. It was officially over.

*

Here's a useless expression: time heals all wounds. Time, like erosion and nuclear decay, has another agenda. It doesn't announce itself. You don't notice it like you don't notice your hair or fingernails growing. A relentless force, time knifes through your mortal flesh with its inexplicable purpose. It happens as you dally, as you fret about your situation, as you make decisions, wallow in indecision, as you buy things you don't need—except for time, which is not for sale. Its price tag is your last day, your last breath. I've seen people take their last breath. They will often make a farewell gesture, a clasping of the hands over their heart. Sometimes they sing to some invisible entity, maybe the angel that's come for them. Or they make a soft movement with their lips, a benediction for their loved ones. There is no bargain in life; no redo, there is just what you do, or what you don't do, and what you ignore at your own peril.

And then it was October, a year and a half later. Time, the great escape artist. I'd finally made good use of my degree in English Literature with a minor in Philosophy. With Nicolas' support, and a fairly generous grant from the town government, we'd established a tutoring program in the community center for middle school and high school students who were struggling with their course work. We ordered a GED curriculum, workbooks and computer programs, covering all the essential subjects needed to earn a high school equivalency diploma. I coordinated the program, taught, and encouraged the kids. Every time one of them got their GED, the community threw a party. I learned that teaching was not teaching, it was encouraging. It was just the simple act of revealing to a "failing" student that that was not their reality. Not their future. There was something else for them, something much better. And many of them succeeded, went on to the community colleges and four-year schools after that. Some of them came back and taught with me, which was a great help. There were four of us now making it happen. When Samaya, a nineteen-year-old female student, got into law school, the people erupted. They threw a parade for her in the parking lot.

I guess I could say I've given back to these people who gave me a place to stay, fed me, after I arrived with nothing but a skewed sense of direction and a desperate need for something meaningful, something that was worthwhile. And no questions asked, no positive ID, no background check. They were just people struggling to get by and give their kids a better life.

Happiness? Am I happy? I'm happy that I'm not selling people mansions that sink into a swamp. Happy that I'm not taking more than my share anymore, trying to do what the Tongva call *living lightly on the earth*. Happy to be almost rid of the corrosive guilt that was eating me up inside. In the last six months I've finally been able to get my own apartment near Rudy Ortega Park. It's a short bike ride to the community center. There are drought-tolerant plants and trees, a mission style plaza, a historic water tower, and huge boulders and stonework throughout the park, carved with native symbols. I spend a good amount of time sitting there; my meditation spot.

I still think about going back east, but without a clear idea of what I'd do there, what would be the point? My purpose? I'd say my immediate purpose is helping as many kids from the center as possible get through grade school, and the high school kids, who seem to be most at risk, to get their GED's. Not allowing the system to fail them, to help them rise above the pervasive cultural and racial prejudice that shadows them. That's the reward, the payoff. I get letters from the students telling me about their college experiences. I write letters of recommendation for the ones applying for jobs. One young man, Mateo, recently joined the local fire department. My job: opening doors for kids who might just be left standing behind them. If I'd said that two years ago, I would have been laughed out of the office by my associates.

And the big question I'm still struggling with: Who are you? Do you know who you are? It helps to know who you are not. I've made some progress on that front. The "fake you" can eventually fall away like dried wallpaper if you let it go. It leaves a bare, clean surface to draw a fresh image upon, a healthier one. I stopped drinking about a year ago. Not in twelve steps, just one. Dr. Van Tragen put it simply, "Drink less." Or not at all, I finally decided. She, the doctor, said she knew people who knew who they were—who they really were. Toypurina knew who she was and she tried to help me see who I am. She called me Robin Crow Man. And where is Robin Bell Zoitner? What happened to him? Did he drown in the Nom de Plume Swamp?

Sometimes, just before dropping off into the void of sleep, I hear two voices, two sisters chanting: *There is no separation. In nature we are fixed between the earth and the sky. We leave and we return. As spring returns from winter. As dawn is born from night. There is no death.* I find much needed solace from those words, flawed and earthbound as I am, still seeking to know the person I might become—and with whom I might finally lie down in peace.

ABOUT THE AUTHOR

Mark Morganstern is a native of Schenectady, New York. He studied at the Manhattan School of Music, played bass fiddle, and toured with jazz and classical ensembles before deciding that music was not his best choice of profession. An avid reader and writer, he switched majors and graduated from the City University of New York with an MA in English/Creative Writing. His fiction has appeared in *Piedmont Literary Review, New Southern Literary Messenger, Hunger Magazine, Expresso Tilt, Mothering Magazine, Scarlet Leaf Review*, and other journals, and was anthologized in *Tribute to Orpheus II*. He received an honorable mention for his story, "Tomorrow's Special," published in the *Chronogram* 11/06 Fiction Contest issue, selected by guest judge, Valerie Martin. His collection of stories, *Dancing with Dasein*, and his novel, *The Joppenbergh Jump*, are available from booksellers everywhere.

Mark lives in a small Hudson Valley town and enjoys walking his dog on tree-lined streets. Contact him at dorsey1156@gmail.com.

A REQUEST AND MORE

If you enjoyed this book, its publishers and author would be grateful if you would post a short (or long) review on the website where you bought the book and/or on Goodreads.com or other book review sites. Thanks for reading!

Other books from Recital Publishing:
Voices in the Dirt: Stories by Ian Caskey
Our Lady of the Serpents by Petrie Harbouri
Voyages to Nowhere: Two Novellas by Tom Newton
The Lame Angel by Alexis Panselinos
The Joppenbergh Jump by Mark Morganstern
Ponckhockie Union by Brent Robison
Seven Cries of Delight and Other Stories by Tom Newton
Saraceno by Djelloul Marbrook
Dancing with Dasein by Mark Morganstern
The Principle of Ultimate Indivisibility by Brent Robison

And please check out **The Strange Recital**, a podcast about fiction that questions the nature of reality.

Made in the USA
Monee, IL
18 September 2022

14158966R00187